The Forest Infirmary

The Forest Infirmary
A Tale of Enadir

Rhydian King

I'r coblyn gyntaf, diolch

Tales of Enadir

A Key to a Throne
The Forest Infirmary

Enadir

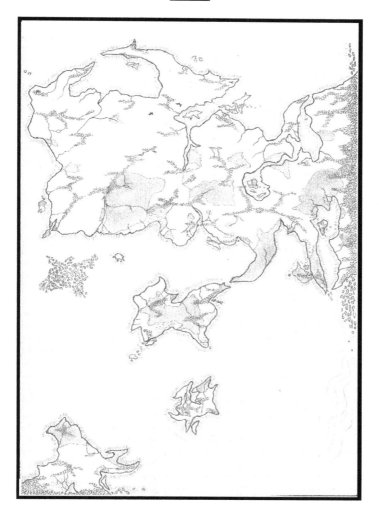

The Midlands and surrounding countries

1. Dailas Forest
2. Pine Wood
3. Cysgodgors Marsh
4. Crisiaddwr River
5. Bramble Plain
6. Critanna Marsh
7. Tarin Swamp
8. Tarnegrefur Mts.
9. Black desert
10. Ioer Rivers
11. Eoli Lake
12. Gwenal River
13. Dantwenn River
14. Atrael River
15. Saraman Woods
16. Pawal Woods
17. Cracket Mts
18. Hostaa Rivers
19. Ahanemis Lake
20. East Jaws
21. Mts of Iadden

22. Jagged Isles
23. Sea-neiad Isle
24. Werlit River
25. Daiwen Jungle
26. Coeddu Forest
27. Haq-nel Mts
28. Ailunel River
29. Silin-ae River
30. Crastalan
31. Council
32. Morgenal
33. Tonnis
34. Muranath
35. Imhara Pass
36. Denran (ruins)
37. Eastern Barrier
38. Arfan (ruins)
39. Bletta Castle
40. Maralen
41. Setarack Temple
42. Cadaran

Northwest Dailas

Prologue: Outbreak

'Bring him in!'

'Acute breathlessness, irregular pulse at the radial, reduced capillary refill.'

'Onset?'

'Acute on chronic. Gradually worsening over the past week and a half but now with a sudden deterioration. No obvious trigger. He collapsed in the marketplace, lives in the shanty town.'

Dafan nodded slowly. His aspirations of retiring early to bed dwindled and extinguished with the patient's hacking cough. Pity. He followed the trolley down the corridor to the ward with his referring colleague, their apprentices dawdling after them in a cluster.

'What else?'

'Productive cough, yellowish-brown sputum. Some crackles on auscultation but nothing dramatic. Reported worsening episodes of frank haemoptysis. Generalised lymphadenopathy, mild jaundice.'

'Hepatosplenomegaly?' Dafan asked.

'Yes, but only slight,' his colleague shrugged apologetically. 'We were worried it might be tubercle sickness.'

'With hepatic involvement?' he raised his eyebrows.

'We think so,' she shrugged again. 'Apologies, Dafan, I know it's not what you want, but we heard Healer Azek sent you a similar patient last week from his infirmary?' she left the question hanging between them.

He glanced at her. Funny how word spread so quickly in their world, almost as quickly as the diseases they treated.

'You heard right,' he confirmed.

'So you'll take him?'

He shrugged and nodded at the patient trolley disappearing around a corner. 'Seems he's already on the way to the ward.'

Relief released the tension in her shoulders and softened her frown. Responsibility handed over, she even managed a small smile, a mixture of gratitude and triumph in the curl of her lip. He had half a mind to change his decision, but that would be unfair on the patient to lose out due to politics.

1

'So working diagnosis is tubercle sickness,' he grunted. 'What treatments have been attempted so far?'

'We initially suspected a hypersensitivity bronchospasm, so we tried theophylline syrup and concentrated ephedra essence, but it didn't do much good,' she shook her head and jerked a thumb over her shoulder. 'The initial assessment was done by one of the apprentices. When we got round to him we noticed the lymphadenopathy and hepatosplenomegaly, noted the history of haemoptysis, and brought him here.'

'Weight loss or night fevers?'

'Both, over the past week. None beforehand.'

He scratched behind his wide calefin ear. The bony claws at the end of each finger were not only excellent for opening letters and prising apart tightly-adherent objects but also perfect for grooming. Not that he needed much grooming nowadays, decades of torment in exile from his homeland took its toll on his balding head and sagging skin.

'Any exposure?'

She grimaced. 'None that we could discern from the history. I doubt you'd get much more out of him for now, but maybe when you get him back on his feet you can figure it out?'

He snorted. Judging from the presentation, there wasn't much hope of that, but there was no use telling her. She had it in her head that she'd done a good job bringing him here, no point bursting that bubble with the knowledge he had little more to offer.

They reached the ward, half a dozen wooden cots lining each wall, ten of them empty, one with their new arrival, the other with Healer Azek's former patient. They stopped at the end of the new arrival's bed, observing in silence as the acolytes transferred him from trolley to bed, coughing and spluttering all over their masks and gowns. Laundry costs would be going up for the foreseeable future.

'Fast onset as well,' he murmured.

'We thought so too,' she admitted. 'But Azek's patient had a similar presentation, no?'

'Seems you know a lot about Azek's referral.'

She flushed. 'My partner works with him. It's how I knew.'

2

He nodded. Now it made sense.

'Could it be an aberrant strain? A particularly aggressive type?' one of the braver apprentices offered his cautious thoughts.

Dafan grimaced. 'Perhaps. He certainly seems like a tubercle sickness patient, but end-stage, not acute. Strange.'

'Perhaps he's immunocompromised?'

He nodded. A good thought. It would potentially explain the rapid onset, it could also result in a co-infection with another illness to affect the liver. He hoped it was. If the tubercle sickness is what caused the hepatitis there was no point even trying. It would be kinder to just kill him and be done with it.

His eyes wandered to the other occupied cot, the patient connected to multiple tubes, two from his mouth, one from his bandaged chest. It was too much of a coincidence to put it down to a faulty immune system. Two patients with aggressive, disseminated infections within the space of a week? Something wasn't right.

'How's he doing?' she followed his gaze to the tubed patient.

'Badly.'

'What did you do?'

'Tried an artificial pneumothorax initially, then converted it to a thoracoplasty last night. We're just trying to rest his chest as much as possible to induce remission in the lung, but it won't do anything for the disseminated disease,' he paused and sighed. 'He'll be dead by next week.'

'So why bother with the thoracoplasty?'

'I had a feeling,' he trailed away. He could feel the judgmental eyes of his apprentices on the back of his head. Fine for them to have idealistic views, but they lived free of his responsibilities, free of his memories of this ravaging disease across whole communities in the Jagged Isles.

'Yes?'

He shrugged. 'I had a feeling we might be seeing more of the same. The tubercle sickness rarely comes in isolated cases, as you know. I thought it best to practice the procedure, track its results, see where we can improve to better guide future practice.'

'A test patient?' she raised her brows. Her disapproval might have affected him a few decades ago, but not anymore.

'It seems I was right.'

'And *his* suffering?' she nodded to the tubed patient again.

'He's heavily sedated, doesn't feel a thing.'

'Healer Dafan, you're walking a fine line between healing and experimenting,' she shook her head.

'You're more than welcome to take him back?'

She quailed and shook her head. 'I best be going.'

'Indeed. You know the way out.'

The sound of her retinue's footsteps echoed down the hallway. His acolytes and apprentices bustled about the bed, preparing various tinctures and potions, following his mumbled instructions. His eyes wandered from the cot to the window behind. Crastalan's dark cityscape stretched away to the partitioning wall maintaining the seclusion of the third level. On the other side of that wall was the crushing bustle of the second level, where thousands lived virtually on top of each other, a suffocating mass of bodies pushing and rubbing against each other every minute, trawling through one another's sweat and waste, breathing in each other's rancid and disease-riddled breath. He shuddered. As bad as the second level may be, the thought of the squalor of the shanty town outside the curtain wall was even more desperate. If someone brought a strain of contagion into this environment, the city would be on its knees within a month.

The patient's hacking cough snapped him out of his daydream, thick brown sputum spraying from his open mouth, chest heaving spasmodically in its futile effort to draw breath.

'Get the laudanum, let's sedate him. Prepare a tube for intubation, let's give his chest a bit of a rest. Quickly now.'

They jumped away to do his bidding. His gaze returned to the window. An aggressive new strain of the tubercle sickness? A cramped, overpopulated city? He grimaced. A recipe for a catastrophic outbreak. All outbreaks had their origin, but what poor, damned fool brought this one to the Midlands?

4

Chapter 1

'You'll fall and break your neck.'

'I won't.'

'Don't expect me to carry you home when you do.'

'I don't.'

Ash stretched his hand, inching closer to his prize. The poppy-scarlet skin of the apple shone with the glistening beads of morning dew. For the best part of a week, he'd watched it with his sisters, waiting for it to drop to their waiting bellies. Somehow, it clung to the branch, tenaciously denying them its sweetness. He'd taken matters into his own hands. The apple tree was old, more ancient than Grey Phell, approaching his ninth decade. According to him, the tree was old even when he was young, as young as Ash, but there was a strength in its gnarled, twisted trunk, a strength that kept it growing.

The branch beneath him dipped as he edged his foot further along. His knee buckled with the unexpected movement, drawing a gasp from the onlookers below. Dem would love it if he fell. She'd look at him with that condescending expression, the smug twist of the lip as she waggled her finger, goading him. No sympathy would be offered for any bruises or broken limbs, such injuries would only make her smile even wider. Then, of course, she would run to Ma, to tell her how her only son was putting himself in danger, again. He'd be told off, slapped around the wrists, and sent back to work, or worse, the healer. That wouldn't bother him, going back to work, or Ma's half-hearted reprimand, no, what bothered him would be the insufferable look of victory on his sister's face as she watched the fruits of her labours. Tightening his grip on the branch overhead, he steadied himself. The apple was his, and it would be his turn to smile smugly at Dem.

Stretching further still, his calloused fingers brushed against the prized fruit, setting it twisting lazily on its stalk. There were plenty of other apples ripe for picking, his ascent dislodged a fair few which Hent collected and placed in a wicker basket. None, however, had the same lustrous, tantalizingly perfect appearance as this one. Hent was ten years younger than him and Dem, the son of the village cobbler,

5

and idolised Ash. He should probably be sent away, so he wouldn't get any ludicrous ideas of following him up. Of course, he would never do so. It was nice to have someone down there cheering him on, someone to balance the crowd.

Aside from Hent and Dem, there were three others; Geri, Arnol, and Mett. The three sons of three miners, still too young to be put to work. They were neutral, here for the show. Whether he returned victorious or fell and broke an arm, it was all exciting to watch. They would cheer whatever the outcome.

He shifted his weight again, creeping along the branch. It bent dramatically as it took his weight. Its downward tilt took him even further from the apple, and he was forced to retreat. Pausing for breath, he looked for another way across, gripping the overhead branch with both hands. There was no way of swinging over to it, the branches were far too thin and flimsy for such a feat. He considered climbing higher up, coming at the apple from above, but again, they were too thin and would collapse under his weight. Not that he was overweight, far from it, he was as skinny as an alley cat in Crastalan, but also tall and lanky, all gangly limbs and narrow shoulders. Certainly not built for the mines. That suited him perfectly. As soon as his growth spurt saw him grow nearly two feet in six months, the chief miner gently informed Ma that he would no longer be suited to work underground. She seemed disappointed he wouldn't be following Da's legacy. He was not. Steben, the woodsman, offered to take him on board, with the promise of 'Filling out his baggy clothes,' but he refused. He settled quickly and comfortably with Geohn, the craftsman, who'd been crying out for another apprentice for years. The work could be as simple or as intricate as he wished, and he enjoyed it. It gave him the calloused hands he needed for climbing this apple tree without fear of blisters.

'Stuck up there?' called Dem, sarcastically.

'Not a chance,' he called back.

A bit of a lie, there was a very good chance he was stuck. Try as he might, he couldn't find a way across to the apple. Twisted between the leaves above was an old crow's nest, now inhabited by a little owl. His eyes met those of the bird, who glared at him, irritated this gangly creature was disturbing its rest. He flicked his hand to shoo it away, but the furious little ball of fuzz didn't move, knowing it was well out of his reach. Cursing under his breath, he looked for a branch he might break off to poke it away, to teach it a lesson for staring at him. As he struggled to break off a surprisingly-resistant twig, an idea formed. Abandoning the twig, he searched his pockets for some string. He normally carried a roll with him for emergencies. But, of course, it was down below with the onlookers, in his jacket pocket. There was only one thing for it.

He unbuckled his belt, slid it out of his trousers, and tied it again, as a hoop. Stretching out with his hand again, he tried looping the belt around the apple. It worked. Now to draw it in. Nice and slowly.

'Oh dear,' he whispered. His trousers slipped. They were made for someone with a greater girth around the waistline than he, and that belt was the only thing keeping them up. He tried straddling his legs further apart to save his dignity, but as he did so, the branch buckled again and the apple bounced free. With a sigh, he regained his balance and the trousers fell to his ankles. Hent giggled, the three lads laughed hysterically, and his sister cried out in disgust. A bit of an overreaction, after all, it was only his undergarments.

Hooking the apple once again with his belt, he drew it in far enough to twist it free. It popped off with a satisfying spring of the branch, and he held it up triumphantly. The boys below were still laughing too hard to cheer, so he slid his belt back in place and climbed back down, the apple safe in his shirt.

As soon as his feet touched firm ground, Hent threw his arms around his waist, beaming.

'You got it!'

He pulled the apple from his shirt and handed it over. 'Just for you, H.'

The boy's smile grew even wider, if that were possible, and took a bite. Juice dribbled down his chin, but instead of the satisfied slurp he'd been expecting, he pulled a face, and spat out his mouthful. Rubbing his tongue childishly in an attempt to scrape off the remnants, he looked up at Ash guiltily.

7

'I'm sorry,' he mumbled. 'It's not nice.'

Ash frowned. It should be perfect. He took the fruit back and examined it, identifying its shortcoming with a glance. A hole at its base, where a worm, or caterpillar, or some other insect had found a way in and spoiled the flesh inside. He grimaced, no kind gesture went unpunished. That apple looked perfect in every way, it should've been the sweetest thing the boy had ever tasted. Apparently, the insect had the same idea.

He shrugged and ruffled Hent's hair affectionately. 'Sorry, H, at least it looked pretty, eh?'

Hent nodded sadly and took the apple back. 'Can I keep it?'

'Of course, I got it for you! It'll go brown soon, though. Throw it out once it does.'

'I will, thank you for getting it.'

'Something wrong with the apple?' asked Dem, her smug voice oozing around a viper's smile.

'Leave it,' he nodded at Hent, whose cheeks were flushed with disappointment.

She put her arm around the boy and hugged him. 'Come on now, wipe away those tears. It's not your fault Ash wasted our time with a rotten old apple!'

He rolled his eyes and turned away, ignoring the jibe. She must have noticed, as she stood and called after him.

'It's true. I told you to just wait for it to fall, but you had to play the hero and get it.'

'I wasn't playing the hero,' he snapped.

'Of course you were. You wanted little H to see you as big brave Ash, climbing the tree for him.'

'I was being nice? Perhaps you should try it?' his cheeks burned.

She snorted, knowing she was annoying him. 'Oh of *course* you were, how noble of you, always helping others. *Such* a brave man.'

Clenching his teeth, he turned to look past her at Hent. Jerking his head, he motioned him to follow them back to the village. The three boys had since wandered off, now the show was over they needed something new to entertain themselves, and the forest had plenty to offer.

Instead of heading directly back home, he detoured to the Clearbed river so he could wash his hands. They passed Ffed's hut on the outskirts of the village, but she wasn't there. The hammock she usually lounged on hung limp and empty between the two hornbeams outside her porch. A shame. She would've understood his quest. A few squawks from the woods sent them scurrying along. Jal, her pet duck, was a terror. Many an ankle bore the scars of her savage bill. He'd personally nearly lost a toe to her incessant pecking.

As they strolled through the forest, Dem held hands with Hent, swinging back and forth to his delight. All the while, she goaded Ash, using the boy's presence as a shield to his retaliation.

'Of course, being the big brave man that you are, you were obligated to go and get that apple, weren't you? Didn't matter how dangerous it might be, or how many ideas it might give H, you had to go and get it. Who shall we blame if one day H tried to climb a tree, tried to copy you, and fell to his death? It won't be my fault, that's for sure.'

'I wouldn't fall!' laughed Hent, happily jumping over a rotting log. 'I'd go all the way up to the top, like a squirrel!'

'All the way up to the top, would you? Hear that, Ash? He'd go all the way up.'

'Right into the clouds,' laughed the boy, innocently. 'As high as the birds! Just like Ash!'

'Just. Like. Ash.'

He didn't turn around. He didn't need to. He knew a hideously slimy grin would be plastered over her face. Breathing slowly, he struggled to maintain his composure, ears burning and heart thumping.

'And how would you get down, H? Once you were up high like Ash, hunting after rotten old fruit? Did you see him climb down?'

'Yes.'

'Wasn't as good climbing down, was he? It was more difficult than going up, wasn't it?'

'Maybe,' mumbled the boy.

9

'So once you were up there in the clouds, with the birds, how would you get down?'

He paused, 'I'd fly down!' he giggled hysterically as she tickled him.

Ash closed his eyes, shaking his head. Hent was still giggling behind him, as was his sister. He turned, blood boiling, and stared at her. She held his gaze, smirking self-righteously as she tickled under the boy's arms. An arrogant glint was in her eyes, mocking him with Hent's words. It was all he could do not to jump on her there and then, to teach her a lesson.

Struggling to compose himself, he knelt next to Hent.

'Alright, H, I want you to listen to me now.'

'I'm listening,' he giggled, squirming under Dem's fingers.

'You mustn't do what I just did, alright? It's dangerous. I only did it because I'm bigger than you.'

'Oh is that why you did it?' she asked, pointedly.

'Alright, H?' he asked again, ignoring her.

'Yes,' he giggled again, rolling around to escape Dem's nimble hands.

'Can you say it to me? H? Say that you won't climb anything like I just did. Alright? Oh by the four winds, Dem, cut it out!' he shouted, and was rewarded by her widest smirk yet. She lifted her hands and raised her eyebrows. He hated her so much in that moment. It was only Hent's presence that restrained him.

'Say what, sorry?' asked the boy, crawling to his feet, grinning at Dem as he watched her hands cautiously.

'Say that you won't go climbing like I just did.'

'I won't go climbing like you just did.'

'Good boy. And you never climb alone, not even easy ones, alright?'

'Yes. No climbing alone.'

'Good boy,' purred Dem, stroking his hair affectionately. 'Only stupid idiots climb like Ash just did. Stupid, idiot little mongrels trying to show off. And you're not a stupid mongrel, are you? You're a clever boy.'

'I *am* clever,' he said, proudly. 'I can count to one hundred!'

Ash smiled. Dem saw his smile and quickly replied, 'That's a lot, H! Twice as much as Ash can count to, but what can you expect from an idiot mongrel like him?'

'Mongrel!' shouted Hent, laughing. 'Mongrel! Mongrel!'

Ash smiled through his teeth at his sister. His fist curled. She noticed, and gently turned her head to expose her cheek, inviting him to strike. Their eyes met, and they held each other's gaze for what felt like an age. She had the same colour eyes as Heb. He forced himself to think of their mother, what they'd say if she returned, eyes full of tears, crying at how brutish her violent brother was. Slowly, her face changed to that of his oldest sister's, and he relaxed. It was a trick Ma taught him whenever Dem baited him; to look into her eyes and imagine it was Heb. She knew he would never hold any ill will towards his eldest sister, no matter how much Dem bit and poked and goaded. His fist unclenched, and he rose to his feet. Dem looked mildly disappointed, but it was quickly replaced by the familiar sanctimonious curl of the lip. She turned to Hent.

'That's right, you tell him what he is.'

'Mongrel! Mongrel!' he danced around, waving his arms in the air wildly.

Ash forced a smile and turned away. 'Come on, trouble, I need to wash my hands.'

'Dirty mongrel needs to wash!' Hent called, to Dem's delight. Suddenly he paused, and looked at him. 'What's a mongrel, Ash?'

'Ash is a mongrel,' called Dem.

'It's a dog,' said Ash, ignoring her. 'But people use it as a nasty name.'

'But dogs don't climb,' said Hent, brow furrowed in thought. 'So, you can't be one. You're a dirty squirrel instead!'

Now Ash laughed properly, as Hent continued dancing around them. He glanced at Dem, whose smug smile was somewhat diminished. That'll teach her for trying to use Hent against him.

Washing his hands clean in the river, he tickled Hent to dry his hands, laughing as he squirmed. It was approaching midmorning, time to get home. Geohn opened his shop at noon, and it was his turn with the sanding-mill today.

Taking a hand each, they escorted Hent back through the narrow stretch of forest to the village.

Starforge's town wall was a simple encircling dyke, with a dry moat at its foot and a simple wooden palisade on top. The village watchtower was manned by two guards, with an additional one above the gates. Normally, there would only be a single guard manning the watchtower, and a gatekeeper only at night. Recently, however, the forest had become more dangerous. Fewer travellers arrived by road, and those who did kept in larger caravans. Rumours of hidden rebels and disloyal outlaws infiltrating towns, stealing supplies, kidnapping honest folk, and infecting seeds of treason were rampant. Some of the few isolated settlements in the region were under constant threat. Last week, the miller's wife and daughter came to their village gates begging for help from a gang of rogues who'd burned their mill and beaten her husband to death. They were far from the first to arrive at Starforge fleeing the chaos of the forest. Only a few days ago, Ma even mentioned an orphan child running half-naked through the woods, lost in the trees before any of the panners could reach them. Of course, he was yet to personally meet any of these so-called rebels, and Geohn flat out denied their existence despite the evidence to the contrary. After all, who in their right minds would rise up against the might of King Stolach? Nevertheless, the unit of soldiers stationed at their village had their duties doubled, and a distinct air of suspicion hung heavy on their frowns.

The gatekeeper recognised them and let them through. After walking Hent back to his house, he and Dem went their separate ways without saying a word. If he could have a whole day, a week, or better yet a month without her, he would bless the four winds and give prayer to their glory for the rest of his life. Ma would try to convince him it was only a phase, and they would eventually grow out of their bickering, but how long could a phase realistically last? No, this was just how she was. Hopefully she'd get married to some unassuming idiot from their neighbours at Clovercream and be shipped off promptly. As if anyone would take her, ugly, stout, and spiteful as she was.

Arriving at Geohn's workshop, he went around the back. They may not open until noon, but he could get going with some work. He had enough projects on the go, after all. A dimly-lit storeroom opened up to the larger showroom, the various wares stacked in piles, shelves, or hanging from ceiling-hooks. From the workshop to the left, he heard Geohn tinkling on his latest project. As the master craftsman, Geohn was responsible for making the finer items out of the silver lore from Starforge's mines. As an apprentice, he was still only allowed to work with wood. One day, however, he would be the one making the delicate doorknobs, candlesticks, spectacle-frames, cutlery, and jewellery that was the village's signature exports. One day, he'd be the one they all respected, the one they went to for help. Until then, he'd be the best wood-carver Geohn ever employed.

His small desk was covered in a thick layer of sawdust, half-finished projects balanced precariously on one end, his chisels at another, and a heavy vice in the middle. Geohn's other assistant, Tano, was also there. He nodded a brief greeting, but as usual mostly ignored him. Tano was good, only a few years away from starting on the silver, but wasn't particularly social.

Picking up a half-finished drawer for a cupboard he was making, he settled into the familiar rhythm of measuring, filing, and sanding. Hours trickled by, and he replayed Dem's smug smile at his failed apple-gathering attempts over and over in his head. He was only trying to do something nice, there was no need for her to react like that. Hent had neither siblings nor parents, and his grandparents were always grateful when they took him off their hands for a few hours every day. In many ways, he was like a little brother to him. How dare she suggest he was being disingenuous in his attempts to make him happy.

Geohn popped his head into their workshop just before noon.

'Tano. Opening time,' their eyes met, and Geohn recoiled. 'Ash! Why're you here?'

'Working,' he held up the half-finished drawer.

'No but, your mother?' Geohn shook his head.

'Ma?' he frowned. Had she said something to end his apprenticeship early? Well he wasn't going out to be a woodsman, that's for sure.

'Yes, she – well – I didn't expect you here,' Geohn stammered.

'Why?'

The craftsman wandered over to his bench and placed a hand on his shoulder. 'She's not well, Ash. The healer's assistant came around this morning looking for you, I told her you could take the day off. I'm sorry.'

'Not well?' he frowned. 'What's wrong?'

'I don't know. I think it's best you go home. Tano and I will be fine here, don't you worry.'

He was already out the door. It was only a couple of minutes from the workshop to his home, and he ran the whole way, feet pounding the cobbled streets like a charging destrier. She was fine last night. It was a normal family dinner, good bread, good stew, a few squabbles with Dem. Nothing to suggest any ailments. She was a bit quieter than usual, yes, and perhaps went to bed slightly earlier, but nothing else. Now the healer's assistant was getting involved?

Reaching his home at the bottom of the baker's street, he tore the door open. The healer was there already, he could see the hem of her coat through Ma's room door. Heart pounding, he approached. Before he reached them, Dem appeared in the doorway, barring his way.

'Where have you been?' she demanded.

'At the workshop. How is she?' he tried pushing past. She didn't move.

'Hiding, were you?'

'Don't be stupid,' he pushed again, she resisted.

'I don't think so. You can't just come marching back in after neglecting–'

'Just let me see her, Dem? She's my mother too? I came as soon as I heard,' he interrupted, treating her with the condescension she deserved.

'Let him in, Demsai,' Heb appeared over her shoulder. 'Come on, Ashil, she's just through here. We sent word to Geohn.'

'I know, I just got it. Thank you,' he shouldered past Dem, who gasped dramatically as he clipped her. Heb frowned at him in disapproval. He didn't care. She deserved far worse than a hard shoulder.

Her room was warm despite the open windows. The stench of diarrhoea and vomit hit his nostrils as soon as he walked in. Soiled bedsheets lay bundled in a corner, waiting to be cleaned. Ma was in the cot, skin glowing with the sheen of sweat, blankets drawn up around her chin. Her eyes fluttered in a fever dream, whimpering and shaking.

Oskra the healer nodded to him. He'd never liked her much since she forced his mouth open as a child to retrieve a fishbone stuck in the back of his throat with her long tweezers. He'd screamed the place down even after it was done and the bone was out. Ma was embarrassed that day. He never forgot Oskra's calloused hands around his cheeks. Never liked fish either.

'Just gave her some medicine,' Oskra said, her singsong Southland accent as strong as the day she'd arrived, before he was born.

'What's wrong? A fever?' he knelt by Ma's side, feeling her burning forehead.

'Among other things. She been out recently? Complained of any bites by insects or animals?' Oskra asked, washing her hands in a basin.

'She's always out,' he snapped.

'Ash!' Heb gasped. 'The healer is here to help!'

'But she knows Ma's job. Obviously she's out with the other panners,' he shrugged.

'You need to learn some respect,' Dem sidled up to Oskra, handing her a fresh towel to dry her hands.

'Shut up.'

'Ash!'

Heb seldom rose her voice. When she did, it was enough to make him shut up instantly. It showed she was particularly angry or particularly worried. Now was one of those times. Probably just worried about Ma, so he'd let off Dem for now. Not that Dem would

15

return the gesture. Her slimy grin returned for a victorious second, before falling off again when she remembered Ma.

'Sorry,' he muttered.

'It's okay to be worried, young man,' said Oskra. 'I need to know in case she mentioned something so we can figure out what this is.'

'It's not just a fever?' he asked.

'Not just a fever.'

'She never mentioned any bites or anything to us,' said Heb.

'Any unusual food she might have eaten?'

'Just our usual,' Heb shook her head.

'Is there anything in particular you'd like us to look out for, Healer Oskra?' asked Dem, sweetly.

Ash rolled his eyes. She wanted to be a healer so sucked up to her at every opportunity. Embarrassing, really. Oskra tolerated it, she even let Dem help her out a couple of days a month when her main assistant was off. Probably only did it out of guilt for what happened all those years ago with Da.

'I've already examined her. Lots of bruises, reduced muscle power, mildly altered peripheral sensation, vomiting, diarrhoea, throat full of secretions, blood in her urine... And all come at once. Very unusual.'

'Bruises?' Ash gently pulled the blankets down from Ma's neck. He recoiled. Black, angry marks around her shoulders, down her arms, extending under her bedclothes. He put the blankets back. They weren't there before.

'I'll be back later this evening. I've left medicines for you to help her symptoms, but I don't know what's causing it.'

'You don't know?' Ash demanded, louder than he'd intended.

'Ash!'

'Sorry,' he mumbled again, looking at Heb.

'I don't know,' confirmed Oskra, looking at his sister. 'She's not well, Hebda. She needs looking after. The deterioration is... surprisingly severe. Nothing I've seen before.'

16

'Okay. Okay. So what do we do?' Heb spoke quickly. She was panicking. The way she wrung her hands proved it. It was the way she wrung them when Elain, their youngest sister, was born.

'For now, we'll see how she gets along with the symptom control,' Oskra rubbed her chin, studying Ma carefully from the end of the bed. 'If she doesn't get better, we'll need to send for help.'

'Help. Okay. From whom?'

'There's an infirmary. About a week's travel, beyond Muddylan and Yewbar, by Whitewater Lake. They're very good there. Or they were, it's been years since I had anything to do with them. We'll send word to them. Ideally, I'd go myself but Kenn's child has the whooping cough and Old Sosen has an infected wound, plus with the risk of something happening in the mines... I'm tied here. My assistant as well.'

'I'll go,' Ash stood. He knew what she was alluding to.

'Wait now, are we sure?' Heb put her hand on his arm. 'Things aren't the safest at the moment...'

He nodded. 'Oskra can't go. Everyone else is busy. You need to stay here to look after Ma and Elain. It has to be me.'

'I don't know,' her hands rubbed harder. 'We can ask one of the guards to go with you? It's just not safe in the woods lately.'

'I'll go too,' Dem announced.

'No chance,' Ash shot her down.

'No chance you get to tell me what to do.'

'No chance I'm taking you.'

'You're right. I'm taking you.'

'No you won't. I said it first that I'd go.'

Dem shrugged. 'What does that matter? Besides, we'll need someone who *actually* knows something about healing to go, make sure the right information is given and received. I'm much better suited.'

'I really don't think it's complicated information?' he muttered.

'It wouldn't be for me, no,' she smirked.

His ears burned again. Damn her. Calling him dumb. She always did. Thought she was so much cleverer than him. He looked at Heb in protest, but his big sister was nodding slowly.

'I'd feel better if both of you went,' Heb looked at him hopefully. 'You can look after each other, yes? Make sure you both get back safe.'

He looked between the three of them. His two sisters and the healer. The decision was already made, he could see it in their eyes. No point fighting the inevitable. No point making a scene. That was Dem's style if she didn't get her way, kicking and screaming and being a child. He had to be better than her. Stronger. He looked at Ma again.

An easy decision at the end of it. Hardly a decision at all.

Chapter 2

She rocked back and forth in the hammock. The hornbeams creaked gently, leaves rustling in the light wind, the morning sun bathed her in its summer bliss. Crumbs from her biscuits were still on her chest, but today was too peaceful a day to bother brushing them away. Let everything sit where it was until it was time to move. Hopefully they'd be there all afternoon. Her hand dropped to the table by her side. A nice mug of milk, fresh from the cart. She closed her eyes. Peaceful.

But something wasn't quite right. One of the cushions was digging in awkwardly. She'd have to move it. But she still wasn't comfortable, now her leg was all tangled in the hammock. She made the necessary adjustments, one after the other. Her collar, her trousers, her cushions again. A fly buzzed in her ear.

She gave up. Peaceful afternoons never lasted. But then again, she was a goblin, and nothing with goblins ever lasted. Families, cities, alliances, lives. Nothing lasted.

Apart from her.

She was still waiting for her end. It would come eventually. No goblin lived for long. Too many foes, too many people who hated them, too much danger outside their pine groves. Goblins knew the whole world was their enemy. Her people lived in anticipation of that final moment, of the breath of the Great Hunter they called death on their napes. It was out there, somewhere in the woods, tongue lolling from its mighty jaws, sharp fangs glistening. She could hear its paws pacing the earth, smell its breath at night. Sometimes close, sometimes distant, but never gone, always waiting.

She stepped back into her hut, spilling more crumbs on the ground. Jal honked and squawked at her heels, snapping up as many as her bill would allow. It was a simple structure, four walls and a roof, nothing more. She built it as she lived; day by day. Any project that had no immediate reward was pointless. What good was it to dedicate months of her life to making one of the grand settlements of men, calefs, or minotorrs when something would probably kill her tomorrow? Better to get by with what she had and enjoy it while it lasted, because it wouldn't be for long.

It's how she'd lived for nearly thirty years.

Taking her whittling knife, she sat on her porch step and set to work on her latest project. Nothing complicated, just a bowl. Holding it firmly in her calloused hands, she slowly carved deeper and deeper lines into the wood. She made them at random, without a specific design in mind. Let the knife and the wood make the decisions. It might look good at the end, it might not. The result wasn't the point. Carving the wood was. Feeling the blade glide through the grain, seeing the shavings peel off, watching it take shape in her hands. Once it was done, she'd give it to one of the craftsmen in Starforge. Sometimes they gave her a silver for one, sometimes a handful of coppers. She didn't know what they looked for, didn't care what they wanted. All she did was carve and see what came of it. Any coin was a welcome bonus.

Nobody told her what to do. Nobody expected anything from her. It's how she liked it. Once, the crafter Geohn gave her three silvers for a delicate spoon she'd made, inlaid her grooves with his fine silver to make an elaborate piece of cutlery. He wanted more from her, offered a deal with a contract to manufacture more for his shop, a partnership. She refused. The spoon was what the wood and the knife wanted to make. She wouldn't force something to change into what it wasn't. She wouldn't be forced to do anything.

The scarred, hairless rings on her wrists and ankles glistened in the sun. Twenty years since the manacles were broken. Since Cadaran and the glacier mines.

No, she'd never be forced to do anything again.

A shout from the overgrown path leading to the village. A visitor. Two. Not especially uncommon. Although the villagers knew she wouldn't be forced into anything, it didn't stop them asking for favours. Not just for her carvings, either. Steben asked for her help more often than not, tracking animals or clearing the wood. Sometimes Oskra asked for help gathering herbs for her medicines. As long as they asked politely enough, she usually agreed to such requests. It was nice to do a good thing, and spending time in the forest was always welcome.

They came around the bend. She raised her brows. Ashil and Demsai Nalbens. A funny pair. Ash sometimes came to watch her carve, tried to copy her work. Dem joined her on her herbology expeditions. Neither knew the other visited her, each thought they had their own special, secret friendship. She didn't correct them. Each as friendly as the other.

Surprising to see them together, however. Unless they were here to settle once and for all who was her favourite. Neither was the answer. Their older sister Hebda was much gentler, like their poor mother.

'Ffed!' Ash raised his hand in greeting.

She nodded back.

'Dear Ffed,' Dem smiled politely. 'We need to ask for a favour.'

It's how every conversation with the villagers started. Always a favour. Their attempt to make it obvious it wasn't an order. Must have had a village meeting or something to discuss how she should be spoken to. Not that she cared. As long as it wasn't forced, they could ask her however they liked.

'Ask,' she replied, as she always did.

'I need to get to an infirmary for help with Ma,' continued Dem, as Ash glowered at the back of her head. Bickering again, it seemed. They always complained to her about their respective sibling. Each as bad as the other. 'Oskra doesn't know what's wrong and wants me to get advice from the other healers.'

She nodded. Lelan Nalbens was a kind woman. She knew about her sickness from overheard conversations between the guards. Only ill for a day and already nearing death's door. She pursed her lips. You never knew when it was your turn. Two things impossible to outrun were the Great Hunter and direwolves. Goblins knew this. Like all goblins, she didn't fear it. Why fear the inevitable? It would come to her soon enough. Once it had your scent, there was no escape.

'Where go?' she asked.

21

Their speech was difficult. All twisted tongues and strange shapes with her lips. Goblin speech was far simpler, more intuitive. Screeches, yips, natters, and warbles. The exact sound made was less important than its substance. Not that she couldn't understand them. There was plenty to infer from the tone and cadence of their words that let her understand, but forming them back was always difficult.

'There's an infirmary by Whitewater Lake, about a week away,' Ash stepped up, ignoring his sister. Two children vying for authority. Each as naïve as the other. 'We need to get there as soon as we can, but with recent troubles with the woods, Heb wondered if you'd come with us?'

'Where Heb?'

'She's with Ma and Elain, looking after them while we're away.'

She rubbed her bald wrists. Twenty years later and they still hurt from time to time. Mostly when she faced a decision. They were right to name the woods dangerous. Rebels were all over the place, some with the Council, some out for themselves. Both dangerous for different reasons. The lone rogues would just kill them. The Council might try to recruit them to be killed later.

True, death was inevitable, but that didn't mean you should look for it. These two children would meet the Great Hunter if they wandered the woods on their own, them and poor Lelan. If she were with them, they might get another day or so before the inevitable found them.

Another day was always worth having.

'I come today.'

Dem nodded slowly, brow furrowing softly. 'And tomorrow?

Tomorrow? What good was tomorrow when today was here? Tomorrow could bring anything. It might never exist. Why worry? Planning futures, bright and miserable, was for other races.

'I come today.'

22

Chapter 3

Saturated with a cocktail of damp and woodsmoke, belches and vomit, roast pork and spilled ale, Dem's nose ran uncontrollably, no matter how many times she blew it. She rubbed it furiously with her wrist. No difference. The snot poured out again a few seconds later.

'Want kerchief?' Ffed offered her own.

'Thank you,' she took the cloth square.

Ash sniggered behind his trencher as she blew again. Damn him. He never stopped to think how she'd feel in the inn. Just danced into the village and declared loudly and confidently they'd be staying overnight in the 'Golden Acorn'. Ffed just went along with him, probably assumed the buffoon knew what he was talking about. He didn't stop to consider what kind of place it was, whether it was safe, what the prices were, what food they served, if they had a private room for the three. No, the decision was made and in he sauntered, banging through the doors like he owned the place.

As predicted, it was a dive. More of a hovel for fiends and degenerates than an inn. Muddylan was never the most glamorous of towns, but Ash had somehow picked its worst as their lodgings for the night. Drunkards, drug addicts, and men with particularly unsavoury looks sat at the ramshackle, stained tables. More than one cast mischievous glances their way as she tried to stomach the miserable excuse for a meal the crooked barmaid served them.

Soggy trenchers, overboiled vegetables, and pork. At least the pork was cooked through, albeit so full of fat it left a sticky film on her lips, which mixed with the discharge from her nostrils into a foul slime on her top lip. She wiped it away with Ffed's kerchief. Disgusting.

Ash seemed to be enjoying himself. Probably thought he was so world-wise and honourable, drinking and eating with the decrepit degenerates of Muddylan. The fool. He didn't see the glances, didn't hear the murmurs. Most of the glares directed at Ffed, the jealous looks of resentment at Ash, the lecherous leers at her. They could've picked a smaller, quieter place to berth up. Even a stable. Anything to avoid the people.

Hunching lower into her chair, she made herself small. Despite the heat of the tavern-room, she kept her oiled cloak on. No point revealing her fine travelling clothes to the other patrons. The brushed leather and soft cotton was too much of an advertisement among the stained linen and torn animal-hides of the locals. Starforge's wealth was written all over them. Not that her hiding mattered much. Ash had cast his cloak over the hook by the fireside, and sauntered to and from the bar ordering more drinks and food, watched all the while by frowning faces and glittering eyes. At least he had the common sense to keep his purse hidden.

The rivalry between Muddylan and their home was decades old. Ever since the silver mine was discovered in the foothills by their village, even the poorer inhabitants such as Ma had suddenly come to a modest wealth, even by just panning the Clearbed for ore missed by the miners. But as much as their wealth grew, so did the hostility from their neighbours, for whom there were no silver lines, or copper, or iron, or anything. Just the mud. Perfect for cultivating their mushrooms and housing their pigs, good enough to grow tough grains, but hopeless for amassing any wealth. Due to a simple chance of geography, the resentment they bore festered and grew. Now here they were, two children, as good as advertising all the wealth they had to their bitter neighbours.

Ash slurped his drink and licked his greasy fingers with an arrogant grin.

'Lighten up, would you? You wanted to be out the rain so here we are.'

'We should've talked about it before coming in,' she hissed, pushing away her half-finished plate.

'What's to talk about? Roof, food, fire, bed,' he ticked them off on his fingers. 'It's got them all. Just like you asked.'

'It's not *safe* here though, is it?' she snapped, voice barely above a whisper as she kept an eye on the others. 'Not with you prancing around like a peacock.'

'Winds! I'm just getting us food and drink and paying for it. That's literally all,' he shook his head, as if she were the unreasonable one.

'No, you're painting a target on our backs. Look at you in your fine jacket and boots. Look at them,' she flicked her eyes to the locals. 'You think they haven't noticed?'

'Please,' he rolled his eyes. 'So, I have good clothes. Doesn't mean they're going to rob us.'

'Quiet!' she hissed. Bloody idiot. 'They'll all know we're from Starforge by the end of the night. You still want to sleep in a cold room with nothing but a rusty latch keeping them out?'

'So they know we're from home,' he shrugged again and took another swig. It held nothing stronger than apple juice, but he no doubt liked to pretend it was cider or ale to feel like a man, not the boy he was. 'I don't mind. I've got nothing against Muddylan. We should really be helping them more, anyway. Isn't really fair that we have so much more wealth just because our ancestors built a village next to a mine and theirs didn't.'

'I'd rather not help by getting us robbed,' she seethed.

'Nothing's going to happen, by the four winds! Just because you don't like it that I picked the place, seriously,' he laughed falsely.

'No, it's because it isn't safe,' she glared at him.

He slammed his tankard on the table, making her jump. A couple of locals from the closest tables raised their eyebrows at them before returning to their muted conversations. She ignored them. Ash stood abruptly and retrieved his coat. More eyes followed his angry strides. She covered her face with her hand as he stood over her.

'Come on, then!' he snapped, trying to pull her chair back. 'Off we go. Decision made. Dem gets her way.'

'Sit down,' she muttered, feeling more and more stares into the back of her head.

'No, no. You're not happy so off we go. Make sure *you're* making all the decisions.'

'Oh yes, because that's what this is about,' she sneered back, unable to contain herself.

'Both sit, quiet,' Ffed stood as well, trying to shepherd them back to their seats. They ignored her.

'Yeah, it is. I reckon. Don't like me doing anything, have to have your say in whatever I do,' Ash spat.

'Oh because you're *such* a responsible man. So big and strong, swaggering about and paying for little old me. You're only doing this to make yourself feel important, not because you actually *care* about Ma getting better.'

Ash stared at her, mouth open. She stared back, cheeks flushing. The hubbub of the tavern continued in the background. His fists were clenched. Go on then, use them. She stuck her cheek out, daring him. Let the bully use the only weapon he had over her. Dumb clout. He thought he was so much better than her, and when he couldn't prove it, he'd resort to violence. He knew it too. She saw the calculation behind his glare, whether the satisfaction of the punch was worth the moral loss. She hoped he would. Sure, she might get a black eye for a few weeks, but she'd win.

'Sit. Quiet,' Ffed's vice-like fingers were around their shoulders, forcing them back to their seats. She didn't even realise she was standing.

The goblin increased the pressure in her fingertips. A flare of pain and she plonked into her seat. Ash did the same, fury diminished with the goblin's squeeze. They stared at each other across the table, her final accusation hanging between them.

'Apologise now,' Ffed ordered.

Silence. She snorted. Ash would never apologise for what he'd done. He'd made a scene and would be too embarrassed to admit it. She raised her brows at him, waiting. He glowered back.

'Dem. Apologise.'

She blinked and turned to Ffed, her smile vanishing.

'Me?'

'Yes. Unfair. Ash love Lelan.'

Now Ash grinned at her. Smugness dripped from his pallid, ugly lips. How dare Ffed take his side! How dare she! The horrible little goblin. No wonder she wasn't allowed to live in the proper village if that's how she treated people.

'Well, Dem? Where's my apology?' Ash purred.

'Shut up,' Ffed snapped. They both raised their eyebrows. Unexpected. Perhaps she wasn't quite as much on his side as they'd both assumed. 'You apologise too. Dem right. Too loud.'

26

'I've not raised my voice,' he pouted.

'No. Loud in other way. Keep clothes hidden. Keep rich secret. Unfriendly eyes.'

'You're taking her side? So why follow me in?' he demanded.

'No side. Good tavern. Roof, food, fire, bed, people,' she imitated him, ticking them off on her fingers. She wiggled her fifth finger. 'People good. Want people around. Other taverns too quiet. Here locals and visitors. There just locals. Good tavern with company to watch us.'

She pursed her lips. She hadn't thought of that. Many of the patrons had the look of travellers, their cloaks and sticks either by the fire or by the door, their packs by their feet. They wouldn't hold the same animosity towards their home as the locals would. Another inn may be quieter, but they might stand out that much more. As Ffed said, it was easier to hide in a crowd than an empty room.

'So you like the tavern, just don't like me,' Ash rolled his eyes.

'Like you fine. But too loud,' Ffed repeated, jabbing her finger at his brushed leather jacket.

He sighed and fixed his gaze on her, jaw clenching and unclenching as he struggled to spit the words out. She waited patiently, knowing it would be her turn to endure the ordeal in a moment.

'I'm sorry, Dem.'

'I'm sorry, Ash.'

She turned away, back to her cold food. Hearing his apology didn't make her feel any better for offering hers. Ffed nodded, satisfied. At least someone was happy. Ash sheepishly threw his cloak back around his shoulders, concealing his clothes.

'Good. Sit quiet. Eat. Sleep soon.'

Best suggestion of the night so far. Two nights of trudging after the goblin and sleeping wild was enough to make her miss her soft feather bed dearly. Her previous expeditions into the forest with Ffed had only ever been around Starforge itself, never any further. This time was different. The goblin was mistrustful of the roads and struck through the dense undergrowth on her own path. She'd been hard-pressed to follow. Ash had it worse, his lanky, gangly frame unsuited to navigating through the spindly branches and uneven turf. Not that she cared. He deserved a bit of humility. Always thought so much more of himself than was warranted, seeing him fall flat on his arse in a puddle was more satisfying than summer's first strawberry.

She glanced at him again, staring into his mug. Perhaps her comment was worded unfairly, but it held an element of truth. He wanted to be important, wanted to do some grand gesture to gain standing in the community. Right now, as a crafter's apprentice, he was scraping the bottom of the barrel. What use was a gangly, freaky, clumsy oaf of an apprentice in a village full of master craftsmen with decades of experience working silver? He wasn't even allowed to touch the metal yet! No, he was a nobody. He was jealous of her, the only village healer's second apprentice. She had an invaluable role, and within a few years would start learning the ways properly. He always played it down, of course, claimed she was nothing more than an errand-girl. Jealousy, nothing more. She almost felt sorry for him, toiling away at his mediocre projects while she was out there actually helping people. He saw Ma ill and jumped at the opportunity to go and ask for help. As if he'd be able to give the same quality history as she could? As if he'd have the faintest idea what they advised? Not a chance. He knew he was out of his depth. That's why he was so annoyed with her. She'd called him out on his pathetic attempts to gain standing and now, inevitably, he was taking it out on her.

He looked up at her. She curled her lip. He didn't react, kept his eyes steady. She frowned. Not looking at her, but at someone directly behind her. Ffed glanced over as well, frowning, hand straying to her belt where she kept her whittling-knife. She twisted in her seat.

The man smiled broadly, revealing a glistening wall of perfect ivory teeth.

'Evening, my friends. Might I join you?'

'No, we're all good,' she turned away, glaring at Ash. Now look at the trouble he's brought.

'No? I reckon I can squeeze in, just next to your lovely goblin friend, aye?'

Ffed took another swig, leaving a milk moustache clinging to the hairs of her upper lip. She narrowed her eyes at the stranger.

He chuckled. 'Perhaps not. Next to you, then, my dear.'

Firm hands around the back of her chair moved her as easily as a napkin to make room at their table. Ash stood uneasily, his frown growing deeper as the stranger sat down with a sigh. He looked around the table and smiled again.

'My apologies, I've not introduced myself. Name's Nariton Selkaharr. You can call me Nari.'

'I'll call you a cur for sitting at our table uninvited,' she snapped.

'Plenty have called me worse for less, my dear,' Nari chuckled again. 'So, what we eating?'

He reached over to Ffed's plate of vegetables. She didn't see Ffed's hand move, only heard the smack of the spoon against Nari's hand. He withdrew with a yelp.

'No worries, not a fan of boiled vegetables anyway, not when there's meat available.'

'Take Dem's,' Ash pushed her cold plate to the stranger.

She shot him another glare. Bloody idiot. What did he think he was doing, inviting the cur to stay? If she could've kicked him she would, but there were too many legs under the table to be sure which was his. She settled for a glare instead. He ignored her. Nari didn't.

'Don't think she's too happy with that suggestion,' he chuckled.

'I was coming back to it,' she lied.

'Maybe,' he leaned across the table and scooped up the bowl in one hand. She moved to stop him, but too late. He sighed contentedly as he shovelled cold pork and soggy bread into his mouth. He winked mischievously. 'That being said, it's been sitting there for a while and you didn't seem to enjoy it when it was hot. Best not leave it to waste.'

He scooped up the rest of the meat and trencher, leaving a miserable pile of overdone vegetables at the bottom of the bowl. He sent it skidding across the table to Ffed.

'There you go, gobs, all yours.'

Ffed held his gaze, ignoring the bowl. She wouldn't eat it. Dem had tried to share plenty of meals with her in the past but she never touched food that came into contact with meat, not even leftover bread from an underfilled sandwich.

'Not to my taste either,' Nari shrugged. 'What's that you're drinking there, son?'

'Apple juice,' Ash mumbled. Typical. She could practically hear his knees knocking under the table. No spine.

'Eh? By the four winds! That's no drink for a lad. I'll get us some ales.'

'No,' Dem said, firmly.

'No?' Nari glanced at her, eyes gleaming.

'You heard.'

'That I did. Just for me, then.'

He stood and signalled to the crooked barmaid, who acknowledged his raised hand with a nod. Nari sat back down, smiling again.

'What do you want?' she demanded. Better to just get to the point.

'Ah, we know who wears the trousers here, don't we?' he nudged Ash in the ribs.

'Well?'

'Well, Dem, that's your name, yes? Well, Dem, you three strike me as not being from around here.'

'I wouldn't say that,' Ash protested, deciding to show who *he* thought wore the trousers, as Nari put it.

'No? You don't strike me as Muddylan folk?'

'No, but we're from close by.'

'Ah! Where exactly?'

'None of your business,' Dem snapped, glaring at Ash again. What did he think he was doing? This wasn't a bloody game, the idiot. People didn't just approach you in taverns for a friendly chat. Not ones who looked like this cur, anyway. She'd seen the sword at his flank when he signalled the barmaid. Ffed's hand was still by her knife.

'Perhaps not. I know you're from Starforge anyway, but I won't tell, don't you worry,' he tapped the side of his nose conspiratorially.

'What does it matter to you?' Ash demanded, all but confirming what Nari was presumably only guessing. She closed her eyes. He really was a clout.

'Nothing at all. I have a proposition for you.'

Here it was then. Doubtless it would be an unsavoury one. She wished she'd packed a knife. She wished Ffed's hatchet wasn't with their packs by the door. She wished Ash had never come. It was all his fault. The idiot. The unthinking, clumsy bastard. Damn him. She'd hated him the moment Ma pushed him screaming into the world, although she couldn't remember it.

'What?' Ash asked.

The barmaid wobbled over with a frothing tankard. Nari took it with a broad smile and flicked her a coin. She caught it with surprising dexterity and shuffled back to her bar.

Nari took a deep draught and sighed.

'Winds! That's what I needed. Well, my friends. It seems to me that you two are on something of a journey and have employed your fine goblin friend here to be your guide. Am I right?'

Ash shrugged. 'What of it?'

Nari's smile broadened again. 'Well, my friends, you're in luck. I humbly offer my services to act as your second guide and bodyguard through these forests to your destination.'

'No,' Dem dismissed him.

'Why, we may live under a tyrant but I didn't expect to find another one here!'

Tyrant? Bastard! How dare he. King Stolach brought peace to the lands. How dare he suggest otherwise. Life might not be easy, but compared to the stories of how it was before, they were all living like kings. And to suggest she was one was unfair, he was just intimidated by her. She opened her mouth to say as much, but stopped herself. The sword, the comment, the weather-worn clothes. He was a rogue. Her mouth closed slowly. There were guards around Muddylan as well. Not as many as Starforge, but certainly a small contingent. They had to tell them. Get this cur arrested before he caused any more trouble in the forest.

31

'We're heading to an infirmary,' Ash said, oblivious. 'Our Ma's sick. Very sick. We need their help to get her better.'

Nari nodded slowly, mouth grim. 'I see. Sick mother.'

'Yes. Do you know the place?' Ash asked.

'Vaguely,' Nari rubbed his chin, suddenly serious. 'You know the way?' he asked Ffed, raising his brow.

'Little bit. Not been before. Know area less well,' Ffed admitted. Why was she entertaining it? Why disclose she didn't know exactly where they were going? She stared at her pleadingly. No more information, by the four winds, just get rid of him.

They ignored her.

'It's not easy getting there,' he kept rubbing, playing with his coarse goatee. 'I was hoping you'd be heading further north.'

Ash frowned. 'It is north, isn't it? By Whitewater Lake?'

Nari's eyes widened and he nodded quickly. 'Ah! That infirmary! Apologies, I was thinking about another one, down by Yellow Castle.'

'Yellow Castle?' Ash laughed. 'Winds! We'd be going a fair way if we went there!'

Nari chuckled. 'That's what I thought. Whitewater Lake is about five days away. I can take you.'

'How much?' Ffed asked.

'How much? Oh! Well,' Nari settled back into his chair, smiling wolfishly. 'I'm not cheap, you know. You're from Starforge so I reckon you can afford my premium price. Two silvers per day. Ingots, not coins. Starting today.'

Dem blinked. Was that all? For less than two weeks' work, he'd be earning the equivalent of Ash's monthly wage. Not a bad price. Definitely suspicious. She glanced at Ash, finally catching his eye. He had a soft smile of victory on his lips. Didn't suspect a thing.

'A bit of privacy to discuss, please?' Ash asked. Well, at least he had the insight to know they needed to discuss it. The bar really was set low.

'Of course, take your time, I'll be over at the bar.'

She watched him carefully, looking for any signs or signals to any other patrons. There didn't seem to be any. Nobody paid him much interest, he didn't stop to converse with anyone. He took a high stool by the bar and stared into his tankard. She turned to the others.

'What in the four winds are we doing?' she demanded.

'Negotiating,' Ash shrugged.

'With him? He's a rogue! I saw his sword. You heard what he said about the king.'

'Yeah I know, so?' Ash shrugged again.

She stared at him. Sometimes, despite everything she knew about him, his stupidity still impressed her. Was he really so naïve? She stopped herself. Of course not. He didn't know he was a rogue, he was just trying to save face.

'What do *you* think?' she asked, pointedly. 'I wonder why that would matter?'

'Means he's lived out in the woods for a while. You can tell that from the state of his clothes. He'll know the way around the place, know where the other gangs are and how to avoid them, plus he probably knows how to handle a sword. Nothing bad there.'

Well, apparently he really was that naïve. She rolled her eyes. He thought he was so clever, picking up on those details, but he didn't think what they actually meant.

'How many rogues go about on their own? They're always in gangs, aren't they? He's trying to lure us out there and get his cronies to jump us. Can you get that into your thick head?'

'I don't think so,' Ash shook his head. 'The amount he's asking for is way more than what we have on us. If we promise to pay him once we're back, it'll be worth more to him to keep us alive.'

'What, a few silver ingots? You think that's enough to buy his loyalty?'

Ash laughed. Right in her face. An arrogant snigger that rolled into a smug chuckle. Like he knew so much more than her. Even Ffed giggled. She felt her cheeks flush again. Damn them both.

'What?' she demanded.

'Dem, you really have spent too much time at home,' he wiped his eyes with his sleeve, still sniggering.

'Shut up. You think I'm wrong?'

'Starforge rich. Dem rich. Forget normal prices,' Ffed laid a soothing hand on her arm.

'How much do you think this meal cost?' asked Ash.

'What does it matter?' she hissed, brushing Ffed's hand away. Here he was again, pretending to be worldly where she wasn't, pretending to be a man of the little people, not a snobby Starforger, as they saw them. She looked between the two. She'd guess low, show them up. 'One and a half silver coins?'

Ash snorted like a horse. 'Winds! It was thirteen coppers for the food, drink, and beds for the night. Would've been fourteen if Ffed had some pork.'

She blinked. Coppers? Where did he even get coppers from? Nobody even used them in Starforge. A half silver coin was the smallest currency they used. She looked back at Nariton on his stool, waving his legs back and forth. If that's how much a handful of coppers got you out here… his request seemed far more unreasonable, which paradoxically made it more reassuring. Perhaps he was just a greedy bastard not a murdering one.

Admitting that, however, would mean admitting Ash was right. That was a step too far.

'What do you think?' she asked Ffed.

The goblin played with the last broccoli in her bowl, one hand rubbing the other wrist. 'Don't know woods well. Here to protect. Nari seems… untrustworthy in good way. Greedy. Protect us for silver, I think.'

She looked between the two of them. 'And if he does lead us to his gang?'

'Please, he doesn't have a bloody gang,' Ash rolled his eyes.

Ffed ignored him and looked her in the eye. 'Here to protect.'

She turned back to Nariton. He raised his tankard happily in acknowledgment. Her lip curled. Ash smiled smugly. Ffed held her gaze. If not Ash and Nari, she trusted the goblin. It's why Heb wanted them to go with her. If Nari really was just a greedy bastard out to make a quick penny, he'd be useful in the forest. As good a woodsman and survivalist as Ffed might be, she lacked the brawn of a proper fighter. Scrappy and fierce, no doubt, but could she really protect

34

them? Besides, Nari claimed to know the way. If they could trust Nari's sword to remain on their side, she reluctantly admitted he would be useful.

*

Nariton watched them closely. Easy pickings. A few days up towards Whitewater Lake for a chance to settle his debts. Damned lucky. From the looks of them, they'd have plenty hidden away in their packs to see him through and settle his score with Kirkin. Provided he could get the money to him in time.

He took another swig of ale. He had a week left. One measly week. If their destination were closer, he would've really taken them there and collected the fee. Honest money. It would've been good to pay his debts with it. But no. Needs must, and money was money, honestly won or stolen, it all paid the same.

Things never quite worked out as planned. He'd been half-considering just running, leaving his brother to Kirkin's vengeance. It was his fault he got caught, after all. But something made him stop by this dump of a tavern, and there were these three. Soft children in expensive clothes and a skinny goblin, of all people.

An old Cadaran prisoner, from the looks of her scars. Their manacles left a mark on everyone. He looked at his wrists. How would they look in irons? Was Nat bound and chained to a wall as he sat here enjoying a tankard of ale? Would he endure the stress and anxiety? He was a gentle soul, for all his lawbreaking, mixed up with the wrong crowd. He looked at the goblin again. Not like her. There was iron in those limbs, fire in her chest. Old scars. Perhaps from before the pits and slave mines were liberated by Stolach. One didn't survive Cadaran without having something to them, that's for sure. She was one to watch, the complicating factor. Not that he was too worried. He had plenty of experience with hard men and women, they were all behind him. Everyone needed sleep, and when they did, light fingers would do their work.

His weren't the only eyes on the three. More than a few of the tavern patrons were eyeing them up. Some more subtly than others. Locals and travellers, drawn to the boy's flashy clothes, the girl's innocence, the goblin's existence. They all saw them as easy pickings.

He sighed and yawned. A busy night lay ahead deterring the more...
persistent patrons. These were his marks, and nobody was spoiling
them before he got to work.

He stared into his tankard. His amber reflection stared back,
ringed with heads of foam. Once this was all done, his thieving days
would be behind him. Him and his brother's.

Chapter 4

The forest was as dark, damp, and uncomfortable as the first two days' travel, however now it felt that little bit more bearable. Muddylan's squalor was behind and things looked brighter ahead. As predicted, the night was uneventful, and despite Dem's fretting and whining, they slept the whole night through without a disturbance. Apart from a few scrapes and bumps outside their door as drunkards stumbled to their respective rooms, it was as peaceful as any night at home. Ash reckoned she almost wanted to be robbed, just so she could prove him wrong. But then, that's how she was. Being right was more important than things going well.

She was trudging behind him now, breathing hard after that last hill. They'd barely spoken since their miserable breakfast of lumpy porridge with nothing but salt to flavour. At home they'd have fruit preserves to sweeten it, but the Golden Acorn didn't strike him as the type of establishment to sell damson jam.

A particularly dense thicket lay ahead. Nari wove his way through with the expertise of a cat. He wasn't so lucky, his long limbs caught in the branches and his head bumped against the trunks. Sliding through the undergrowth wasn't his style, better to just push through and hope there weren't too many thorns. As he pushed past a particularly reluctant branch, it whipped back behind him. Dem yelped and cursed.

'Sorry!' he called over his shoulder. He wasn't.

'Shut up,' she snarled. 'Be more careful.'

'Will do!' he called back, cheerfully.

'Git,' she muttered, loud enough for him to hear.

'Bitch,' he muttered in return.

'What was that?'

'You heard.'

'Bastard,' she stepped on his heel, making him stumble.

'Damn you!' he turned on her. Or at least he tried, the thicket caught his arms, left him snared in an awkward half-turn. A branch dug into his flank, stopping him from getting any further. 'Damn you!'

She saw his predicament and smiled. 'Having some trouble, you little bitch?'

'Damn you,' he spat back.

She picked up a dead stick and wedged it between his stomach and one of the entangling trees. 'Now, now, not when I'm trying to get you out.'

'Get myself out,' he muttered, tugging at his sleeves.

She ignored him, digging the branch in harder, putting her weight against it, using it as a lever. What did she expect? For him to pop out? Stupid idiot. It was under his jacket anyway, scraping against his skin.

'You're making it worse,' he growled. Her stick dug into his stomach, burning.

'Just let me get it in the right place,' she twisted and jerked the stick, digging deeper.

He struggled again, small twigs whipping against his cheeks.

'Stop.'

'Just a bit more of a wiggle,' the stick pressed harder.

'Stop!'

'Now, now.'

'Dem!' Ffed's voice from behind. The pressure on his stomach eased. He couldn't see her, his head wouldn't twist that way.

'Just trying to get this big lump out,' she replied, sweetly.

'Not that way.'

The goblin's hard fingers worked their way around him, twisting and pulling at the branches. Twig by twig, he was released. It was all he could do not to punch her right there and then, twirling her damned stick around her wrist. Ffed held him back.

'Do that again...' he started.

'Yes?' she stuck her chin out again. Inviting. One day he'd take her up on it. Not today.

'Shut up. Just get going,' he turned away.

She snorted and slunk through the trees. Nowhere near as easily or gracefully as Nari, but better than him. Far better. He watched her, fists clenched.

'Show you,' Ffed beckoned him back to the entangling thicket. She demonstrated how to part the branches, which ones to push to bring the others away like a curtain. He tried to take it in but couldn't concentrate, his stomach felt raw, no doubt it was grazed and torn thanks to Dem's little trick. What was she thinking? Was it her half-formed plan to gut him and leave him tangled up, as if Ffed and Nari wouldn't notice? Or was she hoping he'd turn back so she could have all the credit herself. Probably the latter. If anything, he was surprised she was only doing it now. But that's just how she was, always looking for credit. She probably thought this would put her in better standing with Oskra, give her more responsibilities. Idiot. This was far from a glamorous quest or epic journey, it was just a walk to an infirmary and back, hardly the stuff of stories.

Ffed opened up the thicket for him and he followed her through into a clearing. Nari was waiting for them on the other side, leaning nonchalantly against a tree. Dem was halfway across, hands trailing in the long grass.

Ffed stopped short of the clearing, watching it carefully.

'Not without looking,' she muttered, nodding to Dem, wandering peacefully through the grass.

'How come?'

'Ambush risk.'

He raised his eyebrows, watching Dem's progress.

'What about Dem?' he asked.

'Too late to warn.'

'What do we do?'

'Wait. See.'

He watched her, suddenly tense. They remained a foot within the shadows, the bright sunlight of the clearing a barrier they wouldn't cross. He couldn't take his eyes off his sister, scarcely breathing. She was oblivious to it all, walking without a care in the world to Nari on the other side. His mouth dried. A lump he couldn't swallow stuck in his throat.

Only a few metres until she reached the other side. Nari called something out to her. She replied, their voices too quiet to decipher. He gripped Ffed's shoulder. If anything were to happen, surely it would be now. Would they have time to intervene? Ffed's hatchet was still strapped to her pack. Should be get it ready for her?

Dem made it to the other side, pointing over her shoulder. Nari seemed to laugh, shoulders twitching. Dem leaned against another tree, waiting.

He exhaled slowly. Seems this clearing was safe.

Ffed nudged him in the flank.

'Dem safe, don't worry.'

He sniffed and shrugged. 'I wasn't.'

Ffed grinned, pointed face splitting. 'Sure.'

Despite the apparent safety, Ffed still led them around the fringes of the clearing, keeping to the shadows of the trees.

'Took your bloody time,' Nari grunted as he rose from his leaning position.

'Stuck to trees,' Ffed shrugged.

Nari looked her up and down. 'I wasn't going to lead you into an ambush.'

'Maybe. Still not safe.'

Nari shook his head. 'The day I take lessons about trust from a goblin is the day I'll quit it all and become a bloody monk.'

Ffed shrugged her wiry shoulders again.

'Why'd you let me walk into it?' Dem demanded, turning on Ffed.

'Too late. Halfway across.'

'Could've told me to come back?'

'No difference. Halfway,' she ushered them on. 'Go, follow Nari.'

Dem huffed in frustration and scurried after their guide. Ash followed. No point taking it out on Ffed. If she was careless enough to wander into an open clearing without checking it was safe first, that was her problem! He conveniently forgot the fact he only learned about the potential dangers a few minutes earlier.

He did his best to continue as Ffed showed him, separating the twigs and branches instead of bludgeoning through. It was useless, he just couldn't get it right. No matter how he tried, he always got an elbow caught awkwardly, a foot stuck in the curve of a root, bumped his head, or lost his footing completely. The goblin hovered around him like a wasp, pushing and shoving the right branches around, slapping his hands and feet when he put them wrong. She was getting frustrated, growling and yipping in her native tongue at his clumsy attempts. Her irritation was contagious, and he was soon growling with her as Dem and Nari stretched further and further ahead. By mid-afternoon, it was too much even for his fine coat, the leather torn in several places and the seams starting to fray.

'Supposed to be good quality,' he grumbled as Ffed untangled him from the latest trap.

'Not. Doing. What. I. Do!' she moved the branches, less carefully now than at the beginning.

'I'm trying!' he snapped. 'Never claimed to be a woodsman, did I?'

'Not listening to advice,' she pushed against a low bough and the whole thicket rose up before him in a perfect passage.

He rolled his eyes. She made it look so easy.

'I'm trying. I'm just not used to it.'

She didn't say anything, just gestured to the opening. He ducked his head through. It wasn't the end. A few paces ahead was another squeeze through the trees, a sharp holly filling the majority of the gap between a chestnut and an alder. He saw Dem's pack slide between, barely caressing the holly's points. No point even attempting it alone.

'Can you please show me?'

Ffed scurried past and beckoned him over. Silently, she pulled one of the alder's branches up, simultaneously gathering the majority of the holly along its length, leaving a narrow corridor through to Nari and Dem. So simple, yet if it were him, he'd have been pricked and scratched a hundred times already.

High-pitched screams suddenly erupted from the other side. Loud enough to clamp his hands over his ears. Ffed released the branch, her batlike ears flapping in pain. He recovered, trying to see past the brush. Nari and Dem were nowhere to be seen. The screams continued, high and shrill, splitting his ears.

Damn it all! He'd left Dem on the other side of this barrier with Nari. She was right, after all. A rogue. Waiting for the perfect opportunity to do evil. And here they were, perfectly separated by the forest. The screams grew in pitch, then slowly faded as they fled.

Good, run! As long as she kept screaming, he could follow. As long as she kept screaming, she was still alive.

Nariton. Damn the bastard! He'd make him pay for this. They should never have trusted him. It was always his weakness, his naivety, his assumption of good intention. Now his sister was in danger, murder and worse at the hands of the man he'd invited into their company.

He pushed against the alder branch as Ffed had. The holly didn't move. He adjusted his position. A bit better, but not quite right. The gap was too narrow. It would have to do. He pushed through, ignoring the sting of the holly against his cheek as the leaves scratched deep furrows into his cheeks. The vegetation pushed back, denying him entry. He pushed again, arms scrambling for purchase, something to pull through against. Dem's screams faded again. Going too far! He'd lose her. Snarling, he tore at the bushes. Damn them. Damn the forest.

A hand on his shoulder. Ffed pushed the branch again and the passage opened up. No time for thanks, he wriggled through the last few inches, popping out the other end.

His foot caught. He fell heavily, arms still wedged awkwardly against his side. With no protection to cushion the blow, he fell heavily on his face, whacking his head on a stone.

Pain exploded. His head was caved in. His skull was fractured, splintered, shards of bone digging into his brain. Blood poured. He rolled around, groaning. Dem at the mercy of Nari, him brought to ground by the forest itself. What failures.

Something giggled next to him. He opened his eyes. Blind. How long until he died? Until the accumulated dirt and loam made the wound rot, his exposed brain turning to mush as it fell apart in his head.

'Clumsy idiot.'

Dem's voice.

He whimpered, a mixture of confusion, pain, relief, and rage taking power of linguistics from him. Or was it because of his broken skull? Would he ever speak again? What would they tell Ma? Her son was dead, her daughter broken, and no cure to offer. Tears welled at the corner of his eyes. As they burst forth, a glimmer of light. Four winds! His sight was recovering. Perhaps all was not lost.

'Up you get,' firm hands under his arms hauled him to a sitting position. Nari's voice. He growled and swung. How dare the bastard touch him. Blind or not, sword or not, he'd kill him. Throttle him, beat his skull in with a stone.

'Whoa! Steady!'

'Bastard!' he spat, or tried to. His tongue felt swollen, thick. It came out as a muffled blubber.

'Winds! He can't even speak. Must've hit his head worse than it looks.'

Dem again. Did she come back around?

Firm hands around his face squeezed his cheeks to force his mouth open. He tried bucking his legs and swinging his arms, but they were pinned to his sides.

'Bit tongue.'

The hard hands pressed against his head, sending another surge of overwhelming pain. His limbs lost all power as his body threatened to faint from the pain. He fought against it. Cold water splashed over his face, hard hands rubbed his eyes.

'Open up, now,' Ffed's voice, right in front of him. He opened his mouth again. She chuckled. 'Eyes. Open eyes.'

He did as he was told. The world opened up before him. Beautiful trees, their leaves a full palate of greens, their barks wonderful shades of brown, black, and silver, a grey sky of soft clouds through the lush canopy, and his companions. Ffed, her hand on his forehead. Dem behind her. No bruises, no wounds, shaking with laughter. His relief quickly soured. Laughing at him? He'd teach her a bloody good lesson for her dirty tricks.

Struggling to rise, his arms remained pinned. Was this her idea of a clever joke? Bitch. Last time he'd ever try to help her.

'Steady on, lad, a bit of a tumble there.'

Nariton. He bucked again, trying to get free. Only for a moment. Why was he angry at Nari? This was all Dem. He hadn't done anything. All those accusations he'd dreamt up were Dem's doing, her stupid joke with her screams to make him worried. He relaxed. Nari was fine, a good choice of companion. Dem, on the other hand...

'My head,' he mumbled, tongue aching.

'Little cut,' said Ffed, releasing the pressure of her thumb on his head for a quick look before returning it. 'Blood in eyes. Only small.'

Of course. His cheeks grew hot again. No great wounds. No fractured skull or damaged brain. Just a cut, a bit of blood sticking his lids together. Winds! This was all Dem's fault, getting him all worked up with her screams.

Her screams.

He could still hear them, echoing through the trees, but Dem's mouth was shut. He let Ffed fuss over him in silence for a few more minutes, ignoring Dem's incessant giggling at his expense. She didn't seem the least bit concerned about the noise. It would've been reassuring if it were anyone else.

'What happened then?' he blubbed, spitting a mouthful of blood past his swollen tongue.

'We were just waiting here for you two when a pig-driver came through,' Nari helped him to his feet. 'One of the hogs got spooked by us and ran away screaming. Not sure why they're still making that racket.'

'Hogs,' he repeated.

'Aye.'

He shook his head, but the motion made it hurt. Ffed tutted and rummaged about her pack for a bandage when blood trickled again.

'What was that all about, anyway?' Nari nodded to his head. 'Could've hurt one of us as well!'

He didn't reply, clenching his jaw as Ffed wrapped his head. Dem's giggles rang in his ears. Damn her.

'Ash worried. Rushed.'

44

'Worried?' Nari glanced at Dem. 'Ah! I assure you, no harm was done. It was all the pigs, I promise.'

He shrugged. He didn't care. If he wanted to do something to her now, he wouldn't stop him. That'd teach her some humility.

'Worried for little old Dem, were you?' she batted her eyelids and pouted like a child. 'Big strong brother coming to save the day? How sweet.'

'Piss off,' he spat. He shouldn't have given her the satisfaction of a response, it was exactly what she wanted.

She grinned even more smugly, cackling in delight.

'Strange screams,' muttered Ffed, ignoring their exchange.

'The screams of one hog are as much the same to me as any other,' shrugged Nari. 'None of our business.'

'Sound scared.'

'I'm not!'

Ffed tutted. 'Not you. Scream. Scared animal.'

Nari looked over to the direction of the cacophony. 'You reckon?'

'Did you see the pig-driver?' Ash asked. Someone had to be an adult out of him and Dem.

'No, heard him though, chasing after them,' Nari snorted.

'I reckon we should go to help.'

'Agree,' Ffed nodded.

'I think it's a waste of time. Let the farmer tend his livestock. None of our business,' Nari shouldered his pack and gestured to the opposite direction. 'We ready?'

A fresh bouts of screams echoed.

'We should go,' said Ash. 'If we can help, we should offer.'

'You're just trying to save face after your tumble,' Dem snorted. 'We don't have time to go looking for pigs.'

'You don't think we should try to help someone in need?' he asked, flatly. Barely a question, more of a statement to reflect her callousness.

She leaned forward, speaking slowly, condescendingly. 'We're here to get help for Ma. Remember? That's why *I'm* here, anyway. To get to the infirmary and get back as soon as possible so our Ma doesn't die. You remember that? Or did you forget? Got a bit excited on your big man adventure?'

'I know why we're here. We can easily detour back on course. The guy could use our help, that's all.'

'No, you're just trying to save face, turn this into something it isn't. Brave Ash rescues the pig-man. What a story. What a man. Meanwhile, his Ma shivers and vomits in bed, wondering why her mighty son never returned with the medicine to save her life. Not that you care. Just like Da and his mines.'

'Dem!' Ffed barked, turning on her faster than Ash could have. 'Apologise!'

'Not to him. He knows I'm right,' she flushed but held her ground, the adversity strengthening her resolve, her pride.

Ash glared at her. Mentioning Da was low, even for her. Bringing up that whole ordeal. What was she trying to achieve? Make him feel guilty, of course. Make him question the right decision.

'Animal scared. Why? Maybe make us scared too? Need to know,' Ffed took her hatchet from her pack.

Nari looked from axe to goblin, to him, to Dem. He rolled his eyes. 'Winds! Let's go, then. They don't sound too far, I guess.'

'You guess?' Dem demanded, ears red and lips drawn back in a near-snarl. 'Guessing with my Ma's *life*!'

'It won't take long,' he muttered at his sister. Damn her childishness. She was only doing it to contradict him, and was throwing a tantrum because Nari and Ffed took his side. This was the right thing to do. Let her compare him to Da if she wanted to, ultimately he was a good man, dead before his time. If the pig-driver needed help, here were four pairs of willing hands to offer assistance. He glanced at his sullen sister. Maybe three pairs.

It didn't take long to find the hogs. All shapes and sizes, some pink, some black, some hairy, some bald. They milled about the lip of a small crevice, squeaking and snorting in agitation. Their arrival only amplified their distress, running about with renewed vigour. A dog appeared from the brush, barking at the top of her voice at them and the pigs, caught between her duties of herding the livestock and warning these strangers away.

'Who goes? Worrying me hogs?' A gruff voice called from the crevice. It was followed by a beefy hand, big shoulders, and a bald head housing a furious frown. 'You the ones what scared 'em?'

'We're the ones,' Ash raised his hands in apology. He stepped forward to help him from the crevice, but the dog charged forward with a growl, staving him away. He backed up. 'We wanted to apologise and see if we could help.'

The pig driver hauled himself from the crevice with a grunt like one of his stock. Grabbing a thick staff from the ground, he tapped a rock. 'Away, Libs, away.'

The dog trotted back to her master's side, tail wagging at a good job well done.

'So, can we help?' he offered again.

'Maybe,' he regarded them carefully. 'Funny bunch to be around here in the woods. Who are ye?'

'My name's Ashil, this is my sister Dem. We're from a village to the west. Our Ma fell sick so we're heading to an infirmary in the forest for help. Ffed came to help us through the woods. We met Nari here in Muddylan, he said he knew the way.'

'No infirmaries around here, lad,' he took a cap from his jacket and placed it low over his brows, staring at them from under its peak.

'By the Whitewater Lake,' clarified Nari.

'Oh! A few days away. So yer a guard, are ye?' he gestured to Nari's sword.

'Just a traveller,' Nari shrugged.

The pig driver shook his head. 'Aye, and I'm a horse-tamer. I know a rogue when I see one. Stay where ye are. I've left more'n a few of yer lot behind me in me time,' he brandished his staff. 'Want me hogs, do ye?'

'Want to help,' said Ffed.

'I'll take no help from a rogue and a goblin,' the pig driver slammed the butt of his staff a few times on the ground. The dog growled at them, lips drawn over her teeth. Even the hogs snorted angrily.

47

'Then from us,' offered Ash. 'Ffed's been a part of our village since I was born. Nari's led us true this far. We want to help. What's your name, sir?'

'Ye look an honest lad, I'll give ye that,' his face softened. 'That ye sister? Ye have the same nose.'

'Unfortunately, yes,' Dem picked her jacket disinterestedly.

'She's the one who scared your pigs,' said Nari.

'Aye, has the look of me wife about her, they know not to mess with her, make no mistake,' he chuckled. 'Alright. Name's Bib. As it happens, could use a hand, and some long legs.'

'I've got that covered,' Ash laughed.

'Aye, lad. Step up here, if ye would. That's it. Just up here. See down there, bottom of the creek? Twenty-Four is down there, bless her. I can't reach her. Too wide and short. Need someone a bit more stretched out, like.'

He glanced over the edge. At the bottom was a hoglet, snuffling about the steep sides of the crevice. He glanced at Bib. He certainly wasn't the shape for such a rescue attempt, hardly taller than Ffed. He'd barely make it halfway up the sides.

'No problem,' he braced himself on either side of the crevice and swung his legs over.

'She can be a mite feisty when a fright's took her,' warned Bib. 'Watch her nippers, like.'

He nodded and lowered into the depths of the crevice. Even for him, thin and gangly as he was, it was a tight squeeze. Round and robust as Bib was, he never had a chance. Even Nariton would've been hard-pressed to get to the bottom. Ffed would've been fine, but would be too short to climb back out.

Twenty-Four panicked as he approached, screaming and whining all the louder. The hogs above echoed her distress, screeching and crying. Libs and Bib did their best to quell their distress and keep them from the edges, but now and then a snout would pop over to investigate.

Lucky for him, Twenty-Four's attempts at taking a chunk from his fingers were in vain. He distracted her with one hand and scooped her up with the other, holding the portly thing between her legs. She wriggled furiously, snorting and screaming like a child without its mother. It was all he could do not to drop her as he lifted her over his head to Bib's waiting hands. Once in the pig-driver's grip, she calmed almost immediately, and was returned to the merry snorts and grunts of her fellows.

Now to get out. The lip of the crevice was too high even for him to reach, and the narrow gully precluded him from twisting around to a proper position to jump. He tried bracing himself against the walls, but it was in vain. The muddy sides were too slick to get a proper grip on. As he chewed his lip, Bib's beefy hand returned over the lip.

'Here, lad. I'll pull ye up.'

He closed his fingers around Bib's slab of a hand with its wide palm and chunky fingers. His shoulder was practically yanked from its socket as Bib heaved him from the depths. Scrambling with his legs and free hand, he was returned to level ground.

'Solid effort,' Nari clapped his shoulder.

'Good job,' Ffed yipped happily, petting Libs, much happier in their company now her master seemed to have accepted them.

'Oh, yes, very brave, putting his freakish gangly limbs to good use for once instead of slowing us down,' Dem muttered.

'Ye did well, lad,' smiled Bib. 'Thank ye. I'd be mighty sad to see little Twenty-Four lost. Back safe and sound, as long as she doesn't go running off again!'

'Glad I could help,' he beamed, wiping his palms on his jacket. It was already ruined, anyway, what was a bit more mud?

'Ye want some food?' Bib offered. 'Glad to share a bit of me own?'

'Very kind, but we need to get off,' Dem tapped her foot impatiently.

'Aye, aye, up to the infirmary. Well, here's what then. I can head up there a while with ye, spend a night in ye company, then part ways come morning. We'll share an evening supper, aye?'

'I'm happy to,' smiled Ash.

Ffed paused long enough in her petting to agree.

Nari grimaced, 'We wouldn't want to take you out of your way, kind as the offer is.'

49

'I insist,' said Bib, firmly.

'It's no trouble, we have more than enough provisions.'

'Alright,' Bib tapped the butt of his staff again. 'I tried being polite. I'm escorting ye away from me stretch of the woods. Gottit? Lad got me hog out of bother which is why I'll share me supper, but I want ye and yer goblin friend away. Only way to be sure is to take ye there myself. No bargaining.'

Nari threw his hands up in defeat. Dem kicked a stone into the gully. Ash smirked. It was all working out well.

*

Bib made pleasant company. He took a slightly irritating shine to Dem, despite her best efforts to be as unpleasant as possible, and had plenty of gratitude to Ash for his rescue attempts. His path through the forest was well-trodden, far easier to follow than their previous battle through the brush. Although Ffed initially voiced concerns over following a road, on seeing the tangled, overgrown trail, she relaxed, being a far cry from the roads teeming with bandits she apparently feared.

He trudged along beside the driver, who used his staff to gently encourage any stray hogs back to the path. Not that they needed much. For the most part, they were happy to follow the known trail, saturated with their familiar scent. Any who strayed away were coaxed back in line by Libs, circling their line in her ever-present vigil.

'Twenty-Four?' he asked. 'What kind of name is that?'

'Name for livestock, lad,' said Bib, gravely. 'Never give them proper names if they're bred for slaughter. I couldn't tell ye how many Twenty-Four's I've had.'

'Makes sense,' he muttered. 'So they're all for slaughter? None of them for mushroom hunting or anything?'

'No, no, me truffle-hogs are back home with me wife, bless her. I've got these ones on the go, making the rounds, getting 'em fed and fat, selling a few, buying a few. I'll be back home after I see ye off.'

'Isn't it dangerous wandering the woods alone with just a few pigs?'

Bib nodded knowingly and nodded ahead to Nari. 'Yer not wrong there, lad. Plenty of nasty types around. Should watch yer back with that one. I know his sort.'

'He'll get paid a lot when he gets us home,' Ash shrugged. 'I reckon that's more than enough motivation for him.'

'Oh, aye. He might be in it to get paid. Might just capture ye and ransom ye both back to the village.'

Ash paused. He hadn't thought of that. He assumed the promise of good payment would be enough to deter any wrongdoing. Perhaps not.

'He's been good to us so far.'

'Aye, always are. Ye need sharp eyes nowadays, lad. Sharp eyes and a sharper blade, or a big stick. Libs and the hogs keep me safe, just as I keep them. No worries for me safety. As I said, I've seen off a fair few rotters in me time.'

'Apart from when they run away,' he smiled.

'Apart from that, aye!' Bib laughed, knocking something from his belt. Ash stooped down to pick it up. A curious thing. Bundles of twigs woven together into a crude person. Four limbs and a torso, wrapped in a tattered cloth.

Bib snatched it from his hand. Libs whined from nearby.

'Sorry,' he mumbled, drawing his smarting hand away.

Bib stared at the figure for a second, brushing dirt from the cloth, then returned it to the folds of his cloak.

'Sorry, lad. Didn't mean to catch ye. It's a personal thing.'

'A doll?' he asked.

'Aye. For me little 'un. No longer with us. I keep it, sentimental, like.'

'I understand,' he nodded sympathetically. 'What happened?'

Bib shook his head. 'She's gone, lad, that's all there is to it. Life can be hard. Losing something so precious... I reckon she might've grown up to look something like ye sister,' he stared fondly at Dem, trudging ahead behind Nari. Sniffing loudly, he wiped his eyes and glanced at Ash. 'So yer Ma? What kind of sickness?'

'Don't know,' he sighed, glad to change subject. 'Our village healer doesn't know either. That's why we're going for advice.'

51

Bib nodded and scratched his head under his cap. 'Can't say I know which infirmary yer heading to. Me wife and I go to one way down southeast.'

'Oh yeah,' he recalled Nari's assumption. 'By Yellow Castle?'

'No, not that far. That's only a little one. Tiny. Might not be running anymore, if I'm honest. This one's by the Piglick River.'

'The Piglick? That's ages away!'

'Aye, but good pig farming country, as the name suggests. Down to Holevale is a good market, we go twice a year. Tend to try to visit the infirmary at the same time if we need it. Good place. Seems a bit ominous when ye go in, like, but the folks know what's what. Helped me wife get over her malady after the little one... well you know how it goes.'

'But you've never heard of one by the Whitewater?'

'Well, just don't know it. Only moved here a few years ago, like. Might be a specialist one or something? For complicated patients like yer Ma.'

'Maybe. Oskra said it was this way anyway.'

'Well, as long as yer not just going by that one's advice alone,' he gestured to Nariton again.

'I promise, he's fine,' he chuckled.

'Aye,' Bib narrowed his eyes. 'A fine one alright.'

*

The snores of pig, driver, and dog filled the camp. Bellies full of cheese, bread, wild mushrooms, and last year's roast chestnuts, his companions slept with them. Every movement he made, one of the hogs would wake and snort loudly, threatening to wake the bastard driver. He settled back down. No point even trying it tonight. One sniff of suspicion and he'd be at the receiving end of that staff, and the squat little pig driver seemed to know how to handle it.

Damn his luck. Of all people to run into, why this meddling little fool with a better nose for mischief than his own hogs for acorns. Another day probably wouldn't make a difference. Well, two days by now, accounting for the additional time to backtrack to Kirkin. Tomorrow, then. The night after at the very latest. Just enough time to get back. He just needed a bit of peace and quiet. He played with the small glass vial in his cloak pocket. A few drops of this and they'd all be asleep. No chance to use it today, but tomorrow would be different, with no hogs or dogs to distract him. He glanced at Ffed, sleeping with her arms around the mongrel. Not even the goblin would wake up after this.

He watched them sleep, peaceful as a bunch of kittens in a basket. No doubt, they'd curse his name to their deathbeds after he'd robbed them. Not that he'd ever hear it. As soon as the deed was done and the debt was paid, he'd take his brother away from here, down to Morgenal, start a new life in the Jagged Isles. An honest one. Perhaps that would make up for everything he'd done so far. If that meant bearing the unheard curses of the children, they were welcome to say what they wanted.

They should be grateful, really. He'd spent the whole night camped outside their room door, scrapping with all the mean buggers trying to rob and murder them in their sleep. Not that they'd ever know or thank him for it. No matter.

Their purses would be thanks enough.

Chapter 5

Day four of mud, leaves, and bad company since leaving home. Apart from Ffed, of course. But Ash and Nari? Four winds spare her. A night of lying with the stinking pigs and snoring driver did little to improve her mood. Well done Ash, condemning them to the mud with the hogs. She'd woken to one wet snout nuzzling her neck and another chewing her boots. Filthy things. It was a good moment when Bib waved them away.

At least one good thing came of it; it confirmed her suspicions of Nari. For a simpleton like Bib to recognise his threat demonstrated how foolish their decision to keep his company was. She didn't expect any better from Ash, but Ffed? She should have known, but seemed content to let him lead them on. Had the years spent outside their village walls harboured a festering bitterness towards them, and now was the opportunity for indirect vengeance? Was she in it with Nari, having met him in the woods on her wanderings?

She caught herself. No. That was unfair. True, she wasn't allowed to live in Starforge itself, but she'd never shown any resentment for it, or any desire to do any different. The goblin was content in her little hut in the woods, surrounded by the trees and wildlife she held so dear. Her decision to follow Nari was a practical one. He knew these parts better than she did, that was all.

Not that it made it any easier. Bib's livestock had more charm than the rogue. His attempts at humour were crass, his false gallantry an afterthought. Underneath it all was a certain... unease. Sad stares into the distance, musing frowns in silence, soft sighs at night. An air of regret surrounded him. For something done, or something yet to do.

Or perhaps she was just imagining it all.

'Will we stop at Yewbar tonight?' she called ahead.

'Wasn't planning on,' Nari grunted.

She grimaced. 'Why? I wouldn't mind a bed.'

'Not everyone's cut out for life on the road,' Ash piped up.

'No. that includes you,' she looked him up and down. What a state. Torn clothes, mud up to his knees and elbows, bandage around his head. He looked like a mummer's attempt at a wounded veteran, wearied from a hard trek home. Exactly what he wanted, of course. Ffed's handiwork with the bandage was decent, by all accounts. She could have done better, of course, but he refused. Not that she cared. If he didn't want to utilise her experience and knowledge, more fool him. let him wander about with a lopsided bandage half-obscuring his vision. If it made him feel braver, who was she to argue?

'Doing better than you,' he scoffed.

At that moment, his foot slipped in the mud. He managed to grab hold of a branch before landing on his rear, but it dipped dramatically under his weight, sending a shower of dew and dead leaves over him. She smiled. Perfect timing.

He corrected himself and glared at her, face like a beetroot.

'Piss off,' he spat.

'I didn't say anything,' she purred.

'Face says enough. Bitch.'

What a child. She rolled her eyes and looked back at Nari, watching with raised brows.

'Well? Are we stopping at Yewbar?'

'As I said, I wasn't planning on. Quicker to just head straight through the forest to the lake instead of detouring around to Yewbar. We can if you want to, but–'

'How much will it save us?' she interrupted.

'If we head directly there, as much as a day,' he shrugged. 'Do what you like, it's just more silver for me.'

Damn it all. The few handfuls of silver were meaningless. Did Ma have enough time to spare another day? Best not risk it. Despite Oskra's medicines, her symptoms were no better the morning after they started, the morning they went to Ffed. The bruises were worse, the smell of vomit and diarrhoea more potent. Heb's tearful face, trying to hide the stained bedsheets and towels from them. Elain's bitter sobs when nobody gave her attention. She shuddered. They needed to get back.

'The quickest way.'

'I thought as much,' he turned back into the brush, weaving his way between the trees.

'How does he know where he's even going?' she muttered, dropping back behind Ash to Ffed. 'One tree looks as much as the other.'

'Tell direction from sun and time of day,' nattered the goblin, pointing her hairy arms.

'And we're going in the right direction?'

'Right direction to Whitewater.'

She nodded. 'And you definitely can't take us there yourself?'

Ffed wiggled her head from side to side. 'Could take, yes. Could follow direction easy. Don't know best route.'

She sighed. Did Nariton know the best route? It seemed to her like he was just following a general heading as well. No hidden paths, no roads or shortcuts, just a steady slog through the underbrush. Perhaps she was wrong. After all, they'd avoided any gangs, Hobb, and creatures. Maybe that's what his experience brought.

'Ffed,' she spoke quietly. Best not to let Ash overhear. 'What do you think is wrong with Ma?'

Ffed shrugged. 'Didn't see Lelan. Not healer. Dem know better.'

'But I don't know at all. Nobody does. I thought maybe you'd have an idea, maybe you'd seen something in the past?'

Ffed shook her head and put her hand around her back in an awkward embrace. 'Seen much sickness, yes. But same always. Cough and dysentery. Slave sickness. Lelan sound different. Infirmary know best.'

She looked at her. Rare for her to mention slavery. She looked at her bald wrists, the knotted scar tissue glistening. She must have looked particularly sorry for her to open up about it, however briefly.

Raindrops pattered against her head, tinkling softly against the leaves. She looked up. Black clouds moved to hide the sun, plunging them into darkness. Ffed smiled at her.

'Go, go. Stormy soon.'

*

It fell in sheets. Unrelentingly wet. A constant, freezing torrent of water, even though the clouds waxed and waned in their downpour, the collected droplets in the canopy ensured it was a persistent onslaught of fat, freezing drops pattering against her sodden hood and shoulders. It probably would've been better to leave her cloak in the pack where it would stay dry for her once the storm passed. Now she'd be soaked for hours. Ffed certainly had the same idea, and remained in the same shirt and breeches, her spare clothes safely nestled away in her pack. Soaked through as she was, the goblin's wiry frame was exaggerated, the coarse pelt of wiry hair covering her body lying flat for once, giving her an almost-skeletal appearance. She seemed happy enough, though. At least that made one of them.

Ahead, Ash and Nari were equally miserable, hunched over and wrapped in their respective waterlogged cloaks. Even Ash's previously-hilarious attempts at navigating the forest had lost their charm. Each sudden stop as he got tangled or slipped or tripped just fuelled her frustration further. How much further could they feasibly go? Was there any point engaging the elements in this hopeless battle?

Lightning forked and thunder boomed. She shivered uncontrollably. She used to love storms. The heaviness in the air preceding it, the way your hair stood on end, the excitement when it broke, the smell when it passed. She loved watching it from her room, safe in her blanket with a mug of tea.

Being caught in one in the open was quite a different experience. The dancing rain was cold and persistent, working its way through your clothes to chill every part of your body. The wind swung the trees in increasingly-erratic directions, held upright only by the strength of their roots. The spark of lightning gave the world flashes of light and shadow, distorting the bushes and branches to monsters and ghouls. The boom of thunder after each flash was the pounding footsteps of a monster, slowly gaining.

Shelter. A cave, a ledge, and overhang, a few dead trees. Anything to escape. But Nari doggedly led them on, tolerating the elements as best they could. She longed for warmth and comfort. To sit with the merry blaze of a fire, but there would be none tonight, no fuel in this waterlogged forest.

A black pine swayed back and forth like a pendulum ahead, its boughs shivering as the wind tore through. If such a mighty thing like that could suffer so much, what hope did she have?

Ffed's hard hand gripped her shoulder.

'Doing well!' she shouted over the howling wind.

It didn't feel like it. Every step was a battle to keep her feet, the uneven ground a sludge of mud and loam. Ash fell down again ahead, his arms flailing and legs kicking hopelessly. Any other time, she'd have laughed. Not now. Now it seemed so much more dangerous. She rushed forward carefully, supported by Ffed, and helped him to his unsteady feet.

'Pissing storm,' he muttered.

'Worse than the time we went fishing with Da,' she smiled.

'Almost,' he grinned back.

A sudden groan cut across. She looked around. Like a sick dog, a yowling cat, and an angry bear all rolled into one. Was something after them, to top it all off? Was it because she'd mentioned Da, Enadir decided it was time for the offspring to meet the same end? She clutched Ash's hand tight, heart hammering. He gazed at her, eyes wide and glassy. He was thinking the same thing. Winds above! She'd cursed them!

Lightning flashed again, the thunder boomed with it. The monstrous storm was right above them. The trees shook and waved like wheat. The groan continued.

She looked at Ffed, but the goblin ignored her, staring into the woods. Her hatchet was still in her bag. If there was something out there, she wouldn't have time to get it out, wouldn't have a way to protect them.

She grabbed the goblin's bag, started tugging the axe free. Ffed turned angrily, slapping her hands away. She ignored her. She needed her weapon! If Ffed wouldn't take it, let her, she still had her whittling knife, what little good it would do.

'Dem! Stop!' Ffed grabbed her wrists in her iron grip.

'There's something out there!'

'No! Storm!'

The groan changed pitch. Simultaneously deeper and higher, whistling and sighing. Creaking. Splintering. Crashing.

The black pine teetered at the brink of its wave, the storm straining at its mighty trunk. Wood battled wind. The storm won.

'Nari!' Ash screamed, tearing his hand free of hers and crashing through the shrubbery after their guide.

'Ash!' she called after him.

'Dem!' Ffed called after her, catching her wrists again before she could get far, stopping her from following.

'Let me go!' she wriggled and bucked, trying to escape the goblin's vice.

'Falling!' Ffed shouted, wrenching her back.

Like a sick child heaving up its final bellyful of vomit, the black pine groaned as it fell. Impossibly slowly, it crashed through the canopy, tearing branches and boughs from its neighbours as it made its inevitable descent to the forest floor. No stopping it. No changing its course. It fell across their path, as it always would have, right across where Ash disappeared.

The crash of trunk meeting ground was deafening. Reverberations shook her, making her stumble against Ffed, held up by the goblin's solid stance. Splintering cracks and tears as thin boughs crumbled under the trunk's weight, showering them with wood chips and pine needles. She closed her eyes. It stopped.

Howling winds and lashing rain continued overhead, but the groan was gone. More flashes of forked lightning and booming thunder, but they seemed smaller, somehow. She opened her eyes and stared. The tangle of pine roots were ahead, the broken, twisted remains of the trunk not twenty feet away.

She couldn't move. Ash went in there.

Ffed gently coaxed her along. She stumbled, oblivious to the pounding rain. The haze of dust and fine splinters was quickly disappearing. The mighty trunk lay on its side, more than a hundred feet of it, half-buried in the mud.

Lying where Ash went.

She didn't want to look. How could she? If he was in there, lying as twisted and broken as the rest of the tree, how could she accept it? She clenched her fist, nails digging into her palm. Oh yes, now she could grip tight, but when her hand-held Ash's? Weak as a babe. Too easy for him to tear himself free.

Ffed climbed up the trunk as nimbly as a squirrel. She stood dumb at the bottom. It must weigh tons. Hundreds of tons of wood and needle. The broken boughs of oak, sycamore, alder, and chestnut lay around her, torn free by the trunk as it made its descent. Ash was a fraction of their width, their strength. He'd be ripped to shreds, crushed to a pulp, eviscerated.

She put her hands on the pine, Rainwater ran down her face, imitating tears that would surely follow.

'Here!' Ffed yipped, jumping from the trunk to the other side.

Her heart caught. She didn't move. She couldn't. Not until she heard... a groan! A string of curses! The sweetest curses she'd ever heard. Scrambling for footholds, she clambered over the mighty trunk to the opposite side.

Ffed knelt a few paces away, arm around Ash's shoulders. Nari lay beside him, rubbing his head in a daze. A sob escaped her throat, lost in the roar of the storm.

'Idiot!' she jumped down and punched his arm. 'Idiot!'

'Ow! Stop!' he pushed her away.

'What would I tell Ma?' she demanded. Her voice was shrill, strained. She didn't care. He needed to know. 'What would I tell her?'

'Tell her what?' he pushed her away again, rubbing his torn knee. 'I didn't do anything wrong.'

'I'd say,' said Nari, smiling sickly. 'I didn't even hear it, just the storm. Saved my bloody life!'

'You could've... you might have been... what would I tell her?' she shouted.

'Nothing,' he shrugged. 'I did a good thing.'

'Lucky,' said Ffed, matching Nari's sickly grin.

'Lucky!' she shouted. 'Why, Ash?'

'Just leave it off,' he pushed her away again, grimacing.

She wouldn't let him off so easily. The others might think this was okay, they might think he'd done a good thing, but she knew better. So did he, deep down. A stupid risk. Running under a falling tree in a storm, with him barely able to walk through the forest on a good day. As stupid and pointless an act as he could have done. She choked. As stupid as running into a collapsing mine shaft. How could he be so selfish? To risk leaving her alone to bring the news back to Ma. He really didn't care. Just like Da.

She opened her mouth so say as much, but Nari cut across.

'Saved my bloody life,' he repeated.

Ash grinned at him. 'Thought it was better if we kept you around. Who'd we give the silver to otherwise?'

She felt sick. How could he joke and smile after that? Nearly killed himself. His legs could have been crushed, his lungs filling with dirt and dust, leaving him to slowly asphyxiate over the next few hours. Her hands shook, not from the cold. Ffed put her hand on her shoulder again. She shrugged it off roughly.

'Stupid idiot.'

It was all she could manage. There was too much to say, too many thoughts and anger to vocalise properly. She sat back against the trunk, suddenly exhausted.

'Rest for a bit,' suggested Ffed. 'Shelter in pine. Storm will go.'

They did as she suggested, stumbling to a reasonably sheltered area beneath one of the fallen pine's intact boughs. Ffed quickly patched up any gaps in the natural canopy with additional broken branches. They sat in a line against the trunk, waiting for the storm to pass.

Dem sat with her knees drawn up to her chest at the end of the line, as far away from her brother as she could.

The storm continued into the evening, and the makeshift canopy seemed better than any other shelter they might find. A miserable supper of cold apples, hard cheese, and soggy bread. It would have been a beautifully simple meal on any other day. Today, it tasted bitter and foul in her mouth. They spent most of the time in silence.

At one point, Ash and Ffed wandered off to relieve themselves in the forest, leaving her with Nari. She watched him carefully, wrapped up in his cloak, glowering at the trees.

'What're you frowning about?' she demanded.

He blinked, returning to reality. 'What's that?'

'What's wrong? Why the frown?'

'Nothing, just thinking about things.'

'Like what?'

'Nothing important.'

'Like how my brother almost died because of you?'

He sighed. 'It crossed my mind.'

'It was stupid of him.'

Nari nodded slowly. 'I agree. But I'm grateful for it. Tackled me out the way a second before the trunk would've flattened me.'

'Instead he could've been flattened,' she spat.

'Yet here we both are, to live another day,' he raised his water-skin to toast the statement.

'One more day always good,' Ffed returned from the wood, sitting between them.

'Aye. You don't realise how sweet it is until it's nearly taken away,' Nari drank deeply.

Ffed nodded slowly, purposefully. 'Always good. One more day.'

'At what cost?' Dem asked, tears filling her eyes. She blinked them away in case they thought they were tears of sorrow, not rage.

'Anything,' said Ffed, firmly. 'Always fight for another day.'

'Anything? I don't think Ma would agree, not if it meant one of her children killing themselves for a stranger.'

'Winds, Dem!' Ash returned, plonking himself between Nari and Ffed. 'Still going on about it? Just accept I did a good thing.'

'No! An unnecessary risk. We're here for Ma. Anything we do, we should do thinking about *her*. That includes our own safety.'

'Well, I reckon we'd be safer with Nari than without, so even by your reckoning, I did the right thing.'

She bristled. 'You're twisting things! You know what I mean!'

'By the four winds, Dem. Just stop it. If you're jealous because I actually saved someone's life, then–'

'Jealous?' she clenched her fists, her teeth. How dare he.

'Yeah, you're always going on about saving people's lives, well I'm the only one who's done it so far, aren't I? Didn't need to desperately try to be a healer to do it either. Just a decent person.'

'Stop. Both stop,' Ffed snapped. Ignored.

'How *dare* you,' she whispered. She couldn't think.

62

'Oh come on, you know it's true. You're just sour you didn't do it,' he shrugged flippantly, as if he held all the answers.

'If you died. Ma would be crushed. I don't know why, you're an evil bastard, but she would,' she spat.

'Stop it. You keep using her as an excuse. I did something you don't like because you couldn't do it, so now you're taking it out on me. You always do.'

'That's not true,' tears threatened again.

'Both stop. Unkind words,' Ffed snapped again. Ignored again.

'Yes it is. You always want to control what we do. That's why you've been in such a pissy mood, because we're not doing what *you* want, because *you're* not in control. Here's a suggestion. I live my life, you live yours. How does that sound?'

'You're such a bastard,' she whispered.

'Nope. I'm just calling you out on who you are. Jealous because I saved someone and you couldn't, angry because I did it without your permission. Ma has nothing to do with it.'

He sat back, ignoring her. He thought he knew her so well. Thought he was such a grown-up. Nothing but a child. A fool. Selfish and uncaring. Why did she ever worry about him? How could she have cared about such an awful, arrogant, evil boy?

Accusing her of jealousy? Petulant child. If that's how little he thought of her with his overly-inflated ego, then that was his problem. Healing wasn't just about saving lives in big, dramatic actions. It was the small things, the soothing lotions and tinctures to settle a stomach, relieve a cough, disperse a rash. Things that not just saved a life, but made it better too. Oskra told her several times how their role was far more to do with the mundane tasks of relieving little complaints than it was about curing a dangerous disease. Sure, sawing off limbs and suturing ugly wounds were exciting to watch, but surgeons did that bloody task, not the village healers. Their role was more subtle, their influence quieter, but no less important.

Accusing her of being controlling? It was called responsibility. It was called empathy. Maybe he couldn't understand how Ma, Heb, and Elain would feel if she returned without him, but she could. She remembered it. Ash's dusty, dirty face from the mines getting carted

63

back, Da's mangled body next to him. He was still that rescued child, saved by his father's courage, while the rest of them remained the grieving family. How she'd wept that day, wept with the knowledge that Da risked his own life and safety for her brother and three other miners, how he'd propped up the falling roof by the strength of his back, buying just enough time for them to be dragged to safety before tons of rock and dirt crashed down on him. She'd wept, knowing Da put the lives of Ash and three miners above her, Ma, Heb, and unborn Elain. What was worse, they'd been forced to watch him die. The rescue team dragged his mutilated half-carcass free, and he clung to life long enough to be carted home and laid in his cot, gasping and spluttering for air as the dust clogged up his airways. She remembered Oskra's knowing expression as she consoled Ma and the emptiness in the house when he fell silent. She remembered the hopelessness of it all. No, Ash couldn't remember any of that. He was the darling, rescued child, the prized possession of his courageous father. He didn't understand.

She glanced again at Nari, rubbing his chin, deep in thought. Thinking about what? A slippery character, to be sure. Caution. Ash had none of it, so she'd have to make up for his deficiencies. Perhaps he was happy traipsing around after Nari, perhaps Ffed understood its practicality, but she knew better. It might have been better if he was crushed by the tree. She watched him again, staring sheepishly at the flooded ground, hands in his cloak pockets. There was more to him than he let on.

She wiped her eyes with her sleeve. Ash wasn't worth the tears.

*

A grey morning followed. They didn't say much about yesterday's events. Packing their gear in silence, they left the pine and followed Nari once again.

The rogue was in an unusually foul mood, grunting and snapping at them whenever approached. So much for appreciating another day.

'What's the matter with you?' she spat after he barked at them to hurry up.

'Didn't sleep well,' he snapped.

'Why? I thought you were used to sleeping wild?'

'Things on my mind,' he hissed, curling his lip.

She left him. If he wanted to be foul, let him. She was content to walk in silence. Yesterday's prolonged rest put them behind schedule, and Nari drove them relentlessly through the woods. Fortunately, there were no more storms, and although her clothes were still damp from yesterday, at least the wind wasn't too fierce.

Ash struggled to keep up. She didn't offer any help. She could hear Ffed's encouraging words from behind as she demonstrated for the hundredth time how to get through the tangled branches, but the idiot was just too dim to get it through his thick, swollen skull.

They crossed a road at midday. She hoped they might follow it for a while, but Nari walked right across, back into the depths of the forest. She kept her pace, watching his broad back. What was it about him that charmed Ash so? Why was he so keen to keep him alive, to win his favour? Was it because he was a rugged old adventurer, complete with scars and a sword? Did it appeal to those deep-set boyhood fantasies of his, about adventure and excitement in the forests? Or was it just that he offered different company to her, that he was anyone else but his hated sister?

The day passed slowly. In the evening, they camped around another fallen tree, taking shelter in its bare, twisting roots. This time, Nari lit a fire and toasted their food over its flames.

He handed her a slice, crunchy bread topped with melted cheese.

'A peace offering and my apologies,' he said.

She raised her brows. 'For what?'

'I know we've not seen things the same way. I'm sorry for any offence I've caused or any wrongs I've done. It's not my intention.'

She snorted. Easy enough giving a blanket apology without specifying what you were apologising for. It was just a statement, a gesture of goodwill. Didn't mean anything. Didn't change anything. But then, her argument wasn't really with him, it was with Ash, Nari was just the latest object in their feud.

She took the offered slice.

'Thank you.'

He smiled and nodded, handing out the other slices to Ash and Ffed.

'We made good distance today,' he announced. 'Made up for lost time yesterday. The lake is about a day away, then it'll be one more day to reach the infirmary.'

'Then home,' she said.

'Aye.'

'And you'll get paid,' she rolled her eyes.

'Aye,' he smiled briefly.

'What? You want more now?' she narrowed her eyes, finishing her bread and cheese. Was this his game all along? To lure them out into the wilderness until they were hopelessly lost, and demand even higher fares to get them back to civilisation? A sneaky trick. She wouldn't put it past him.

'No, no. No worries. Here, why don't you all set your jackets and boots over here, over the fire? Just sleep under your cloaks for tonight. I know mine got all soaked yesterday and they're still not dry.'

'Yeah good idea,' Ash shrugged his worn jacket off and slung it over one of the roots. 'Not quite how it looked when we set off,' he grimaced.

'Nothing a bit of care attention won't fix,' Nari reassured. 'Dem? How about your things?'

She relinquished her gear, feeling suddenly tired. Ffed stumbled slightly as she helped hang them up. Nari caught her gently.

'Careful, now! You must be exhausted, helping Ash here all day. Have a sit by the fire, there you go. Don't you worry, lad, you'll get the hang of foresting soon enough. Perhaps we should all get some sleep.'

She nodded. An excellent suggestion. His first to date, truth be told. Warm food in her belly, a nice fire by her side, Nari's curiously soft and soothing voice all around them. His words were meaningless, just a jumble of soft sounds, muffled by her exhaustion. She tried to concentrate on what he was saying. Useless. It was too difficult and she was too comfortable. Ffed stirred beside her, grunting softly as she fought to stay awake. She shushed her gently. Just let it happen. It was inevitable.

*

Muttered curses. The crash and scuffle of things tossed aside. She stirred, glimmers of light penetrating her heavy lids. It must be morning. She settled back, drawing her cloak tighter around her. A ball of warmth. Just let her rest for a few more minutes.

Another curse. Something clattered away into the forest. She scrunched her eyes tighter. So noisy! No need for it. The lake would still be there, just let her have a few more minutes.

Rough hands shook her shoulders.

'Dem. Wake up.'

She groaned and shook her head.

'Yes. Wake. Now.'

What did she want? No need to shake her about like this. Opening her eyes slowly to avoid the sting of the sun, she rolled to her front, preparing to rise.

'Yes. Wake now. Nari gone.'

Her eyes snapped open. Gone?

She rose in an instant, her cloak falling to the floor next to the long-dead fire. Bile rose to the back of her throat, bitter and foul. She stumbled away and vomited up last night's meal, chunks of partially-digested bread and cheese spattering the floor.

'Good. Get rid of it. Nari poison sleep.'

She wiped her mouth with the back of her hand and stumbled back.

'Check your pack, Dem,' Ash's voice was hoarse, strained. He'd been vomiting like her.

She fell on her knees and rummaged through. More than half-empty. A few cotton shirts and sparse provisions left. Medicine pack, spare travelling gear, and purses all gone.

She looked at her brother. His pallid expression told her all she needed.

Ffed played with the remnants of her hatchet, its iron head missing, just the handle left.

They stared at each other. No jackets, barely any food, no money, no boots. No sign of Nariton.

67

She shook her head. Something rose in the pit of her stomach. An urge. Vomit? No. It moved into her chest, making her shoulders shake and spasm. Her throat heaved, her chest wheezed. Ffed sprang to her side, frowning.

Laughter bubbled out. Harsh, guttural, bitter laughter. Ffed and Ash stared at her. She couldn't help it. It was too funny. Too typical. She'd been right all along. A rogue and a cur. Inevitable.

'Dem...' Ash approached her gently, concern in his red-rimmed eyes.

'If we meet him again,' she spluttered between her chortles. 'He dies. The *bastard* dies!'

Chapter 6

Jacketless, bootless and shivering, they stood outside the remains of the infirmary. As abandoned as a half-formed child in Cadaran's pits.

It shouldn't have surprised them, really, to find the building in such a decrepit state, not after their luck. But it was too much for the children, who sank to their knees by the overgrown doors, defeat finally reaching their hearts.

Ffed watched them silently, nothing to say. What comfort would any of her clumsy words give? If these were goblin children, she could soothe them with her croons and growls, hold them close so they'd feel the reverberations of her chest. Not these. There was a line she couldn't cross. Intimacies that nobody would accept from one of her kind, even in these circumstances.

She settled for a hand on their shoulders. After a while, they both took hold, almost simultaneously. Dem rested her tearstained cheek against it, Ash hung his head.

A difficult journey for them. Her gear and provisions were mostly intact, being of little value as they were. Nariton had an eye for quality, after all. So she shared her clothes with them, for what it was worth. Not much, as it turned out. None of her things fitted Ash, and although Dem could squeeze into her bigger jacket, she couldn't button it up. The biggest loss was their boots. She always walked barefoot so had no replacement to offer, other than tearing up one of her leather breeches and wrapping it around their feet. It wasn't much help. By the end of the first day, their soles were swollen and bleeding, cracked skin caked in mud. She'd washed them clean in the Whitewater Lake, soothing their yelps at her touch with a grumbling tune from her painful childhood. She wasn't sure if it helped. This morning, they followed the lake around until they found a path leading from a small forgotten jetty. The path led them here. To more disappointment.

Such was the world. If she were with other goblins, they would have nodded to each other knowingly and shrugged their loss away, for this was the way of Enadir. The whole world was against goblins. In all matters of life.

But these were human children. Entitled to a better life than she. They didn't expect disappointment. They didn't know defeat. It was not their birth-right to kneel in the dirt and be humbled by the world. It was not in their nature to see the death that stalked Lelan and acknowledge its inevitability. They did their best, they fought for another day. They did well.

Sometimes, most times, the fight was in vain.

She couldn't tell them these truths. She could only offer her hand, and give what solace she could in her firm grip.

'Well,' Dem rose first, wiping her eyes. 'Shall we go in? Might be something we can take back, at least.'

'Take what?' Ash mumbled, still on his knees. 'Mouldy herbs? A dead rat? Why bother?'

'Because we've come all this way! I won't go back with nothing!' Dem shouted, startling the flock of sparrows nestling on the roof.

She walked up the wide stairs and put her hand on the tarnished doorhandle. She paused. Ffed watched her from below. The girl didn't move. Frozen in place. Too scared to open it and face the emptiness inside, the darkness, the defeat.

She followed her up, nudging her aside. She wasn't afraid of an empty infirmary. Few things scared her at all. But she didn't like thinking about those things. Things like the cold. The ice.

Shaking her head, she opened the door and stepped inside. Dust and cobwebs, rot and mould. Forgotten and damned. The shadow of abandonment and fear, and something far more ancient and malevolent. But old, stale, like the lingering stench of a lanced abscess clinging to their skin, of a rotten carcass long removed from the crawlspace under a hut. It drew her, called her close. More than curiosity. Instinct. The same instinct that drew vultures to carrion, that made dogs howl to the moon. A part of her very being yearned for it, a blight on her soul hooked its claws into her breast. She took another step. It was faint, faded, years old, clinging to the walls and beams in its desperate attempt to survive the passing years. Dem followed, keeping close to her heels. Ash joined them, ducking his head through the low door. Did they feel it too? Probably not. Something about its scent, no, its *touch*, told her it was for her. If it affected these human children as well, they were unaware of it.

Together, they explored the rooms. The feeling prevailed. In several places, the roof was collapsed, letting in pools of merry sunlight in the otherwise gloomy ruin, chasing away the ominous disquiet in her stomach. Birds, rats, mice, hedgehogs, a couple of foxes, all made their new homes in this strange place, abandoned for so long. She smiled and greeted each one she saw, for animals knew the goblin truth of death and suffering at the hands of others. The animals only inhabited the rooms open to the elements, where the presence was all but insensible.

Some rooms were filled with cots, some with shelves bulging with books, some with cupboards filled with empty glass vials, an old operating theatre, the smooth table at its centre empty and clean. At least in appearance. Here the feeling was at its strongest, as palpable as dipping her feet into the sea. Surely the children would feel it here? But no, they passed through. Curiosity and wonder in their eyes, but nothing more. No dread. No emptiness. No... hunger. There was a garden in the back, once carefully-cultivated, now overgrown and full of squirrels. She wanted to watch them for a while, scurrying back and forth over the walls, taking relief in the sunlit respite, but Dem and Ash wanted to move on. They explored three floors of dusty rooms, dirty corridors, and crooked stairways. Nobody was here.

Returning to one of the rooms with vials, Dem looked for an itinerary for any useful medicines. She found one, but the shelves they led to were empty, cleared out. She tried some of the books, but there were too many, and her knowledge too shallow to know what to look for. She gave up with a grunt of frustration, slamming the covers closed with puffs of dust, catching the sunbeams in swirling clouds of sparkling memories.

There were a few old leather aprons and gloves in a storeroom which they commandeered, but no shoes. A fruitless search. The children grew more and more restless, more and more disheartened. Each as hopeful as the other at every new room. Poor things. The

71

memory of whatever was once here, its footprint, was far too malevolent and awful to leave room for hope.

They settled in one of the wards, taking a dusty cot each. The bedclothes were too dirty and rotten to use, but the wooden frames were comfortable. Tall, cracked windows let in enough light and air to dispel the miasma, felt as little more than a slight pounding in the back of her head. She shared out some of their provisions. The last of the cheese, a few apples, and some tough bread apparently not to Nariton's taste.

'So what now?' asked Ash, hopelessly.

'Head back,' suggested Dem, flatly. 'We tried our best. It's been for nothing.'

'Damn it all,' he muttered. 'The bastard led us here for nothing. He knew it was empty. Just wanted us out the way.'

'Maybe,' she shrugged.

'I'm sorry. We shouldn't have trusted him. If we hadn't brought him along…'

'It wouldn't have made a difference,' Dem sighed. 'We'd have come here anyway. Oskra said it's been years since she's been here. They must've moved.'

Ffed looked through the splintered doorway at the dark corridor. Moved, or chased away? What could fill her with such dismay yet simultaneously draw her so close? A shadow of the past lay on the place, on her. She drew her cloak tighter. Not even the breath of the Great Hunter on her nape would make her so cold.

'Damn bad luck,' Ash continued, oblivious as his sister. 'We failed Ma.'

Dem nodded silently.

Ffed sighed. They were accepting the truth. It wasn't easy, but that's the way of things. She remembered when her mother died, the lashes trailing blood, her back open in tatters, the thump of the whip into her body long after her screams were silenced. The Hunter fed well that day. Well enough to forget her, huddled and shivering in the corner, her young hands clutching an oversized pickaxe, hugging it tight as she once hugged her cradle-toys.

72

'No,' Dem looked up. 'Bib mentioned another infirmary, right? We'll head there.'

Ash shook his head. 'It's way down by the Piglick River. We'll never get there and back to Ma in time.'

'What would you rather do, just go back? Not me. I won't give up on her.'

'We don't have any shoes, Dem.'

'We'll go to Yewbar first. It's on the way, or thereabouts. We'll take whatever we can from here that might be valuable and trade it. They might be able to tell us something about this place as well.'

'Is it worth it? She might not be around by the time we get back. Do we risk not being there at the end?' he grimaced.

'If it means giving her a chance, yes. We took that risk the moment we left.'

They both looked at her. Hopeful. Determined. She nodded slowly. They had grit to them, these two. A will. One to fight for another day, for them and Lelan.

Goblins knew it was unwise to mock the Great Hunter. It only grew hungrier the longer it prowled on your trail. It only grew angrier. A goblin who cheated death too many times, who stole too many days, was bound for a particularly horrific end. It was a wise old goblin who stopped running and faced the inevitable.

But then again, as she said all her life, another day was always worth having.

Chapter 7

Unlike Muddylan, Yewbar was a tolerable settlement. Nowhere near as fine as Starforge, of course, but certainly pleasant. Neat houses, cobbled main roads brushed clean daily, a bustling marketplace, and guards who were less afraid of the civilians. It was enough to make her feel out of place in her weather-worn, torn rags of clothes and swollen, bleeding feet of three days' walk from the infirmary.

They were very nearly denied entry. The guards took one look at them and judged them urchins looking for a place to beg. A second look at Ffed brought their spears down half a foot. Other travellers and visitors passing through the gates stared and whispered. The shame of it made her ears blaze.

Fortunately, her skills extended beyond simple healing. She explained their plight, and although the guards only half-listened, mention of a bag of delicate glass vials to trade was enough to see them through. Praise the four winds for her initiative and silver tongue. Not that it received any recognition from her brother. Ffed at least clasped her arm gratefully for her efforts.

A pang of guilt flared in her stomach at the thought of their friend, confined to the stable, but who were they to argue with the rules? Goblins weren't allowed in the inn, the keeper made it perfectly clear. They even had a poster next to the door highlighting the right to refuse service to any customer. Not that Ffed seemed to mind. She went happily enough to where the animals slept. True, the stable-hand's fares for the night were nearly triple what they were paying for their tavern room, and that was without any food or water for her, but he made the point it took up a stall and there was no telling how the other livestock would react to a goblin in their midst. The townsfolk reacted unkindly enough. By the end of the morning, she wasn't sure whether it was their dishevelled appearance or Ffed's company that drew the glares and harsh words.

Fortunately, the money they made trading the vials from the infirmary was more than enough to cover the costs. An enthusiastic perfumer gushed at the range on offer, practically emptying half his

74

purse as soon as they opened the case. Ash may have grumbled and whined all the way over at the weight of it, but he was happy enough now he had a new pair of boots, a jacket, and a place to stay the night. No thanks was given, of course, but that was the ungrateful swine's way. Selfish to the end.

In their desperation to recover a semblance of dignity, the opportunity to investigate the state of the infirmary hadn't yet presented itself. Now fed, watered, and clothed, pressing matters at hand returned to the fore.

The tavern, this time her choice, was quaintly pleasant. A few quiet figures dozed in one corner next to their tankards, in another was an able minstrel with his lyre. The other tables and booths were mostly unoccupied, a scattering of villagers and travellers spread around the room, some singly, some in groups. Most smiled at her now she was more presentable, some ignored her.

The first group she approached were travellers, unfamiliar with the area. Sympathetic croons and apologies were offered for her tale, but nothing of value. A grizzled old man glared at her over his tankard, best avoided. The minstrel was new to the village, having only settled a few months previously.

'Never had a cause to head there,' he smiled, voice smooth as caramel. 'You never know, though, I run the risk of catching something nasty whenever a pretty young girl passes through, if you get me.'

She didn't, despite his knowing wink. 'So you've not heard anything about it?'

'Wish I could help, but no. Ask Myld behind the bar. She might know. Here,' he tossed a coin at her, winking again and giving his best smile. 'Have a drink on me. Maybe tomorrow I'll need their services, aye?'

'Wouldn't count on it,' she muttered, approaching the bar.

Myld's staggeringly circular form leaned precariously on a dainty milking stool as she surveyed the room, playing with a small length of knotted string in her podgy hands. Her kindly face lit up from its brooding frown as Dem approached, and she rolled off the stool with a creak and a thud.

'More apple juice, dear?'

'Not for me, thank you. My brother might want some.'

'I'll send my boy over.'

A snap of her fingers and her obscurely thin and wiry son scurried behind to collect the order.

'Anything else?' she smiled again, features practically lost in the folds of rolling fat.

'Actually yes. I need some help. My brother and I were looking for an infirmary, our Ma's sick. I wondered –'

'Oh, the closest one is by the Piglick River,' she half turned, pocketing Dem's coin in the fold of her bulging apron.

'Yes. We hoped to find a closer one. Our village healer mentioned one by the Whitewater Lake?'

Myld stopped.

'Whitewater? You've not been there, have you?'

Dem nodded faintly. Myld's hands shot to her mouth, covering her gasp.

'What happened? It was abandoned.'

'For good reason! You poor things, going to that old place. We used to use it all the time,' she dragged the stool across, already out of breath from the exertion of standing and talking. 'Nice and convenient for us, it was. Mighty shame when it closed.'

'But why?' she sat on one of the bar stools, hooking her feet around the legs.

'We don't know. They were good healers, very kind, very clever. Cost a fair bit, don't get me wrong, but it was worth the service they offered. A sickness of some sort drove them all out. Don't know where it came from, don't know how, but some blight took hold of the place. Us folk stopped going before long. They didn't have time for our ails and complaints, all their time was taken up treating this… whatever it was. Within a few months, they'd shut the place down and fled!'

She frowned. 'Fled? Why?'

Myld leaned closer, voice dropping. 'We don't know. There were plenty of stories around the time, mind you. Asked around the other villages and nobody reported anyone getting sick of anything new, it was all just in the infirmary.'

'As in the healers themselves?'

Myld shrugged. 'Some of them. Their assistants, their apothecaries, their cleaners and cooks. But not enough to account for all the patients in their beds. There were rumours…' her voice dropped lower. 'Travellers going missing, fishermen and woodsmen never returning to their homes. Snatched away. *Some* reckon those healers were experimenting with things, ran out of real patients so took to gathering their own. When that didn't work, they tried their weird medicines on themselves. Brought a curse on the place.'

'But you said they were good?'

'They were! This all happened within a few months. Perhaps a new healer arrived and influenced the rest, perhaps they worked alone. Only takes one bad apple to ruin the barrel.'

'And it's closed ever since?'

'The rumours stopped circulating, travellers arrived safely at their destinations, up until recently with the rebels, that is. A few folk went to the infirmary but it was all closed, locked up, the good healers gone with the bad. It's been empty ever since.'

Dem played with a splinter in the bar. It all sounded like overblown stories and unfounded tales of a superstitious, untrustworthy town.

'So you went in the infirmary itself, did you?' Myld babbled excitedly, caught up in the joy of her gossip.

'We did.'

'See anything in there? There were stories of patients left strapped to their beds when the healers fled, left to rot. Cupboards full of skeletons clawing to get out. Jars of organs and pickled people. Anything like that?'

Her piggish eyes gleamed in grisly delight. Dem turned away. Vile woman, taking such pleasure in the perceived suffering of others, real or imagined. She'd seen no sign of wrongdoing, no evidence of any such experiments. An abandoned infirmary, nothing more. This woman had nothing more of value for her. She couldn't trust her tale. Parts were far too outrageous to give it any credence, too fantastical to hold even the most basic points with little more than contempt. A fool looking to thrill her customer with a story.

'Nothing like that. Just empty.'

Myld settled back, disappointed. 'Pity,' she mumbled. 'We all love a story about Whitewater Infirmary. Not had a good one for a while.'

'Whitewater?' her boy piped up next to her elbow, returned from his serving duties. 'That bloke over there mentioned coming from thereabouts. He might know some more?'

She looked over her shoulder. The boy pointed to a hunched traveller facing a wall, inconspicuously gathering his gear into a bag as he prepared to leave.

'Two from Whitewater on the same day!' Myld exclaimed. 'Coincidence! Must be something in the air.'

Coincidence? Not likely. She watched the precise movements, the broad shoulders hunched over in pretence of meekness.

'Bastard!' she shouted, recognition dawning.

The inn startled, the patrons turning to stare. She ignored them, scarcely even saw them. Her eyes were on him and no other. Ash rose from his table, mug and plate forgotten before him. He approached with her, no words or commands needed to understand.

Nari glanced at the door, Ash was already in the way. He looked to the window, but she was there. Dirty, split fingernails dug into her palms. Her heart pounded, her stomach somersaulted. Here he was, in all his arrogance. Not a chance he didn't see them. The bastard sat here in this room, mocking them with his proximity.

'Bastard!' she seethed.

Nari held up his hands placatingly, glancing between the two, over their shoulders at the other end of the room. No escape there, swine. None at all.

'Easy, now,' he muttered, voice strained.

'I'll *kill* you,' she seethed. Her hands trembled, her shoulders shook. 'You left us!'

'Easy, just settle down,' he backed away, not meeting her eyes, constantly looking over her shoulder to the far corner. Meek and cowardly, for all his bravado. An overgrown slug, no mettle when it came to facing his foes.

'Settle down?' her temples ached from her clenched jaw. 'I'll kill you!'

Where was Ffed with her hatchet when they needed her? In the bloody stable with the animals, her hatchet head stolen by this scum. Damn it all, but they didn't need her. She snatched a knife from a table. She'd gut him. Open him up from groin to neck.

'Just calm down, no need for a scene,' Nari mumbled, a hint of hysteria creeping into his voice. Pathetic.

She brandished the knife. Ash crept closer, arms wide, ready to sweep him up.

'Just give the word,' he muttered.

She nodded, turning the knife over. She'd never killed before. Never been in a fight, apart from with Ash. They never ended well. He was too big a lump to get the better of, surprisingly strong despite his skinny appearance. Now it worked to her advantage. Let him tangle the bastard up and she'd stick him with the blade. Right between the ribs.

'Let's just walk away quietly. Nice and quiet,' Nari backed up to his table, speaking softly. 'No need for a scene, please? Please. Just calm down. Please.'

Filth. How dare he. No amount of grovelling would do. It was an insult. To be robbed by such a spineless degenerate.

'Thieving bastard!' she shouted, spitting at the floor between his feet.

'Nariton Selkaharr!'

The booming voice reverberated from behind. She stopped in her tracks. Chairs and tables scraped as they were pushed aside. The dozing figures in the corner were on their feet. Burly, rough men with twisted grins. She looked back to Nari. He was pale, sweating.

'By the four winds! You been up to no good again, Nari? Making more friends?' the closest figure approached as the others covered the exits. Three of them. Travellers. A glint of chainmail under their jackets, the bulge of weapons at their hips. Rogues.

Nari swallowed, his stubbled throat bobbing.

'Look, Pit, I already gave Kirkin what I had, just ask Damid…' he spoke over them, ignoring her and her brother, eyes locked on the approaching rogue.

'Oh I heard, Nari! Heard all about it. Still short though, aren't you? Well short of the mark. Poor Nat won't be happy, we'll make sure of that.'

Nari swallowed again, his voice turning hoarse. 'Kirkin said it was enough to buy another couple of weeks. It's only just short of what I owe.'

'Interest, Nari, interest,' Pit, if that was his name, flexed his fingers and slowly put on a studded gauntlet, grinning all the while. 'You know how it goes. Boss gave you a couple of weeks, maybe, but that doesn't teach you a lesson, does it?'

Nari scrambled to back away, but he was already pressed against the table. Pit passed between her and Ash, shoving them aside contemptuously.

'Out the way, girls, you can have your stab at him when we're done.'

'Girls?' Ash pulled a face. Everyone ignored him.

'Look, Pit, just ask Kirkin and he'll give you your share from what I've already paid,' Nari tried manoeuvring himself between another table and Pit, but one of the others drove him off. 'He's not long gone, alright? You'll catch him outside somewhere. No need for this.'

'Probably, but it's a bit of fun, aye? For that time back in Clovercream? It's only been a few months.'

'Look, I'm sorry about that, it was a misunderstanding.'

'Oh, all forgiven, dear Nari. It's all just a game.'

'I said I'm sorry, it'll never–'

'All forgiven! We just want another laugh, me and the boys.'

The crunch of the gauntlet into Nari's face made her gasp. The way his head whipped back like a dead bird. For a moment, his nose was a pale, broken thing, misshaped like a twisted mushroom. A moment later all she could see was blood, gushing from the nostrils and from the open wound on the bridge where fragments of bone poked through the skin. Pit followed it up with a savage knee to Nari's stomach, doubling him over, then cracking him again with the gauntlet, this time smashing into his shoulder. Nari barely had time to voice his strangled, nasal groans when Pit kicked the wind out of him. Again. And again. His companions joined in, adding their boots to the mix. Pit lifted him from the floor, limbs toneless as an empty sleeve, head rolling on his neck. Pinned against the wall, they set about him again. His head dropped forward, blood and drool spilling from his broken mouth and pooling on his bloodstained tunic.

She watched with satisfaction. Exactly what he deserved. At least at the start. As the seconds wore on, his grunts and groans became more muffled. Suddenly it was less gratifying. Her stomach turned. She looked away. Like butchers tenderizing a steak. The brutality was too much, even for scum like Nari.

Ash caught her eye, frowning, mouth twisted in disgust. He looked ready to cry. She felt the same. Why? He surely deserved it. Up until a few seconds ago, she'd have given anything to be the one wearing that gauntlet.

She looked back. Another punch to the gut. Nari vomited, spraying the rogues with the bloody, bilious, stinking stomach contents. They recoiled with cries of disgust, then set about him with renewed vigour, fuelled by their distaste, driven by their stained clothes. She caught his eye, already red, glassy with tears. Another stinging blow across his cheek snatched his head away.

The tavern door banged open. Rough hands shoved her aside again. Guards, their blue surcoats emblazoned with the king's manticore. A brief struggle with the rogues ensued and Nari slipped to the puddle of blood and vomit at his feet. Pit and his companions shoved the new arrivals away and fled through the open doorway, pursued half-heartedly by the guards.

'Them three were in on it!' Myld blabbered away, pointing her podgy finger at them in excitement. 'The girl and boy included! All came from Whitewater, I tell ye!'

One of the guards faced them, all bristling moustache and puffed-out chest. She recognised him from the gate.

'Trouble makers! Zero tolerance. Out or gaol.'

'Trouble makers? They're the ones who beat him half to death,' Ash protested.

'She was threatening to kill him! We all heard it!' Myld's boy piped up from behind his mother's bulk.

'Zero tolerance!' the guard repeated, hand on his sword. 'Out or gaol.'

'We're going,' she snapped, gathering her meagre belongings.

They were escorted out to the night. Dem half turned in the street to look for Ash, but the guard shoved her forward. She heard him stumble along behind her, cursing all the way. Where now? Better not be the gaol, they'd complied the whole way. People watched them again, turning and staring in the street. It was almost worse than before.

'Where are we going?' she complained, trying again to turn to her brother.

'Out or gaol, like I said,' the guard replied, gruffly.

'And the ones who actually beat him up? What about them? You gonna do something about the actual criminals?'

'We'll catch them. We've already caught you.'

'You haven't caught anything. We were just there. We've done everything you asked. Just let us find another inn.'

'Not a chance. Your options are out or gaol. Keep struggling and I'll assume you want the latter.'

Realisation dawned.

'Out the bloody village?' she shouted. 'You're throwing us out this late?'

'Zero. Tolerance.'

Each word was punctuated with another shove.

Outrageous. Downright criminal. They'd done nothing wrong. In fact, their contribution to the village in their brief stay was far greater than their cost. To throw them out for being nothing more than bystanders.

But there was no point arguing. Better to risk it in the forest than the lecherous degenerates of the town gaol. Who knows what manner of scum lurked behind those bars.

Through the village gates, they pushed them into the road. The few travellers still waiting for admittance shuffled away, eyeing them suspiciously and clutching their provisions close. Fools. The real criminals were in there.

They threw Nari's half-conscious body next to them. He lay panting and rattling in the dirt, blood still leaking from his nose.

'Go find their goblin friend. Should've known better than to let her in. Can't trust them. Bloody animals.'

'You're the animals!' Ash snarled. 'We did nothing wrong.'

'We have plenty of witnesses who say otherwise. You stay down!' he shouted at Nari, struggling to a sitting position by leaning on his sword.

'He's hardly a threat, is he?' Dem rolled her eyes.

A scuffle from inside as a pair of guards marched up with Ffed between their arms. She hung between the two, feet above the ground, a look of passive acceptance on her face. She brightened when she saw Ash and Dem waiting, even managing to untangle one of her hands long enough for a small wave.

They tried shoving her roughly to the ground like they did with Nari, but she skipped neatly away as soon as their grips relaxed. They settled for throwing her pack into the mud, grinning spitefully.

'Now piss off,' the guard folded his arms while his companions tightened their grips on their spears.

'Better than being here,' Ash muttered, slipping an arm around Nari and helping him to his feet.

Ffed glanced between the battered thief and Dem, raising her brows. Dem shook her head. It would take some explaining.

*

Logs and leaves crackled and popped as the hungry flames went to work, chewing away at the wood and loam to release the heat within. She watched the tongues lap and roll, confined by their ring of stones. Nari's groans and whimpers continued long after her tending hands grew tired. His thanks left her conflicted, guilty. He didn't deserve her care, but it wasn't her place to deny it. A person in need. Oskra would have done it. That being said, it wasn't her best effort at suturing. The scar made the broken and partly-reset nose look even

83

worse. All things considered, it was far more than the bastard deserved.

'You have some nice friends, Nari,' Ash muttered, half-heartedly.

'Surprisingly, they're not my friends,' Nari whined, voice muffled and congested, with a hint of a lisp from his broken teeth and swollen lips.

'Never would've guessed that,' Ash smirked, warming his hands on the fire. 'Did a proper number on you. Who were they then?'

'Nasty bastards.'

'Scum tend to stick together,' Dem sneered.

Nari was silent. The thievery hung between them. As yet unacknowledged. She snorted and turned back to the fire. Ffed's soft snores and the crackling flames the only sound from their camp, surrounded by the myriad other sounds of the living forest. Scurrying rodents, hooting owls, rustling leaves, creaking boughs, and whistling wind. She settled back, moving the sleeping goblin's boots to one side. How lucky, to have the ability to sleep after such events. The shame of being thrown out the village still stung, but Ffed accepted it as easily as she accepted a cloudy sky or muddy road. How did she live with the shame?

'So who were they then? Really,' Ash repeated.

'Bad folk. Kirkin's men.'

'Who's Kirkin?'

Nari was silent for a moment. 'He's a rogue. The big man around these woods, the guy in charge of most of the rogues with his gang of enforcers.'

'In charge? Didn't know rogues were organised enough to have people in charge? I thought you were all just out for yourselves?'

'Some are. The lucky ones are. It isn't always so easy. Kirkin used to be with Pahag, you heard of him? Pahag Keweit?'

Ash shook his head. Dem did the same. Nari shrugged.

'Guess you wouldn't have. Starforge is pretty sheltered. He's a rogue in the southern woods, got a big gang down there. Kirkin used to be with him, now he isn't. Or maybe Pahag just sent him up here to continue what he's doing down south.

'Say you're a road robber, or a mugger, or a lone thief. Plenty of freedom, you can do what you want. You rob whoever you come across. Not always the best idea, as it turns out. You rob a member of a gang and suddenly you have two options. You run and keep running until you're out of that gang's territory, or you pay them back. A gang like Pahag or Kirkin's can't be outrun, you get a hundred leagues away and the scoundrels in the back alleys are still talking about them. So you try to pay them back by effectively joining the gang, paying off your debt bit by bit, thereby making the gang grow even bigger. If you run out of time and you're still in debt, well, look at me now.'

'Winds...' Ash breathed. 'Kirkin, you said? Would it work if we met a rogue and just said we were one of the crew? They might leave us alone if we did?'

Nari snorted, leaving a blob of blood and snot on his upper lip. 'Risky. If it's a gullible idiot like me I might leave you alone. Run into one of Kirkin's lapdogs like Pit and you're in a world of trouble.'

'But there's no way they can keep track of all their members?'

'You'd be surprised. They're not dumb, people like Pahag and Kirkin. They're just as cunning and clever as the Barons of Morgenal. Even the king. Clever enough to survive among them, get strong despite them. Cleverer than those Chancellors in the Council by far. Only an idiot would directly oppose Stolach. Pahag and Kirkin just want their little underworld empire.'

'So all the rogues in the forest are a part of this network?'

'No, the lucky ones are still out for themselves, but it isn't safe. At least if you're a part of the gang you won't get bothered by them.'

Dem laughed sarcastically. 'Like they didn't bother you?'

Nari was silent. 'I've just run out of time. To be one of them you need to pay off your debts. I've been a bit... short.'

Dem shook her head. 'Well, it's what you deserve, really. Thieving honest folk. We just wanted to help our *Ma*!' she shouted, fury making her mouth twist. 'You stopped us, led us to an abandoned infirmary. If she dies, it's because you killed her.'

'I didn't know about the infirmary.'

She snorted. 'Sure.'

'I didn't. I thought you'd be safe. You only had a few more days to go. How was I supposed to know?'

'You thought we meant the one by Yellow Castle at first,' Ash shrugged. 'Looking back, you seemed surprised when I mentioned Whitewater. Judging by its reputation in Yewbar, you must've known.'

Nari shook his head, then clutched his temples in pain. 'The pig-driver didn't know either, did he? Or do you reckon he was in on it too?'

They were silent for a while. Maybe he knew, maybe he didn't. Did it matter? Ultimately, the result was the same. He'd led them on a merry chase through the woods and robbed them blind. Then she'd stitched his face up and reset his nose. He should've done the decent thing and walked away as soon as he was able to. But no, here he was, a parasite feeding off their meagre supplies. Bloody and pathetic. His weakness was sickening.

'Guess it's too much to ask for our things back?' Ash ventured.

'All gone, lad. Had to,' Nari clutched his nose gingerly.

Dem snorted again. Bloody cheek of the man! 'Hardly had to. You could've just accepted your lot as a thief and a cur. Didn't have to drag us through it as well, did you?'

'It's not that simple.'

'Sounds pretty simple to me. You robbed your way through the forest, picking on innocents, then eventually tried something on with the wrong people and got mixed up with Kirkin. Now instead of paying the price, you're just still robbing more innocents. You haven't learned a thing.'

'I've learned plenty. I'm trying to leave.'

She laughed. 'Course you are. One more time and all that, one last job, as they call it. Well I've heard plenty of stories of liars, thieves and murderers just like you, and "one more" is never enough. You always go back to your old ways. This is what you are, Nariton. Give all the excuses about Kirkin that you like, but I know what you are.'

'I had to. If I want a chance of putting it behind me, I need to pay him off and get away from here.'

'You could've just run away in the first place, left us alone.'

'No.'

'Yes.'

'He has my brother.'

She paused. This was new. 'What was that?'

'Kirkin has my brother,' he looked between the two of them. 'Natirad. Nat. He's holding him until I pay the rest of our debts. The things I stole from you... it wasn't enough. Only got me another two weeks. I don't know if they'll keep Nat alive, but I have to try.'

'All our things only got you two more weeks?' Ash whistled softly. 'How much did you owe the guy?'

'More.'

'And if you just did what we asked and got paid honestly, would that have been enough?'

Nari sighed deeply. 'Wasn't enough time.'

'You left it pretty late, didn't you?' Ash looked confused. Typical of him. For all his flaws, he was pretty organised. Leaving things until last minute wasn't in his nature. It was one of the few things they had in common.

'I got lucky–' he stopped abruptly, glancing at her. Damn right to stop, before he said another bit of idiocy. If that's how he saw them, a lucky break for his criminality and poor foresight, then perhaps his beating wasn't such a brutal thing after all.

'Is your brother a thief?' she asked.

Nari stared at her.

'Well?' she cocked her head. 'Is he a thief?'

'He's a good man,' Nari whispered.

She laughed mirthlessly. 'That's a yes then. No sympathy from me. If you're stupid enough to get mixed up with a thug like Kirkin, you deserve what's coming.'

'You think I deserved this?' Nari spread his arms wide, gestured to his smashed face, pulled his shirt up to reveal the ugly bruises lacing his torso. She ignored them. The last time she saw such extensive marks were from a sickness, not a beating. She didn't need reminding of Ma's condition. Then again, maybe she did. It put his actions into perspective. It reminded her of what he'd cost them.

'You deserved every blow.'

87

Nari stared at her. She couldn't read his expression. His eyes were too bruised and swollen to see anything behind them.

'Your brother's right. You are a bitch.'

She smiled stiffly. There it was. Resorting to name-calling. Beaten. So similar to Ash. Luckily, she knew exactly how to deal with it. Derision and contempt. Say one thing for Ash; he'd given her enough practice to deal with this nonsense.

Snorting, she locked eyes with him. Challenge him. Make him face her, see the person behind the insult. Let him hate her, make him angry. He was in no state to do anything. She saw Ash shake his head from the corner of her eye. He knew what she was doing. He was as experienced as she was. It was getting increasingly difficult to bait him nowadays, he just ignored her. Nari had no such experience.

'What you staring at?' he demanded. The lisp of his broken dentition gave the words more comedy than threat.

'A child, apparently,' she kept her voice low, demanding his silence.

'Keep staring.'

'I will.'

'Just keep staring.'

'Alright,' her smile broadened. She didn't have to force it.

Nari grimaced as much as his battered face would allow. His lips twisted and split anew, leaving streaks of blood on his fractured incisors.

'Keep staring and see what happens.'

'I'm curious.'

'Leave it, Dem,' Ash whined.

'Don't tell me what to do. Stay out of our conversation and go to sleep,' she glared.

He recoiled with a sigh, settling against a log to watch what happened. He knew not to challenge her now.

'Curious?' Nari continued, ignoring the interlude.

'I'm just looking.'

'How well do you think you'll see through a black eye?'

She cocked her head and grinned. 'You tell me.'

Nari sprang up like a grasshopper, swinging his scabbarded sword. Or he would have. He barely made it halfway before collapsing awkwardly, twisted on his side, clutching his temple. He groaned meekly, rolling his head from side to side.

Pathetic. Snorting, she turned away.

She jumped. Ffed crouched next to her, eyes narrowed.

'Ok?'

She nodded briefly. She'd been asleep only seconds ago. Now she was awake as she was, ready to pounce. Taking a new place next to her brother, she eyed her warily. Was she ever asleep or just pretending? Crouching like a hawk, the goblin watched Nari, one hand next to her knife.

'Nari ok?'

'What do you care?' he groaned, face buried gently in his hands.

'Checking. Hurt,' she shrugged, settling back to her previous position.

What was going on in that pointy little head? One minute poised to gut him, the next asking how he was feeling. Perhaps she'd never understand her. Never mind, she knew her better than most people knew goblins.

'You know he robbed us, yeah?' Ash chuckled.

Ffed bobbed her head. 'Did what he needed. Lived another day. Us three here.'

'Here in the rain and the mud again. No beds for us, no stable for you. Thanks to him,' Dem chuckled emptily.

'Nice stable,' Ffed agreed. 'Nice forest. Both good.'

'Glad you like it,' Ash grinned. 'Wish I had your outlook on life, Ffed, I really do.'

'Don't know if I do,' Dem muttered.

To forgive and forget so easily might seem noble, but some things didn't deserve absolution. This was a man who drugged them and left them for dead in the woods. You didn't let such a transgression go by. You didn't accept it and move on.

'What's your plan to get the rest of the money?' Ash asked.

'No idea, damn it all. Nobody'll trust me with a face like this. Not that I'd have much chance of robbing them in this state anyway. I've just bought Nat two more weeks of waiting before they kill him.'

'Two weeks good,' Ffed nodded approvingly.

'It's not good when you know what's coming,' Nari choked, half-sobbing.

'What coming? Not here.'

'What's that supposed to mean?'

'It's a goblin thing, I think,' Ash cut across. 'It's how she, how *they* think. But I get you.'

'Stop speaking to him,' Dem snapped. If they ignored him, he might just leave, give up and die in a ditch with his scumbag thief of a brother.

'I'm just thinking...' Ash trailed away dramatically. She ignored him. If everyone just shut up, Nari might piss off sooner. With nobody picking up on the trail, Ash started up again. 'You know the way to this other infirmary?'

'No,' she sat upright, glaring him into silence. How dare he suggest it. How dare he even contemplate it. Inviting the wolf back into their farm, the adder into their boots.

'Yes,' Nari glanced at Ash, voice muffled, hoarse, whistling, and whining at the same time.

'Not a chance. Not if the four winds fell still and the sun turned cold. Never!' she hit Ash's legs, unable to reach his shoulders or ears. The fool! Now the bastard thought there was a place for him here. Now he'd linger, a malady never healed. A recurring scab at your lip like the travelling whores bore, a weeping sore from the dead bone of a stubborn veteran unwilling to amputate. Damn him for suggesting it. Damn Nari for pouncing on it.

'Just think about it, Dem,' Ash protested.

'Never! Are you so naïve?'

'Just think – stop! Stop it. Just think. He knows the area.'

'We'll find it!' she kept slapping his limbs, trying to reach his head, trying to knock some sense into his thick skull. His gangly legs kept her at bay.

'He knows the way. He won't do anything to us now. Look at him. Even you could take him.'

Her heart hammered. Ears burning, she snarled and hit him harder. Damn it! By the four winds, how was this even a conversation?

'We'll vote,' Ash lurched forward and grabbed her by the wrists, stopping her assault. 'What do you think, Ffed?'

She stopped, nostrils flaring, fighting to control the thundering pulse in her ears. Let her see sense.

Ffed watched Nari, eyes narrow, one hand rubbing the bare ring of the opposite wrist. She rummaged into her pack and took out her hatchet handle. Nari flinched at the sight, the hope instilled by Ash's suggestion evaporating as quickly as it formed.

'Nari no trouble. I watch.'

'So that's a yes?' Ash grinned.

'Nari trained pig. Sniff out infirmary,' Ffed's lips twitched in a half smile.

'What's in it for me?' he called out.

'We don't bloody kill you, you bastard!' Dem screeched. Or at least she meant to. She was too worked up, too angry. It came out as a squeak, about as threatening as a dormouse.

'We'll pay you, like we initially agreed. Enough to free your brother,' Ash nodded gravely.

Dem shook her head. 'He poisoned us. You can't be this stupid.'

'We'll get there sooner if he's with us. For Ma.'

She turned away, disgusted. Using her name to get his way. He was only doing it to spite her, or to make himself feel strong and magnanimous. Selfish reasons, either way. Stupid reasons. She looked at Ffed. The goblin held her gaze. Calm. Confident. She said she'd protect them. Promised it.

'He'll kill us.'

'I protect.'

'What if you can't? You didn't do such a good job last time.'

Ffed raised an eyebrow and glanced at Nari, snivelling and grovelling in the dirt. Dem smiled, despite herself. Nothing more needed saying.

*

Something tickled his chin. He brushed it away with a groan. It returned. Warm breath against his cheek. he tried moving his other arm. Trapped to the floor, painfully held in place by boot or knee. His eyes snapped open.

'Dem?'

'It's this easy,' she whispered, glaring at him.

'What? Oh.'

The blade glittered in the dying embers of the campfire, tickling his stubble.

'Easy,' she breathed.

He held her gaze. A child with a knife. No. an angry child with a knife. A fine distinction. Dangerous one, too. Especially with a motive. Playing this properly required guile and tact. But what angle to take?

She increased the pressure on the blade.

'Cross us again, and I won't wake you up next time.'

Sweat trickled down his flanks. Angry as she was, she always seemed rational. Appeal to reason.

'I'm going to help you,' he whispered. Her brother was asleep. He couldn't see the goblin.

'You're going to betray us and play the same trick again. My brother's a fool. I'm not.'

The thought had occurred to him, but no. For one, they didn't have the wealth he needed. Two, the guaranteed payoff for getting them to the infirmary and home was enough to pay his debt. Three, his vial of tranquilizer was smashed in his beating, so he didn't have the means to do it anyway.

She pushed harder, hard enough to make speaking even more difficult than it already was. Time to push back.

'Keep me alive and you'll get back to your Ma quicker. That's what you want?'

She stopped, eyes simultaneously growing wider and frown deepening. The knife drew back a fraction. That's right. Keep pushing.

'I'm your best chance of seeing her well again.'

'*Bastard*,' she hissed. The pressure returned, greater than before.

He gulped. Perhaps mentioning her Ma wasn't the most tactful. She already blamed him for the delay. Best not remind her of it.

'Ash and the goblin trust me,' he wheezed. Perhaps peer pressure was her weakness? He moved his free hand to his belt, looking for his knife. He might be able to fight her off. In his current state, he was in no state for a knife-fight, but still more than capable of handling the girl. Probably.

'My idiot brother, maybe. I'd think again about Ffed. She just knows you're no more threatening than a louse.'

'So why the knife?' he couldn't help himself.

'Lice need removing. They can spread disease if you're not careful. Best rooted out and crushed.'

She pressed. A burn as the blade pierced his flesh. He tried swallowing. The blade scraped against his throat as it moved. She sneered.

'What would they think if they found me dead in the morning?' he stammered. Would guilt be the angle to safety? He scrambled around his belt. Where was his knife?

'I doubt they'll care. Ash'll be annoyed. Ffed'll understand. We'll just move on.

'If I call out, he might wake up. What will he think of you if he sees you murdering me? It's one thing to find the body, quite another to see it happen.'

She snorted. 'He didn't help you in the inn, did he? You can stop looking for it, by the way, it's right here.'

She wiggled the blade in his neck. Of course. Silly of him not to recognise his own blade. The beating left him muddled, foggy, fragile. He could barely remember most of it. Dem grinned smugly.

He started. The beating. One thing he recalled amid the thud and crunch of fist and boot was catching Dem's eye in the midst of it. She didn't grin so smugly then. She didn't grin at all. A child, unfamiliar with violence and murder. Angry, hurt, and frightened. She had the motive, the opportunity, the means. But not the stomach. For all her posturing, that's all it was. In the heat of a moment, she might do it, but not in cold blood. That took a different type of bastard. He was safe.

He met her eye.

'Do it, then.'

She paused, fury blazing. Her hand was still. He pushed his neck further into the blade. She drew back the same amount.

'If you want to do it, go ahead.'

'I'm warning you. If I wanted to do it, I wouldn't have woken you up,' she sneered, trying to look menacing. 'This is to remind you I can.'

'Can you? I saw your face when they beat me. You think you have the stomach for that?' he smiled, swollen lips pulling lopsidedly.

'If it means protecting us from scum like you, why don't you find out?'

'Why don't you?'

They remained as they were, faces inches apart, glaring at each other. But it was already over. He'd called her bluff. The threat was dead and buried. She knew it too.

Huffing, she withdrew, throwing the knife by his side.

With a satisfied chuckle, he returned it to his belt. 'Sure you want to give me this?'

She ignored him, taking her place between her sleeping brother and the goblin. He sneered at her. Stupid child. Empty threats were a sign of weakness, not strength.

His smile faded.

The goblin stared at him, yellow eyes glittering.

Turning, he wrapped his cloak tighter. He felt her eyes bore into his skull, making his neck twitch, his ears burn.

She didn't need to say anything to make her threats.

Chapter 8

The Piglick gurgled by on its tortuous path, sparkling waters dancing in the dull sunset. Clouds of midges swarmed the muddy banks, its shores turned to sludge by the passing of countless trotters. Ffed wrinkled her nose. It was a strong odour and no mistake. Even for her. The children wouldn't enjoy it. A quick glance at their grimaces confirmed her suspicions. She suppressed a snigger. There were far worse stenches than a bit of pig waste. Ash slipped on the bank, landing heavily on outstretched hands. He cursed and spat, wiping the pasty sludge on his stained boots. Dem chuckled, but stopped when she saw Nari's smile.

'What you laughing at?'

'Same as you,' Nari sneered.

'He's my brother. I'm allowed to,' she faced him, hands crossed, face full of violence. 'You're not.'

'Give it a rest,' Ash slid in the mud, ignored.

'I don't need your permission to laugh,' Nari chuckled falsely.

Dem looked him up and down like a piece of dirt on her shoe. 'If you're laughing at us you do.'

Ffed shook her head and skipped over to Ash, her bare feet finding purchase where their clumsy boots could not. This was how it was. Dem and Nari at each other's throats, threats and insults every other sentence, Ash largely caught between the two, Ffed mostly ignored. At least it put a stop to the children's bickering, for the most part.

'How much further?' Ash asked, leaning on her shoulder.

'Don't know. Nari knows,' she nodded over to him.

'Nari?' Ash turned to the rogue.

'What?' he kept his arms crossed, glaring at Dem.

'How much further?'

'Tomorrow.'

She nodded approvingly. Soon. Very soon. Then they'd be on their way back to poor Lelan, assuming she'd evaded the Great Hunter for this long. Hopefully, she was alive. If not, well, the Great Hunter needed to feed as much as anyone. If it didn't, the world would soon be overrun.

Still a little daylight left. The surrounding woods were full of hedges and bushes with spindly, wiry branches and sharp leaves, a pain to walk through, it was easier to just go down the river itself. With their new boots, the children kept their feet dry, even when wading through the water. She didn't know what state Nari's boots were in. He didn't complain, at least. Not that he should. Even if he had holes in the soles that let in the water and mud, it only meant he could relish in the smooth clay and crisp river. She grinned as her toes wrapped around the rocks and pebbles of the riverbed, as sand and mud pushed between them, only to be washed away a moment later by the current. A good river.

They passed a few hogs on the way. She couldn't tell if they were wild or farmed, certainly they passed no pig-drivers like old Bib, but perhaps they were just waiting a bit deeper in the wood. They left them alone in any case, snorting and tossing their snouts as their beady eyes followed them on their way.

Barely two miles later and it was time to set up camp. She helped Ash back up the slippery bank to firmer ground, and they made it to a small clearing in the underbrush. The dense cover of the shrubs concealed their flame well enough, and they huddled around the campfire in silence.

But something was wrong. A gnawing in the pit of her stomach, a hunger not settled by their provisions. She peered into the darkness. Something in the shadows.

The others carried on their nightly routine. She tried to follow, but the feeling persisted. Unease. Like staring at your reflection and seeing something move behind you, then turning and nothing was there. A sickness in her stomach, making it turn and wobble. She glanced at the others. It wasn't the food. They were fine with it. Could she be ill? She rubbed her wrist briefly, feeling her pulse while she was at it. Strong, rhythmic, slightly quicker than normal but that might be her anxiety.

'Goblin, forgot to give you this.'

She turned to Nari, holding her hatchet head in his outstretched arm.

'Mine!' she muttered. A welcome surprise. She'd assumed it lost with the other gear.

'Couldn't sell it,' he read her mind. 'The smiths knew it was goblin-work and wouldn't touch it. Tried flogging it off to a tinker but he refused. Kirkin obviously wasn't interested.'

She took it from him. It was good to feel its iron between her fingers once again. She rummaged in her pack, her fears momentarily put aside. The handle was in here somewhere... there! She brought it out triumphantly. For a few minutes, she lost herself in the task of resetting the head to the handle, cleaning the eye of splinters, hammering it in place, slipping in a few wedges and nails to secure it, trimming away the excess. She gave it a few test swings. It was shorter than before, what with her trimming, the balance a bit off, but not bad. If she added a bit more weight to the other end it might make it better.

She nodded to him. He settled back with a sickly smile, a sheen of nervous sweat on his forehead. Perhaps he meant it as a peace offering? Perhaps he thought it would gain favour with her? It was neither. She bore him no ill will. He did what he could to survive, to save his brother, to live another day. No harm had come to any of them from his antics. Just people surviving in the world. But his threats and sly looks needed watching, and the children needed defending.

Stiffening, she looked back around. Free from the distraction of her returned axe, the disquiet of the surrounding forest bore down on her. Nari wasn't the only one with dark intentions. The usual scuffles and scurries of night-time sounds were still there, but altered. Something scuttled in the twigs and leaves that sounded very much like a hedgehog, but not quite. Something squeaked and snuffled almost exactly like a rat, but not quite. Something scratched and sharpened claws on tree trunks exactly like a badger would, but not quite. She gripped the axe tighter.

'You gonna put that away?' Nari swallowed nervously, staring at her.

97

She blinked, focussing on him. She'd been staring past his shoulder. In the darkness, he probably thought she'd been staring at him. No point correcting him.

'I look around.'

She stood and slipped into the trees before they could protest. The campfire was obscured almost immediately. She breathed in the night. Leaf, dirt, pig-waste, pine, a hint of early honeysuckle. Beneath it, something else. Something familiar. Her stomach lurched again. A feeling. Something tugging at her heart, willing it forward.

Circling the camp, she listened, her broad ears flapping. The others muttered from the other side of the shrubbery, mystified by her behaviour. Why couldn't they feel it? It didn't matter. She could. A pervasive, oppressive weight on her chest. A net of anxiety, trapping her limbs in its attempts to paralyse. A fear.

Movement in the dark. A snapped twig. Too heavy for a rodent. A harsh breath. She raised her axe with one hand, pushing aside a branch with the other. Nothing. Only the bare forest floor, a snapped branch with jagged splinters, green leaves knocked from their perch.

Sliding on through the twisting trunks, ducking beneath the boughs, clambering up and down fallen logs, she worked her way around the camp in an ever-increasing spiral. Nothing there. Only the signs of something recently passed by.

She paused by an alder, its trunk scored by narrow claws. Running her fingers along it, she frowned. Deep enough for a badger, but too small for one, and there were no burrows nearby. They were like four blades, straight and true. Unnatural.

Her nape prickled. She turned slowly. The sound made her freeze. A giggle. Faint, light, like a child. No, not *like* a child, but a child. No doubt. A human infant. She stopped and smelled the hand that traced the claw marks. Sap and loam, and something else. Something that made her eyes sting and her stomach seize. Rot and mould. Death and decay. She peered into the night, heart hammering. The stench of the infirmary.

Between the partly-illuminated trunks, the shadows stared back as dark as pitch. Something stared back at her. Something unseen. A malevolent and malicious force in the night, sinister intent behind its

98

featureless mask. The cold sweat of terror broke through her pores. She felt it come close. There was no sound, no rustle of leaves or snapping of twigs. All that was a charade, a game for it to lure her out here, alone and exposed. It was a miasma. Ethereal and incorporeal, leeching through the heavy darkness and through her pores, working its way to her frantic heart.

Another tug at her breast. The oppressive feeling subsided for a moment. She took a breath, stepped forward. She wanted to see it, to meet it. She wanted to listen to its voice, its true voice, unmasked from its childlike giggle.

A faint keening came from the woods. High-pitched and soft as gossamer, rising in pitch as it approached. She understood its meaning, its welcome. It was like the songs her mother once sang when she was a babe, nestled in her arms. A song of safety, of belonging. It drew her forward, beckoned her on, commanded her limbs to move.

She paused. Wrong. All of it. She wouldn't be commanded to do anything. She'd suffered her years of servitude and slavery. Now she was free.

Blinking her eyes, she stared again into the darkness. The keening stopped, replaced by another giggle of curious delight. A child finding a new toy, or an old one long-forgotten. The darkness became oppressive again, leaning in on her from all sides. A chill on her nape, more terrible than the inevitable breath of the Great Hunter's pursuit. The rank breath of something poised to strike.

She whipped her head around. Whatever it was disappeared into the canopy above with a rustle of twigs and a scattering of leaves. She backed away, axe held in a sweaty grip. She kept her eye on the tree for as long as she could, heading back to their little campsite. Something told her the thing would go now, its hunt aborted by her sudden arousal. The tug at her breast gently abated, and the normal sounds of the forest slowly returned.

Slumping next to the fire, she ignored the questions of the others, batting them away with shrugs and grunts. They eventually gave up, falling asleep one by one.

She couldn't bring herself to close her eyes. It was gone for now, but she couldn't forget what she saw. Every time she closed her eyes, the flash of that terrible, pale, tortuous limb sprang before her eyes, each child-like finger ending in jagged black claws.

Chapter 9

Ash nodded with satisfaction. This was more like it. A well-kempt garden and a heavy iron perimeter fence, keeping the forest away from the mighty building at its heart. Red sandstone walls built into mind-bending arches and spires, heavy leaded windows glowing gold from the torches within, towering storeys of solid stone competing for height with the surrounding forest and winning easily. Clean as a cotton sheet, reassuring as the arms of a parent.

He tried the gate. Locked. Of course, it was dark already, it made sense to keep it closed. A chain to one side attached to a bell. He yanked it, tolling the brass. Stepping back to the others, they watched the building through the black iron bars.

He grinned at Dem. She smiled back. He couldn't help it. This was it. Nothing like the decrepit, run-down ruin of the Whitewater infirmary. There was life here. You could see it in the shadows moving behind those illuminated windows, the well-kempt lawn, the neat bushes and tidy orchard in the corner. Even the path was of carefully-raked stones, winding through the green gardens to the heavy porch. A series of cabins and huts lay within the complex, presumably for some of the workers to inhabit, but were mostly dark.

He glanced back up at the bell and pulled the chain again. Perhaps they didn't hear the first time.

Nari groaned and leaned against a tree, cursing under his breath. Surprisingly, he'd made it the whole way without falling behind once. Ash half-hoped that in his battered and bruised state, he might be a little slower, slow enough for him to keep pace. A fool's hope. Even injured, Nari was still far quicker through the forest than him. It just wasn't his climate. Perhaps even more surprisingly, apart from the quibbles with Dem, there'd been no more sign of betrayal from their guide. Whether it was out of loyalty to them, to the promised payment, or due to his injuries, or fear of Dem's wrath, he couldn't tell.

Ffed nickered from the forest behind.

He grimaced. Maybe it was Ffed's wrath he feared. Her peculiar turn over the past day and night puzzled them all. Stealing off into the darkness then returning with a face like she'd seen a ghost, only to jump at every shadow or snapped twig during the day, and skulk through the trees with her axe at the ready when the sun set. It was enough to put anyone on edge. Who could say what instincts being back in the deep woods might have ignited in the goblin's brain? Years of living next to civilisation might have dampened her primal instincts, but after a few weeks in the wild was she becoming like the other goblins again? She certainly spoke less, returning to her own speech of yips and titters more often than not. There was no telling what she might do.

'Try it again,' said Dem.

He pulled the chain a third time, harder now. The sonorous peal echoed in the night, startling a flock of crows into a flurry from the rooftops.

Ffed growled softly at the sound. He glanced around instinctively. She was well away, her back to them, facing the darkness.

Nudging his sister, he nodded to their friend. 'Should we bring her in or leave her out here? I don't want them to think…'

'I know,' she nodded, chewing her lip. 'I think it's best if it's just the three of us. I'm sure she'll understand. I don't want a repeat of Yewbar.'

Still no answer from the infirmary. He frowned. 'That wasn't Ffed's fault, was it? I could try climbing the fence, by the way.'

'No, just wait, I'm sure they're coming. And no, it wasn't directly her fault, but you don't know how much having her around might have influenced the way they treated us. If it was just you and me, that guard might not have thrown us out.'

'Maybe,' he tapped his chin. 'You're probably right.'

'I think so. Look!' she grabbed his arm. 'Someone's coming! I told you.'

The main gates opened and a figure bobbed down the path, lantern held aloft.

'Alright, I'll tell her.'

Dem nodded and pulled Nari to his feet. Ash approached Ffed cautiously.

'Ffed?'

She grunted but didn't turn.

'We were thinking it might be best if you stay out here, if that's alright? It's not that we don't want you coming, we just don't know how they'll feel about having a goblin around.'

'You go. I stay,' she said.

He grinned with relief. They were the first intelligible words she'd uttered for hours. At least she was still there.

'You'll be alright out here?'

'Fine here.'

'Hopefully we won't be too long,' he returned to the others.

'I wait. Watch.'

He nodded. She seemed happy enough, in her own way. Something must have spooked her last night, but if it were serious, she'd have told them. Who knows what superstitions and beliefs she maintained from her old culture? Best to let work it out alone, they had important things to do.

A gaunt, pale face swung in and out of the lantern's shadow. A woman. No, a girl. Barely older than Dem. The shadows exaggerated the pocks and acne scars on her cheek and chin. She paused on the other side of the gate, holding her lantern high.

'Hello?'

Ash stepped up. Dem beat him to it, practically trembling with self-importance.

'Hello, we're here for the healers, we need their help!' breathless in her excitement, her words were nearly lost in the night.

But the girl had keen ears and nodded earnestly, staring at Nari.

'Of course. Bring him in. We don't normally take admissions at this hour, but we'll make an exception for this one.'

Dem flinched, brows furrowed. 'Admissions? Oh, yes, you can take a look at him as well, I suppose.'

The girl paused for a second from unlocking the gate, hand hovering over lock and key. 'As well? Either of you hurt too?'

'No, our Ma's sick,' Dem said.

'She's not with us,' Ash clarified.

'Ash, please, don't interrupt,' she rolled her eyes at him. Arrogant cow. 'As I was saying, we need advice. Our Ma's sick and our village healer said it needed your expertise.'

'Not mine,' the girl chuckled. 'But I'll see that you get seen by the ones you need. Let's get your companion sorted first.'

'Aye,' Nari grunted, barging past and shoving the gate open. 'Give me something nice and strong. Head's killing me.'

The girl saw them through, locking the gate behind them. Ffed remained unseen and undiscovered. Hopefully it would remain that way. Hopefully she'd be safe.

Carefully-tended stones crunched underfoot. As they approached the infirmary, its bulk and enormity became that much more obvious. Half as tall again as the tallest tree in the distant forest, kept at bay by that black iron fence, the ruddy red walls rose as a bastion of architectural superiority among the log cabins of the sprawling gardens. The craftsmanship that must have gone into it! The sheer skill and knowledge immortalized in the curving arches and weight-bearing columns, the delicate spires and lofty staircases. It would have taken many lifetimes of genius craftsmen to complete such a building, with only the final ones realising the completed work of art. It was more like a temple than an infirmary, a grand, exquisite chapel of enormous proportions.

The girl reached the porch and pushed the heavy door open on silent, immaculately-balanced hinges. More stone arches and pillars were on the inside, made warmer by rich wooden panels, flooring, and rafters. Muddylan's hay flooring was as crude here as it was in Starforge. This was a place of class, of richness and elegance. Dem gazed about with her mouth half-open, eyes wide in wonder. He probably had the same expression, stumbling through the corridors after the pockmarked girl.

'Oh aye, looks pretty enough, but where's the medicine?' Nari grumbled.

Before Ash could stop her, Dem turned and punched the rogue's shoulder. Her little fist wouldn't have done much damage, but the shock of it made Nari stumble.

'You shut your mouth. They're getting your help.'

'There's really no need,' the girl interjected, placing herself between the two. 'We're coming to the ward now. It's a big place.'

'Touch me again...' Nari growled, pointing over the girl's shoulder at Dem.

'What?' she challenged him. 'Think I can't take a concussed, broken coward? You're here because I *let* you here. Now behave.'

'I'm here because you don't have the stomach to do what you want to do,' Nari growled.

'You're going to get us thrown out,' Ash grumbled, joining the girl between the two. He turned to Dem. 'We need their help. Can you just leave him alone for a little?'

'Exactly, we need their help. Him insulting them won't do us any favours,' she sneered.

'It's really no insult,' the girl stammered. 'Let's just get to the ward and get you sorted? You've had a long journey and it's late, that's never good for tempers.'

Dem snorted and turned away. Nari hawked as if to spit, but the intent dissipated when Dem's glare turned even harder. He swallowed lamely and trudged down the corridor. Exhaling with relief, they followed. Dem grabbed his arm after a few steps, pulling him down to her level.

'Don't you *dare* speak to me like that again. Don't you *dare*!'

Typical. Called out for being an idiot and now she was taking it out on him. He tried pulling away but her hands closed tighter, painful around his arm.

'Just leave it.'

'Take his side again and we're done,' she spat. 'You're no brother of mine if you side with the person who robbed us and left us for dead. It's disgusting.'

'We're here for Ma,' he prised her fingers away. 'You arguing is only making that more difficult.'

'Him insulting the healers will make it difficult. Him being anywhere within a hundred leagues of us makes it difficult. *I'm* the one thinking about Ma. Don't you *dare* use her against me. You know I'm right.'

'In your opinion. I think he can help us. He got us here.'

'No. He betrayed us once, he'll do it again. You just like having someone around to take your side.'

He could have laughed. Was she really accusing him of such pettiness when she was the insufferably childish one? Pathetic. For all her posturing, she was so immature.

'Let's just get to the healer.'

'Don't tell me what to do.'

She marched off after the other two. There was no reasoning with her when she got into one of her moods, she was out for a fight, and four winds protect whoever got in her way.

The ward was cool and quiet, roughly a third of the twenty beds occupied by sleeping patients. The girl pointed Nari to one and he collapsed into the sheets, not bothering to undress.

'I'll get you a tincture in a moment, just need your name and age,' the girl waited at the end of his bed.

'Nariton Selkaharr. Twenty-eight.'

'Any medical problems?'

'Busted head, busted teeth, battered ribs—'

'Unrelated to your injuries?'

'Not that I know of.'

'When did it happen?'

'Dunno. Two days ago? Three?'

'Loss of consciousness? Episodes of nausea and vomiting?'

'Yes to both.'

'Can you remember the events?'

'Vaguely.'

'Any change in sensation anywhere in the body? Loss of vision?'

'Just everything hurts.'

She nodded. 'One of the healers will come around to examine you and administer what medicines they deem appropriate.'

'Good of them.'

Her smile was strained. 'Try to get some sleep. You two, come with me. I'll take you to the duty healer.'

They left Nari, his soft snores already echoing by the time they reached the corridor. Everything was soft and quiet, an oasis of calm

106

and safety. Their shoes tapped along the panelled hardwood floors, the echoes lost in the rafters above. Like three little mice scurrying at midnight, they stole their way down the maze of corridors and passageways.

'Healer Anten in through here,' she gestured to a final door.

'Excellent, what's your name?' Dem asked politely, pleasant as a summer's day, as if her false manners could brush her previous actions under the table.

'Joli. Please, after you.'

She knocked briskly and pushed the door open, gesturing them in before her. The candle-lit room was warm, tables of books and ledgers on one side, a cupboard full of pots and vials on another wall, and a middle-aged man sat at a desk, scratching away with a quill. He watched them enter, brows raised.

'Hello?'

'Visitors, Healer Anten,' Joli followed them through into the cramped room. 'Their friend looks like he was beaten quite badly, he's on ward two. These two have a message from their village healer.'

'Oh. Their friend is stable?' Anten asked, putting the quill down and watching Joli over the rims of his crystal spectacles.

'Yes, walked in. History of head trauma, but he's a delayed presentation, a few days old.'

'We'll examine him in the morning. You can conduct it, I'll supervise.'

'Thank you, Healer.'

'This business with these two needs doing now, or can it wait until morning?' he spoke as if they weren't there, looking right past them at Joli.

'They've travelled here for advice, something their own healer couldn't manage. I thought it best to check with your first in case it was urgent.'

Anten grunted dismissively. 'Travelled far?'

'Esteemed healer,' Dem cut in with a lame curtsey. Ash stifled a snigger at her attempted gallantry. 'We've travelled from Starforge, at the banks of the Clearbed. Our healer–'

'Starforge is well over a week away,' Anten interrupted. 'A few more hours until morning won't make much difference.'

He felt her bristle next to him. Careful now, don't explode.

'Our Ma is gravely ill,' her voice was low, doing her best to keep calm.

'There are many ill patients here. I can't see why we need this conversation now. Please, have some sleep and I'll have someone speak to you in the morning.'

'We've travelled a long way,' Dem continued, speaking through gritted teeth. Ash took a half step away.

'And you must be exhausted. Sleep. Rest. Recover. This is not the hour for discussion.'

'We just want advice,' she protested.

'You'll have it. Just not tonight.'

'You're not even doing anything!' she snapped.

Ash rolled his eyes. It was only a matter of time before she cracked. Predictable. When things didn't go her way, she lost her temper. When people didn't do what she perceived to be the 'right thing', she bit their heads off.

Anten pushed his glasses up the bridge of his nose and settled back in his chair, staring at Dem over his steepled fingers. She glared back, nostrils flared like the bull she was.

'Young lady, I don't expect you to understand the intricacies and pressures of a healer, you lack the experience and intellect to grasp our complex work. It may seem to you that I'm sitting here doing nothing, but in reality I am conducting the *most* important part of my busy schedule. Without proper documentation of our assessments and treatments, our care is wasted,' he tapped the pile of parchment on his desk. 'I'm not even halfway through my paperwork for the night, and I have an infirmary full of patients who may require further treatment at any point, generating yet *more* documentation.'

Dem opened her mouth to respond but he held up his hand for silence.

'No! I don't want to hear it. You're not entirely to blame, Joli gave you an unfair expectation by bringing you here when she should know better than to disturb the duty healer for such trivialities. This conversation is over. I'll send someone to see you in the morning.'

They stood for another moment in stunned silence. Dem stared wide-eyed at the healer, lip curled. Ash shared a glance with Joli, who shrugged apologetically. No harm done, really. A bit more of a wait was nothing to him, if they could only get Dem out the room without murdering the healer.

'Apologies again, Healer,' Joli murmured, gesturing them to the door.

He glanced at Dem, still staring at Anten, who studiously ignored all three. He was half-tempted to give her an encouraging tug on the sleeve, but touching her was risky, he might not get the hand back. By a stroke of luck, he didn't need to, and she turned slowly to exit the room, eyes wide and mouth shut tight, nostrils doubled in size.

Wincing, he followed. By the four winds! He'd only seen her this angry once before as a child, and back then Ma and Heb were around to soothe her for the loss of her favourite doll, its dress sacrificed for the sail of his newly-constructed toy boat. Back then, she'd nearly scratched his eyes out, screaming and spitting like a wildcat, clawing at his face with her nails, her face purple with the effort of containing such rage. Anten may live to regret his dismissal. Her fury would inevitably be unleashed, he just hoped it wouldn't be on him.

'Many apologies, friends,' Joli offered lamely in the corridor. 'I thought he might give you a few minutes.'

'It's alright,' he replied, hurriedly, keeping his eyes on Dem. She remained silent, motionless, staring off into space.

'I'll take you to a relative's room?' she muttered, glancing between the two, an appropriately-concerned frown on her brows.

'That's great,' he replied, following her down the corridor. If they were single rooms, he might just survive the night. Dem shuffled along dumbly behind him, her expression unchanged. Best not to engage at the moment, just get her somewhere with no sharp objects, lock the doors, smother your ears, and pray the thunder passed.

*

Ffed kept her back to the tree-trunk, axe in hand, ignoring the sweat trickling down her temples. Silence all around. As if her ears were plugged, as if she were underwater. A pervasive, encompassing, suffocating stillness. Oppressive as a black leather bag over your head. She dared not breathe too loudly for fear of what might spring forth once the silence was broken, what sinister force prowled behind this deaf barrier, stalking.

Through a gap in the trees was a clearing. Only a few feet wide, a small ring of stones at its heart. Why was she here? What drew her to this place? What made her swim through air as heavy as marshwater to this clearing? A gnawing in her gut. A hunger. She closed her eyes. Judgement battled with instinct. Please, let her go.

Her foot inched ever closer to the opening, exposing her to ambush, her body moving entirely against her will.

Or was it? Curiosity tugged. She crept forward. She shouldn't be doing this. Yes she should. Something needed looking at. Something needed investigating.

The clearing was empty, no activity at its peripheries, no flashes of light from poorly-concealed weapons or reflected from the back of watchful eyes. No rustles of leaves or swaying of branches. Nothing at all. Still. Silent. Muted. Frozen in place by an absence of... everything.

Stepping forward, she looked at the stone circle. They were once whole. Pieces of a jigsaw scattered on the forest floor. Judging by their blunted edges, they were old, lying here for years undisturbed, washed by countless rains and changes of season. But no moss. No overgrowth of the underbrush to hide them. An absence of life. She looked carefully at the grasses holding them up. Different to the grass further back. Preserved, as if they'd been pressed. An absence of death as well.

Something told her not to touch the fragments, not to disturb them. She didn't want to. She didn't want to be here, exposed and frightened in this clearing, with only the veiled moon and stars to provide her with a semblance of light. But she couldn't take her eyes away from the shards, piecing the jigsaw together in her mind. It built slowly, carefully, turning the fragments around until they slotted together into a whole. An artificial shape. Corner pieces and straight walls. She knelt again, her nose nearly touching one of them. Clay. A clay box, shattered for some reason. But why? Why leave it undisturbed for so long? Why did it call her?

Her heart skipped as the silence shattered.

A giggle.

No matter where she turned, she felt the eyes on her back. Malevolent, malicious eyes. This was not the gaze of the Great Hunter, who stalked out of necessity and service to the world. It was a gaze of hatred, a gaze of torture and despair.

She took a step back. Her foot brushed something hard. Her breath caught as a spark of pain shot up her calf, as if she'd stepped on a nail. Turning, she skipped into the cover of the forest, sliding and ducking through the boughs, up a bank, down a creek. She fled through the remains of a campsite, recently used from the looks of it, a discarded blanket and empty pack still there, but there was no time to investigate further. Probably just a traveller on their way to the infirmary. She rounded a cluster of rocks, jumped over a few ditches, slid under a bush, and over a rotting log covered in slippery moss.

Panting, she stared wildly into the darkness. Nothing. But it was there. The child. Its sibilant laugh echoed in her ears, the false innocence giving it an even more terrible note. It played as any child would, laughed as any child would, followed and imitated her as any other. But it was all a lie.

Her foot and calf continued to throb, but she couldn't inspect it, not while the thing was still out there, still searching. It would find her eventually. It always did. There was no escape. Why it followed was a mystery. Perhaps it was just a game. Perhaps it enjoyed the chase. More than the chase, the fear.

The gnawing in her stomach returned. The compulsion to get up and move. She fought it. The closer they got to the infirmary, the stronger it grew. The closer the stalker approached, the stronger it grew again. Then there was the broken clay box. Something connected them. A memory she didn't know she had. Something ingrained within her very being, sleeping until now.

It was a weak pang now. Weaker than it had been all night. Perhaps she'd managed to throw it off her tail for a while. Perhaps it was playing in the remains of that old campsite. She hoped so. If she could sense its approach without ever seeing or hearing it, surely it could do the same to her. It only had to follow its gut to find her. It always found her.

But not for now. A shuffle of a hedgehog gave her relief. Animals shunned the thing just as surely as she was drawn to it. If the forest was safe enough for the hog to come out of its den, it was safe enough for her.

Twisting, she inspected her foot. The skin was unbroken. She massaged her calf and the gnawing pain gradually ebbed away. All that pain from just touching the clay. There was something to it, something evil. A greater mind might have gone back to uncover its secrets. She had no such ambition. Let her be a simple goblin leading a simple life. Let her day be bright and merry, and her night warm and silent.

Ash and Dem were in the infirmary. She wasn't sure how she felt about that. The scent was there. If she hadn't been so distracted by the stalker, she might not have let them enter, but what was done was done. She had to trust their iron to see them through safely, and as they rightly said, goblins were unlikely to be welcome. Perhaps this was why, because they could feel things others could not. Their awareness of unpleasant things might remind other races of their existence, and some beings prefer to live in ignorance than fear.

Not her. Not goblins. The whole world was against goblins. The stalker was a mighty foe, but no matter how cruel it was, how awful, it was not her ultimate fate. Like all goblins, she was promised to the Great Hunter at the start of the world, along with all other races. Only the daemons and dragons were powerful enough to deter it, to negotiate a different arrangement, and now the dragons were gone. The Great Hunter didn't claim them, as it didn't claim any daemon. Even when they seemed dead, they remained in another way. She didn't know how, she didn't care. All goblins knew this and accepted its truth, and she'd seen no evidence to counter her beliefs.

112

But she didn't know the stalker, or the absence of life and death around the clay box. Could it be that this thing was like the daemons and dragons, negotiating and evading the Great Hunter? She'd never met a daemon. Perhaps this was how it felt to be near a Negotiator.

She shivered. Unlikely. This felt unnatural, whereas the daemons and dragons were the very essence of nature. It whispered of terrible things, of forbidden pacts made with the emptiness beyond the world. Magicks.

All goblins knew the dangers of magicks. The other races accused them of forgetting the scourge of the Magus Herikik, but it was not so, for who suffered most at his hands if not his own people? It was the thing of destruction and corruption. A thing to be feared.

She looked up. The hedgehog was silent again. Gripping her axe, she peered behind. An unbroken floor. A still canopy. An unassuming forest. She kept watching. The nearest hornbeam swayed in the wind, rustling the nearby branches. Nothing obviously untoward, but the gnawing was back.

A prickle at the nape of her neck. She turned. Nothing. Back to her trail. It was all clean, no sign of any passing feet, no disturbed leaves or broken branches. A warm, still, summer night. At any other time, it would have seemed perfectly safe. But something nagged at the back of her mind. Something whispered of danger.

If only she'd kept an eye on the hedgehog, she might have been reassured. But she didn't hear any cries of pain, no crunch of bones or snap of twigs, nothing to suggest its demise. Everything was still. No owls hooted, no insects buzzed, no leaves or branches rustled, apart from the hornbeam.

She froze, eyes locked on the spreading boughs. It alone moved, a poor mimicry of wind. The forest was devoid of all tracks, including her own, including the hand-print left on the rotting log when she mounted it. All meticulously brushed away. Too clean. Too perfectly undisturbed. Its perpetrator kept rocking the boughs.

A sudden thump as something fell from the rustling branches. The hedgehog. Half of it, anyway. Its lower half lost, its upper half ending in fleshy rags, quills snapped and bent.

She closed her eyes.

Laughter filled the night. Soft and light. A child at play.

Chapter 10

'Describe the symptoms to me again, please?'

Dem spelled it out again, using over-complicated medical terms that went straight over Ash's head. He drifted off. She was in her element, giving a perfect timeline of events surrounding Ma's deterioration and the results of treatments attempted by Oskra.

He wouldn't admit it to her, but it was probably for the best that she came after all. He would've been lost with all the technicalities they used to scrutinise the case. If it were him alone, he probably would've been brushed off by the first junior healer sent to clerk them in. Through Dem's knowledge, it was escalated up the chain to one of the most senior healers in the infirmary. Each step required the story to be repeated, with more complex and curious questions added with each iteration. Funny, really. For all Anten claimed the importance of documentation, half of what they wrote down in their file didn't seem to get read, otherwise they wouldn't have asked them the same damned story four times already.

'Definitely no bite-marks?' the healer asked.

'Definitely none,' Dem replied, the fourth time she'd answered the same question that morning.

'And nothing to suggest any illness in the days leading up to it?'

'Nothing. Fit and healthy.'

'Interesting,' the healer rubbed his immaculately-trimmed goatee. Semon was one of the most experienced, the same grade as Anten and one other called Awis. 'Most interesting case.'

'As we tried explaining to your *esteemed* colleague last night,' Dem smiled sarcastically. It was a wonder she was able to speak at all, really. He'd been worried her constant screaming that night may have ravaged her throat into uselessness. But here she was, vocal cords intact. More than could be said for his sleep. It was a shared room, after all.

'Our apologies again. Anten did not mean to insult. The pressures of being duty healer at night...' Semon trailed off. Ash nodded politely in acknowledgment. Dem did not. Semon cleared his

115

throat. 'Well, anyway. Obviously it's difficult to make any diagnoses without reviewing the patient ourselves, and it's been what, two weeks since you last saw your mother?'

'About that much.'

'Two weeks. With such rapid progression, we're probably working on outdated information.'

'So what, you're just giving up?' she demanded, a flash of colour rising to her cheeks.

'Not at all, we just need to decide how to proceed. This needs discussion between us healers. Ideas need exploring. Books need studying. I assure you, this is an exceptional case and we need to prepare for it.'

'Right, good,' Dem nodded, satisfied.

'Good. Now, if you'd give us some time?'

Ushered out by another acolyte, they prowled about the gardens to pass the time. In daylight, they were even grander than he'd expected, with trimmed bushes and carefully-arrayed flower-beds of botanical wonders, a beautiful orchard with its own little pond, supplied by a diverted creek from the Piglick, more plants and herbs than he'd ever be able to name. The paths of fine white stones crunched under their boots like frozen grass, tended as carefully and precisely as the rest of the grounds.

'Should we check in on Nari?' he suggested on their third lap, breaking the silence of nearly two hours.

'What do you think?' she snapped.

'Probably a no from you.'

'I think so.'

'Well I might.'

'No you won't.'

He glanced at her, but she didn't look at him.

'Alright, no visitors for Nari.'

She grunted. Some battles weren't worth fighting. Amusing as it may be to tease her, after last night's impressive display of pent-up fury his desire to poke the bear was somewhat diminished. He failed to stifle a yawn as it crept up on him.

'Kept you up last night, did I?' she snapped, sharp as a needle.

'I'm just tired,' he muttered.

'Stop complaining.'

No winning with her. She was probably embarrassed for her behaviour. Better to leave it unacknowledged. He might bring it up sometime in the future if she ever accused him of overreacting, it was good to have a few arrows in the quiver, but not today. He'd rather leave her well alone, but as soon as he was out of her sight she'd probably just accuse him of visiting Nari in secret. He shouldn't have mentioned it.

They passed the row of huts. A few of the workers waved half-heartedly from their porches. He waved back, Dem ignored them, trudging around with folded arms. They looked happy enough, in a resigned sort of way. Probably exhausted from years of tending to the meticulous garden.

One of the men held a stick figure in his hands. Vaguely familiar. Where had he seen it before? They passed the final house, another stick figure placed on the chair on their porch. Of course! Bib had one just like it. The doll's garments for these ones seemed cleaner than Bib's tattered rags, but it was definitely the same type. There must be a supplier in the nearest village, Holevale or whatever it was called. Funny things, very simplistic, but perhaps that was their attraction. He tried pointing it out to Dem but she ignored him. More fool her. Little H back in Starforge might like one to make up for the disappointment of the rotten apple. Winds! It seemed so long ago!

'They seem alright here, apart from Anten,' he ventured.

'Now they're taking us seriously, yes.'

'Shame we had to say the same thing so many times.'

'That's just how it is. They need to hear the story.'

'Yeah, but they could just read the notes, right? Save a bit of time.'

Dem rolled her eyes. 'You get a lot more from hearing the story in the patient's own words, Ashil. I wouldn't expect you to understand.'

He flushed. Really? Condescension? When half of last night's fury was because of Anten's patronising comments about her lack of understanding of the intricacies of his work? She could piss right off. Smarmy cow.

Taking a breath, he calmed himself. Just pretend it's Heb, not Dem. You wouldn't want to punch Heb in the face, grind your fist into that stupid, flat nose until it crunched like a snail's shell, the pulp dribbling out between your fingers…

He relaxed, tension leaving his body. She was sensitive today, stung. He had to tread carefully.

'Oskra would like these gardens,' he gestured to the flower beds. Perhaps reminding her of home would help.

'Obviously.'

Perhaps not.

'What do you think these are for?'

'Why would I know? I've not even started my learning. Not properly,' she huffed. She brightened. 'Oh, wait. That's mandragora, you can use it for analgesics and anaesthetics, depending on the preparation and the dose. That's henbane, black nightshade you might call it? Can settle nausea and vomiting and help with bowel spasms, depending on dose you can mix it with mandragora for an anaesthetic.'

'So you do know a bit,' he smiled. Apparently this was the way to cheer her up. Success. Just don't let her get too arrogant with it all.

'Just the simple stuff,' she sniffed. 'Well, simple for me anyway.'

And there was that arrogance. Typical.

'Shall we go through there?' he pointed to a gate, partially-hidden behind a rosebush. 'We've not been yet.'

A secluded section, high stone walls topped with an iron grille, keeping the small ring of flowerbeds in shadow. Nowhere else to go through. He turned back, disappointed by the meagre discovery. Not nearly as exciting as he'd hoped. Dem grabbed his arm, frowning.

'These are odd.'

'They all are to me, simpleton as I am,' he shrugged.

'No, seriously. I recognise most of the plants outside, can't necessarily name them or their uses, but at least I've seen a lot of them. These are different.'

'So what? I'm sure there are millions of plants in the world you've never even heard of. The Jagged Isles, the Southlands, the Northlands, the Westlands, the Kingdom of the calefs and Far Eastlands. There's a lot more to the world than Dailas Forest.'

'Maybe,' she pursed her lips. 'I don't know, they don't look right.'

'Ah! Coincidence to find you here!' a voice from behind. They turned together as Joli walked through the gate.

'Why a coincidence?' Dem asked.

'You're in the private garden of the man you need to see,' Joli smiled politely.

'Oh? Who's that?'

'One of our healers. He's only been here a few years. I'll let Healer Semon and the other elders explain. If you'd follow me.'

'Strange plants,' Dem gestured over her shoulder as Joli escorted them out.

'Hybrids. You won't find them anywhere else in the world,' Joli nodded. Dem shot a smug glance at him. He hated it when she was right. 'He grows them himself. Brilliant mind. A bit eccentric, though.'

'Eccentric?' Ash asked. Didn't sound promising.

'He's not really allowed to be duty healer anymore. Amazing at what he does, of course, but we mostly just keep him for very special cases. The really complex stuff.'

'And we're trusting him with Ma?' Dem asked. 'This eccentric one who isn't allowed loose on other patients?'

Joli shrugged. 'You can discuss it with the Healers.'

'You're damned right I can.'

Back through the cool, arched corridors of the infirmary, polished hardwood all around. She led them back to Semon's office in the eastern wing, two floors above Nari's ward. Inside were Semon, Awis, and Anten, watching them once again over the rims of his crystal spectacles. No mysterious eccentric to add to the company. Perhaps they were planning a dramatic entrance for the fellow? Ash smiled at them, but it went unacknowledged. Was it a prerequisite for a healer to be a miserable arse? Taking the offered seat next to Dem, he folded his arms. No doubt, she'd do all the talking.

'Afternoon, children,' Semon nodded pleasantly.

'Afternoon,' replied Dem, curtly. She nodded to Awis and pointedly ignored Anten. The old healer didn't seem to mind, or care, but studied the set of notes before him with the intensity of an academic.

'We've had an extensive discussion between ourselves, searched through our texts and old cases, and we have a few more questions for you.'

'Can't have been that lengthy a discussion, we've barely been gone three hours.'

Semon smiled thinly. 'Any neurological deficit in your mother?'

'No seizures or anything. She responded to voices, although it was a bit variable. Oskra conducted a full examination and mentioned reduced muscle power, and mildly altered peripheral sensation.'

'Which muscles, which areas of skin?'

'It was generalised, no specific pattern.'

'Altered sensation in what way?'

'Reduced pain and crude touch. We couldn't really assess proprioception because of compliance. Upper and lower limbs.'

'Change in her pupils?' Awis asked, his rich Southland accent rolling over his tongue.

'Equally reactive to light. Direct and consensual reflexes intact,' she confirmed.

Awis nodded. 'At least they were two weeks ago, eh?'

'We came as soon as we could. It's been a difficult journey.'

'Any photophobia or neck stiffness?' Awis continued.

'Yes to the first, no to the second.'

'Bleeding gums or dysentery?'

'Yes to both.'

'For how long?'

'From the onset of symptoms. Two days. Nothing before or after.'

Awis settled back, looking over Anten's shoulder as he recorded their answers, nodding silently.

'You mentioned generalised abdominal pain, started a day later?' Semon picked up the line of questions.

'Yes, she kept clutching her stomach.'

'How did she examine?'

'Oskra said her abdomen was normal, apart from the bruising.'

'Jaundice? Was she yellowed?'

'Yes.'

'Dark urine?'

'Yes, but it was so bloodstained it's difficult.'

'Pale stools?'

'Yes, well, it's difficult to judge. Profuse diarrhoea and dysentery.'

'And definitely generalised pain, not specific to any particular part?' he pointed under his right ribcage.

'Definitely.'

'And no trauma?'

'None that we noticed. We asked the other panners in case she had a fall at work, but they all said it was a normal day for her.'

Again, mostly repeated questions. At least he thought so. Perhaps a few were new. They'd been through it so many times he couldn't remember what was said and what wasn't. They were silent for a while, looking over Anten's shoulder at his looping handwriting, the scratch of his quill the only sound as he crossed out lines and added new ones to the parchment, presumably working through a list of diagnoses. They murmured to each other in low voices, indistinguishable from one another, barely moving their lips. Ash glanced at Dem but she ignored him, keeping her eye on the healers.

'What do you think?' he asked.

'It's difficult. She has such vague symptoms it could be a number of things happening all at once,' Semon rubbed his goatee. 'It's often the case with older people to get multiple co-morbidities flaring at the same time, but your mother is quite young, unless it's an aggressive infection–'

'Any tubercles?' asked Anten, suddenly, piercing them both with his glare.

'Pardon?' Dem blinked, surprised by his sudden interruption.

'Tubercles? Lumps. Groin, neck, or axillae.'

Dem shook her head. 'No, nothing like that.'

Anten sighed and crossed off another line from the parchment, settling back into the chair and rubbing his spectacles with the hem of his sleeve.

Semon and Awis exchanged a knowing look and smiled sadly at them.

'You've got us stumped. Between us we have a rather extensive experience of most disease, and although we can fit a number of diagnoses into your mother's puzzle, none fit perfectly, even when we consider multiple co-existing disease processes. It's also a problem with timing, sometimes it helps to have a bit more of a timeline to appreciate the way the symptoms develop, which we don't have. The truth is, between the three of us, we don't know.'

'Hence referring us to this other healer,' Ash nodded.

'Don't interrupt him,' Dem frowned.

Such an arse. Even now, clamouring for favour with these people. It wasn't like he'd cut him off mid-sentence, anyway. It was just an observation.

Semon smiled. 'No, it's fine. He's right. I think all we could offer your mother is symptomatic treatment, then cautiously start treating her through the possible list of differentials. It would take time, and the treatments for some could worsen other possible conditions. Healer Gerath's services are needed.'

'Healer Gerath,' Dem nodded, pretending as if she knew who they were talking about.

Awis raised his brows. 'You're familiar with him?'

Dem flushed, making Ash smile. 'No, I'm just happy to speak to anyone who might help us.'

'We'll see,' snorted Anten under his breath, but loud enough for everyone to hear.

'Well, is he here?' Dem asked, ignoring the comment. 'I understand he's quite specialised? We saw his herb garden outside.'

'You didn't touch any, did you?' Anten leaned forward, suddenly, grabbing her hands.

'No, we just had a look,' Dem recoiled, snatching her hands away.

'Forgive our caution,' Semon rested his hand on Anten's shoulder. 'Gerath's herbs are potent. As with all medicines, they are essentially poison that we titrate to benefit not harm. Taking them from the source might lead to particularly high doses.'

'Right, well we're not stupid enough to touch random plants, thank you. We may not understand all the *intricacies* of medicine, but we have some common sense,' she said pointedly.

Ash winced, peering out the corner of his eye to see Anten's reaction, but the healer ignored it, busying himself with organising the paperwork on the desk.

'Of course. Joli?' the pockmarked acolyte stood up. 'Take them down to Healer Gerath, would you? Anten, are you finished with the notes?'

Anten handed the file wordlessly to Joli, ignoring the two of them once again.

'If you'd follow me?' she gestured to the door.

'He's not here?' Dem asked.

'Gerath can be a bit...' Semon waved his hand in the air.

'Eccentric?' offered Ash.

'Indeed. He prefers to stay downstairs. It's been like that since he arrived. Unfortunately, it's why we had to take him off the duty rota, I'm sure Joli told you.'

'She did,' Dem nodded, pushing her chair back to leave. She curtsied to the healers. 'Thank you for your time.'

'Neat curtsy,' Ash sniggered after her, following Joli down the corridor.

'Piss off. Pays to be polite.'

'Like making sarcastic comments to Anten?'

'He doesn't deserve my politeness, or respect. Conceited old fool.'

'If you say so.'

They followed her down the stairs and back to the main entrance, where they took a right at the crossroads to head to the north wing. Instead of ascending the stairs, Joli led them to the lower level, past the storerooms and wine-cellars, past the kitchens and pantries and to a final, solid mahogany door. She stopped and smiled apologetically.

'Here we are. A lot of his herbs and plants thrive in darkness, it's why his garden is so shaded.'

'You're making me question this decision,' he was only half-joking. Putting their trust in a crooked, pale ghoul of a man in his damp, dark cave of an office seemed a significantly poorer choice than going through the painstaking list of differential diagnoses with the other healers. A healer who grew poisons potent enough to make Anten jump out of his chair. Pride was the only thing keeping him from running straight back that corridor to the pleasant craftsmanship of the infirmary above.

'Be quiet,' Dem snapped at him. Such an over-inflated sense of self-importance. Impressive, really.

Joli knocked heavily on the door. They waited in anticipation. A click as the latch was flipped, the door swung open on well-oiled hinges. He tensed, prepared to face the monster within. The arthritic, warty, anaemic freak locked away in his dungeons, safe from the prying eyes of good and normality above.

He blinked. Unexpected. Not a monster at all.

Just a man. Balding, with a hook of a nose and a rash around his ear, but nothing else to distinguish him from anyone else. He glanced between the three of them and held out his hand expectantly, snapping his fingers.

'Well, come on. A referral from upstairs? Let's get on with it.'

Joli handed the pile of notes and he disappeared into the darkness, leaving the door open. They shared confused looks. At least it wasn't just him.

The man called from within. 'Well, are you coming in or not? No, not you, Joli. Go back to those crooks upstairs, see if they need help with the sniffles and bumps they spend all their time with on the wards. Someone might be dying of a stubbed toe that needs their urgent attention.'

Joli smiled again at them. 'As I said, a bit eccentric. You know the way back? Just follow the corridor when you're done.'

She retreated along the corridor as they stepped into the darkness of the doorway. Perhaps the true monstrosities were within, hidden from sight, luring unsuspecting fools into the bowels of despair with its façade of innocence.

'Shut the door, please. It's just a latch, don't worry, I'm not locking you in here with me,' he called again.

Ash didn't move. Monster or no monster, it still wasn't right. Dem pushed past him to do as requested, plunging them into momentary darkness. He panicked, grabbing for the latch but missing, punching Dem in the shoulder instead. She cursed and pushed him away. He stumbled into something hard and waist-height. Heavy objects thumped in the darkness and glass shattered, making him jump again and hit his head on a rafter, sending a cloud of dust tumbling into his wide eyes. Yelping, he struggled to clear them and blundered blindly into Dem again, falling to the floor in a heap.

'You bloody idiot,' Gerath hissed from nearby. 'If you waited another two seconds I'd have lit a torch. Now look. Two hours' work on the floor. Go on, look! See it? Two hours of distilling and titrating contaminated by dust and dirt.'

'Sorry, Healer,' Dem muttered from the floor. 'He's not the brightest.'

'Piss off, Dem,' he growled, still pawing blindly at his eyes as she bucked free from his gangly limbs.

'Shut up,' a thump in his side as she kicked him. 'You're embarrassing us.'

'Aye, kick him again if he tries smashing any more of my work.'

'Sorry, Healer,' her voice was further away. He wasn't as blind anymore. There was a dim glimmer of light all around, but everything was still too blurred from his streaming eyes to make sense of it. He kept rubbing.

'Sending down two clumsy children to my workshop… what's this place coming to? What am I, a wetnurse? Do I look like I have any milk?'

'No, Healer.'

'Damn right I don't. Now sit there and shut up while I read through this load of nonsense and see what they've sent me. When the lump wipes the filth from his eyes, tell him to do the same. I've got work, plenty of it, and they always send me rubbish. But if I don't see them, it's always *my* fault they can't diagnose anything, it's *my* funding they dock, *my* supplies they cut.'

His rambles trailed away into silence, Ash kept rubbing. Eventually the blurred shapes focussed, revealing the dim contents of the room. Nothing exciting, nothing different to any other storeroom. Shelves and tables, glasses, vials, and tubes on top, dusty books and tomes, clouded jars with indistinguishable labels marking their contents. In the far corner was a tiny fireplace, with a pile of equally pathetic sticks by its side, presumably for firewood. There wasn't a single wall not utilised by shelves, drawers, cabinets, or other peculiar paraphernalia of metal tubes and orbs and glass containers. A single high window cast a narrow band of light to a taut sheet, which blunted and dissipated the light into a soft glow.

Dem was perched on a stool, watching Gerath patiently as he flicked through their notes, resting his elbows on the very table Ash had disturbed in his flailing panic. Whatever material he'd been titrating soaked the edges of the dossier. Presumably it wasn't corrosive or harmful in any way. Or so he hoped.

Gerath wasn't alone. A few acolytes, distinguished from the white-clad healers by their brown hoods, milled about the shelves, coming and going like bees. He tried following them to pass the time, but for some reason he kept losing track. There were at least four. One tall, one small, one fat, one merely stocky, but at any moment he could only see two, even though there was nowhere else they could go to. He shook his head. He must have hit it harder than he thought.

'No tubercles?' Gerath suddenly asked, sharply. 'You're sure?'

'None,' Dem confirmed.

'Absolutely sure? You checked everywhere?'

'All the usual places where lymphadenopathy occurs.'

'Not lymphadenopathy. Tubercles. Distinct lumps.'

Dem paused. 'We checked everywhere. Oskra did a thorough examination of all the major groups. Axillae, groin, cervical chain, we–'

'No.' Gerath interrupted, slapping the table. '*Not* lymphadenopathy. You're naming lymph node groups. I'm asking for other lumps. I'm asking if you *specifically* checked the entire body, head to toe, for lumps or nodules.'

Dem flushed. 'I didn't personally, no.'

'Didn't personally?' he huffed in distaste. 'Who are you? Neglecting a proper examination in a poorly patient. Who trained you?'

'I'm not, Healer. I'm yet to begin my formal teaching.'

'So why are you here? What good are you?'

'I'm – it's – Oskra sent me,' her face simultaneously flushed and paled at the dressing-down. Ash sat back, trying not to enjoy her discomfort too much.

'And who's Oskra? Village healer, couldn't be bothered coming here herself?'

'She's busy,' Dem protested.

'So she sent a child with half a story, no medical training apart from a minimally-extended vocabulary from her dimwit brother. And you expect me to work with this?' he shook the dossier under her nose. 'I need the hands that examined, I need solid signs and symptoms, not the second-hand blithering of an emotionally-clouded girl. Who are you to tell me what this Oskra saw or felt? How can I trust your report?'

'I studied her notes before coming. Memorised them word for word,' her voice dropped lower, timid and hesitant.

'Oh brilliant,' Gerath rolled his eyes and clapped mockingly. 'You can read a report of an examination. Doesn't mean anything, does it? Normal to one could be vastly abnormal to another. I need the first-hand account! For something of this magnitude to come from the mouth of the uninformed…'

'I'm sorry, Healer,' Dem whispered.

'Keep it, it's no good to me.'

She sat stiffly, straight-backed, but her chin lowered with every cutting word the healer spoke. Her eyes lost their glimmer. For whatever reason, Gerath's tirade cut her more deeply than Anten's crude dismissal, possibly even more than Nari's betrayal. She withered before Ash's very eyes, like a scrap of paper tossed into a furnace. Had anyone else spoken to her like that, she'd have retaliated with the fury of a savage. Not today. Perhaps it was the environment, exhaustion after their journey, or just the fact she was finally realising the limitations of her knowledge. Despite her condescension and arrogance, the sharp words and kicks and torrents of abuse, her obsession with controlling as many aspect of his life as she could, seeing her like this was somehow worse. It started out as fun to see her put in her place. This was well beyond that.

He should say something. Do something. Defend her from this bully. As he opened his mouth to say as much, something changed. A chill ran up his spine and doubts collected. Who was he to question this man? A man so revered in his abilities that the three most senior healers in this acclaimed infirmary deferred to his opinion on the case? If he said he needed Oskra's account, that's what he needed. If Dem's report was insufficient, that's just the way it was. His would have been even worse. He had nothing to add to the story. There was no value in him coming at all. An apprentice crafter, nothing more. He didn't even understand the language they used in this place. Speaking up was pointless. Suddenly as dejected as Dem appeared, he hung his head and was silent.

Gerath stirred and looked over his shoulder at the acolytes behind him.

'Stay here.'

They nodded dumbly. Better to sit and do as they were told than suffer his displeasure. Dem may have been the one towards whom Gerath's anger was directed, but Ash felt its sting just the same. They'd come all this way with insufficient information to help Ma. Wasted time going to the Whitewater infirmary, allowed themselves to be led along and robbed by a rogue, then thrown out of a village for a further altercation with the very same man! They were fools.

Children, nothing more. Unversed in the intricacies of real life, sheltered in their corner of the forest with their riches and privileges.

Gerath wandered over to the shelves and disappeared. Ash blinked slowly. A hidden alcove, leading to another room. Foolish of him not to notice it, really, but an overlap of the corner of the loaded shelves obscured it from this angle. Shifting his position, he could see Gerath's robe as he discussed with someone, or seemed to anyway. Another acolyte? No. he could finally see all four of them at once, standing smartly as Gerath conversed. It must be another healer, although he couldn't see one. He leaned forward again, trying to catch a better glimpse.

His hand slipped on the wet table, jarring his elbow as he fell. Gerath glanced over momentarily. He didn't see anyone. The notes spread out untidily, some falling to the ground or deeper into the puddle of whatever he'd spilled on the table.

A numbness washed over him, a helplessness. Would they return to Starforge empty-handed? Two failures on an extended trip to nothing. All because they were too inexperienced to understand the information they carried. If it was too complicated for an experienced healer like Oskra, what hope did they have? A sudden burst of anger flared. Why did Oskra send them anyway? As Gerath said, he needed the first-hand experience of the examiner. As a healer she should have known. Instead, she willingly sent them on this useless journey, first to the wrong infirmary, second bearing the wrong information. It was her fault as much as theirs!

'Idiot!' Dem snapped, gathering up the parchments. 'Can't you just sit still?'

'Apparently not,' he snapped back.

'Just shut up and sit over there. You're making things worse.'

That was damned rich of her. He wasn't the one cocky enough to give half a story to the healers and look smug about it as he did so. Perhaps it was her fault, after all. Had it just been him and Ffed, Oskra might have given clearer instructions and spelled it out for him. Dem's arrogance and overconfidence probably gave the impression of knowledge she didn't possess. Oskra trusted her with a responsibility beyond her capability. Little bitch.

He opened his mouth to say as much when Gerath returned, his frown somewhat diminished.

'Anyone else ill?' he asked, as if his previous tirade never happened.

'No,' Dem confirmed.

'You both feeling well? No aches or pains or anything?'

'Nothing.'

'And you were with her in close proximity for how long?'

'A day.'

'How close a proximity?'

'I bathed her, dressed her, and assisted Oskra examine her. Ash helped feed her a little.'

'More than a little,' he muttered. He'd cradled her head and spooned broth into her cracked, bleeding lips. Dem did none of that. She didn't wipe the spillage from her chin or listen as she choked on half-swallowed pieces.

'No symptoms after a day,' Gerath grimaced. 'Her co-workers? The other river-panners. Anyone else unwell?'

'Not while we were there.'

Gerath glanced over his shoulder again at the acolytes. They remained still. Was that a movement from the alcove? Or just his imagination? Gerath turned back to them and caught his eye. A look of displeasure crossed his face for a moment.

'I know what it is.'

He brightened, despite everything. 'You do?'

'Those nose-wipers and back-rubbers upstairs don't keep me around for nothing. Bastards don't like my work, but they know I'm the one who keeps this place's name. They won't admit it, but they know,' he chuckled. 'Oh yes, Gerath has all the answers to their questions. Even miserable old Anten. Without me, they're just another bunch of fools.'

He spoke to himself more than to them. 'Eccentric' didn't do him justice. There must be a madness of some kind in that head, straining at the seams to break out. Perhaps that's what he was doing when we went to the alcove; having a conversation with the voices in his head.

Gerath snapped back to focus, treating them to another glare. 'The treatment isn't easy. Neither to manufacture nor to take. An unpleasant thing.'

'What is it?' Dem asked, quietly.

'I don't trust your village healer's examination, but your history was good enough to diagnose. Inexperienced hands will miss it. A type of tubercle sickness. Less contagious than usual. Much less contagious...' his voice trailed away, the displeasure softening for a moment into almost a look of pity as he spoke in a low voice, more to himself than to them. 'But far more aggressive. Too aggressive for its own good.'

'What do you mean?' asked Ash.

Gerath glanced at him, interrupted. 'Diseases don't necessarily *want* to kill you, not ones like the tubercle sickness. They want to spread as much as possible. If it's too aggressive, it'll kill before it can disseminate itself within the population, limiting its own spread. The most successful diseases are the slower ones, the creeping death with no signs or symptoms, spreading like unseen rot within the population. This one is loud and obvious. A peacock of a disease. Doomed to fail,' he shook his head disapprovingly.

'By fail you mean it'll kill Ma?' Dem asked.

'If we don't treat it. This is a bad strain, very bad. It needs eliminating. We'll get her better. But as I said, the medicine is complex. We don't have the supplies to hand.'

Ash closed his eyes. He knew exactly where this was going.

'What do you need?'

'I have most of them, in fairness. Some of them I can substitute with my own hybrids, but not one. There's a type of fungus, a mushroom, it only grows in swampland. We had a supply but recently ran out. Your best bet is Tarin Swamp.'

'Too far,' Dem shook her head, regaining her voice now hope was returned, albeit only slightly. 'It'll take us another fortnight to get there and back to Starforge.'

'Go to Trottmire, then' Gerath shrugged. 'It's smaller and you're less likely to find the mushroom because of it, but what do I know? How confident are you in your foraging skills?'

131

Dem glanced at him. Ash smiled.

'We know someone.'

*

Clinging to the boughs, she watched the underbrush. Her blistered hands smarted, raw skin from torn callouses burning against the rough bark. She couldn't let go. No matter how much it hurt, she had to keep her place.

It was down there.

The thing waited for her, scurrying about the grassy tufts and bushes, reminding her of its presence with the purposeful rattle of leaves and snapping of twigs. As if she could ever forget it. The wound on her cheek was only just scabbing over, the blood finally congealing.

She did her best to keep awake, to stay alert, but there was only so much she could do, only so many hours her body could keep going. It waited for her breath to become steady in the early hours of the morning before striking. Not killing, no. If it wanted her dead, it had the opportunity to do so. Her slashed cheek was testament to that. She didn't know what it wanted, other than to see her suffer.

Yet she was still drawn to it. Whenever it approached, the hunger intensified. The compulsion grew. Despite the ache of her cheek and the pull of dried blood down her face and neck, despite the long nights of pursuit and terror, she couldn't keep away. If not to the stalker, then to the infirmary. Even if Ash and Dem weren't there, she would have stuck around the forest, just to be close to that dark, arched building.

Her foot slipped momentarily on the bough, sending something tumbling to the floor below. A sudden scurry as the thing jumped on it in the shadows below, squeaking with malevolent glee. Savage growls followed, then silence.

Why did it wait? It was a brilliant climber, whatever it was, it could have come up here and dragged her down whenever it wanted. But no. those weren't the rules of this particular game. This was one of patience and endurance. Would her hands last the hours it took for it to grow bored and leave? By the grace of Enadir they might.

She'd been keeping watch on the children whenever possible, staying within the shadows at the border of the iron fence. A few glimpses here and there as they wandered the grounds earlier that morning, but nothing else. A few patients came and went, the workers milled about on their tasks, and that was it. Something called for her from the bowels of the building. Stronger than the stalker or the clay box, infinitely greater than the remnants within Whitewater infirmary. There was the source of it. A magnet to her iron.

A scratch at the foot of the tree as serrated claws gripped the bark. She strained to see, but risked dislodging herself from the bough. Better to keep still. Thuds and tears sounded as the thing climbed.

Something knocked her foot. She tightened her grip, straining to look over her shoulder. Nothing behind. It was beneath. Nothing but a flimsy bough between her belly and its claws.

She struggled again to take another look. Just a shadow against the trunk. The canopy parted momentarily to allow moonlight into the forest. Her breath caught.

Two orbs of eyes, dark as torture, rimmed with fire. Pale limbs, black claws. If she saw anything else, it was too horrific to understand. The moon hid behind the canopy again. She tried shuffling forward but the bough started dipping under her weight. Nowhere to go. Another cuff of her feet sent her legs flying, cutting loose into thin air.

A thud to the forest floor as the thing jumped down, anticipating her fall, darkness within darkness watching her flailing limbs with evil excitement.

The bough bounced, trying to shake her off, trying to throw her into the waiting jaws below.

She gripped tighter, a new warmth between her fingers as raw skin finally split. Blood dripped from her fingertips, lost to the forest floor. Something scurried directly beneath, slurping and gasping, moaning in black ecstasy as it gathered up the stray droplets. The cold breath of the Hunter kissed her nape.

Not today. Not like this.

Her legs swung back over the bough, relieving her tattered palms for a second as she swung upside-down. The forest floor danced and jolted beneath her. Just a puddle of darkness and shadows.

She vomited green bile, filling her throat and stinging her nose.

Laughter echoed in the darkness.

133

*

'Trottmire?'

'It was that or Tarin.'

'Piss off. You're not dragging me to bloody Tarin. Do I look like I have a death wish?'

'Exactly why we're going to Trottmire, idiot.'

'Good. I have no desire to be eaten by trogs.'

Nari's day and a half in the infirmary was apparently not what he expected. Other than the obvious diagnoses of fractured ribs, broken teeth, and a probable concussion of some description, there was nothing to be done for him. Even the painkillers were apparently ineffective, giving him a worse headache and making him nauseated. Safe to say, he was ready to leave.

'We're going tonight?' the rogue asked, reaching for his pack.

'What's the point of going tonight?' Dem curled her lip even further than it already was at the prospect of conversing with him. 'We'll head off at first light.'

Nari groaned and sat back in his bed. Ash smiled sympathetically. He'd be similarly frustrated at being told there was nothing to do. No treatment except rest and recuperation, a few more dressings and sutures for his wounds, and a nice warm bath. Nothing else. Even a set of new teeth from the surgeons would take days to manufacture out of extracted teeth, wire, bone, and ivory. So here he was, gapped-toothed, bruised, and sullen as the day they'd arrived.

'Every hour we waste is another one closer to Kirkin's deadline,' Nari warned, voice still congested, although the whistling lisp was slightly reduced. '*And* another hour without help for your mother. There are two lives in the balance here.'

'If you *dare* try to make me guilty about this,' Dem rose her hand as if to strike him, her voice dangerously low. Ash grimaced. Her punches and kicks were generally weak, but she'd long since perfected the art of a stinging slap across the ears. But not today, not for Nari. She controlled her urge and left it hanging as a warning.

'Semon and Joli are heading back to Starforge tomorrow,' Ash explained. 'They'll help Oskra manage Ma's symptoms while we're gathering Gerath's supplies. Hopefully it'll give us a bit more time.'

'Oh great. No offers to help me out, were there?'

Dem shook her head in disgust. 'A sick person and a criminal in over his head are hardly equitable, are they? These are healers, not thugs. What do you expect them to do?'

'They're doing *you* a favour. Why can't they lend me the money to pay Kirkin? We can pay them together at the end when it's all done.'

'This isn't a money-lender,' Dem rolled her eyes and stood to leave. 'Why don't you ask them in the morning, see where it gets you?'

'I might just.'

'Good. Ash, we're going to bed. Come on.'

He glanced at Nari. Back to Dem. Stay for a pleasant chat or go with the viper? Difficult decision. He glanced back to Nari, who raised his brows. Back to Dem, her frown deepening. Well, too late now. His hesitation would result in a stern telling-off. If he was going to be shouted at anyway, he may as well make something worthwhile out of it.

'I'll be there in five or ten minutes?'

Dem inhaled sharply. 'Stay for as long as you need to.'

Frosty as a winter morning.

Nari chuckled as soon as she was out of sight.

'Brave of you, lad, I wouldn't have done that if I knew we'd be sleeping in the same room tonight.'

'I'll probably live to regret it.'

'That's assuming you live.'

He smiled. 'What's it like?'

'What?'

'Doing what you do for a living. How do you feel about it?'

Nari shrugged. 'Feel pretty shitty about it at the moment, I'll be honest. Brother's got his neck on the block with mine next in line, and my only hope of getting us out of it lies in the hands of your bitch of a sister, no offence.'

Ash snorted. 'She means well. You *did* betray us. Bastard,' he added, half-jokingly.

'I'm a bastard for sure. As for what's it like, being a thief and a scoundrel, a scallywag? Highs and lows. Constantly. The thrill of the job, the low of the consequence, the high of the plunder, the low of the debts you sink into. One day you're in the best room in the tavern, a bottle in one hand, a full plate in the other, and a whore balanced on each knee, the next day you're scrounging for scraps in the pigsty. I've been in four different gaols on seven different occasions, I've travelled over half of Northern Dailas. To do what I do, you have to be a bastard. What you and your sister have is the real life. What do you want to do?'

'Craftsman,' Ash nodded, confidently. 'Always have.'

'Creative type, knew it. Quite a few miners in your village, aye? All miners and craftsmen. You don't have the build for the former.'

'That's right,' he chuckled. 'I'm good with my hands. I'd make you a lovely cutlery set.'

Nari snorted. 'How nice,'

'How will you find Kirkin?' he asked. 'Once we give you the money for helping us through this, how will you find him to pay your debts?'

'He'll either find me, or I'll look for one of his representatives, like Pit back in Yewbar. It isn't difficult when you know where to look.'

'And it'll be enough for your brother?'

'Should be. As long as your sister agrees.'

He nodded slowly. 'Thank you for helping us, Nari. I appreciate it. I'll help you as much as possible with your brother.'

'Thanks, lad. The four winds know how much he needs us.'

Chapter 11

Dem waved goodbye to Joli and Healer Semon as they turned down the western path. Their route would take them past the Halfmount hills and old iron mine, up to Muddylan, and eventually back to Starforge. Provided they kept a steady pace, it wouldn't be much more than a week before they arrived, they even took a pigeon with them in its wicker basket to send an update as soon as they arrived, in case they hadn't already set out home by then. At last, Ma was getting the support she needed. With the added expertise of the two from the infirmary, her symptom control should see her through to the cure. Everyone would be relieved when the healers arrived, her handwritten letter in hand. It made her sick to think how worried Heb and Elain would be for them at that point. They'd surely assume the worst, especially with the current state of the forest, but they'd be back soon. Just a few more detours and they'd be back.

Turning back to their own path, she grimaced. Nari hobbled along, making good use of the walking stick he'd purloined from the infirmary's stores. Not that he needed it. She checked his notes last night when he and Ash were chatting, and there was no record of any lower limb problems. The bastard was just doing it to glean more sympathy from her gullible brother. Not her. She knew exactly how far the cur could be trusted.

Just one more thing before they could set off.

'Ffed!' she called, looking into the trees. 'Ffed! It's us! We're off!'

No answer. A flaw in their plan. No thought was given to reuniting once their business at the infirmary was concluded. They could probably make it without her, but she was reluctant to leave their friend behind. It didn't seem fair to lean on her so heavily up until this point only to abandon her without warning.

'Ffed!'

Still nothing. She could well be on the other side of the infirmary, spying through the windows or something. Could they spare the time to start circling the perimeter calling for her? If they were spotted by the workers, or worse the other healers, questions would certainly be asked. Explaining a concealed friend probably wouldn't put them in the best light, and they had to keep Gerath sweet. Who knew how someone as cantankerous as he might react to a goblin?

'Ffed, we're leaving!'

'She'll catch up if she wants to,' said Nari, face screwed up from her shouting. 'Just leave her to roll around in dung or whatever it is that goblins do in their free time.'

'Don't say that,' Ash tutted. 'She's actually quite clean.'

'I bet she stinks if you get too close,' Nari muttered.

'Far less than you,' Dem snapped. She put her hands to her mouth as she shouted. 'Ffed!'

'Ffed!' Ash joined in, calling as they walked.

For now, the easiest route was to take the path down to Holevale, and from there find the Piglick again and follow it down to Trottmire. If she were with them, she might have insisted on going through the forest the whole way to avoid potential rogues, but the healers reassured her the path was safe and regularly patrolled. It made Nari twitch at the thought of meeting soldiers, but she didn't care. If they took him off her hands, all the better.

'Ffed!'

She recalled the goblin's peculiar behaviour the night before arriving at the infirmary. Ash mentioned something about reverting to her natural tendencies after being away from civilisation for so long. Could it be possible? Had these few nights in the forest pushed out the years of order and civility ingrained into her by Starforge's inhabitants? Surely not. It must be something else. Or were they really just calling for a feral pine goblin to attack them from the trees? The thought made her hesitate. No. This was their friend. She'd have a good reason for behaving strangely.

'Ffed!'

A rustle ahead and the branches parted.

'Here.'

Her lips broke into an automatic smile. It was only a few days apart, but seeing her alive and well brought a strange comfort to her. Skipping forward, she embraced her, ignoring the scratch and tickle of her coarse hair in her ear. Ffed awkwardly wrapped her arm around her shoulders in return. Something hard dug into her back. She wriggled free, eyeing the goblin.

'Hatchet out?'

Ffed nodded sombrely. 'In case.'

'In case of what?'

She eyed the goblin's face closer. She had cleaned the hair on her cheeks of dried blood, but the new wound was still obvious beneath it, the linear scabs glistening.

'Danger.'

'The road should be safe, don't worry,' Ash approached and embraced her. 'The healers said so.'

'Perhaps wrong,' she kept her white-knuckled grip on the axe, eyes flitting past them into the forest.

'To be fair, I don't think soldiers would take kindly to a goblin,' Nari sneered. 'They'd stick her as soon as they saw her.'

'You'd rather go through the forest with your walking stick?' asked Ash.

Dem snorted, Ffed's wounds momentarily forgotten. 'Oh aye, essential item for Nari, that.'

The rogue scowled at her. 'I think I'll manage. For Ffed's sake as well.'

'Somehow, I don't quite think Ffed's wellbeing is on your mind here, Nari. Your own skin tends to take priority over ours, doesn't it?'

'You stay on road. I stay in forest,' Ffed stated, firmly. 'Easy passage. Safer. I keep watch.'

'You're sure?' she chewed her lip. 'I'd rather have you around?'

'Right here, just in forest. Keep watch.'

Dem nodded slowly. 'Keep watch for what?'

Ffed looked at her. She couldn't read the expression, couldn't understand what she was telling her with those yellow eyes. There was suspicion there. Dread. Axe at the ready. Danger. From what? Surely not the guards? Something in the trees? She nodded slowly at her. She knew more than they did. Infinitely more. It would be foolish to ignore her advice. With a final nod, she disappeared back into the brush, hatchet still in hand.

*

In total, they passed two patrols on the road to Holevale. Six soldiers to each, spears and shields over their shoulders as they trudged up and down the road. Both stopped and questioned them, but they were allowed through without any issues, even Nari knew to keep his mouth shut and let her do the talking. Outside the town was a bigger unit, and the king's presence was plastered across the streets, with soldiers stationed at practically every street corner. While Nari shrank deeper and deeper into his cloak, she held her chin high. Finally, some civility and order. It was needed, after all. Holevale's bustling town square was a heaving market and different consumers of all manners of life attended every day.

It was the safest she'd felt since leaving Starforge. Even the infirmary fell short. Something about the presence of soldiers gave a sense of security, of confidence, they treated them with more respect than Yewbar, nodded politely and let them through without obtuse questioning or thinly-veiled threats. Far superior to the timid contingent in Muddylan, whose presence was little more than a token. A better class, just like home. Apart from the pigs. Hundreds of them. Perhaps thousands. Squealing, squeaking, snuffling, and snorting from their mighty pens, screaming from the dark abattoir in on the town's fringe. Cleaners worked up and down the streets in teams, fighting a constant battle against the stream of filth the livestock left behind, but it was never enough, the eye-watering odour permeated every part of the town, from the mud of the roads to the tiles on the roofs.

Ffed was the only one unconcerned. Somewhat unexpectedly, she gained entrance to the town without issue. Out of caution, she hung back from them and made sure there was a buffer of a few other groups of travellers before approaching the gates, just in case of another bout of discrimination due to association, but it was unnecessary. True, the soldiers gave her a bit more attention than the others, but that was just extra vigilance. No harm done in taking a cautious approach.

Dem made sure to choose their inn again. Ash initially veered to one of the dingier establishments, probably in hopes of scrounging a proper drink from an unsavoury barman, but she soon put a stop to his wanderings. He sipped at his apple juice quietly, watching the flames dance in the fireplace. Nari had his leg stretched out dramatically and his head cradled in his hands, searching in vain for more sympathy. Ffed wisely kept her hood up to remain as inconspicuous as possible. It would have raised eyebrows at Starforge, but Holevale attracted all sorts of characters, so even a hooded individual indoors drew little attention.

'Strange in infirmary?' Ffed suddenly asked, making them jump.

Dem shrugged. 'A few were a bit standoffish, but not too bad, why?'

Ffed shook her head. 'No. See strange things?'

'Not especially. Just standard things you'd find in an infirmary, really. Medicines, herbs, wards, beds. There were a few operating theatres but we didn't have a reason to go. Healer Gerath was a bit of an eccentric.'

'Putting it lightly,' Ash muttered into his mug.

'Superior minds are often peculiar,' she hissed. 'I wouldn't expect a slug like you to recognise greatness.'

Ash stretched. 'Well, if that's what you call greatness, I'd rather be average, thank you very much.'

She glared at him. How dare he! After everything Healer Gerath was doing for them, here was Ash, big dumb Ash, slating and mocking him. No wonder Gerath locked himself away in his cellar to avoid the insipid behaviour of lesser minds.

'There's a reason why the other healers defer to him for the complex cases,' she sniffed.

'There's a reason why he's not allowed to treat the other patients,' Ash chuckled drily. 'If he's so great, how come Semon went home instead of him?'

'Because he needs to stay with his equipment to manufacture the medicine? Bit obvious, isn't it, even for you?'

Ash rolled his eyes. A look passed between him and Nari. They smirked. So that was it. Ganging up together to put her down. How very mature. Two boys poking fun with their inside jokes and childish exclusion. Pathetic.

'Gerath is a proper weirdo, Ffed. Half-mad, I'd say, strangest thing in the whole building,' Ash sniggered.

'Just. Stop,' Dem raised her finger in warning. 'He's helping us. We *need* him. Anten, Awis, and Semon all trust him with Ma's case.'

'Only because they have no idea what's going on.'

'Exactly. Nobody does. Apart from Gerath.'

'So he says.'

'And so do I.'

'Oh, great. Healer Demsai approves the crackpot.'

'You've got no respect. Why come if you're so opposed to him?'

Ash shrugged. 'Couldn't be bothered with the fight.'

'What's your idea, then?' her ears burned. Her face must be scarlet by now. 'What's you great strategy to make her better?'

He shrugged again. 'Just leave it with Semon and the others to move through the other treatments.'

'So the option the very people involved thought was inappropriate?'

'Yeah, what of it?' he demanded, tone changing. 'It's supposed to be a discussion, isn't it? Between the healer and the patient. Supposed to give the options and decide on what's best.'

'Which is exactly what we did?' she meant to say it gently to avoid antagonising him, but her frustration gave it a condescending note. He picked up on it, bristling with frustration.

'What *you* did. I wasn't asked.'

Now she chuckled, despite herself. 'Why would we ask you? You don't know anything about it.'

His eyes widened and he smiled emptily, leaning forward across the table. 'You're really going to comment on not knowing enough? After your *humbling* conversation with Gerath?'

Gritting her teeth, she held his stare. Sly weasel. He knew exactly how small that made her feel, her deficiencies and weaknesses exposed so publicly in front of a master healer like Gerath. He knew *exactly* how much she wanted to be good, to do the best possible job in her role. He knew *exactly* how much more it hurt when Ma was the subject at the heart of her failure. His lip curled minutely in a sneer. Damned snake. She could have killed him there and then.

'Strange how?'

Ffed's voice pierced the gathering clouds of rage like a rare sunbeam, bringing her back to reality.

Ash blinked and turned to her. 'What's that, sorry?'

'Strange how?' Ffed repeated.

'Just a weird guy. Lives alone in a dingy cellar, refers to himself in the third person, grows weird hybrid plants that are poisonous in an infirmary–'

'All medicines are technically poisonous,' Dem interrupted under her breath.

Ash ignored her. 'Works in near darkness, insults the other healers, has a bunch of weird kit and equipment in his little dungeon to make his weird potions. Even his room has a bunch of alcoves and recesses in there to hide whatever he wants.'

'Hide what?' Ffed asked, frowning.

'Don't know. I thought he was speaking to someone in the shadows of his little cellar. Maybe he was just speaking to himself, I don't know.'

'You see something?' Ffed leaned forward, nearly knocking over her glass of spiced milk.

Ash leaned back in surprise at the goblin's sudden movement. 'Not really. He's a weird guy. He might have been speaking to another of his acolytes, maybe he wasn't. I couldn't see.'

She rolled her eyes. Typical Ash. Making monsters out of nothing, just because he disliked the man. He used to do this when they were children, make up stories about people in the village. Ffed would blush if she ever recounted some of the stories Ash used to tell about her when he was a child.

'Why you asking?' Nari growled.

Ffed settled back into her chair. 'Saw something.'

Dem raised her brows. 'In the infirmary?'

'In woods. Last few nights. Following.'

143

'What?'

Ffed shrugged. 'Don't know. Something small. Skinny. Like a child but not. Something bad.'

'Like a child?' Ash grimaced. 'Can't be too dangerous if it's a kid, right?'

'*Like* a child. Not a child. Strong. Sharp claws.'

Dem looked at her. 'Your cheek?'

Ffed's hand lifted and touched the scar. 'Yes.'

'An animal?' Ash ventured. 'There are apes in other parts of the world.'

'Not ape,' Ffed shook her head. 'Cunning. Trickster.'

'What does it look like?' Ash asked.

Ffed was silent for a while, taking the occasional sip of her milk. All three watched her anxiously. If this thing caused Ffed such concern, they would all do well to pay heed.

Finally, the goblin shrugged again. 'Not had proper look. Skinny. Pale. Black claws, cruel face, full of hate. Gave me bad feeling.'

'Kolgatha,' a voice muttered from behind.

They turned in unison. A solitary drinker stared darkly into his steaming mug, rough hands wringing.

'Did you say something?' Nari challenged him. 'Or was that just a cough?'

'You heard,' the drinker's voice was gruff and hoarse, perhaps from years of drink, perhaps from the pipe, perhaps from over-use.

'We didn't,' Ash leaned forward with a frown, cocking his head for a better listen.

'It's what it sounded like,' the drinker shuddered, wriggling deeper into his matted fur-lined jacket.

'You been listening to our conversation?' Nari challenged again.

'Only what the goblin just said.'

Nari sneered unpleasantly. 'Oh yeah? Not just spying on us for someone? Getting paid by a certain rogue?'

'Stop it,' Dem waved him away. 'Let him talk.'

144

Nari turned on her, brows raised and eyes wide. 'You don't think Kirkin would send someone looking for me? He has eyes everywhere.'

She kept her eyes on the drinker. 'I'm sure he does, I just don't think this is one of them, he doesn't look the type.'

'Which is exactly what makes me suspicious,' Nari crossed his arms and sat back in his chair, shooting daggers between her and the drinker.

She turned back to him, voice barely above a whisper. 'The thing you said. What is it?'

He shook his head, clenching and unclenching his hands then wiping them on his breast. 'You don't want to know. I shouldn't have said it.'

Dem huffed. 'Clearly we do otherwise we wouldn't have asked.'

The drinker stopped his fidgeting and stared at her for a moment. His dark, puffy eyes seemed sad, the downward curl of his lip giving him a constant grimace. He shook his head.

'Just stories. Like dragons and daemons. Small, hateful things that go around doing evil.'

'But daemons are real,' Dem muttered.

'Mm. That they are. So it's not too much of a stretch to say these are real too.'

'I've never heard of them,' Nari shrugged dismissively.

'Unsurprising. They crop up in old legends, mostly. The bad ones,' he brought his chair around his table to be closer to theirs, speaking in low tones, making them lean forward to listen. She looked into his mug, anticipating the reek of alcohol, but it was only tea. At least he wasn't just talking out of his cups. He looked between them. 'Evil servants of daemons to help them with their magicks, to complete the dark tasks they don't want people knowing about. They look like children but... aren't. Your friend here said it; they're tricksters. Cruel and malevolent. In the legends, they're an omen of a bad ending. People don't like them. I read about a play once that featured one, based on one of the legends, but the troupe playing it all disappeared, never to be seen again. They're bad luck. Even talking about them is bad.'

'Kolgatha?' Ash repeated, loudly.

A few of the other patrons at a nearby table jumped and stared at them, hissing under their breath. The drinker raised his hands.

'Quiet! I said they're bad luck. Not many people have heard about them nowadays, but those who have wish they hadn't, especially around here. What good is knowing something bad? Better to live in ignorance.'

'And we have one following us?' Ash squeaked, and edge of panic to his voice. They turned to Ffed for confirmation, who shook her head slowly.

'Don't know. Never heard before.'

'But you've seen it?' he insisted.

'Don't know. Saw something. Might be something else.'

'Like what?'

Ffed was silent, staring at the cinnamon and cloves floating on top of her milk. Dem scratched her head and looked at the drinker.

'Have you ever seen one?'

'By the grace of the north winds, no. But… I've heard plenty. I've seen the signs. We all have.'

He stared into his mug again, eyes glittering in the torchlight beneath his heavy brows. Sniffing loudly, he wiped his eyes and drained the rest of his mug.

'I'll take my leave. I'm sorry I frightened you.'

'You didn't–' she started, but he was already pushing past the tables on his way out. She watched him to the door, where he retrieved his cloak and pack. No sword or cudgel to suggest he was one of Nari's rogues, just the familiar trappings and trinkets of a pig driver, he even had one of Ash's favourite little stick dolls poking from a side pocket. He left without a backwards glance.

Nari snorted and shook his head. 'Crazy drunk.'

'He was drinking tea, actually,' she corrected.

'With stories like that, seems pretty unlikely.'

She scratched her head and glanced at Ash, recalling what he said before.

'You reckon Gerath was speaking to something in the alcove?'

He glanced back at her, still annoyed. 'Maybe. Couldn't get a proper look.'

'Could it be a daemon?'

The question hung between them. They stared at each other in turn. Daemons. Once the second-most powerful race in Enadir, chief advisors to the giants, their numbers now dwindled to practically nothing. One of the world's few remaining mysteries. Knowledgeable beyond the wildest dreams of even the wisest human. They'd all heard the stories of Deia and his people, of Godan, Gwahl, Dwerel, Karanydd, Dwrelian, and the rest. If ever there were a legend or story worth hearing, you could bet there was a daemon involved somewhere, with the same names cropping up each time. Grey Phell said he'd seen one once, just wandering the woods without a care in the world. Nobody believed him, of course, but there was that possibility.

Could it be that Healer Gerath, the wisest in the esteemed infirmary, was in fact under the tutelage of one of this race? That his extensive knowledge came from an ancient source? Could it be that his hybrid plants and various strange equipment was all due to some daemon magicks?

'I've never seen one,' Ash mumbled, rubbing his chin and frowning. 'I don't know what they look like.'

'Just think about the drawings in our books,' Dem insisted.

'They all looked different, didn't they?' Ash shrugged.

'Maybe,' she conceded. 'Different but similar at the same time.'

'What does it matter if there is a daemon? They're normally good, aren't they? Fought on the right side.' Ash asked, naïvely.

Nari snorted again. 'Depends, lad. They're on their own side, for the most part. We all know anything involving magicks is never good,' he glanced at Ffed, the implication clear.

Dem watched her. Magus Herikik was another legend from two centuries ago, eventually killed by the minotorrs, and in some iterations with the aid of the daemon Karanydd. She didn't know what reputation goblins may have had before his scourge, but his

147

intervention certainly hadn't helped. Ffed didn't seem to hear, and kept her attention on her milk, lost in her own thoughts. Nari was right, anyway, daemons were a suspicious lot, always with ulterior motives at play. It's what made the stories so interesting; trying to piece together the clues to figure out what the daemons were up to while all the other events happened around them. There were scholars who'd spent decades trying to decipher the stories, chief among them the academic priests in their chapels to the winds. They may have fought with the giants against the cockatrice in the Cataclysmic War, but why? In the end, the giants and cockatrice destroyed each other and the daemons remained. There was one scholar, she couldn't recall his name, who accused the daemons of manufacturing the war itself to rid Enadir of its two greatest races, leaving it free for the daemons to take. Was it possible? Perhaps. Another, Brother Ikdis Sawein of the Knights Garia, theorised there were two types of daemon, possibly in opposition to one another, and the war may have reflected this division of their race. Brother Narg of Starforge's chapel once lent her a copy of the weighty transcript, of its sad conclusion that insufficient evidence was available to confirm or deny any of its claims. An interesting read, all the same.

'When we return we can keep an eye out,' Dem nodded.

'So we're still going ahead with it? Getting his supplies?' Ash asked, the edge still in his voice.

'Yes. I still think he's our best chance. The other healers advised it. We should listen. Just because there may or may not be a daemon involved doesn't mean we shouldn't do it,' she caught herself, jumping to conclusions like a novice. 'We don't even *know* if there's a daemon. It's all just speculation. We don't know what Ffed saw, we don't know what you saw. We don't know anything. All we know is Gerath said he'd help us and we need to get him this mushroom. Those are the facts.'

'I don't trust him,' Ash shook his head.

'Do you trust Healer Semon?' she asked.

'Obviously. Thank the north winds he's on his way home.'

'As I said, he trusts Gerath. That's also a fact. Let's all remember that.'

*

An uncharacteristically cold and foggy morning awaited them. As they trudged across the town square, the stalls only just opening, the fires only just starting, Ash pointed to one of the houses.

'Look in the window there, another one of those stick dolls.'

'Great,' Dem ignored him.

'I meant to have a look for one for H. I thought he might like one. Do you reckon one of the stalls will have them?'

'We really don't have the time, Ash,' she scolded. 'You should have remembered last night. We're not stopping to look.'

He huffed and groaned like the child he was, but didn't say anything. Too right. He'd had plenty to say last night and her patience this morning was still suitably thin. What did he think this was, a shopping trip? Sometimes, he behaved as if Ma's sickness wasn't even real.

On the way out, they passed a school for young children before they went out after their apprenticeships, its gates flanked by four guards. It was a surprisingly large building for so few pupils, lining up miserably before the schoolmaster in the yard. She smiled at the sight of their sullen pouts. Starting lessons at such an early hour would have made her far grumpier at their age. Strange to have guards stationed there, but perhaps with so many travellers coming and going, one couldn't be too careful.

Passing the school, the made it to the town gates. Nodding politely to the guards as they left, fresh faces from their warm barracks half-hidden behind their round helmets, they left Holevale behind. Out again into the woods, a small trail led to the Piglick, used by the various pig-drivers to bathe and water their livestock at the riverbank. Ffed followed a few minutes later, again to avoid any association with them while in the town.

'How was the stable?' Ash asked.

'No stable. Pig pen.'

'Oh. Was it alright?'

'Warm. Hay not too stale,' she nodded with what may have been a hint of resignation. 'Good for me.'

'That's good,' Dem smiled. 'As long as you got the rest you deserve.'

'Probably.'

The riverbank was wide and flat at the turn, well-worn ground used for decades by the respective pig-drivers. A few were there already, making their final preparations before herding the animals to market. They waved half-heartedly in acknowledgment, but their concentration was on their pigs; their livelihoods. Ffed and Nari led them downriver, beyond the well-trodden paths and into the underbrush, keeping the trickling, splashing river within earshot. The temperature rose with the sun, chasing away the fog and replacing it with clouds of midges. The stench of pig slowly diminished, replaced first by the fresh loam of the forest, then the sour note of a bog.

Around midday, Ffed stopped suddenly, peering into the woods, ushering her and Ash behind. Nari stood to one side, frowning. It must have looked comical, with her stout frame and her brother's gangly one cowering behind a skinny goblin half their size, but Nari didn't laugh. His hand strayed instead to his sword, his frame suddenly tense and poised, his wounds forgotten.

'See anything?' he growled, scanning the woods.

'Heard something,' Ffed nipped.

'Where?'

'Behind. Over there.'

The minutes stretched by. Ash obtained a stick from somewhere, though what he intended to do with it was anyone's guess. The thing was half-rotten and covered in more moss than a boulder under a waterfall. She curled her lip at him, but he ignored her, trying to look brave and helpful. He was neither, of course, but if it made him feel better, let him hold the thing. Every child had their own version of a comforter.

Nothing approached, nothing moved, just the sway of trees in the wind and the incessant blur of midges. No snapped twigs, no rustles of displaced leaves. No mutters, murmurs, or curses in the shadows.

A blackbird perched on a nearby branch and sang its greeting. Ffed relaxed and stood. Nari followed suit. They shared a glance and moved on, sandwiching the children between them in the column.

'What was it?' Ash whispered, rotten stick still in hand, its end already bowing under its own weight.

'Don't know,' Nari grabbed the stick from his hands and threw it into the woods, exchanging it for his old walking-stick. 'If you want to hold something, take that one.'

'Leg feeling better, then?' Dem couldn't help herself.

He ignored her. She smiled to herself. All lies eventually exposed. All it took was a little pressure.

Ffed stopped them multiple times throughout the day, always watching carefully for a few minutes, her hatchet drawn more often than not, shielding her and her brother with the other hand while she watched. Nothing ever materialised from her caution. It became routine, stopping and staring, waiting for the all-clear. By the fifth time, the danger lost its edge. Ash played absent-mindedly with the walking stick, Nari hadn't even drawn his sword, and even she found herself staring disinterestedly at the ground instead of following Ffed's gaze.

'I think it's clear,' Nari muttered.

Ffed nodded slowly, body still tense.

'Shall we be off? Looks like we're nearly in Trottmire. Smells like it too.'

Ffed nodded again, lowering her arm to allow them to continue. She kept her hatchet in hand.

As Nari predicted, they reached the bogs and wetlands of the swamp within a few minutes. The ground dropped away into grimy pools covered in algae, the sludge at the bottom masquerading as firm floor. She knew better than to trust it. The sour, putrid stench of rot hung around like a dead carcass around her neck, cloying and heavy in her nostrils. The clouds of midges and flies intensified, biting any piece of exposed skin they could find in their desperate greed for living flesh. She beat them away half-heartedly, rummaging in her pocket for the stained, worn, torn-out book-page provided by Gerath with an illustration of the required fungus.

151

'Alright, so it's no more than ten centimetres in diameter, and tends to grow in shade and dampness,' she read. 'Pale yellow colour, with a few red streaks around the edges. Happy?'

'Not really,' Ash prodded the pool floor with his stick, grimacing as it disappeared up to his wrist.

'Happy you understand what we're looking for,' she clarified. Pedantic child.

'As much as a simpleton like I can.'

'Then let's get looking.'

Ash grumbled and plodded along, trying in vain to evade the pools, parting reeds to search for their prize. Ffed took the page from her hand and studied it for a few minutes, tracing a finger over the picture.

'Is that alright, Ffed?' she asked. 'Do you know it?'

She shook her head. 'How big?'

'Ten centimetres at most,' she tapped the page where it gave the dimensions.

'Can't read.'

She blinked. How could she not know? 'Oh! I'm sorry. It says here, you see, apparently most are between five and eight centimetres,' she estimated with her fingers.

'Look like picture?'

'Yes.'

Ffed nodded. 'I look,' she smiled reassuringly.

They spread out, moving through the pools and bogs, under the mix of gnarled, living trees and their dead counterparts, the trunks tilting and listing at crazy angles. At times, they were forced to wade through the bogs, half-swimming and half-walking through the muddy sludge. Thankfully, nobody got stuck, and they were careful not to take any inappropriate risks.

'Don't wander too far,' she called to Ash, rummaging around in the distance.

He waved dismissively over his shoulder. He never listened. He accused her of being controlling, but she only had his wellbeing in mind. Someone had to take responsibility, and he certainly wasn't up to the task. At least he stopped, if only to spare himself another scolding.

'Something here,' Nari called.

She bound over with Ffed, splashing through the shallower pools and scrambling over the lower logs. Nari pointed triumphantly to a cluster of mushrooms, clinging parasitically to the lower half of a log. She consulted the page. Not the ones. More grey than yellow, with orange spots not red stripes, and pushing it with their size.

Nari saw her deflate. 'Wrong, am I?'

'I think so,' she conceded. 'Have a look. What do you think?' she turned to Ffed.

'Wrong,' the goblin confirmed.

'Well, shit a bastard,' Nari muttered, kicking the head off one of the mushrooms. 'Alright, let's keep going.'

She stared at him as he trudged off, parting reeds with surprising care. She didn't realise he was so invested in finding Ma's cure. Perhaps he was a changed man? She caught herself. Of course not. The sooner they found the fungus, the sooner they'd be back, and the sooner he'd be asking for his payment. How long did he have left, anyway? Why should she care?

The day turned into a dull slog through the swamp. Her back ached from being stooped over for so long, her hands caked in sludge and slime. Sweaty and stinking, she must look a mess. Despite her illiteracy, Ffed's experience in foraging was invaluable, directing them to the likeliest places where fungi would grow, under rotting logs and within the depths of bullrushes, until they were all relatively proficient within a few hours. However, despite their growing confidence, the mushroom remained unfound. Four other kinds lay in their wake, each slightly closer to the desired one than the last, but it was never right. Gerath warned them it might be difficult, but she'd never considered it might not be found. Now, hours in, back a mess, skin gnawed to a bumpy mess by the flies, clothes soaked in stagnant water, sweat stinging her eyes, doubts settled in. Could this all be futile? Was Ma to be condemned by yet another of their failings? Should they have kept those other mushrooms, in hope Gerath could use his genius to concoct a cure with slightly different ingredients? Of

153

course not. He asked for this mushroom specifically. To bring anything else would incur his rage and invite another tirade and commentary on her deficiencies.

'Ffed! Nari!' Ash's voice called from behind.

Had he found something? Probably not. He barely looked at the picture or listened to the description. Typical of him not to call for her help. She wasn't surprised. If he had his way, she'd surely be the last one to know about anything.

'Ffed!' his tone was urgent. 'Nari!'

Then again, perhaps he had found something. He sounded excited enough. A shrill edge to his voice. They headed over. Exactly as she'd warned him not to, he'd wandered off on his own to the far end of a stinking, boggy clearing. Typical. In future, maybe she should tell him to go as far away as possible just for his contrary mind to do the opposite.

There he was, wading and stumbling through the pools, tripping over his clumsy feet. He really wasn't a woodsman. A court jester, maybe.

Her heart caught. Someone followed, splashing through the pools, cudgels and knives drawn.

'Ash!' her scream caught her unawares, instinctively ripping free from her throat. Ffed darted past, skipping over the dead trunks, carving a path through the scarce firm ground to her brother. Nari went by a different path, ploughing straight and true through the mud and water, sword drawn and eyes cold.

There were four of them. Her eyes settled on one, spiked mace in hand. The man from Yewbar. Pit. His two companions were with him, plus a new face. She glanced at Nari but couldn't see his face. Pit grinned and waved his weapon.

'Afternoon, Nari!'

'What do you want?' Nari barked.

'Oh, I think you know.'

Ffed reached Ash as he stumbled and fell face-first into a pool, drawing a chorus of harsh laughter from the rogues. Thrusting her arm around his waist, she heaved him to firm ground and back to Dem.

'You alright?' she asked, looking her brother up and down for any injuries.

'They just came out of nowhere,' he spluttered, eyes like saucers. 'I was looking under a log at the edge of the clearing, stood up, and they were there on top of it, grinning at me.'

'It's alright,' she patted his shoulder. What more could she do?

'Shouted for help and ran as fast as I could,' he blabbered, ignoring her. 'That one shot at me. I don't think it hit me,' he pointed at the new face, small bow in hand.

'You don't have any arrows sticking out of you,' she grinned in false reassurance.

'Winds! I thought they'd get me.'

He clutched Ffed like a raft in a storm. The goblin patted his head, probably about as reassuringly as she'd awkwardly patted his shoulder. She couldn't blame him, he'd been given a fright, how would she react if a group of violent thugs suddenly appeared in front of her? Probably not too dissimilarly. Probably worse.

She glanced between Ffed and Nari. Even to her inexperienced eye, this was a bad situation. She and Ash were useless in a fight. Four against two, and one of those two still reeling from a head injury. She glanced behind at the swampland. Nowhere to run. Not enough time to hide. Pray to the four winds they weren't here for blood, or if they were, Nari's and not theirs.

The four spread out, slowly surrounding them. One with his bow, Pit with his mace, one with a knobbly cudgel, one with a long knife. She felt her pack. Perhaps they could bargain with them? Pretend their meagre possessions were worth enough to bargain for their lives?

'We don't have anything of value,' Nari declared, turning between the four as he backed away.

She rolled her eyes. There goes the possibility of bargaining.

'We don't want anything, dear Nari. Just a bit of sport, like I said.'

'Kirkin won't get his money if you kill me.'

'That's for your brother to worry about, not me.'

'It will if he finds out.'

155

Pit laughed, the sound rumbling from his belly as he spasmed in delight. 'How will he find out? When you're dead and sunk in Trottmire, everyone will assume you ran and abandoned dear old Natirad,' he pouted in mock sympathy. 'It would have been the sensible thing to do, instead of frolicking around with these children.'

'And what are you going to do about them?' Nari quickly glanced over his shoulder.

Pit sighed dramatically and scratched his head. 'Not nice, but I'm afraid we can't leave any witnesses to what's about to happen.'

Heart pounding in her ears, mouth dry as ash, she backed away. This was *exactly* why they should've left him in Yewbar, why they should've left him again in the infirmary. Hang around with scum and more will find you. Now they were going to die for no crime at all, for trying to do the right thing.

She stared at Nari, but he kept his eyes on Pit and his crew. Avoiding her gaze or just keeping vigilant? Both.

'Please,' she called. 'We're just looking for a cure for our Ma. Please let us go.'

The cudgel-bearer laid his hand on his breast. 'Awh, Pit. Hear that? For their mother. Sick mother, aye? That why you went to the infirmary?'

'For our Ma,' she nodded. She didn't expect to find compassion, not after the way they beat Nari in the tavern, but everyone had mothers. Perhaps they'd remember theirs?

'Touching,' Pit nodded, sadly. 'Few things more honourable than looking after your parents. A sad thing indeed, Reger.'

The cudgel-bearer, Reger, nodded solemnly. 'Imagine how she'd feel knowing they were caught up with the likes of Nariton Selkaharr.'

'Probably die of shame. Best we spare her the grief,' Pit winked.

'Doing a kindness, really,' Reger nodded, smiling wickedly. 'Wouldn't want to disappoint your mother with your bad decisions, would you?'

She kept backing away. Of course there was no compassion. These animals didn't know its meaning.

'We won't tell anyone!' she cried. 'We'll keep quiet, we promise. Please. We need to get home.'

'And where's your home? Yewbar?'

'Starforge,' usually, she'd never reveal their home to this sort, but perhaps the name would make them pause, give them cause to consider taking them hostage instead of just killing them. 'They'd give good money for our safe return.'

Pit made a show of rubbing his chin in mock consideration. 'And dear old Nari? What about him? Will your village vaults buy his miserable life?'

She swallowed, mouth dry, palms soaked with sweat. They wanted Nari's blood, not theirs, if she could convince them they could get paid and kill him, surely they'd jump at the opportunity? 'We'll keep quiet, we promise.'

Pit shook his head and tutted. The bowman hawked and spat on the ground. 'That's not nice,' he wheedled, voice thin and nasal. 'Throwing your companion to the dogs. Bastard thing to do.'

'Clearly they've spent too long with this slimy eel,' Pit gestured to Nari with the mace. 'That's the kind of treacherous talk I'd expect of him.'

'He's nothing to us, we swear!' her foot splashed into a pool. Ffed steered her back to firm ground, still backing away. To where, she didn't know, but at least it brought them time. A few more seconds of life before the inevitable. 'We promise we won't tell anyone! Just let us go!'

Ash grumbled something under his breath but she couldn't hear. She didn't want to hear. Now wasn't the time for heroics or loyalty. He was a traitor and a thief. If their places were reversed, he'd sell them without a moment's notice. Courage and bravery were noble concepts in the stories, but when it came down to it in real life, you just had to do whatever was needed to survive. Nari made his own bed years ago when he started stealing, they shouldn't be made to share his crooked fate.

'Hear that, Nari? She's trying to get rid of you,' Reger laughed. 'Can't say I blame her. You're shit on a shoe.'

'We can talk about this. Kirkin will find out. He always finds out somehow,' Nari kept trying. 'All it takes is a drunken comment. He doesn't like missing out on a payday.'

'We both know you don't have the money,' Pit knocked the head off a bulrush with the mace, sending it spinning into the swamp.

'I'll get it to him. He'll want it.'

'Nope. Not buying it. Slippery bastard like you. Besides, we both know the outcome is the same. Whether Kirkin knows or not, you're ending up in the mud.'

'He likes to dish his punishment out himself,' Nari reached them, hand outstretched like Ffed's, shepherding Ash and Dem behind.

'I'm sure he'll forgive us,' Reger smirked.

'Alright, then why not wait a few more days? If you ask nicely enough, I'm sure he'll let you dish it out?'

Pit stopped, barely five metres away. Reger, the bowman, and the knife-wielder formed a half-circle around them. Pit gestured to his companions.

'Why wait? Besides, doing it like this feels so much more *exciting*, doesn't it, lads?' they grunted and sniggered in agreement. 'Like children misbehaving under the noses of our parents. Gives me a right little tickle.'

'Free reign to dish out a proper punishment,' Reger added. 'You won't be walking again so soon, I promise you that. We tried getting you before you reached the infirmary to save those healers the bother, but you were too sneaky.'

'Kept us waiting for a few days, didn't he?' Pit shook his head in disapproval. 'All tucked up in bed while we were out in the forest.'

Nari's throat bobbed up and down as he swallowed.

'Alright. Just let the children go.'

She looked at him. What trick was this? He certainly wasn't noble enough to genuinely try bargaining for their lives. It must be a ploy.

Pit certainly thought so, shaking his head and wagging his finger. 'No, no. I'll make it quick for them if it makes you feel better.

Even the goblin. You can watch it, an appetizer for the fun we have in mind for you.'

An arrow whizzed by her cheek, snatching her hair away. She stumbled back, heart skipping as it thundered in her chest. The bowman lowered his weapon, reaching for another shaft, leering foully.

'Apologies. Old arrows need re-fletching. They always drift.'

'Bastard!' she screamed, finding her voice.

'Now, now,' Pit tutted, approaching again. The noose closed around them. 'He was doing you a favour. Had it hit you, you'd have been lights out before you knew what was going on. That's a damned mercy compared to what's waiting Nari.'

The acrid smell of urine reached her nose. Damp as her clothes were, she couldn't tell if it was hers or Ash's. His face was white as ice, his lips trembling, tears on his cheeks. She took his hand in her own, if nothing else to stop it trembling. This was it, then. she didn't want to see the bowman's draw. Just let it be quick.

'What the–'

A thud, followed by a string of curses, splashes and grunts. Nari jumped away in the corner of her eye, leaving her and Ash exposed. She stared at her brother's face, anticipating the punch of a weapon between her shoulder blades, in her neck. More scuffles. Growls. Grunts and clashes of metal on metal. Ash's eyes widened, his mouth dropped, the tremble in his lips gone.

She turned.

Ffed whirled between Reger and the knifeman, her hatchet a blur, parrying and deflecting their weapons while simultaneously landing her own. Nari tussled with Pit, hands clasped around each other's wrists, struggling for control of mace and sword. The bowman knelt in the pool, breathing forcefully as he struggled to stem the gushing wound at his shoulder.

Ffed broke away for a second, leaving the two rogues breathless and red-faced. Reger pushed his companion towards her.

'Get the bitch!'

He dove at her, knife held underhand. Ffed swung her hatchet, iron thumping into his cheek with a clunk. He fell into the muck with

159

a cry. Before she could recover, Reger was on her again, cudgel swinging overhead in a blur.

Dem lurched forward to shout her warning, but her voice abandoned her.

Ffed saw it coming, catching the club with her axe handle, turning it away. Reger grabbed her with his free arm, drawing her close to his body. Dropping his cudgel, he grabbed her hatchet instead, wresting for control of the weapon, all the while squeezing her closer to his barrel chest.

'Naz, come on,' he called to the knifeman between strained breaths. The other rogue, Naz, stumbled to his feet, blood streaming from his broken face, a flap of skin the size of Dem's hand hanging from the grisly remains of his cheek.

'Shit, man! Come here and stick her!'

Naz stumbled blindly, groaning, blood trickling. His hands were empty, knife lost. Reger growled like a dog as Ffed bucked and snarled. Losing his grip, he bent his knee, wrestling her under the water.

Dem yelped and splashed towards them. She couldn't let him drown her! Ash grabbed her arm, pulling her back in time to avoid Nari and Pit as they continued their tussle.

'Help him!' she squeaked, pointing to Nari. She had to save Ffed.

Ash peeled away, gangly limbs reaching for the wrestling rogues. She couldn't worry about him for now. Ffed's struggles were growing weaker, her limbs losing their fire.

She threw her arms around Reger's neck, trying to drag him back. Too heavy. A bull of a man. He bucked his head back, butting her chin. She stepped back, momentarily stunned as the taste of copper filled her mouth. She grabbed his arm, trying to prise it free of Ffed's head under the water. Useless. Like iron. His eyes met hers, violence and evil dancing behind them. He was going to win. She wasn't strong enough.

A splash from behind as the tangle of Ash, Nari, and Pit collided with Naz's half-blind stumbling, sending them all into the water, rising again with a roar of curses. In the background, the bowman's wails resonated, growing weaker each minute.

Ffed's arms went limp enough for Reger to let go and swipe at her. His slap struck her cheek, sending her spinning. Spitting blood, she wiped her mouth. This pig wasn't going to get the better of her!

Something to hit him with. His cudgel or Ffed's axe. On her hands and knees, she started looking for the weapons. Reger watched her, realisation dawning. He tried reaching her but Ffed wasn't quite done. He tried kicking out at her, but she avoided his clumsy boots. Where was it?

Another scream from behind. Nari clutched his shoulder with his free hand while Pit grappled for control of Nari's sword with Ash, eyes wide and mouth twisted in rage.

Here! Her hands closed around the polished handle of the hatchet. She approached Reger, still kicking and spitting at her, trying to keep her at bay. She kept the axe ready. Realistically, she had one swing. If she missed, he'd probably grab her and take the axe. If she missed, she might even hit Ffed.

Suddenly he wheezed, as if the breath were knocked out of him. His eyes watered and his mouth dropped. She stopped, axe still held high. What was this? Should she swing? Was it a trick?

Reger rolled onto all fours, still gasping.

Ffed rose with a splash, breathing hard, whittling-knife held in her free hand, blood dripping from its tip.

'Axe,' she snapped her fingers at Dem. She handed it over wordlessly. Ffed looked quickly over her shoulder and roughly pushed her aside.

Dem fell next to Reger just in time to avoid Naz's wild swing with his fist. She rolled away, but Reger was no threat. His face was pink with the effort of breathing, hands clutching in vain at the puncture wound in his flank from Ffed's well-placed thrust.

Another splash in front of her as Ffed struck Naz again, this time a hard thrust to his upper arm with her blade, sending him spinning. He fell next to Reger, breathing hard through gritted teeth. Their eyes met for a second. He only had one remaining. Shards of shattered bone had punctured the other, leaving it a swollen, crimson orb bulging halfway out of the socket. He tried pushing himself to his feet, but Ffed's axe hit his knee with a crunch, putting an end to his efforts.

Ffed thrust her calloused hand in front of Dem's face. She took it and was pulled to her feet. Before she could say anything, Ffed was already on the move, finding firm ground in impossible places to spring to Ash and Nari's aid. Pit saw her coming and immediately untangled himself, retreating to Reger and Naz, but not before Ffed got a snapping blow on his shoulder with her hatchet as he barrelled past..

'Ah! Get up, boys,' Pit hissed at the two, clutching his shoulder. 'Come on!'

'Goblin bitch,' Reger wheezed.

'Go, by the four winds! Go!'

They watched the three stumble away, supporting each other as best they could, only five working legs, five eyes, and two good sets of lungs between the three of them.

'We'll be back, Nari!' Pit called over his shoulder as they disappeared into the mud and mire. 'We'll be waiting. We know where you're going.'

'Piss off,' Nari spat.

Dem looked between them. Covered in mud, blood, and algae, breathing like the bellows, faces only just losing their snarls. She smiled. Laughter came next. Uninvited. Unexpected. After surviving a fight to the death, inevitable.

Chapter 12

'What happened to him?'

'Your friend threw her axe. Took him clean in the collarbone. Never seen anything like it. She had it out of him and was attacking the others before I could blink.'

Nari turned the bowman over with his foot.

'Winds,' Ash breathed. 'Just didn't expect it from her.'

'No?' he looked at him.

'No! Why? Did you?'

'Maybe,' he sniffed. More than maybe. He was right to be cautious around her. He saw that iron in her from the beginning, the ability to do anything she needed to survive. If you saw it once, that look, you never forgot it. If the scars on her wrist weren't proof enough of her iron, one good look in the eyes would do it. A simmering rage beneath the surface. A wildfire waiting to be unleashed.

He looked at her now, cleaning her hairy arms of blood and grime, smiling every now and then at the frog sitting a few paces away as happily as a child. Anyone could be fooled. Pit and his cronies certainly were. If they saw what he'd seen, they'd have shot her at the first opportunity, then worried about him and the children. But here they were. Alive. Damned lucky.

He turned back to the bowman. He recognised him from years ago. One of Kirkin's scouts. He couldn't remember his name, Jod or something. No matter. There'd be no words said for him.

Tugging the quiver from his back, he offered it to Ash along with the bow. The boy stared back wide-eyed.

'Well? You know how to use it?'

Ash shook his head, complexion turning a particularly unhealthy shade of grey. 'No chance.'

'No need to be squeamish about it.'

'No,' he shook his head again and turned away. 'Can't shoot.'

'I can teach you? It'll be useful to have someone who can shoot in case...'

He stopped himself. The boy looked petrified enough as it was. No point scaring him even more with the prospect of them returning with vengeance on their minds.

Ash bent double, breathing hard, doing his best to avoid looking at the corpse. Poor lad, probably the first bit of death he'd seen. This wasn't their world. They lived in the fantasy land of Starforge, with silver plates groaning under the weight of mounds of food, feather beds, fine clothes embellished with the silver threads of their mines. As far attached from the real world as he was from theirs.

'Maybe later, not right now,' Ash muttered.

He patted his back. Good lad. Turning, he caught Dem's eye. Frowning, as always. She may not be retching like her brother, but her uncharacteristic silence betrayed her discomfort.

'You alright?'

'Fine,' she nodded, standing next to her brother.

'Any injuries?'

'No, I'm fine.'

He pointed to her swollen lower lip. 'Doesn't look fine. Didn't notice it?'

She touched the wound and winced. 'Must have happened when that rogue 'butted me.'

'Reger. Evil man. You want me to look at it?'

She flinched. Barely noticeable, but he saw it. He let his hand drop and stepped back.

'I'll ask Ffed.'

He shrugged. Suit herself. If she didn't trust him, why should he care? It wasn't like he'd just fought for their lives. Her attempt to bargain his life for theirs hung between them like a pair of soiled breeches. Perhaps she was ashamed about it. Perhaps he should hate her more. He didn't. Honestly, he couldn't really blame her, after everything he'd done to them. The real world was a bitter scrap for survival. Ash may not understand it, still lost in his fantasy world, but Dem did. An ugly world, demanding ugly actions to get by. For all her morals and sanctimonious comments, she wasn't above stooping to betrayal and treachery to serve her own means.

164

A smirk tugged at his lips. The realisation she was no better than him must be eating her alive.

Ffed sat to one side on a dead, fallen trunk, still grinning every now and then at the frog. Waving an arm to chase it away, he sat next to her and pointed at the corpse.

'You won't have to worry about your mysterious follower anymore.'

'Why?' she snapped, glaring at the frog's recently-vacated perch.

'You stuck an axe through his chest,' he sneered. Dumb goblin. 'Him?'

'Who else?'

She narrowed her eyes. 'Him?' she repeated.

'Him. As they said, they've been loitering around the infirmary, missed us in Holevale, and stalked us all day. All those times you stopped before? You were probably hearing this guy.'

Ffed turned her yellow eyes back to him, staring blankly. He raised his brows. Come on, it wasn't that difficult to join the dots, even for an imbecile. She kept staring. His neck prickled. Eyes like a hawk, staring furiously at a sparrow.

She broke away with a shrug. 'Maybe.'

'Not maybe. Jod was a master tracker. Perhaps not the best with a bow, but he was trained. As good as a grey dreyad.'

She ignored him and approached the children. 'Come. Find fungus.'

Dem sniffed and nodded, coaxing her brother to his feet.

'What should we do about him?'

She nodded over her shoulder, avoiding looking at the corpse.

'Leave. Birds, mice, frogs all hungry,' Ffed urged them on.

Ash groaned and stumbled on, shaking his head. Nari patted his shoulder as he passed. Give him a few days and he'd be back to normal. He gave Jod a final look. Skinny weasel of a man, hunched shoulders and spindly limbs, a sunken face with only two teeth left to chew with. Too puny to draw a proper bow, hence his tiny short-bow. No doubt, this was Ffed's mysterious follower, his features distorted by night into a monster of legends. Kolgatha? He spat. No chance. Let

Ffed fret about her phantoms if she wanted to, but he was a man of reason. Ghost stories were fine for children and superstitious old wives, but real monsters were flesh and blood, real monsters could be killed.

He stared after the others. A monster of flesh and blood held his brother, after all.

*

'Another one here!'

Dem rushed over, studying the mushroom, looking back and forth to her reference page. Her shoulders slumped. Ash muttered curses under his breath and let the log drop.

'Not quite stripey enough?'

'Too stripey. These stripes only go halfway up the hood, that one had stripes the whole way.'

He rolled his eyes and huffed. Probably thought she was being pedantic. Probably thought this was all pointless. Probably would have made a hundred mistakes and condemned Ma if she weren't here in charge.

'These things matter,' she said, firmly.

'Sure they do,' he wandered off to the next log, up to his knees in mud and algae.

'Subtle differences are important.'

'How subtle though? Don't you think they could be variations of the right ones?'

'I'm sure. It's enough of a change to be significant.'

'So what was that one, then? If it isn't the right mushroom, what kind of mushroom is it?'

She shrugged. 'I don't know. I know what we want, everything else by definition is what we don't want. Look; I've circled the most important features. Diameter, colour, habitat, and distinguishing features. That one had three out of the four, but failed on the last.'

'Too many stripes.'

'That's right.'

'Sure.'

Heaving the next log aside, he inspected its underside. More of the same ones, stripes extending all the way to the tip. He quickly glanced over his shoulder at her. She pursed her lips. Ash sighed dramatically and released the log, which plopped back into the mud. Reaching behind, he took out the stick doll he'd been making for H. It was quite good, to be fair to him, his rudimentary crafting skills coming through to twist and bend various twigs into a roughly humanoid form. A few more hours' work and it would be as good as any of the ones they'd seen, it just needed the rough clothing and that would be it. Better than wasting time searching for one in the market.

A night and a day of trudging through mud and swamp-water chased away his initial shock. He was moodier than usual, true, but that might well be down to the aforementioned muck combined with the stifling summer heat slowly cooking the foul swamp-water into increasingly complex layers of stinking sludge. Their continued fruitless search probably didn't help the matter. Making the doll for H was a good idea. It must be therapeutic for him, manipulating the twigs to the desired shape, giving him a sense of control after a chaotic few days. She should have suggested it sooner, really, but then again it was probably for the best he made it himself.

The deeper they delved into the swamp, the more fungi they found, but one remained elusive. There was always something missing. The stripes too long, the colour more pink than red, the diameter too large. Despite her scolding, Ash was right to have doubts. She had them herself, but Ffed agreed. Better to be safe than sorry, especially with fungi, especially with Healer Gerath.

Separating a bed of reeds at the base of a bay willow, she found another contender. The right habitat, a good size, pale yellow, red stripes extending halfway up the hood. She leaned forward excitedly. Four out of four! She stopped. No. A few pale blue spots around the head. She looked back at the reference page and her circled features. No mention of dots. Sighing heavily, she retreated, letting the reeds snap back into place.

Ffed called her over to have another look at the picture, fan-like ears flapping softly. She handed the page over and Ffed took a hard look, tracing her finger over the illustration.

'Found something?'

'Just reminding.'

167

She nodded sadly and looked around. How much more swamp did they have? Surely they'd run out of it eventually? This was probably the absolute depths of it, judging by the wealth of different flora and fauna. As soon as it started thinning out again, it was a bad sign.

'Wouldn't mind stopping for a bite to eat in a bit,' Nari called from behind.

'Good for you,' she called back.

Ash splashed up to them, still fiddling with the would-be-doll. 'No, I wouldn't mind some either.'

She threw her hands up in exasperation. 'Sure, why not then? Picnic in the woods for us!'

'Nice picnic,' Ffed smiled, either missing her sarcasm or choosing to ignore it.

'Great,' she snapped, plonking herself down on the nearest hummock. 'Let's all sit around and have a nice civilised lunch.'

'Good idea,' Ash grinned and sat next to her, rummaging about his pack.

'Lucky they're waterproof,' Nari grinned, recovering a bread roll from his provisions. 'Few things worse than soggy bread, especially swamp-soggy bread.'

'Never tried it, thank the four winds,' Ash spoke around a mouthful.

No point sitting around and watching everyone else eat while she went hungry. Making a point of being as rough as possible, she thrust her hand into her pack and ripped out a wedge of cheese. Tearing off a chunk of bread, she ate it methodically, alternating bites between the two, glaring at Nari and Ash.

'How about we try a few shots with the bow?' Nari handed the weapon to her brother.

Ash swallowed his mouthful and took it hesitantly. 'I'm really not much good.'

'Practice won't make you any worse. Come on. You know how to nock an arrow to the string? Just like that. Face sideways with your left foot to the target. Let's use that log there, see it? Now, holding the string not the shaft, draw back. This is where it gets technical and where the good are separated from the bad.'

'So what do I do?'

'Not really sure, to be honest. I'm not much good at it, but if you keep going you'll probably get better at it.'

'Great.'

'So you draw with your back, arm, and shoulders all at once. That's it, press your shoulder-blades together. Pull the left arm back while pushing the right arm forward on the bow. Nice! All the way back to your cheek if you can… oh.'

The arrow dropped off the weapon and fell to the ground. Ash and Nari stared at it dumbly. Dem sniggered. Now she was glad they stopped for lunch.

'How did that happen?'

Nari rubbed his chin. 'I think you're too tall for the bow. Probably. Jod was a tiny little rat. His draw length is probably much smaller than yours. The draw weight will be low as well, a wimp like him couldn't possibly draw anything too heavy. Just go to where the arrowhead meets the shaft.'

'Alright I'll try.'

Ash retrieved the arrow and drew the bow again. This time he kept it in place.

'Hmm,' Nari scrutinised him, cradling his chin in his hand. 'Definitely too small. At full draw the arrow should be at your cheek. yours… isn't.'

'Just a bit short,' Ash grimaced, the bowstring quivering half a foot before his nose.

'Alright, no matter, better than nothing. Sight down the shaft at the target. Hold it in place, exhale slowly and… release!'

She held her breath as the arrow whizzed through the air towards the target… and beyond. It splashed pathetically into the swamp twenty feet behind and to the left of the log.

'Good start!' Nari declared, triumphantly.

'Was it?' asked Ash, sceptically.

'Was it?' sniggered Dem.

'I try some cheese?' asked Ffed, softly.

169

'Yes, first shot, went in the right direction. Good start from my point of view. Go get the arrow before it's lost for good and we'll try again.'

'Better believe I'll be standing well behind him if he whips that out,' chuckled Dem as Ash stumbled off to collect his arrow.

'It's a start. He'll improve,' Nari sniffed.

She laughed again. 'Can't get worse, can he?'

'Dem? I try some cheese?'

A small tug at her sleeve as Ffed stared inquisitively at her pack.

'Yeah sure, help yourself,' she handed her pack over.

'It's difficult when the bow's not the right size. Ideally he'd have a longbow, given his height,' Nari continued.

She shook her head. The bowmen in Starforge were easily the burliest soldiers in the garrison, with shoulders so wide they had to walk sideways through doors. Ash's beanpole physique was a far cry from a longbowman.

'Not a chance he'd ever be able to draw one of those.'

Nari grimaced in reluctant agreement. 'Just needs a bit of feeding and we'll make an archer of him.'

'You'll do no such thing,' she snapped. What was he thinking? 'Ash is a craftsman, not a fighter. It's what he wants,' she picked up the half-finished doll from where Ash left it and waved it at Nari. 'See? This is what he's good at. You might want to mould him into some sort of rogue archer thief, but that's not who he is.'

Nari shrugged. 'He seems enthusiastic enough. Maybe he wants to learn a new skill.'

'Maybe he's doing it because he wants to impress you,' she snapped.

'Not a bad thing.'

'Isn't it?'

Another tug at her sleeve. 'Dem. Need reminding again.'

She turned to Ffed. 'What?'

'Picture. Need reminding,' Ffed took another bite of the cheese, straight from the main wedge.

'Here,' she handed her the page. 'Keep the cheese as well, if you like it that much.'

'Perhaps the boy wants a good role-model in his life, eh? Strong male figure and all that.'

She stood and pointed a finger at him. 'Don't you dare. I know what you're getting at. Don't go there, Nariton.'

He looked at her. She expected him to argue back, to say something inflammatory about Da. But he didn't. Something about the look on her face must have discouraged him. He backed down with a shrug. Nodding slowly, she sat again, ears burning, heart hammering. A step too far, even for Nariton.

Ash trotted back, oblivious.

'Alright let's go again!'

Nari smiled softly and kept his coaching as Ash missed again and again. If he was getting any better, it was by minute margins. Dem only half-watched, her head still spinning from Nari's thoughtlessness. He should've known better.

'Spots on mushroom?' asked Ffed suddenly, her nose inches from the page.

'No, just stripes,' she muttered back. Ash missed again, his worst one yet, sending the arrow flying way above the log. Even Nari covered his eyes at the useless attempt.

'Sure? Words say so?'

'Yeah, I've circled the features.'

Ffed handed the page over, pointing with her long fingers, 'What this?' she tapped the illustration.

Dem glanced at the picture. 'Just staining. Someone probably spilled something and it's dried a different colour.'

Ffed held the page close to her nose again. 'Don't think so.'

With a sigh, she took the page back. Ffed tapped again on the stains. She shook her head. Definitely a stain. They just so happened to be on the illustration. A small cluster of droplets near the top.

She stopped. Could it be?

She scanned the page again. Definitely no mention of spots in the distinguishing features. Just the stripes.

'It doesn't say anything,' she muttered. 'Look, I've circled all the distinguishing features. It doesn't mention it anywhere.'

'Words outside of circle, maybe?' Ffed suggested.

Her cheeks grew hot. Had she really overlooked something? She forced herself to read the page in full. It was difficult not to scan the rest and skip straight to the circled sentences. It was how she learned things; she identified the important points and picked them out, the rest was all just noise. She read carefully, Ffed watching her closely. Nothing so far, but now Ffed mentioned it, the supposed stains were looking more and more like a faint, purposeful feature. But still no mention of spots. Penultimate paragraph now, nothing. Final paragraph.

Her heart skipped a beat.

The final sentence was cut off midway, but it said enough.

"In summer, a seasonal change occurs with pale turquoise spots on the vertex–"

She jumped to her feet with a yelp.

'Ffed! You've done it!' she seized her by the arms and spun her around. 'You've done it!'

'Yes, yes,' Ffed muttered, smiling softly.

'It's here!'

She stopped spinning. Where was it? Next to a bay willow. She scanned the swamp, ignoring Nari and Ash's puzzled looks. There it was! Rushing over, she parted the reeds again.

On an unceremonious cushion of mud and slime, the pale golden crown glinted back at her, its peripheries streaked with rubies, its crown finished with sapphires.

*

'Making a habit of these nightly visits, are we?'

'We just need to see Healer Gerath.'

Anten peered at them over his steepled fingers. Muddy, weather-stained, and probably stinking to the four winds, they certainly weren't dressed for an audience with a Chief Healer. Somehow, she didn't care. Haste was more important that propriety in these circumstances.

'You found what he wanted?'

172

'In my pack,' Dem confirmed.

'Remarkable. May I see it?'

'Why do you need to?' asked Ash, frowning.

'Curiosity, nothing more.'

'Don't you think it more pertinent to inform Healer Gerath of our return? He might be anxious to get started,' she suggested.

'A message has already been sent. If he is awake, he'll make his intentions known, I'm sure.'

She shrugged off her pack. No harm in showing him. Retrieving the precious package, she handed it over, along with the reference page.

Anten received it delicately, unwrapping it with a surgical precision and laying it on his enormous pile of notes.

'A curiosity,' he whispered, whipping out a thicker pair of spectacles to examine it more closely, turning back and forth between the page and the specimen.

'The blue dots are a–'

'Seasonal variation, yes, I saw,' Anten nodded.

'Nearly missed it,' she smiled, wryly.

'An easy mistake to make, I'm sure. There are very similar mushrooms in the swamp, you did well to forage the right one.'

'What is it?' asked Ash. 'What's it for?'

Anten leaned back and covered the mushroom up again. 'Not a clue. Anything Gerath asks for is generally an enigma to the rest of us. He does things differently.'

'Differently to whom?' Ash asked.

'Everyone.'

Ash glanced at her. She ignored him. Why was he questioning it again, after all they'd been through getting it?

'Perhaps you'd find the books he reads useful, in that case?' she suggested, sweetly. 'It might be useful to see where he gets his ingenuity from?'

'We would love to, except he keeps them all to himself, dear,' Anten sighed. 'He has a whole hoard of information down there, but he doesn't share it around with the likes of us.'

'Where did he get them from?' Nari asked, lingering in the background.

'Brought them with him when he arrived. No matter, he doesn't use our library either.'

Dem snorted. 'Well, maybe that's why. If you opened yours to him, I'm sure he'd let you use his.'

'Ours is open to anyone,' Anten sniffed. 'He chooses not to use it. I assure you, when he was permitted to work on the wards we positively *encouraged* him to use it, for the sake of patient safety. But, Gerath is who he is.'

'Thank goodness for it, otherwise we might not have gotten an answer for Ma,' Dem snapped.

A knock on the door. One of the assistants, bowing deeply.

'Healer Anten, sir. Healer Gerath requests the children and the package be taken to him as soon as they're ready.'

'Good. Take them with you, I have more than enough to do here without one of Gerath's wild treatment plans to confuse my thoughts.'

He waved them away. Old buffoon. Just because he was too narrow-minded to accept any new thoughts or ideas didn't make her trust Gerath any less. She curtsied neatly and followed the assistant down the familiar set of passageways and staircases to Gerath's basement. Ash and Nari trailed behind, dragging their feet and muttering between them. She ignored their mumblings. After their break-neck journey from Trottmire, they were all exhausted. For fear of running into Pit and his companions in Holevale, they bypassed the village altogether and made the whole journey through the woods in one feverish flight, Ffed leading the way and Nari behind. Free from the burden of searching, they made it back to the infirmary in record time.

Struggling to keep her eyes open, she waited by the door as the assistant knocked tentatively. The door swung open almost immediately, and they were ushered into the darkness by one of the hooded acolytes.

'Didn't expect you back so soon!' Gerath huffed.

'We thought it best to make haste. Ran into a bit of trouble along the way as well,' she handed over the package, a new surge of excitement keeping her standing.

'Well, trouble's all around, what did you expect?' Gerath muttered as he snatched the fungus from her hands. He stopped suddenly in front of Nari, looking him up and down in disgust. 'Who's this lump?'

'Nariton Selkaharr, pleasure to meet you,' Nari yawned.

'Is it? Can't say it's a pleasure to meet you. You stink. You all do.'

'Swamp muck,' Dem explained, apologetically.

'I know what it is. Doesn't change your stink, does it? You can leave.'

He unpeeled the mushroom with the same delicacy as Anten and rushed over to one of his instrument-laden tables, setting candles and spirit-burners alight as he went. His acolytes milled about him, pulling various pots, pouches, and other receptacles from the surrounding shelves.

'What?' she blinked.

'Leave. I can't work with your stink filling the place. Go on, out, all of you.'

She paused, trying to get a glimpse over the shoulder of the acolyte shepherding them back out the room. 'But, I wondered if I'd be able to–'

The door slammed shut in her face. Ash and Nari stumbled over each other, nearly falling. She kept her feet, staring at the shut door inches from her face.

'What an arse,' Nari muttered.

'Shut up,' she snapped, looking down at her soiled clothing. 'He's right, you know. We really do stink.'

*

Ffed curled her knees up to her chest, shivering uncontrollably despite the residual heat of the day that still saturated the evening forest. Not since the glacier mines had she shaken like this. Not since those frozen nights on the surface, nothing but her mother's frail arms around her shoulders to keep her warm.

If only it were the frost that made her shiver now.

Her crude shelter faced the infirmary through a gap in the trees. Not the front entrance where the children went in, something drew her to a small backdoor to a lower level. A familiar instinct, by now.

A knock and scuffle on the flimsy branches behind her. She ignored it as much as she could. It was here. Found again. Inevitable. Nari was a fool to think a man could replicate this thing, that a man could pose such a fierce challenge to her. His reassurances fell on deaf ears. If only he were here to witness this.

If it wanted her, all it needed was a quick thrust through the ramshackle walls and her back would be exposed to its claws and pointed teeth. Its footsteps circled, hardly making a sound. She sat stock still, hatchet balanced on her knees, ears erect. Any moment now, it would cross the shelter entrance, revealing itself at last. When that happened, she would die. To lay eyes on this evil, this terror of the night, would seal her fate, as surely as staring into the abyssal depths of a cockatrice's gaze.

She released the breath she didn't realise she'd been holding. Perhaps if she wounded it somehow it wouldn't go after the children. One last act of protection, even if they'd never know.

The faint footsteps rounded closer, closer. Every instinct told her to close her eyes, to shut out the night and hope her blindness would be her salvation. But as soon as they closed, the darkness became oppressive instead of comforting, the unknown evils of the world seizing the opportunity to creep closer. She snapped them back open, staring wildly into the darkness, anticipating the first clawed foot to step into sight.

Heart thundering, sweat dripping, she kept control of her bowels, for now. A ragged breath from outside sent a chill through her body. It knew she was here, it knew she knew it was there. Savouring her fear, feasting on her dread, both such exquisite delicacies for the creatures of darkness.

A movement in the distance caught her eye. Anything to distract from the inevitable.

The infirmary's backdoor swung open.

She clutched her chest and gasped. Invisible hooks tore at her breast, drawing her out of her shelter. Searing, burning, scalding her beating heart, drawing her in as surely as any minnow on a line. She fell forward, face pressed into the earth, fighting with her limbs as they moved involuntarily to draw her from her shelter. Useless. Like fighting a bull with one arm tied behind your back, like swimming in treacle. A long, low groan extracted itself from her chest. Her neck shook and strained with the effort of the battle. Her eyes spun in their sockets, sending the world into a kaleidoscopic blur of shadow and light. Digging her palms and knees into the earth made no difference, she was dragged forward regardless, a bodily force wrenching her on, leaving furrows in the loam.

Something stopped her in her tracks. It pressed into her face, cold and rough as a pillar of ice. Back in the glacier mines? Manacles, whippings, back-breaking labour, and constant unremitting cold. Enough to scald her red-raw fingers, enough to freeze the tears even as they left her streaming eyes. Whimpering, she forced her lids open. Better to face it than fear it.

Not the brilliant blue of the glacier, not the perfect whiteness of an ice storm. Black iron. Just the infirmary's perimeter fence, nothing more.

Her heart skipped painfully. She'd left her shelter! Nothing separating her from the follower. For all its flimsy uselessness, that thin wall of sticks and leaves was enough at least to conceal her from it, something to hide behind. Out in the open, she had nothing.

Panting, she waited for it. For the patter of small feet, the childish giggle, the burn of tearing flesh.

Nothing.

She stole a glance over her shoulder. Let her know her enemy, if nothing else.

Denied again. An empty forest, her small shelter staring sad and empty back at her. No sign of anyone else. Two furrows led from the entrance to her knees. Dragged indeed. But by what? Did the follower take her out then discard her once it saw how pathetic she was?

Another tug at her breast spun her back around to the infirmary, pressing her face and breast against the fence, trying to tear her through the iron. Hardly able to breathe, she forced her hands around the bars, pushing herself away, giving her ribs more room to expand. It worked. A trickle of air into her tortured lungs, and another. Enough to calm her thundering heart and trembling limbs.

Whatever it was that entangled her heart lay on the other side of the fence, doing everything it could to drag her to its slavering jaws. Tears of effort welled at the corners of her eyes, blurring her vision, making the world swim.

Blinking them away, she gritted her teeth. Not like this, caught in invisible manacles. She'd never be made prisoner again, clawing at the bars of captivity for solace. Pushing harder, she brought her feet in front of her, bracing them against the iron, pushing back, enough to take a proper breath.

The infirmary came back into focus. The open door. Empty. A deeper, more impenetrable darkness within than should have been possible. An oscillating, pulsating, inky blackness. A dancing shadow.

Another pull, but she was prepared, pushing back with all four limbs, mouth open in a silent scream. The wave passed. She kept looking.

Next to the open door crouched something small, hunched, and pale as a half-rotten corpse. Ape-like and twisted, staring into that open doorway, nodding, twitching, cowering at odd intervals as it bowed, no, *prostrated* before the darkness. She narrowed her eyes and stretched her neck, straining for a better look.

The pale thing gave a final nod and sprang away, scurrying like a foul, twisted lizard over the garden wall.

Emptiness faced her from the doorway. The emptiness of infinity, of death and destruction. No ordinary darkness, but an absence of sound, smell, and touch in addition to light. A hole in reality. A void, ravenous for the delicacies of the world, desperate to fill that bottomless, ever-expanding emptiness at its heart. She held her breath, knowing what was to come.

Stronger than ever before, the hooks and claws sank into her breastbone, crushing her, suffocating her, closing its burning grip around her heart, savouring the moment her worthless life was lost. The Great Hunter howled behind her, racing to sink its fangs into her neck. Her heart skipped again, and again. Her face burned. The Hunter's footsteps boomed.

The door slammed shut. She dropped to the floor. Gasping, sweating, shaking, but breathing.

Dragging herself back to her feet, she stared at the stained, weather-worn door, heavy brass latch still as the grave.

What lay in the impenetrable darkness? What phantoms haunted the shadows to give them such menace?

She shivered. The follower was gone, at least for now, she was sure of it. Whatever connection they had faded with each second as that pale twisted thing stole away on whatever task it was appointed by its dark master.

Collapsing her shelter, she shouldered her pack and circled back around the perimeter fence. Where she'd been drawn to it before, suddenly that door repelled her more than anything she'd ever encountered. As visceral as a pungent stench, it offended her senses in a way she couldn't explain.

Even in her new shelter on the opposite side, this one overlooking the main entrance, she couldn't shake the dread she'd faced in the doorway. Every shadow danced with its threat. Even the night sky, where once she'd see the moon and stars, now all the saw was the infinite emptiness in between.

Within it all, two indigo eyes, glimmering with malice.

Chapter 13

With a final twist, he held the doll at arm's length, simultaneously admiring and scrutinising his work. If anything, it was probably too perfect. Glancing out the window at the hut outside, he compared his work to the doll on the porch. Definitely a higher quality than his reference piece which was little more than bundles of sticks bound together with rudimentary twists and lengths of twine. His was a work of art, carefully intertwined twigs that kept their shape without the aid of string. He'd even positioned some of the knots and knobbles to replicate a crude nose and brows. H would love it.

'What do you think?' he showed it to Dem.

'Very good,' she nodded, disinterestedly.

'Nari?'

'Yeah, lad, looks fine.'

'It's not as crude as the ones we've seen,' he explained. 'Admittedly, their simplicity is part of their charm, but I couldn't help but make a more intricate one.'

Neither replied, absorbed in their own thoughts. More fool them. If they didn't want to appreciate an artist and his work, he wasn't going to force the matter. They'd barely said a word since arriving, although that was mostly down to exhaustion. He'd nearly fallen asleep in the bath Dem forced him to take before bed. Made a difference, of course. Clean and warm, with the scented oils of the lavish bathroom still lingering to his skin, it was probably the best he'd ever slept. A deep, dreamless slumber right up until he woke around an hour ago. He had no idea what time it was, probably mid-afternoon by the looks of it. Dem claimed she'd been awake for hours but he didn't believe her, she was as exhausted as him.

A knock at the door had Dem on her feet in an instant, practically tearing the thing off its hinges.

'Yes?'

The assistant healer blinked rapidly. 'Healer Gerath sent for you.'

'Finally.'

She was half out the door before remembering to stop and turn to him and Nari.

'You coming?'

'Just give me a minute to get my shoes,' he scrambled under the bed for his stained boots.

'How about you?'

'No, no I'll stay here.'

Dem paused, glancing between Nari and their packs. Ash snorted. The man literally fought for their lives, yet she still accused him of treachery at every opportunity. She'd never learn.

Nari raised his brows, reading her thoughts. 'They're safe, don't worry. I promise.'

'It'll be fine,' Ash pulled his boots on and scrambled after his sister, ushering her into the corridor. 'We can trust him.'

'Sure,' she muttered, pulling a face. Still suspicious, of course, but she allowed herself to be pushed away from the room without recovering the packs. 'I don't like leaving our things with him.'

'I noticed,' he rolled his eyes.

She slowed. Fantastic. Now they'd have to take their packs all the way downstairs just to appease her paranoid delusions. 'Why would he stay behind, if not to do something bad?'

'Maybe he just didn't want to get insulted by Gerath again?' he suggested.

'Maybe. I suppose. Alright, let's go.'

Easier than expected! They followed the assistant to the end of the corridor.

'We can make our own way down, if you have other things to do?' he asked.

'Really? If you're sure?' the assistant nodded enthusiastically.

'Of course, we've been a few times now,' he smiled. 'We'll find our way.'

'Alright, thank you!'

They watched him scurry away down another passageway, no doubt already putting them out of mind. Dem turned to him and raised her eyebrow.

'Well?'

'Well nothing,' he shrugged, leading the way.

'No, no. What are you doing?'

'Well,' he shrugged again for dramatic effect. 'I thought we could try to take a look around his lab? We can sneak in unannounced and have a bit of a rummage.'

She scoffed, rolling her eyes. 'Oh right, piss off the guy who's helping us. Great plan.'

'Oh please, like you don't want to have a look around his cellar.'

'I don't actually. I respect his privacy,' she turned her nose up at him with a level of superiority only she could muster.

'So you'd rather get yelled at for something, palmed off with his little potion, and never see him or his weird workshop ever again?'

'If that's what it takes to save Ma, then yes.'

'You'll never see any of those books Anten was talking about,' he sighed dramatically. 'I guess it's alright. Anten, Awis, and Semon have gotten along fine without any of Gerath's secret books, I'm sure...' he trailed away suggestively.

Dem stopped in her tracks and eyed him suspiciously. He flicked his eyebrows and grinned. Her jaw clenched and her eyes narrowed further. Try as she might, she couldn't fool him. He had her. Anything to distance herself from her new arch-nemesis Anten.

'If I asked he might let me have a look at one of them,' she said it more to herself more than to him, doing her best to talk herself out of it.

He snorted as they rounded the last corner before the stairs. 'Oh yeah, he really strikes me as the reasonable book-lending sort.'

'I guess just a little look wouldn't do any harm?' she whispered, their footsteps echoing down the stairwell.

'Exactly! Just a few minutes, right?'

'Obviously I won't take any, I'll just write down some of the titles for future reference. Maybe I'll find them somewhere else.'

Into the cellar, the warm summer air of the upper levels suddenly cooled and dampened, stone floors replacing the polished wood above. The closer they got, the faster his heart beat. Past the storerooms and barrel-filled wine-cellars, past the bustling kitchens and cool pantries, and finally outside the familiar mahogany door

'Good idea. You'll need them if you want to build up your future medical practice,' Ash nodded, voice barely audible even to him.

'It might be locked,' she said it half-hopefully.

'Probably will be, to be fair,' he agreed, reaching for the latch. His hand shook. Why? Scared of getting shouted at by the mean man? He set his jaw. Get a grip and open it. Time to find out what he was hiding down here.

A soft click as his thumb pressed down. He pushed. No movement. Relief flooded his heart. Locked after all. No snooping today, then.

Turning to Dem, he shrugged, giving a sickly grin as his hand withdrew. She didn't return it, but kept staring at the door. His fingers tugged gently on the handle as he uncoiled them, his sweaty skin sticking to the metal. The slightest tug, and the immaculately-oiled hinges swung open a fraction. He froze. Pull, not push.

The crack between the door and its frame widened. They stared at it in silence as it grew. First a crack, then a crevice, then a gorge, inviting them in. No shouts or challenges from within. No irate acolytes or seething healers. Just two children facing the darkness.

Sharing another glance, they stepped over the perimeter, closing the door behind them.

They stood still, scarcely daring to breathe. Ash felt Dem's anxiety radiating from beside him. They hadn't done anything wrong, going through a locked door wasn't a crime, was it? No harm in having a look. It wasn't like there were any patients down here to protect their confidentiality.

As they waited, his eyes adjusted, the pitch blackness retreating into a gloom of shadows and outlines, illuminated by that solitary window in the back. The heavy desk he'd crashed into on their first visit stood before them, its instruments covered in a dark cloth. Nobody else was around.

'Alright, ready?'

'Where are they?' asked Dem, voice cracking. 'If they sent for us, surely you'd expect someone to be here?'

'We didn't exactly *want* the place filled with people, did we?' he hissed. 'Kind of defeats the point of snooping around.'

She remained still, craning her neck back and forth. 'No, but surely there should be *someone*?'

'If we knocked, they'd have come,' he nodded with a confidence he didn't feel.

'From where? I don't see anyone.'

'Which proves my theory,' he nodded again, growing bolder. 'There's an adjoining room. More to this cellar than what we see here, I'm telling you now.'

'I don't feel comfortable doing this,' she shook her head, voice rising.

'Ssh! They'll hear!'

He tried putting his hand over her mouth but she pushed him away.

'No, we shouldn't be here. Gerath will get angry and might not want to help us.'

'Ssh! It'll be fine, he's not going to just throw it away.'

'We don't know. He's down here because he doesn't want to be bothered. Two outside visitors snooping around his workplace is *exactly* the kind of thing he came here to avoid.'

'Ssh! Winds! Ssh!'

If she didn't shut up, they'd definitely hear and there'd be no choice about it!

'Look, we're not doing anything wrong. We're just looking. Not taking anything or moving anything, just looking,' he nodded slowly, backing away a few steps to give her space. 'If anyone asks, we knocked, waited, when nobody answered we just tried the latch and wandered in. Nothing bad.'

She looked at him uncertainly. 'You promise not to do anything?'

'I'm literally just going to look around and find the other room. If anyone sees me, I'll just say we've been sent for and I was looking for them. It isn't a lie.'

'I guess not.'

'You can stick around here and make that list of books?'

'And if someone comes in and sees me?'

'Just say what I said; we've been sent for and I went off to look for them while you waited here.'

She nodded again, wringing her hands the same way Heb did when she was anxious. He nodded slowly, rounding the table. He could feel her eyes on him, watching him go. Perhaps it was to keep an eye on him and make sure he didn't get into any mischief, perhaps it was to make sure no mischief came to him, or perhaps it was just to remind her he was still here. A quick glance over his shoulder and he gave a thumbs-up. She shook her head and rolled her eyes, turning to the bookshelves. Good. If she was comfortable enough to react with such disdain, she'd probably be alright. No need to worry. Now to find this secret room through the hidden alcove.

Crouching, he followed the shelves around the wall, stopping every so often to make sure nobody approached. No-one. Just him and Dem. The place where he thought he'd seen the alcove was further ahead, but he checked the edge of every shelf and cupboard just in case there were more. There were none, of course, but it was good to be thorough. At the very least, it delayed him actually finding what he was looking for.

Why was he procrastinating? What was he afraid of? He didn't know. Surely not Gerath. He'd been told off by far sterner people in the past. Something else. Something about this place that made him uneasy. Why did Nari have to stay upstairs? It would've been easier with him here.

He got to the gap in the shelves. As predicted, there was a step in the wall, with a narrow, arched gap between the two sections. Heavy curtain were drawn across it, concealing its contents. He crouched in before it, waiting. Waiting for what? For someone to come and stop him, so he wouldn't have to go through. Closing his eyes, he remembered what Ffed said about her follower, he remembered Gerath discussing with a hidden someone. Time to go through.

With a final glance at Dem, tracing her fingers over the spines of books and making notes on a piece of scrap paper, he slid a hand through the curtain and slowly drew it aside. He half-expected them to be thrown aside, for Gerath to stand there with fire and fury in his expression, but no, nothing so dramatic. Another passageway beckoned, equally empty. The gloom persisted, another small window at the far end providing the modicum of light required to prevent total darkness. Crouching low, he continued. Not that crouching would do much good. Even hunched over in his lame attempt at stealth, he was still taller and clumsier than most, hardly a member of the king's Guild of Assassins.

The passageway forked at the end, both at right angles, twisting away in different directions. A decision to be made. Always difficult when faced with two seemingly-identical choices. He could pick at random. In the absence of any information, it was probably the best way to decide. Rummaging around his pocket, he retrieved a coin. Leaf-side for right, tower-side for left. It spun in the air, catching the faint rays from the window and landed in his palm. Leaf-side for right.

He took a few steps along the corridor, and stopped. Why did he stop? For some reason, his feet refused to go on. Something held them in place, rooted them to the spot. He stared down the corridor. Tunnel was probably a more appropriate name for it, twisting away into the darkness with nothing visible at the other end, just shadow, dark as pitch. Suddenly, he felt small, insignificant, a silly boy on a hopeless quest. What was he even doing here, playing in matters he didn't understand?

He stepped back. The feeling lessened somewhat. He stepped back again. He felt twice as good. He looked at the coin in his palm, leaf-side gleaming up at him. Traditional custom would have been to upturn the thing on his opposite hand before revealing the face, after all. He turned it over. Tower-side for left.

Pocketing the coin, he made his way down the opposite way. This felt better. As if this were the way he was meant to go. More high windows provided more light, guiding him down the twists and turns. Damp and cold allowed moss and lichen to cling to the stone and mortar, making it slippery in places, but his weeks in the forest gave him steadier feet, nothing to be worried about.

A sound up ahead made him stop suddenly. Another. Faint rustlings and murmurs of whispered voices. Was someone approaching? He listened carefully. No. They were growing fainter. He struck on, slower than before, keeping one hand on the stone wall for support.

Another curtain stretched across the tunnel after a sharp turn. He skidded to another halt, heart in mouth. It was only half-closed. He ducked back behind the turn. Shadows moved on the opposite side. Had they spotted him? His ears strained for any sound of approaching footsteps. Nothing obvious, just the rustle of cloth and parchment, the faint tinkle of glass vials, and the constant murmurs of whispered voices. He closed his eyes. Many voices, far more than the four or five he'd expected. At least eight different tones, all speaking at once.

Pressing his body against the wall, he peeked around the corner. The half-drawn curtain concealed the room beyond, revealing nothing but shadows. He needed a closer look. It was risky, of course. Once at the entrance he could hide behind the curtain, but there was a stretch of a few feet where he might be spotted. He'd already seen enough to know Gerath and his acolytes were up to something down here, wasn't that sufficient?

Of course it wasn't. He had to know. If they were entrusting this man with Ma's life, they needed to know what was happening.

Taking a breath to steady himself, he slid around the corner, pressing his back up against the wall, moving as slowly as silently as a hunting wildcat. Or so he hoped. He probably looked more like a scraggly mule trying to sneak up on an unsuspecting hay bale than anything else. Either way, he made it to the curtain without any shouts or challenges from within.

Steeling himself, he crouched as low as he could and peered around the cloth.

It was all he could do not to gasp.

A full ward, nearly identical to the ones upstairs, complete with the familiar medicine-cupboards, paper charts, syringes, tubes, and cots for the inpatients. There were at least eight of them, tended by three of the four acolytes he'd seen last time, flitting between their beds on their various tasks. But where the wards upstairs were warm, wood-panelled, and bright, the beds made with clean linen and cotton sheets, this was as gloomy and cold as the rest of the cellar, the beds made with rough wool and stained burlap. Superficial differences, of course, but it set the tone for the main contrast; the patients.

Upstairs, there were a few unwell souls, those with yellowed skin and distended bellies, poor folks with infected limbs and chests full of pus, but nothing like these. Manacled to their cots by iron chains, they pawed deliriously at unseen objects floating above them. Their eyes rolled in their heads, sweat streaming down their pallid faces. He watched one of the acolytes, the tall one, strip the bedclothes off the nearest patient, exposing bare, skeletal ribs and a torso covered in dilated, tortuous veins beneath skin so bruised it was a hundred different shades of blue and purple. Even as he watched, another patient vomited a foul bilious bellyful of greenish-brown fluid over her pillow, while another released an abhorrent discharge of black stool over his red, blistered thighs. Beside him, a skeletal woman lay with her neck distended, a funnelled tube in place to deliver food and tinctures directly into her emaciated stomach. From the far end, one of the patients screamed a torrent of incomprehensible sounds, spluttering violently between ulcerated and peeling lips. He was silenced by a medicine-soaked cloth clamped over his nose, delivering whatever sedative it contained to maintain the smothering reticence of the ward.

He sat back into the corridor, breathing heavily. What sort of place was this, where the infirm were left to the devious machinations of some lunatic experimenter? What business did he have keeping these poor souls prisoner? A heaviness sat in the pit of his stomach. A weight of guilt and disgust. He had to leave. Dem needed to know. Perhaps she'd have an answer for him. By the four winds, let her have an answer for him!

Staggering back along the corridor, he made his way to the fork. It was all he could do to keep from vomiting. The smell of the ward lingered on his nostrils. Death and decay. Rancid as old sweat and blood.

He reached the fork and turned down the first corridor to take him back to Dem, and froze, nearly slipping on a patch of damp moss.

The fourth acolyte. He stood still, mumbling under his breath as he traced a finger down a chart, his back to him.

Winds! What to do? Announce himself and face the consequences, risk getting dragged back to that prison-ward, condemn himself and his sister for witnessing such evil? No chance. But there was no way past him, not without being caught, and he wasn't going back to that ward. He'd be a sitting duck, nowhere to hide or run except into the arms of the acolytes. He felt the coin in his pocket and turned to the right-hand corridor.

The acolyte tutted softly under his breath and turned, heading back to the ward. Ash was already gone, backing down the other corridor, eyes wide and staring as he watched the acolyte disappear. He stood still, his breath as loud as a smith's bellows in his ears. How did he miss him? Did he come from the other room, from Dem? Was she alright? Or did he come from here, from this corridor? Was there something else down here? Another ward, maybe? Perhaps a dark operating theatre for the damned. He turned, staring at the beckoning blackness. That resistance returned, something pushing him away, a sense of unease, of things best left unknown. He turned again, back to the corridor to safety, to Dem. It was easier to leave, to go with the knowledge he already had. That was enough, wasn't it? He didn't need to see more.

Da died putting himself before others, running resolutely into the darkness to save his son and three miners. Gathering more information might give him more clues as to what was going on, on how to help those poor people in their cots. Da would do everything he could to save a helpless person, even if it meant endangering his own life. Da was a hero. If he were here, there was no doubt what he'd do.

Setting his jaw, he forced his legs to move. Reluctantly, they obeyed. The darkness pulsed in front of him, oscillating and growing, flowing over the walls and floors like the tide of a black sea. Its waves engulfed him, the foam in his nostrils. Suffocating. Oppressive. Leaden limbs floundered on, his arms outstretched, grasping and clawing at the immaterial fathoms around him. The currents grew stronger, threatening to tear him off his feet and fling him back down the corridor, but he resisted, digging his heels deeper into the scarred and cobbled stones. The darkness was all around him, inside him, blind to all but the colour of darkness, deaf to all but the hum of darkness, numb to all but the chill of darkness.

He was floating in a black mist. No up. No down. No past, no future. Nothing ahead and nothing behind. Nothing to say he was floating at all, expect the sensation of neither standing nor falling, not moving or standing still. A limbo of nothing and nowhere. An absence of all things. The emptiness between the stars.

'You shouldn't be here.'

The words echoed around him a thousand times, growing louder with each repetition, distorting and folding back on themselves until their words took new meanings immediately forgotten and reinterpreted. He blinked, pawed clumsy hands at his invisible face, felt the bump of his nose between his thumb. He was present, alive, here. Sensation rushed back in a flood. No, it was more like the numbness, blindness, and deafness poured out of him, like those words were the hammer to open to bung in the barrel.

Spat back to reality, he blinked again. An open door was before him, leading to a dimly-lit room. How did he get here? Turning, he saw the corridor, straight and true as an arrow leading back to the fork, barely twenty paces away. No mist, no infinite void. He swayed on his feet, blinking to clear away the remnants of his blurred vision. What happened? Could it be that Gerath and his acolytes had stooped to the forbidden practices of magicks?

He shook his head, rejecting the notion. He must have had a faint or something on the way, nothing more. Just an ordinary faint after working himself into a fit of delirium and fear.

Reality's return brought those fears back with a thundering heart and freezing sweat as the voice spoke again..

'Should have turned back, yet here you are. How tenacious. Just like your friend.'

His friend? Dem or Nari? What did they mean?

'Who said that, sorry?' his voice was as small and meek as he felt. The other's voice seemed far away, somehow muffled, as if his ears were underwater, making things difficult to understand.

'Determined to see what lay at the other end, weren't you? You people never listen anymore, never pay attention to your instincts. Funny.'

'Who's there?'

'Well, I don't normally take to uninvited guests, but I can make an exception,' the voice became clearer, if only by a fraction.

'Healer Gerath?'

'Gerath isn't here. Only me.'

He wasn't sure whether to be relieved or not. 'I'm Ash, I'm – I was just looking in – looking for Healer Gerath,' he stammered. Winds! Why couldn't he speak? Scared like a child. 'He sent for us. Gerath sent for us.'

'Of course. You and your sister.'

'Yes, yes! There wasn't an answer so we came looking. I'm sorry.'

There was a figure in the gloom, watching him. He couldn't make them out. The voice was strange. Deep enough to reverberate in his chest, but quiet enough to make him strain to hear. His hand brushed against the doorframe, making him jump. He didn't remember taking a step closer to the room.

'I'm sorry,' he repeated. 'I must have taken a turn in the corridor, my head's spinning.'

'I'm sure it is. You weren't looking for Gerath, Ash. Curiosity killed the cockatrice. Ever heard that before?'

'I was! I promise,' he tried backing away. Something stopped him, gripping his legs in a vice. He looked down, but there was nothing there. Nevertheless, his legs were frozen, dead to all commands to move. The figure approached.

'I asked whether you'd heard the expression before. *Curiosity killed the cockatrice.*'

'I've heard it,' he nodded. His legs trembled with the effort. By the four winds, he needed to get a grip.

The figure came closer, gliding as smoothly as a swan over a still lake. 'Good. What does it mean?'

'That sometimes we shouldn't go looking for things, that things are best left unknown,' he mumbled, watching the shadow grow larger.

A stench came from the room. Something fouler even than the ward. Acrid and pungent. It took a few seconds to recognise it. Vinegar, or something close to it. Mixed with alcohol. Fermented together into an ugly stench to assault the nostrils and make his eyes water. But not just that. There was something more underneath it all.

'It's a reference to the War,' the shadow continued as he retched emptily at the smell. 'All those centuries ago, before King Stolach and his reign, before your villages, before this infirmary.'

'The Cataclysmic War, between the giants and the cockatrice,' he gasped, fixed to the spot, unable to turn from the stench even if he wanted to.

'Oh, before that, even. The Cataclysmic War was for a taste of long-desired vengeance, not curiosity. Curiosity is what drew the cockatrice to Nefarwy from their island of Uffernen many centuries before that War. Look where it got them.'

'I don't understand.'

'Cockatrice. Cockatrice. Singular and plural are the same. "*Curiosity killed the cockatrice*" doesn't mean one inquisitive creature. It refers to their whole race.'

The shadow emerged, materialised into a person. Short, bald, dressed in neat black clothes with rolled up sleeves. His skin was alabaster-white, like chalk, or lye, or bleached bone. Half his face was covered by a black mask over his mouth and nose.

'I'm sorry, I don't–'

'Understand, no, I know. I'm just amusing myself while giving you a lesson. Curiosity can be a dangerous thing,' he sneered, dark eyes narrowing.

'I'm sorry. I'll leave.'

He tried turning. Again, his legs failed him. Caught. Transfixed. Paralysed by the pale one's penetrating gaze. The part of him that wanted to leave screamed in terror. Another part, a stronger part, knew he had to stay. The pale one's eyes crinkled in a hidden smile beneath the mask.

'Of course, the cockatrice never really had their curiosity sated, did they? Never had a proper chance to enjoy that which they coveted.'

'I was just looking for Healer Gerath,' he whispered.

'He isn't back there,' the pale one nodded over his shoulder. 'He isn't in the ward you visited either. Probably in his garden at the moment, waiting for one of his acolytes to announce your arrival. Shall we go to the ward to get one?'

Ash froze. This was it. One of those empty cots would soon have a new occupant, a fresh new body to be tantalized and tortured with whatever potions and medicines these twisted sadists poured down his throat. He closed his eyes. Why didn't he leave?

'Perhaps not. You can go back to your sister, or you can do what the cockatrice never did and scratch that itch under your skin.'

He released a shuddering breath. Toying with him like a cat and a half-chewed chick. The pale one stepped aside, inviting him in to the gloomy room. Everything told him to turn, to run. The sensible, survivalist part of his brain screamed to flee, to scramble on all fours like a dog if he had to. An even wiser part of his brain knew he'd never make it. His limbs would fail, his chest would seize, and he'd fall into one of those manacled cots. An illusion of choice.

Swallowing, he stepped forward, half-expecting the door to slam shut behind him, for the pale one to swoop him up in a flurry of rotting sheets and burlap blankets, toss him over his shoulder and throw him into a vat of vinegar, to be pickled and preserved for future use. Of course it didn't happen. The door remained open. The pale one slid past him and drew the curtains from his high windows, flooding the room with light.

He wished he hadn't.

Table after table of corpses, some fresh, some less so, some with their organs in jars beside them. Line after line of neat sutures criss-crossed their bare bodies, testament to this twisted creature's sick games at playing maker. Covering his mouth with his hand, he turned to him, perched as neatly as a bird on his high stool.

'Why?'

He would have screamed it if he could. He would have flown across the short distance between them and pummelled him into the ground. But he couldn't, not with such heavy limbs and fluttering heart. The room made him weak as a new-born, helpless before the pale one's condescending gaze.

'It's my job.'

'To desecrate corpses?'

'I'm the examiner.'

'What does that mean?'

'Would you like to find out?'

He stared at the man, looked back to the corpses, back to the man. Examiner? He approached one of the tables and scrutinised the corpse. On second look, there seemed less evidence of wrongdoing. The cuts were identical on every one; a Y-shaped incision of the chest and abdomen, a transverse incision of the neck. A few had additional incisions in their limbs, but only a few. His heart gradually settled. Something at the back of his mind felt vaguely familiar. Dem might have mentioned a type of healer who looked at corpses instead of patients, and how awful a position it must be, to deal solely with the dead. He looked back at the masked man.

'You examine the dead bodies?'

'Among other things.'

'To find you why they died.'

'In part.'

He turned to the bodies again. 'I understand, I think. What's your name?'

The pale one regarded him for a few seconds. 'Lusur.'

'Healer Lusur?'

Lusur chuckled. An ugly sound, like a choking child. A chill crept down his spine again, the tightness returned to his chest.

'Disease is my permit, young Ash, not healing.'

'You must know a lot to identify the causes of death.'

'More than anyone.'

'Gerath consults with you?'

Lusur chuckled again, setting his teeth on edge. 'Sharp one. I knew you'd seen me last time.'

'I thought so,' he nodded. 'You think it's the tubercle sickness?'

194

Lusur nodded silently, watching him as closely as an adder. Ash swallowed an empty mouthful, but the lump in his throat didn't budge. Something awful lay behind those eyes. Something unspeakable.

'Will Ma be okay?' he whispered.

Lusur jumped from his stool, making him flinch. He curled a finger, beckoning him to follow as he glided past the tables. Hesitantly, against his better judgement, Ash followed, dragged by unseen hooks of curiosity.

The room was longer than expected, its length disguised by the pervasive shadows, made worse by the contrast of the opened windows. Table after table of bodies. Some with their cavities still open, most closed. Vials of extravasated blood stood beside the beds adjacent to the jars of organs and boards pinned with specimens.

'Why do you keep them?' he whispered.

'I don't. When I've written my report, they're given to the undertakers in Holevale.'

'So why are so many here?'

'Some are complex cases. I need more time with them than others.'

'Why take their organs out?'

'To study and dissect. To understand the efficiency with which each disease attacks and destroys the tissues of the body.'

'Why?'

'If you understand how a disease works, you understand its weaknesses. In here.'

Throwing aside a curtain at the end of the hall, they entered a side-room. Another dissecting table stood in the middle, occupied like the rest, but it was too dark to see anything more than a lump on a table with four legs. He could practically feel the stench in the air. Not just the vinegar and alcohol, the other reeking miasma beneath it all, saturating the very air with its weight. Lusur stepped to one side and lit a torch. As soon as the first spark of flame ignited, a series of intersecting mirrors amplified the light a hundred times, illuminating the room brighter than daylight, focussing the beams to a curved mirror on the roof that shone directly down on the table.

What was on it made him stumble.

A corpse, of course, dissected like the rest with the familiar Y-shaped incision in the trunk. But the body... Ash shuddered, suppressing a mouthful of vomit. How he must have suffered in his final days. Misshaped limbs twisted like an unkempt thicket into bizarre contortions. Not just at the joints, but the very bones were twisted and turned, with one of his thighs approaching a forty-five-degree angle of deformity, as if mighty hands had twisted and bent them. Black bruises covered his gnarled and leathery skin, where inch-thick lumps stretched it to bursting. His mouth was opened in a permanent grimace, the teeth distorted to protrude at odd angles from bulging, purple gums, around which a hideously swollen and ulcerated tongue pushed like a caged and engorged slug. The eyes were mercifully removed and placed in a jar, but the irregular, gnarled shapes was more akin to a cluster of grapes than a solid globe, the pupils stretched hideously across several lumps, splitting and rupturing in a dozen places at once. On a specimen block was a kidney in cross section, deformed into a barely-recognisable mass of cystic cavities and amorphous, crystalline projections both within and without. The other organs were similarly affected; lungs, liver, stomach, and heart. In a larger jar were the bowels, or what he presumed were once bowels. The twisted, calcified, bulbous masses of knotted and gnarled tissues were barely recognisable as anything at all, expect perhaps a blind artist's abstract view of what the diseased bowel of an unknown creature might look like. Of all grotesque and hideous things he'd seen, this was beyond anything he'd ever imagined.

He glanced at Lusur, who watched him with his viper eyes.

'What is it?'

'As I said. To understand a disease, you must know how it works. Here is what awaits your mother.'

His breath caught. 'The tubercle sickness.'

'That which taints your mother. In its glory.'

He stepped forward for a better look. Ma looked nothing like this, by the four winds. Nothing so foul or evil.

'Not so close!' Lusur's sharp command made him stop. He tapped his face mask. 'Not without proper precautions.'

'It's still contagious?'

'Probably not, he's been dipped in preservative for long enough, but why take the chance? Why risk spreading such a disease? It would only cause panic and dismay if this got out. Disorder and chaos on a scale never before encountered, not since before the giants. Whole villages would burn to contain its spread, this entire infirmary would be purged to dust, its foundations sent back to Enadir's dirt. We don't want that.'

'No,' he stepped back.

'This man had a different strain to your mother, a different type.'

'How many kinds are there?'

'Hundreds! More than you can imagine,' Lusur's voice dropped to a whisper. 'The common types ravaging the Southlands and Jagged Isles are but shadows of its original form, diluted and weakened over the centuries. Every now and then, of course, you find a special strain that's like the cunning original.'

'It changes?'

'Every day, more types are made, each different to the other, but all of them similar, treated in similar ways. But this, this one is a special strain, similar to your mother's.'

'Why couldn't he be treated?' he nodded to the table.

'Presented too late. Lived all alone in the woods as the tubercles ravaged his brain and body, rotting his mind as it rotted his flesh so he didn't even think to attend. Nobody with him but his little child. Dead, now.'

'The child too?'

Lusur nodded slowly, voice almost too low to hear. Paradoxically, the lower his volume, the stronger it reverberated in his chest, almost as if one compensated for the other.

'Worse than the father. You would not have recognised it as human.'

He looked back at the corpse. Black bruises, just like the ones covering Ma. His knees shook.

197

'But you can make them better? The mushroom we got from the marshes. It'll work?'

'Perhaps. Depends on how quickly it grows.'

'So she... Ma could be like this?' he choked, keeping his eyes averted from the hideous thing on the table.

'Depends on what kind of strain we're facing. Depends on your mother's reserves, her mettle. It's difficult to tell with the limited information you and your sister provided Healer Gerath. If it is like this one, and it sounds it, she needs that medicine as soon as possible. Otherwise...' his voice trailed away into a sibilant hiss, echoing in his ears and bouncing around his chest. 'Fire and dust to Starforge and all the surrounding villages, probably even to here if anyone could trace your journey.'

'But you've treated cases like it before?'

'I've seen it a thousand times.'

'And treated it successfully?'

Lusur made his drowning child's chuckle again. 'How endearing to see your concern for your mother.'

'Treated successfully?' he raised his voice. He didn't mean to, but this twisted snake's apparent pleasure at Ma's fate sparked his rage. The fact he couldn't stop his knees shaking didn't help, but it was so much easier to lash out in rage when fear gnawed your spine.

Lusur ignored him, gliding past with what must have been a sneer beneath the mask. He could have grappled him there and then, put his arms around his scrawny neck. He was twice his size, twice his weight. If he got him to the ground, Lusur wouldn't stand a chance.

But he couldn't. His limbs were lead, stuck in tar.

'Let me show you something. You know why it's called the tubercle sickness?'

'Because of tubercles,' his voice. He didn't mean to answer, but something made him speak, made his throat and tongue move, almost of their own accord.

'And what are the tubercles, one might ask.'

'I don't know.'

'Well, prepare for a demonstration,' a gleaming silver scalpel appeared in his hands, held as delicately as a fiddler holds his bow.

198

'See the masses on the skin? I already removed the larger ones and preserved them, these ones weren't worth the effort of dissecting, but I can show you their contents. Behold!'

With a sweep of the hand, he brushed his blade across the skin, opening up several of the swollen lumps. They burst live over-ripe plums, discharging their offence over the skin. Ash's eyes watered as the putrid foetor drowned his nostrils. Heaving emptily, he fell to all fours, body spasming violently in its impotent efforts to purge the evil his nose and eyes had introduced.

'Observe the black discharge,' Lusur continued, his low voice echoing around the room, rattling his heart and lungs. 'Not just clotted blood but a mixture of pus, necrotic skin, and a pigmented discharge unique to the disease. They grow all over the body, from the eyes to the bones, distorting and corrupting every tissue it encounters. Irreversibly.'

Irreversibly? Ash groaned, clambering on all fours. They said it was curable! He crawled to Lusur, still droning on about the particulars of the discharge. It couldn't be irreversible! There had to be a cure!

'Please!' he wheezed between gasping breaths, clawing at Lusur's chest. 'It can't be irreversible!'

His fingers stretched higher. Lusur ignored him, now gesturing to the various pots of organs, talking about transformation of the tubercles into cystic and pseudo-cystic lesions, of internal calcifications, of amorphous proliferations, trans-coelomic spread. A wealth of words and phrases with no meaning, refusing to use the ones he wanted to answer his questions.

His little finger caught on the loop of the mask, Lusur pushed him away and he collapsed to the floor, mask still in his hand.

'And here I thought you wanted to learn about the disease,' Lusur chuckled.

'I don't understand what you're saying,' Ash threw the mask away. 'Just tell me if you can treat–'

He stopped. His heart stopped for a moment, staring in horror at Lusur's face.

There was no nose, nothing but two holes in the middle of his face. His mouth was a mess of scar tissue, extending from the corner of his simultaneously thin and bloated lips to the lower edge of his slitted nostril. What he'd initially taken for alabaster-white skin was just cosmetics, a painted face to hide the blemishes beneath. Lusur raised a bald eyebrow, opening up cracks in the clay-like mask of painted skin, his dark eyes glittering in the bright light of the room.

'Not what you were expecting?'

'Your face,' he breathed, all thoughts of the tubercle sickness momentarily forgotten.

'Work with disease for long enough and something's bound to get you. The rot got me,' he touched his face lightly. 'Nothing you can do when it sets in. Just cut and burn.'

'I'm sorry.'

Lusur sniggered. 'You really don't know anything.'

Ash frowned. What was that supposed to mean? He looked back at the table, at the hideous corpse with its disgusting discharge and abhorrent mutilations. When they returned to Starforge, is this what awaited them, only with Ma's twisted face in place of this stranger's?

'Can it be treated?'

Lusur laughed again. 'Better ask Gerath those kinds of questions.'

'But I thought you advised him?'

'I work with disease, not cure.'

'But the mushroom we found, it'll heal her? The medicine will heal her?'

'Ask Gerath.'

Going around in circles. Perhaps a different question would get the answer he needed.

'Have you seen the disease be stopped?'

'Yes.'

'How? With the mushroom?'

'At a cost. A high one. Some might say too high, leaving the affected… weak. Vulnerable. Open to a long, steady, *inevitable*, reckoning.'

'But they survived?'

Lusur nodded slowly, almost regretfully.

'There were survivors.'

He breathed deeply in relief. The stench of the lanced tubercle made him instantly regret it as his stomach lurched again. Lusur's sad nodding continued. A chill ran down his spine. Was the burden of survival truly so terrible?

'What was the cost?' he whispered.

Lusur chuckled. 'That remains to be seen.'

'If you're not going to answer me, I may as well leave.'

Lusur gestured to the door. Ash glowered at him. He smiled back, ugly face twisting around the mass of scar tissue at its centre.

'Why can't you give a straight answer?'

'Perhaps there is none. Perhaps I don't know.'

He looked him up and down. 'Is that why you study the corpses?'

Lusur's smile broadened. Grotesque. 'Perhaps.'

'Alright. I'm ready to leave now. Gerath will be waiting.'

'He will indeed.'

He paused, staring at the pale healer. Lusur stared back, the smile fixed on his cracked and swollen lips.

'Well? Can I leave?'

'Why ask?' Lusur cocked his head, smile fixed.

'I... don't know. I felt like I should ask permission.'

'Very polite of you. You have my permission.'

He wasn't sure if he imagined it, but his chest felt a little lighter, as if a constricting noose were suddenly released, if only by a fraction. Strength returned to his limbs. The strength of choice, no longer an illusion. The leaden heaviness dissipated, if only by an ounce. His breath caught as he stifled a sob. Lusur's smile remained.

'Been feeling anxious?'

'I don't know why. I took a turn in the corridor. It feels like my legs have only just properly woken up'

'Probably the smell, aye? It takes getting used to.'

'Probably.'

'A bit of nerves too, I'd imagine, being surrounded by so many corpses.'

'Yes.'

'And me with my pretty face,' Lusur held his gaze, unblinking. The noose tightened again around his chest. Come to think of it, he hadn't seen him blink once.

'I'd like to leave,' his voice was small again, like shouting it over the edge of an immeasurable cliff, lost in the wind before it even left his mouth.

'By all means.'

His dark eyes glittered again. Even from this distance, he could see his reflection. A gangly, skinny boy, all alone in a room of corpses, frightened beyond reason, too scared to stay, too terrified to move. Something pulsed behind them, like a swirling, glittering whirlpool of indigo ink, sucking more and more into its iridescent depths. How easy it would be to lose oneself in such a maelstrom, to forget the world and its poisons, to drift back into that blissful void of an unfathomable black sea.

The stench tickled his nostrils again. Disappearing into such a void would mean abandoning Ma to her fate, but was that such a bad thing? Was her end not inevitable, her slow descent into a tortuous, twisted shadow of the person who raised and loved them all these years? Was he strong enough to face the terror of the tubercle sickness within his own mother? He could already picture it, Heb and Elain weeping in the background as he and Dem uncovered Ma's mutated corpse, stifling screams and retches of disgust at the charnel reek poured out.

His nostrils twitched again at the stench, and the vision faded.

Blinking, he stepped back. Lusur's hideous grin was less than a foot away, his foul breath on his cheeks. He wiped his face shakily. When did he approach him? Why? What spell did he have him under to move him as easily as a marionette?

'Tenacious indeed,' Lusur sniggered.

'What do you mean?'

'Run along, Ash, I have work to do.'

He took another step back, secretly relieved the question was ignored. Lusur turned back to the corpse, ignoring his exit. He hesitated at the door, taking a final look over his shoulder. The healer stood still, head bowed over his specimen. A black heart lay in that narrow chest, channelling evil through his twisted limbs, fuelling that wretched brain. He should put an end to him, to all of it. Any advancements in medicine were inconsequential to the black arts conjured in these dungeons, and this living corpse was the ghoul at its heart. All it would take was a quick jump, an arm around his throat, and he'd throttle him, squeeze that last gasp of decaying breath from his lungs. Lusur was tiny, little more to him than the stick doll he'd constructed for H. Easily overpowered, even by him.

As his muscles tensed, his eyes drifted to one of the mirrors. Lusur's black eyes flashed indigo again, watching his every move. Fear turned that tension to a tremble, and he scurried away, barely maintaining control of his bladder.

Ignoring the tables of corpses was easier said than done, but he did his best, ignoring the twitches in the corner of his eye, shutting out the imaginary groans, feigning ignorance to the spasms in their cold fingers. It was all in his head. Just corpses, nothing more. Just his laboured mind racing with terror. Just Lusur and his evil tricks. Fixing his gaze on the exit, he kept walking.

Another side room made him stop just short of the exit. The sensible part of his brain screamed at him again, but he ignored it, or was made to ignore it. Something was different about this room. A feeling told him as much. He peered around the curtain. Tiles of raw clay propped up stacks of wooden boards on one side, barrels of nails beside them. In the middle was a mighty workbench complete with clamps and saws, beneath which was another bucket of thin twigs and sticks, presumably off-cuts from the boards. Coffins of all shapes and sizes lined the remaining walls, leaning against each other, stacked on top of one another, their empty depths beckoning to be filled. He shuddered. One for every corpse in the main room, and more besides.

Some people asked for cremation so their ashes might be carried by the four winds to the fields beyond the clouds. Specific races had their own traditions, such as the neiads and their aquatic ceremonies. Some preferred burial. No matter what the choice, just about everyone got put in a coffin on their way to the undertakers so the body might be prepared for the final rites. It always seemed such a sombre and noble end, to have a custom-made coffin to enclose and protect the body in its final moments on Enadir. Seeing them like this, made en-masse to suit ravaged corpses of any size and shape cheapened it somehow, made it mundane and methodical. Frighteningly so. Death was an integral part to this place. As normal as a cold or headache. No ceremony to it, no grandeur. Just a workbench, a saw, and a few planks of wood. Boxes for goods, to protect the blushes of the squeamish.

Lusur's hand dropped on his shoulder, making him jump.

'See anything interesting, Ash?'

'Just looking,' he squeaked, the healer's death-breath making him gag. They stared at each other, him trembling, Lusur leering. The silence stretched on. He swallowed, unable to tear his gaze away from the black eyes.

'What's the clay for?' he whispered. Anything to break the silence.

'What now?'

'The clay,' he repeated. 'In the corner. What's it for?'

Lusur's sallow lips twitched unpleasantly. 'Parents sometimes want clay coffins for their little ones.'

'I've never heard that before.'

'A local tradition.'

He thought of H, of Elain, lying bare and cold on one of the tables as this sallow sage approached with his keen blades and waiting jars of vinegar, a cold clay box waiting in the corner for each of them.

'And you still... dissect the children?'

'If necessary. They're often easier to cut through, children, their skin nice and supple.'

He exhaled with a shudder. 'I'd like to leave.'

'Nobody's stopping you. It was your choice to have a look.'

A dull ache throbbed at the back of his head as he staggered the final few steps to the corridor, leaning heavily against the wall. By the four winds, he needed to get out of here, to find Dem and take her as far away from this damned place as possible.

'Your friend outside likes looking as well,' Lusur called after him from the doorway, quiet as a whisper, resonating like a drum in his chest. 'Curiosity, eh?'

He froze. 'My friend?'

'Goblins aren't usually so committed. You must have been very convincing when you acquired her service.'

'You've seen?' he stared over his shoulder in disbelief. Lusur was but a shadow again, lurking in the darkness of his dungeon. Although he couldn't see it, he knew he was smiling again.

'Tell her what I said about curiosity. I don't think hers will ever be sated.'

'What do you mean?'

Silence.

'Lusur? What do you mean?'

Nothing. The doorway was dark with no movement within. He wasn't stupid enough to go back for clarification. Taking another breath to steady himself, he forced his legs to move, anticipating another wave of nausea, another plunge into the depths of darkness. It never came. He reached the fork in the road unopposed. Without looking back to Lusur's dungeon, he returned to the main room.

As he staggered in, a series of gasps and curses echoed around the cavern, like a theatre audience at the reveal of an off-stage villain. He barely had time to process before something flew at him.

'Winds! Ash!'

Dem threw her arms around him, burying her face into his chest, nearly knocking him back into the hidden corridor.

'You've been gone for nearly an *hour*!' she mumbled.

As he tried to process a suitable response, more voices flew at him from different directions.

'Where've you been, boy? You been in there? Speak!'

'We didn't see him in the corridors.'

'Definitely wasn't on the ward.'

'We all looked.'

'Only leaves one place then, doesn't it? You been stuck in the corridor, have you? Fainted after a wrong turn, is that it? Damned lucky you didn't do yourself harm, stupid boy.'

He recognised Gerath's voice among his acolytes, beetroot-faced and glaring.

'I guess that's the thanks I get, isn't it? Toil away all night at his medicine and the nosy fool goes poking around places he shouldn't,' Gerath continued his tirade, hands flailing in agitation. 'That's what it means to you, is it? Enough to invade my privacy down here. Makes a man angry, so it does.'

'I'm sorry, we were just looking,' he mumbled, probably too quietly for anyone to hear.

'Gives me half a mind to pour it all away! Teach you a lesson!'

'No!' Dem wailed, hands shooting to her mouth.

Gerath produced a dark, stoppered vial and held it dramatically overhead, ready to cast it on the floor.

'We're sorry! He was just looking, I promise!' Dem pleaded. 'Just like I was looking at your books, nothing else, nothing bad!'

'Aye? What do you have to say for yourself, boy? Snooping around *my* house! Better be a good answer or patient old Gerath might just lose his temper, perhaps then you'll learn your lesson.'

He drew his arm back, vial poised between gnarled fingers, his crimson face ready to burst. A chill spread through Ash's body, running from his toes all the way up to his ears. The vial was the only thing standing between Ma and the corpse on the dissecting table, and now this pompous bastard of a healer was threatening him with its destruction, all because he'd seen his secret torture-ward. Well, there was one thing he hadn't factored in to his tantrum; his apparent master.

'Lusur won't be happy if Ma doesn't get the medicine.'

The vial teetered between his fingers as Gerath trembled, his crimson face blanching to a sickly white. One of the acolytes gasped quietly, the others stared comically between him and the healer.

'What did you say?' Gerath whispered.

'Lusur seems quite keen for the medicine to get back to Ma, to make sure this infection doesn't spread.'

Gerath's tongue flicked out to lick dry lips. 'Lusur?'

206

'I met him. It's where I've been,' he paused, guilty despite the situation. 'I was just looking for you.'

Gerath was silent, his expression unreadable. Was it confusion, awe, respect, or worse? Fear? His eyes watered, lids flickering. His arms dropped from their threatening heights, and he gently placed the vial on a table.

'Who?' Dem looked between them, oblivious.

'There's someone else down here,' he stammered breathlessly, thoughts suddenly jumbled and confused. 'A man called Lusur. Called himself an examiner or something. His room's full of corpses.'

'Corpses?' she gasped.

'Not the worst of it, there's a whole other ward down here! They've got people strapped to their beds, wailing and moaning as they force their potions on them. I swear it, Dem,' he grabbed her shoulders. 'I knew there was something wrong!'

She glanced between him and Gerath, her face similarly changing through a range of emotions; fear, disgust, confusion, before setting her jaw into a grimace of determination.

'Corpses?' she demanded, glaring at the healer and his acolytes.

Ash glanced to the door. If they made a dash for it now, he could barge Gerath out the way, grab the vial, and be out the door. He just needed to communicate it with Dem. Once they were back to the upper floors, he could tell the other healers about what was going on down here on the hidden ward, verify what Lusur said, and be away. Winds! They needed to get out of here and make it home before the unthinkable happened to Ma.

'That's right, corpses aplenty through there,' Gerath waved his hand at the corridor. He wasn't even attempting to deny it. 'For our examiner to do what the role suggests. Examine the bodies and determine cause of death. A pathologist. Heard of that, child? Hmm? Ever come across that big word in your extensive medical studies?'

'Yes I have,' sniffed Dem. 'And the ward of restrained patients?'

'For their own good,' Gerath sneered. 'The infirmary's intensive ward.'

'Intensive ward?' Ash frowned.

'For the sickest patients. Even to the untrained eye, you must have recognised their condition was beyond anyone upstairs, no? When the fools up above fail, they bring them down to old Gerath for his special touch. When I fail, they go to the examiner.'

A tension he'd been carrying suddenly released. An intensive ward for the critically unwell. That's why they were down here in the dark. Not to be cruel or torture them, but because despite the efforts of Anten, Semon, and Awis, they'd deteriorated to the point where desperate measures were required, desperate enough for Gerath. It's why he was so dismissive of them as the healers of stubbed toes and sniffles. Suddenly, everything made sense. A weight lifted from his shoulders. A belt released from around his chest. He stood tall and breathed easily. An explanation for everything.

Gerath saw the change and snorted. 'Oh, now he realises what a fool he's been, sneaking around and playing investigator. You're damned lucky Lusur didn't punish you for disturbing him.'

Lucky was an understatement. Something about him was wrong, something twisted and backwards. Now he was out of his company, he knew he never wanted to share it again. There was something wholly unnatural about the pale healer, something unsettling. The cold touch of fear caressed his nape once again.

'Why would he?'

'You think I'm a cantankerous old git? Nothing compared to him. He must be in a rare mood to show you around his quarters.'

'Why's he down here in the dark?'

Gerath rolled his eyes and sat down on the stool, suddenly looking thin and worn. 'People don't like having corpses around them, do they? Better to hide them away. Besides, it's better down here for practical reasons. Back door is next to the mortuary so we can ship off the bodies to the undertakers in Holevale.'

Dem nodded slowly. 'And the ward? Why keep sick patients in a cold cellar? It can't be good for them.'

'Not just sick, child, the sickest. Better to have the mortuary next to the intensive ward and emergency operating theatres. Easy access to the examiner's services, if and when they're needed.'

'So sick and weak that they need binding?'

Gerath grimaced, the tired face replaced by his familiar shade of beetroot. 'Yes, if I deem it necessary for the safety of my staff! Delirium sets in quite quickly with these patients and I won't have anyone injured for the sake of a few restraints.'

Ash stared at his feet, unwilling to meet anyone's eyes. Embarrassment and guilt mixed with fear and unease. Gerath's explanations made perfect sense, of course, but were they an inconvenient truth for him to swallow, or a carefully-constructed fallacy to evoke the very embarrassment he felt? Was he under- or over-reacting to it all? He felt Dem's glares in his burning ears and cheeks. Of course she believed Gerath, but she didn't see what he saw, she didn't endure Lusur's company. He glanced again at the vial on the table. That's what they were here for, after all. Not for liberating patients or exposing the secrets of a twisted pathologist. For Ma. To stop her turning into one of the bloated, tuberculated, grotesque–

No!

He couldn't let those thoughts linger. She'd be fine. Help was already on its way. They had time.

Looking up at Gerath, he bowed his head in respectful humility. Best to play the admonished child and get out of here safely than make a scene. He'd discuss it with Nari later. Dem was already rattling away her hundredth apology, suitably grovelling to appease Gerath's overinflated ego. He should probably join her to make it convincing.

All the while, the hairs on his nape stood stiff as a rabbit before a drawn bow, the memory of drifting in infinite emptiness still weighing heavily on his mind, the abyss penetrated only by Lusur's indigo stare.

Chapter 14

Nari watched the children scuffle and snap at each other in the entrance hall, as feral as wild dogs over a bone. They had no sense of urgency, no regard for the sands of time trickling away in the hourglass of his brother's life. He sighed, ignoring the nagging voice at the back of his head, the one keeping track of days since Kirkin's ultimatum.

'I *told* you!' Dem seethed, face a healthy shade of purple. Healthy for a grape, at least.

'I know what I saw. There's more going on down there.'

'We nearly *lost* the cure, Ash! All because you were trying to prove some wild accusation against Gerath.'

'It's not a wild accusation,' he turned, flushing to resemble a glass of fine calefin wine.

Dem folded her arms and curled her lip. Winds! If she looked at him like that he'd have a hard time keeping his fists away.

'A mortuary and an intensive ward. Hardly the stuff of criminals.'

'There's more to it than that! There's something wrong with this place, and Gerath and his cronies are at the heart of it.'

'Well look here, why don't we ask someone who knows the place.'

Awis approached, a soft smile on his face as he descended the steps to them. A trail of assistants followed after their mother duck, sometimes falling behind by a few steps, skipping and shuffling to catch up again. Of all the healers, he supposed he was the kindest. It was Awis who managed his head injury and prescribed the necessary salves to soothe his various wounds after his beating. He nodded to him as he approached. If all healers were like him, he might have more respect for them. A pity they weren't. He glanced at Dem, smirking triumphantly, there wasn't much hope for the future generation, either.

'Perhaps I will,' Ash spat back at her.

'Are you children all set?' Awis asked, beaming down on them. A few acolytes tripped over each other as they came to a sudden stop. Nari turned away to hide his grin.

'Yes, Healer Awis, all set to go,' Dem produced the vial of medicine.

Awis's smile faltered for a moment. 'Yes. One of Healer Gerath's tinctures,' he turned to his retinue. 'Nobody ask me what it's made of or what it's for. I'd rather not be embarrassed in front of our visitors.'

The ducklings tittered politely. He caught Nari's eye and smirked. He shook his head with a smile. Here was a man who knew what he was and how to use the power of the moment, even if that power meant telling poor jokes and basking in the strained laughter of grovelling juniors.

'Well, safe travels back to your village. If you need anything, you know where to find us.'

'Actually, Healer Awis,' Ash raised his hand as the group turned to leave. 'I wondered if I could ask something?'

'By all means,' Awis smiled patiently.

'Downstairs, in Healer Gerath's... place. I saw a few things I wanted to ask you about.'

Awis glanced at him again. Nari shrugged. He had no idea what happened in the cellar beyond the overheard snide remarks between the two children. The healer nodded invitingly to Ash.

'I can do my best, as I said, anything Healer Gerath does is more often than not beyond my simple mind.'

More polite chuckles.

'Two things. I saw a ward downstairs where patients were getting treated, well, differently to upstairs.'

'The intensive ward,' Awis nodded.

'Oh,' Ash deflated as quickly as Dem puffed up in triumph.

Awis nodded sympathetically. 'It can be difficult to see, but it's necessary. They require very intensive courses of treatment, more often than not the body can't tolerate such a challenge. It takes a strong character like Healer Gerath's to weather it. Why do you think I stay up here?'

'So it's all normal down there? The restraints, the forced medications and all of that?'

211

'Sometimes, the treatment seems crueller than the disease,' Awis sighed. 'But it's all done with the best intentions,' he turned to his paddling of ducks. 'At some point, you'll all spend a rotation with Healer Gerath and his acolytes. Try to learn as much as you can before he chases you away. The record stands at three days.'

'And the bodies?' Ash blurted out.

Nari raised his eyebrows. Interesting development.

'Bodies?' Awis frowned.

'Tables of them,' Ash grew bolder, glaring at his sister, 'dissected and cut up to different degrees—'

'Oh, the mortuary,' Awis nodded.

'Oh,' the boy deflated again as his sister sniggered behind her hand. Poor lad.

'I'm sorry if Healer Gerath showed you that, it's not appropriate.'

'So you knew about it? About Lusur and what he's up to down there?'

'Of course. I can't say I'm on first-name terms with all of Healer Gerath's acolytes, but the reports they send out are all sound.'

'No, Lusur is the one in charge of it. Gerath said he was the examiner, the pathologist.'

Awis shrugged with a disinterested grimace. 'Makes sense for him to allocate tasks to some of his staff, he has a lot on his plate. I'm sure he oversees everything his juniors do, don't worry.'

'No, honestly I think Lusur is in charge.'

Awis chuckled and walked away, entourage waddling in tow. 'I've never met a person who can control Healer Gerath, I promise you. Now, next we have our musculoskeletal ward. Tell me, Megyn, if an elderly patient presents with a shortened and internally rotated leg following a fall...'

They watched him leave, Ash scowling, Dem beaming. He tapped his foot expectantly. What next? A few more minutes of pointless bickering before they sulked out the door? What a sad existence he lived that his and his brother's lives lay in the hands of these immature idiots.

As they descended into their inevitable petty squabbling, he stared out the open door, tuning out their insipid voices into a meaningless drone. Still plenty of daylight left to the hot summer afternoon to get going. Would they make it in time? It was a push. It was already a week and a half since…

No. Don't go down that path. There was time. At least there would be if these two cretins could put their petty quarrels behind them and move.

'Are you two done?' he snapped. 'Do you think we could *possibly* get going at some point today?'

'I don't know,' Dem looked him up and down like a lump of mud. 'Depends on whether *he*'s happy to admit he behaved like an arse and risked Ma's health for no reason beyond his own prejudice.'

'I *know* there's something going on. Awis doesn't even know Lusur exists.'

'A scary ghoul in a basement,' she stuck her lower lip out in an exaggerated pout. 'Someone's been having nightmares? Scared little Ashil?'

'Piss off. I know what I saw!'

'Both of you shut up or I'll *drag* you out,' he snarled, turning on them.

They stepped back simultaneously, eyeing him warily. He turned away. Not the way to do it. By all means, he could scare them out the infirmary, but once they were in the forest, that damned goblin was waiting and who knows what she'd do if she saw him threatening them.

'Sorry. Can we just leave? I'm sure your mother would appreciate your hasty return.'

They shouldered their packs and filed out in front of him. Dem glared up at him as she passed.

'Don't pretend this is for Ma's sake. You just want your payment sooner.'

'Absolutely right. A greedy bastard to the end. Now, if you wouldn't mind?'

She snorted and rolled her eyes.

Judgemental bitch. She knew exactly why he needed the money. Perhaps she'd forgotten how little time he had. She probably just didn't care.

They waved half-hearted farewells to the few staff members who paid them any heed and left the infirmary. As they reached the gate, his neck prickled with the sensation of being watched. Turning back, he examined the various closed doors and dark windows, but there was nothing to be seen. Just a feeling. His gaze caught on a child watching them from one of the outhouse porches. She stared back for a moment before waving timidly. He smiled. Presumably the offspring of one of the groundskeepers. As he raised his hand in return, the child's mother rushed out and shepherded her back inside, throwing him a suspicious look before closing the door. Shaking his head, he followed after Dem and Ash. Funny, for a place with so many stick dolls, she was the first child he'd seen, even in Holevale. He couldn't blame the mother for protecting her offspring, not in a world where rogues and bandits would seize the opportunity to ransom an infant for a handful of coppers. He'd seen Kirkin do far worse for far less, after all.

Ffed caught up with them at a crossroads, greeting the children with her incomprehensible nips and titters, like a reunited pup. He hung back, watching with folded arms. She seemed unusually pleased to see them. Was her stint in the forest really so unbearable? Surely she should have felt at home in the mud and rotting leaves, just like the rest of her kind.

Dem revealed the vial of medicine to her. 'Look! This is what'll make Ma better.'

Ffed nodded. 'Good. Now walk home,' her eyes flicked to the infirmary. 'Away from here'

'Couldn't agree more,' Nari nodded, waving the children on.

Dem set her jaw and looked him up and down. 'Yes, we're going. Which way?'

'The fastest route is via the Halfmount Hills and old iron mine, then a steady path northeast to Muddylan and Starforge,' Nari pointed to the northern road leading to the hills. 'If we keep a steady pace, we should make it in a few days, even going through the woods.'

214

'A few days?' she raised an eyebrow.

'Only if we get going. I'm not the one with a sick mother.'

Ffed made a sound between a tut and a hiss, but he did his best to ignore her. Better to at least pretend to be unafraid than lose face entirely. Despite her disapproval, she didn't make any other moves and ushered them along, shooting him a dark look as she passed. Winds! The sooner he was rid of their company, the better.

*

'A shadow?'

'Yes,' Ffed nodded.

'I don't know,' Ash shook his head. 'It was dark, but Lusur was real, just a guy.'

'Bad feeling?'

'Awful,' he nodded. 'But I think I fainted or something. I don't know. It felt wrong, somehow, like something was unnatural about the whole place.'

'Unnatural, yes. Something pulling you in?'

'The opposite. Like there was something in there stopping me from getting close, something telling me to stay away, I can't explain it.'

Dem rolled her eyes at their hushed conversation. Two superstitious fools feeding into each other's fantasies. The afternoon was warm, the sky a rich blue, the white sun illuminating the emerald forest. If they were home, she'd be on the Clearbed River with H and Elain, paddling in the shallows, having a picnic of sweet tarts and strawberry cordial. A few more days and the dream would become reality. Just a few more days.

'Perhaps a sense of moral decency?' she suggested, sarcastically. 'A bit of guilt, snooping around where we shouldn't?'

'There was something off about it,' Ash insisted. 'Even Ffed says so.'

'I don't think so. You're both just making something out of nothing,' she shook her head.

'We're *not*,' he snapped, hands clenched. 'You listened when Ffed said we had a follower, you were happy to sneak into Gerath's

215

quarters to see what was going on. How come you've changed your mind all of a sudden?'

'Because there were explanations for both!' she laughed.

'Oh yeah? What?'

'The follower was the little pale rogue dead in the swamp. Even Nari said as much,' she nodded to him, who shrugged impassively. Typical of him not to take her side against his best friend Ash, even when it meant using his own argument. She rolled her eyes. 'The infirmary has already been explained adequately enough. An intensive ward and a pathologist, nothing more.'

'Oh yeah? What about the things we saw? The unnatural things we felt?'

'You had a faint and hallucinated something while your brain was all a blur,' she pointed at him, then turned her finger to Ffed. 'You were exhausted after an impressive sprint through the woods and saw something out of nothing in the moonlight of a shadowy alcove. That's all there is to it.'

'I know there's more to it,' he muttered under his breath like the stubborn mule he was.

'You *want* there to be more to it,' she laughed again.

'Why would I want that?'

'For one, because after everything he's done to us you still don't like Healer Gerath, and secondly, to justify jeopardising Ma's medicine with your sneaking and snooping. Just accept it.'

'Not sure, Dem,' Ffed chimed in. 'Ash right. Something bad in infirmary. Follower not dead.'

'Is it still following us?' asked Nari, tiredly. 'I'd be more inclined to believe it if someone else saw it.'

Ffed narrowed her eyes at him. 'No, left after shadow sent away.'

'Well isn't that a shame.'

'Not a shame,' she yipped back. 'Good thing. Keep away.'

'The point is,' Dem cut across, 'you're both worrying about things that don't matter anymore. The infirmary is behind us and the apparent follower is gone. Let's just make our way and forget it.'

'Stop!'

216

Nari's hiss made her jump.

'Down!'

She dropped at his command. Ash and Ffed did the same, but where she and her brother remained rooted to the spot, eyes wide and hearts thumping, Ffed shuffled to the rogue on all fours.

'What?'

'Someone there,' Nari nodded ahead.

Ffed nodded. 'I go. You stay.'

He didn't protest, and the goblin wriggled away into the undergrowth. Dem lay as she was, her chin resting in mud, a root digging into her flank. She didn't dare move in case a poorly-placed boot set the entire canopy rustling to betray their location. Her mind raced with possibilities. Ffed's follower, less gone than they'd hoped? More rogues, come to rob them? Turning her head, she glanced at her brother. He lay face down, eyes screwed shut like a vice, breathing prayers to the winds. His ambush at Pit's hands was still affecting him, but there was nothing she could do at the moment except hope he didn't do anything stupid.

The minutes stretched on. Nari slunk back to crouch over them, sword drawn. The sight of it made her sick. They really were in danger.

'Who is it?' she whispered.

He ignored her, staring suspiciously into the woods.

'Nari?'

'Quiet,' he shushed. 'We're too open here. I'm going to need you both to crawl over there, to that chestnut's roots. Got it? Keep to the south side, looks like there's a bit of a ditch you can hide in.'

She nodded wordlessly and crawled on her belly. Her pack dragged uncomfortably, threatening to drag her back at every point. She could hear Nari encouraging Ash behind her, his increasingly urgent tone suggested he wasn't having much luck, but she ignored it for now. Once she was where she was meant to be she could turn around and help, but not until then.

A dirty puddle greeted her at the bottom of the ditch. Taking care not to make a splash, she slipped in, disrupting a cloud of midges into the hot and humid air. The chestnut tree's partially-exposed roots formed a natural cage in which she huddled, watching Nari's vain attempts to move Ash's petrified form as the flies buzzed around her.

A rustle in the trees behind them made him turn and Dem gasp, but it was only Ffed. She batted Nari's sword away and crouched next to him, whispering away. She couldn't hear them, but there was no point crawling back after only just getting here. Ffed placed an encouraging hand on Ash's shoulder and whispered into his ear as Nari kept his vigil. Initially, he resisted, trembling in fear even at her touch, but he eventually calmed. With Ffed's encouraging whispers, he made the agonising crawl over to her, even managing to control his long limbs well enough to avoid setting the whole forest alive.

As he slid next to her, face as pale as snow, she gave him an encouraging smile. He looked ill in response. Ffed and Nari joined them seconds later.

'Okay,' Nari breathed. 'We're going to have to turn back very slowly and quietly and back-track a bit.'

'Who's ahead?' she asked.

'Pit's cronies,' Nari sniffed.

Her heart skipped at the name. Ash whimpered softly. So she was right, after all. Nari's old foe was back to torture them again. Damn him. If only he or Ffed had killed them all in the swamp.

'How many?' she whispered.

'Saw three,' Ffed yipped. 'Not Pit, just Reger and two more.'

'Not Pit?' she repeated, brightening. Maybe they'd had a falling out over something. Brutish rogues like them were surely always arguing over the spoils of their black deeds.

'He'll be somewhere around,' Nari shook his head, shutting down her hopes. 'They're all spread out, guarding the way.'

'Guarding it?'

'From us,' he nodded, confirming her suspicions. 'I should've seen it coming. They knew we were in the infirmary, they knew we'd be making our way back to Starforge. This is the best way back, no wonder they're waiting for us.'

'Can we just sneak around them? Go through the heart of the woods? We're in them already,' she suggested.

Nari shook his head, as she knew he would. 'It gets far too thick away from the roads. Where we are now is in cover, but we're still following the path and Pit's thugs are watching the way. If we went through the heart of the woods, Ffed and I would probably make it, but you'd struggle and Ash wouldn't have a chance. It would slow us down too much, take well over a week, maybe more.'

'Well what in the four winds are we supposed to do, then?' she hissed, panic setting in, wiping the sweat from her brow before the buzzing midges could land.

Nari sighed heavily. 'We turn back, head back to the crossroads, and take the road west. It might be clear.'

'How long will that take?'

'A couple of days longer than planned,' he glanced around, tight lipped and tense, his face pink from the heat. 'Past Redgate Ruins, over to Clovercream and up.'

'And if Pit has men stationed there as well?'

He shrugged. 'Then we have to chance the wild woods.'

She clenched her fists, her heart hammering, sweat dripping. If Pit found them, he'd kill them, and Ma would die. If they went directly through the deep woods, Ma might die from the delay. If they went all the way around, Ma might still die from the delay, but it was only a few days. A bit of a no-brainer, really.

'And you can't just... I don't know. Kill them?'

She felt embarrassed as soon as she said it. Nari and Ffed shared a rare look of understanding and regarded her with the same disapproval.

'Too risky,' the goblin muttered.

'All it would take is one slip,' Nari shook his head. 'When there are other options available, it's not worth it.'

'Fine. I don't need your judgement, I was just asking. So we're turning back.'

'Quietly. There may be more about we haven't yet seen.'

She nodded and brought her legs under her in a crouch. Nari and Ffed did the same. Ash twisted around on all fours, hands and knees in the muddy puddle, nostrils flaring and jaw muscles bulging, a sheen of sweat on his face and neck. Winds! He looked on the verge

219

of screaming. She put her hand on his shoulder, but he shrugged it away angrily.

'Are you ready?' she asked as kindly as she could.

Breathing heavily, he nodded and swallowed. 'Nari. Can I have the bow?'

Nari's frown deepened. 'The bow?'

'The bow. The thing you shoot arrows with? Know it?'

'I do,' he touched the weapon on his shoulder, currently unstrung and wrapped in protective cloth.

'Well? Can I have it?'

Nari looked him up and down for a second. He caught Dem's eye. She shook her head. Absolutely not the time to indulge his boyish fantasies. Giving him a weapon in his skittish state was inviting disaster. Who knew what he might attempt in his panic? Nari seemed to understand and gave her a small nod.

'I don't think it's the best idea right now. We'll be going as quickly as possible at a crouch. You'll need both hands to help keep your balance.'

'I need it,' Ash snapped, hot as a kettle.

'I don't think so. Let me hold on to it for now. If they spot us, I'll pass it over.'

Ash paused for a few seconds. 'Make sure you do.'

'Deep breaths,' Ffed muttered to him. 'Keep bent low. I go first, find good way through. You right behind me.'

Ash nodded, snorting like a horse, shoulders moving like a dog about to vomit. Dem glanced at Nari again. He raised his eyebrows again. If they were spotted, handing Ash an unstrung bow was as futile a gesture as nailing a fallen flower back to its stalk. It might seem helpful at the start, but it was certainly going to die. Nari knew it. She knew it. Even Ash probably knew it, but perhaps it would give him some comfort.

Ffed glanced over her shoulder at them, meeting their eyes in turn for a few second each.

'All ready? Stay low. Go!'

*

Four days later, Dem fell into a water-trough. She couldn't care less if it was usually reserved for horses, or if the stable-hands laughed openly, or if the children across the road stared open-mouthed as their parents ushered them away. All that mattered was the water. Cool, refreshing, lapping pleasantly at her sunburnt and scratched ears, taking away the burning heat in her face and neck. A loose bit of straw floated up to tickle her nose, batted away by a lazy sweep of the hand. The repulsive mixture of equine hair, saliva, and other waste mixed with her new bath-water wasn't an issue. This was exactly what she needed. This was bliss.

Someone tapped her back, prompting her to surface with a splash. She squirmed as water cascaded down her aching back, mixing with the stale sweat and muck coating her skin.

'Well's over there,' Ash pointed over her shoulder.

'Winds! Let's go.'

She skipped across the road to the blessed water-source. A splash behind her confirmed Ash's mimicry of her makeshift bath. Clovercream townsfolk parted ways before her as she stumbled to the well, seizing the heavy-bottomed bucket and hurling it into the depths. She turned the winch, but it was so heavy! Heavier than she'd expected. Probably in need of some oiling as well, truth be told. It gave a sudden lurch and twisted out of her grip. Ffed stood on the other side, turning it for her. She leaned against the cold stone wall, watching the darkness for the laden bucket's blessed return. She seized it as soon as it appeared, almost tipping herself over the edge to plunge headfirst into the abyss, but Ash's hand on her collar saved her. Bucket in hand, she drank a deep draught directly from it, ignoring the rough wood on her lips, relishing the spillage over her front. Ash snatched it from her within a few seconds, again copying her actions. Winds! This was good water. Sweet, crisp, and cold. There was a little brook from the Crisiaddwr River under there for sure.

Four days of trudging through the stifling heat of the summer forest, enduring the humming midges and biting horseflies, rationing their water as best they could while maintaining their breakneck pace took its toll. More than ever before, they must look like beggars. Not that she cared.

Belly full, she passed the bucket to Ffed, who made a point of taking a funnel and refilling her empty water-skin instead of drinking directly from the bucket. Nari, red-faced and sullen as she and Ash, did the same.

She stared at the rogue as he filled his water-skin, maintaining a composure she'd long-since abandoned. Although Ffed led their party, Nari set the pace. He drove them like a slaver for three punishing days. He settled on the fourth. She didn't know why, or particularly cared, as long as they weren't driven quite as hard. Perhaps he knew they'd reach Clovercream that day. Perhaps he was finally as hot, sweaty, and tired as they were. She'd tried rebelling against him on the second day, tried going at her own pace instead of his, but his constant cruel reminders of Ma's condition spurned them on, his snarls and furious gaze as efficient as a whip. For once, Ffed didn't come to their aid. She shared her dwindling water and guided them as gently as ever, but wouldn't admonish Nari for his tone or unpleasant comments. Perhaps she was too worried for Ma, but they'd be home soon. Another three or four days, that was all.

'Are we staying or are we going?' she panted, throwing the bucket back for another draw.

'Up to you,' Nari shrugged, looking around disinterestedly.

She narrowed her eyes. What was this newfound nonchalance? Perhaps Ffed mentioned something to him without her realising, after all.

'I wouldn't mind a bit of a rest. We can keep going in a few hours?' she suggested, tugging at the stiff winch.

'Whatever you prefer,' he ignored her struggles with the winch. He really didn't give a damn, but why? She shook her head and kept heaving at the cumbersome mechanisms of the well. He was happy enough to order them around and be a bully when they were in the wilderness, but as soon as they were in sight of civilisation his tone miraculously changed to this impassive helper. Ffed leaned over and turned the winch for her again, moving as easily as a knife through butter. She curled her lip at Nari. If he really wanted to put up this façade of helpfulness and compassion, lending a hand to working the well would have gone a long way, but there he was instead, studying the crowd. Following his gaze, she spotted a guard on the town watchtower facing them. So that was it, after all! Just a bully when the opportunity arose, now scared into timidity at the prospect of soldiers witnessing his transgressions.

'Thank you, Ffed,' she said, pointedly, taking the funnel and filling her dry water-skin. 'If we can just rest for a few hours then set off in the evening? Maybe we can buy some food?'

Nari didn't reply, just kept staring away into the crowd, the majority of them losing interest in the scruffy travellers crowded around the well.

'We can get some cheeses?' suggested Ash. 'Stock up on some for home as well?'

She nodded. Surprisingly good idea for him. Clovercream, as the name suggested, was locally-renowned for its dairy produce. Situated as they were on the fringes of Dailas, they had acres of lush grasslands at their doorsteps for their cattle to pasture between the forest and Long Lake. According to the residents, it was the best in the whole northern forest.

'We'll do that, have a rest and some food, then head out.'

'Yes,' Ffed nodded enthusiastically. 'Cheese.'

She smiled, despite her exhaustion. Thinking about stocking up for home made the trip feel more ordinary, as if they were just visiting. It made it easier to forget everything they'd been through on the way.

'We'll have a look at a few of the cheesemongers,' Ash nodded knowingly. 'Different ones stock different types. We probably shouldn't go for anything too soft or it'll spoil on the way back, especially in this heat. Stick to the harder stuff.'

'Eat soft ones now?' Ffed asked.

'Yeah I suppose,' Ash grinned. 'I wouldn't mind some with bread and tomatoes.'

'We'll eat it on the edge of the forest,' Dem declared. 'We can have a look at the final stretch.'

'Why don't we spend the night?' Ash suggested. 'I don't know about you but I'm pretty spent. We can get up early and get started?'

She fingered the medicine vial in her pocket. 'Hmm... why don't we just see how we feel after some food and rest? We can decide then.'

Ash nodded and shrugged. What was that look he gave her? Disappointment and regret. Was he really that tired he was willing to risk another night's delay? They certainly needed rest, but after so many nights sleeping on nothing but a bed of turf and fallen leaves, she hardly missed feather beds anymore, their short stint at the infirmary was just a bonus. Clearly, Ash still wasn't used to it. The whole journey had taken a far greater toll on him than her, he just wasn't as strong as her. Despite all his faults, Nari was a good judge of ability, her brother would never have made it through the wild woods, he just wasn't cut out for it.

'Alright, we'll have a look for food and reconvene later?' Ash and Ffed nodded. Nari continued to ignore her. 'Hello? Nariton? Is that okay?'

He jumped at his name, shooting her a glare that would curdle milk. 'Yeah, fine.'

How rude. 'Or not,' she gave him her best look of disapproval. 'It's not like we need you anymore. We're quite capable of making our way back without you.'

'Sure, why not?' Nari sighed.

It was true. His services were now obsolete. All they needed to do was follow the edge of the forest north until they came to the Clearbed, then follow it upriver to home. She only tolerated his company out of politeness.

'But your payment?' Ash asked. 'You need to come with us for your brother?'

Nari smiled thinly and raised his brows. She waited for him to say something, but that was the extent of his response. Shrugging, she pushed Ash and Ffed away down the high street.

'If you want your payment, find us later before we set off. You know the route we'll be taking,' she paused and looked over her shoulder. 'We *all* know it.'

Whether or not her comment landed, she couldn't tell, he was staring into the crowd, his mind elsewhere. Let him ponder and

224

ruminate over whatever was on his mind, she didn't care. The sooner he was out of their lives, the better.

Ffed ran up to the first cheesemonger they saw, going from one end of the window to the other, pressing her face up against the glass like a child. They joined her with giggles, staring at the range on offer. White cheeses, yellow cheeses, some with rinds, some without, soft and hard, some speckled with herbs and nuts, some interspersed with eyes, some laced with lines of mould. It was but one of many scattered around the town. The cheesemakers themselves had their lodgings over the leagues of grasslands and rolling foothills across which they'd be skirting on the way home.

They went from shop to shop, buying flatbreads and preserves from one, a few small wheels from another, a large wedge from a third. Ffed remained outside, nose pressed against the window as she pointed to the ones she wanted while she and her brother handed over the coins. Within an hour, they had an ample selection of provisions for an evening meal, the journey back, and to restock home's larder. As they passed a final cheesemonger, Ash stopped and pointed.

'Looks like they sell soft cheeses, you want some, Ffed?'

The goblin nodded enthusiastically, already on her way to the window.

As with all the other shops, the smell hit her as soon as she crossed the premises into the dingy, low-ceilinged interior. Sour and pungent with a heavy underlying creaminess. Strips of tacky paper hung from the rafters, speckled with hundreds of flies, but not enough to completely eliminate the pests from hovering around the precious produce. That produce, wheels of the soft white cheese, lay on the counter, some still within their pale rind, some cut and bulging free, half-melted in the summer heat.

She glanced at the window. Ffed's squashed features stared intently, pointing at one with a herby crust of rosemary and bay. She nodded to the shopkeeper, standing with folded arms and a deep frown at Ffed at the window.

'Friend of yours?' she asked disapprovingly.

'She's been helping us. We're from Starforge.'

'Oh!' her features brightened suddenly. 'Lovely to have visitors to our town!'

Unlike Muddylan, there was no danger in people knowing where they were from here. Clovercream was affluent enough in its own right for its inhabitants to pose no threat to them on account of the regional reputation of its luxury products. Trade between here and home was always good. They weren't quite at the same level as Starforge, of course, but close enough to know their class and offer the appropriate respect.

'We're on our way back home and thought we'd grab some of your amazing cheeses. We've had quite the journey.'

'So it seems, young lady! So what can I get you?'

She pointed to the one Ffed wanted. 'Enough for three people, please.'

'Three, eh?' she eyed Ffed again. 'You be careful with her lot, don't matter how much she might've helped.'

'We will, don't worry,' she smiled politely.

Ash wandered in from outside and pointed to a string of cured sausages hanging behind the counter.

'Shall we have some of them as well? I like them.'

'Straight from Holevale, these, where I'm originally from, that's why I stock them.' the shopkeeper smiled warmly. 'Lovely bit of work. Pork with button mushrooms, hazelnuts, and a healthy load of thyme and black pepper. Gorgeous! You won't get it anywhere else in Clovercream. I got a special arrangement with one of the folks over there, a little business exchange I set up when I moved here a few years back. You'll find the saltiness pairs very well with the cheese your sister's picked.'

She flinched involuntarily. 'How did you know we were siblings?'

The shopkeeper laughed, the rolls of excess skin around her neck and waist bouncing under her loose-fitting dress. 'Young lady, your noses are identical. Not twins, are you?'

'Winds! No!' Ash pulled a face. 'Can you imagine?'

'Brother and sister is quite enough,' Dem agreed.

'No, I suppose your noses are about where the similarities end, eh? One sausage enough for you?'

'Two please,' Ash held up the corresponding number of fingers.

She cut them from the string. 'Two! Big appetite for a beanpole such as yourself. Not like your sister, she's more my shape. I bet you can just shovel it away without gaining a bit of weight, not like us two, eh?' she winked at her in assumed solidarity.

Dem maintained her composure. Plump she may be, but she was certainly *not* a round and flabby mass like this woman. Besides, anyone would look fat next to an emaciated gangly freak like Ash.

'One's for home,' Ash grinned smugly at her unwitting insult.

'Oh! Aren't you good. Here you go. With the cheese as well that'll be... two silvers and a half.'

'I got the last one,' Ash slung his pack off his shoulder. 'You can get this one?'

She rolled her eyes. The last one was only one silver, the one before that she'd paid another two silvers for, and the one before that was only cost him one and a half. Oh, he knew exactly what he was doing, the cheap little git.

'Oh my!' the shopkeeper gasped suddenly, making them jump, her hands shooting to her mouth dramatically. She glanced at Ash, but he was as perplexed as she, pausing from packing the cheese and sausages away. A quick look at the window confirmed Ffed hadn't moved, either. The shopkeeper stared at Ash, face pale, hands slowly moving from her mouth to rest on her chest, eyes already welling with tears.

'Alright?' Ash asked, suitably perplexed.

'You poor thing! Forgive me, you just look so young.'

He looked at her, she shrugged. She had no idea what she was going on about. 'What?'

The shopkeeper grimaced sadly and pointed to his pack, her other hand still over her heart.

'My pack?' he asked, flatly.

'My dear, the doll. I understand if you don't want to talk about it. You just didn't look old enough to be a father.'

'I'm not a father,' Ash frowned, retrieving the stick doll poking out his side-pocket.

'A sibling, then? A little one?'

He glanced at her again. 'Elain?'

She gasped again and shook her head sorrowfully, adopting a sympathetic tone. 'Such a pretty name, I'm sorry. Bless your poor parents, but at least you two are still here, thank the four winds.'

Dem shared another look with Ash. Was this some sort of strangely-veiled threat, or was it just the random ramblings of an old woman? 'I mean no disrespect, but we have no idea what you're talking about. Our little sister is alive and well at home.'

The shopkeeper looked at them dumbly. 'But, the doll?'

'The doll?' Dem asked. 'What about it?'

'I've not seen one for years, not since I moved here. I just assumed you were given it the same way... I'm sorry. Where did you get it?'

She looked at her brother again. Was there something special about the dolls? Something symbolic? Had her idiot brother outdone himself with his little project by unwittingly producing something bad? Ash shrugged, expression mimicking her own befuddlement.

'I just made it for someone,' he said, quietly.

'You *made* it, child? What would possess you to make something like that?' her tone changed, suddenly accusatory, almost angry.

He looked at her again for support. 'I just made it for someone at home. I saw a load of them around the place in Yewbar, Holevale, and the infirmary we'd been to and figured I'd get one for our friend,' he blurted out, in the same way as he would if being told off at home. 'I wanted to buy one but couldn't find anyone selling it so I just made it myself.'

'These, these... *things*,' she pointed at the doll. 'They're not toys, child. They're not bought and sold. They're... memories.'

'Memories?'

'For lost children.'

A chill ran down her back, despite the heat, a shadow fell over the doorway. Ffed stood at the opening, looking in.

'All okay?' the yipped. 'Long time.'

'Fine, Ffed, just wait outside for a second?' she waved her away. The last thing they needed was for the shopkeeper to kick off about a goblin coming on to her premises, especially in her agitated state, but she didn't even notice, her attention fixed on the bundle of twigs in Ash's hand.

'Lost in what way?' Ash swallowed.

'Taken by black hands in the night, to be sure,' her voice quivered. 'It was at its worst a few years back. Dozens of little ones went missing, their parents left with nothing but those dolls. It's why I left for here. The place just wasn't the same without their little voices.'

Dem looked at the doll in her brother's hand. She was right. Looking back, there were hardly any children in Holevale, not nearly enough for the number of people. She recalled the half-empty school, the barren yard and their sullen faces suddenly more sinister, the presence of the guards at its gates suddenly more poignant.

'Why?' she asked. 'Who was taking them?'

'Nobody knows who exactly,' she wiped her eyes. 'But we know what and why sure enough.'

'Why?' she repeated.

The shopkeeper took a breath, grimacing at the doll in Ash's hands. 'Kolgatha,' she whispered.

Her heart skipped, the chill spread over her body, plunging her into icy water, the shadows of the room seemed darker, the droning of the flies akin to those covering a corpse. The drinker in Holevale said the same. She stared at the little figurine. Suddenly, the crude shape lost its innocence. It was no longer a bundle of sticks, it was a bad omen. A thing of evil. Even Bib the pig-driver had one. He'd lost a child as well, he said so himself. No, not lost, had a child taken from him. What strange machinations were at play in the forest to the east? What evils lay in wait? Now more than ever, she was glad the final stage of the journey lay before them.

'A kolgatha?' Ash whispered, staring at the doll in his hands.

'You know them, yet you still carry it?' she shook her head.

229

'Only in passing. We didn't know they had anything to do with this,' he brandished the doll, making her flinch. 'We didn't know they went about snatching children!'

'Perhaps they take them too, yes. Who knows how many are out there? Who knows how many more for all the children they stole?'

'What do you mean? Did a kolgatha take them or not?'

The shopkeeper shuddered. 'Either they or their dark master, whoever it is.'

'Kolgatha,' Ffed growled from the doorway. This time the shopkeeper took notice, jumping at the sight of her and grabbing a slim-bladed knife from her cheese-counter to brandish like the world's most pathetic sword.

'Stay out!' she squealed.

'It's alright!' Dem stood between her and the doorway. 'Ffed's helped us all the way. She's practically a resident of Starforge.'

'She's seen one,' Ash announced, suddenly.

The shopkeeper gasped loudly, dropping the knife with a clatter. 'No! By the grace of the four winds, no!'

'Yes,' Ash pressed on. 'She thinks one was following us in the woods. Tell her, Ffed!'

'That's enough, Ash,' she raised her finger in warning. Working up this poor woman with tall tales wasn't the way to go. Someone had to maintain a level head about them. She turned to the door. 'Ffed, just wait for us outside, please? We don't know what she saw, it's just speculation.'

The shopkeeper had already turned north and was whispering prayers under her breath, hands held aloft in supplication to the winds. She remained as she was for a few minutes before finally settling down. She turned to them with a sickly look about her.

'Please put it away,' she nodded weakly to the doll. 'I didn't think I'd ever see one of them again. If the goblin's seen one after you... I think you'd better leave.'

'But, I still don't understand,' she protested. 'Why do they take the children?'

'Do you know what a kolgatha is?' she came around the counter to shepherd them away.

230

'Vaguely. Servants for evil daemons. They look like children, right?'

'My child, they *were* children,' she paused by the door, massaging the bridge of her nose with trembling fingers. 'When a magus, daemon or not, wants a slave for their magicks, they take a child from its parents and leave such a doll in exchange so everyone knows not to come looking. The child is drugged and locked in a box with no opening except a funnel to their mouths. Through that funnel, it's fed nothing but blood and evil potions for weeks, all the while being worked on by the magus's dark spells and rituals. Can you imagine? The poor things trapped in the darkness of that stifling, suffocating box, force-fed all manner of evil things, lying in their accumulated filth, barely enough room to wriggle. Once the rituals and rites are complete, the magus cracks open the box and spills out its contents. If it survived, it's no longer a child but an evil shadow of one. A kolgatha,' she sighed, half-closing the door. 'Most don't survive. They say for every one made, a hundred other little ones must perish. Winds! I shouldn't be telling you this. Talking about them brings bad luck, but I've had my life. You need to know what you're carrying, what you made, then you might be able to avoid it in future. I know it isn't a real one, but it represents the same. Evil. I'm sorry.'

'Wait, we still haven't paid!'

The door slammed in her face.

*

Nari ducked into the alley to his right. Empty pails lined one side, boxes the other. He wrinkled his nose at the smell. Clovercream had never been his favourite place to visit for that very reason; too much of a putrid stink hanging about the place, clinging to every pebble on the ground and every tile on the roofs. Revolting.

His follower appeared at the alley entrance a few seconds later. There was nowhere to escape to from here, the other end was walled off and piled with refuse. If it came to violence, he'd be a cornered rat. Fortunately for him, his follower was one of the reasonable ones. Far more reasonable than some.

'Nari.'

'Damid,' he nodded back.

'Decent place for a chat,' the satorr nodded to their surroundings. 'Nice and quiet.'

'That's what I thought, if you don't mind the smell.'

Damid wrinkled his nose and shrugged, 'You get used to it very quickly. Doesn't taste bad, either. I've got some with me if you'd like?'

'I'd rather just get this over with,' he sat on one of the boxes and gestured the satorr to another beside him. He took it, stretching out his long legs and cloven feet. Damid fished out a roll from the bag over his shoulder and offered it to him. He declined.

'You sure?' Damid waved it under his nose. 'It's good. Sausage and soft cheese, bit of tomato, bit of lettuce. Tasty.'

He gestured to his broken incisors. 'Nippers aren't suited for crusty bread anymore.'

'So it seems. I can take the crust off for you?'

'I'm fine.'

'Suit yourself,' he settled back against the wall, taking a bite.

Damid was once a scout in the king's army. As a satorr, he wasn't as agile or guileful as the king's grey dreyads, but he was a damned sight quicker. It's why he didn't bother running as soon as he spotted him by the well. Better to just lead him somewhere quiet and have a conversation. After a respectable ten years of service, he'd retired and set out on a number of failed enterprises that eventually saw him tied up with Pahag and Kirkin. Now, just like him, he was trying to buy his way out. So many of them had the same story. If only there were a way for them to reconcile and band together without fear of betrayal, but it would never happen. There was too much fear clouding everybody's judgement for such a revolution.

'I know I'm late,' he stated, bluntly. Better to just be out with it.

'You are.'

'Is Nat still alive?'

Damid kept chewing. 'To my knowledge, yes.'

He exhaled forcefully. Perhaps Kirkin would give him another chance?

'I wouldn't be so relieved,' the satorr swallowed his mouthful and took another bite. 'Death would be kinder than what Kirkin's planning. Word's out that if you don't turn up, Nat gets sold to Cadaran.'

His gut clenched. Kirkin had threatened them with as much in the past, but he never thought he'd do it. Clearly, he was wrong. If Nat went there, he'd suffer things nobody ever should. He didn't have the mettle to survive that place. It didn't bear thinking about.

'And if I do turn up?' he croaked.

'You go instead.'

Winds! Him or his brother. What kind of choice was that? When it came down to it, no choice at all. He couldn't live with himself and abandon his brother to such horrors.

'Is there any other way?'

Damid sighed and shook his head.

'Please, if I just have another five days I can get paid for what I'm doing and I'll have all the money Kirkin needs,' he blabbered, panic seizing his chest. 'I might be able to get more on top of it!'

'Nari, Nari. It's too late for that. You know it is. There's no bargaining here. I don't know why Kirkin gave you the additional fortnight in the first place.'

'If I can speak to him myself...'

Damid kept shaking his head and tore another chunk from the sandwich, stuffing a loose sausage into his mouth before it fell. 'Try it if you want to, but you know what'll happen. You've been careless. You knew what was coming.'

'I'm *this* close to getting a payout,' he pinched his fingers together. 'This close! It'll be more than enough to cover the debts. Kirkin's no fool. He knows late money is better than no money.'

'You're right, he's no fool,' the satorr mumbled between mouthfuls. 'He knows what'll happen if people hear they can dodge their debts without being punished. He can't look soft, not in this game.'

'Winds damn him! So what now? You're going to drag me back?'

Damid frowned and curled his lip in distaste. 'Nothing of the sort. After he got a message from Pit saying you'd been spotted around Trottmire, Kirkin sent a bunch of us out to all the villages, from Pickpat to Oakrin, in case you turned up. He'll be in the Redgate Ruins with your brother three days from today. If you turn up in time, you take his place in Cadaran.'

'And what happens to Nat? The debts weren't just my own.'

Damid popped the final piece into his mouth and licked his fingers. 'Nat will die, Nari. He either dies slowly and painfully in Cadaran, or he dies in three days and you take his place in the shackles. That's how it goes.'

'How it goes, eh?' he hawked and spat, blood thundering in his ears. 'You make it sound so simple.'

The satorr shrugged. 'It is simple, really. There's one rule; pay your debts. He doesn't care how you get the money, all he cares about are the numbers in his ledger. You failed, now you pay the consequences.'

'And you think that's a fair way to live? It could easily be you next time. Perhaps then you'd have more sympathy.'

Damid sighed and nodded. 'You're right, next time it could be me. But this time it isn't.'

He scratched his beard, watching the satorr. A decent person, by all accounts, always polite and pleasant to talk to, never overly judgmental, he just spoke truths and practicalities. Perhaps he was the best person to deliver this news.

'Why does he care so much?' he shook his head. 'A man in every village in the region, all just for me? I don't even owe him *that* much, if you think about it relatively.'

Damid's lips twitched in a half-smile. 'Not that much? Sure about that?'

He winced. Alright, he owed him a lot. He didn't know how he'd accumulated such debts. But that was a lie, of course, money like that was hard to come by but so easy to flush away. A few days of high living with his brother every few months kept them firmly in Kirkin's pocket, and no amount of drink, drugs, food, or whores could ever compensate for the weeks of struggle, of living in the dirt and mud, dreaming about the next indulgent binge. It was never worth it. Like so many things, the anticipation was always more than the realisation. The hope for a better time always hyperbolic to the truth. But for all their transgressions, they didn't deserve this.

'Fine, it's a tidy sum,' he admitted. 'But there's plenty others who owed far more than we did.'

'What can I say?' Damid stood and strolled to the alley's opening. 'Perhaps he just doesn't like you.'

'That might be the sum of it,' he whispered under his breath, then looked up at the satorr. 'So that's it? Nothing else?'

'Message delivered, isn't it?' Damid called over his shoulder. 'It's up to you what to do with it,' he stopped and turned at the opening. 'Why didn't you just run? When they took Nat you had the opportunity to leave and never return. You could be in the Jagged Isles by now.'

'Would it have made a difference?'

'He might have just killed him. When Pit found you, Kirkin knew you were still in the area to exploit. He only made the decision to sell him to Cadaran after finding out you were still around.'

His stomach tightened again, clamping down harder than a steed with the bit in its teeth. 'You saying it's my fault?' he hissed.

'Of course it's your fault,' Damid shrugged. 'You know that. I'm just asking why you stayed. Sure, you got close to paying him, but you must've known it wouldn't happen. You owed too much. Because you stayed, Nat faces a worse fate to punish you. If you were a thousand miles away over the seas, he wouldn't need to do it, would he? Either way, Nat dies. The way he dies is your choice.'

'Thanks.'

'So why did you stay?'

'Piss off, Damid. You delivered your bloody message.'

No reply. He glanced back to the alley opening, but it was empty. He sighed, holding his head in his hands. Why did he stay? A fool's choice to do so. Kirkin knew his ultimatum was nigh impossible. When he initially stole Dem and Ash's fine possessions, he truly believed they might be enough to cover his debts. In fact, they probably were, but Kirkin just wanted him dead anyway. He'd caused too much trouble, was too much of a liability, and it was time to cut the rot away.

So why stay in the first place? If he stayed now, it meant two deaths. If he ran, only Nat died... but slowly and painfully at the hands of Cadaran's slavedrivers. They could keep a bag of bones working for months more than they had any right to live with nothing but hate and barbed whips. If he'd run from the start, nobody would've suffered it. Now one of them inevitably would. It couldn't be Nat.

As he rose to leave, his sword smacked lightly on his knee. That was why he stayed, because deep down, he thought he could fight his way out of this. So, Kirkin waited for him back at Redgate Ruins. He'd meet them there, face his foes, and try to cut his way through them to his brother. He wasn't much of a swordsman but by the four winds, he'd swing it hard enough to make something count. With a bit of luck, they'd both die fighting.

*

Ash sat with his back to the slope, enjoying the sun on his eyelids. His belly was full of cheese, sausage, and elderberry cordial, sitting with a comfortable heaviness in his gut. Taking a lazy swig from the bottle, he belched and grinned at Ffed, sipping her warm milk and nibbling on the bread.

'Winds! That stinks!' Dem slapped his shoulder.

'Sorry,' he smirked.

'You can't just sit here and be nice, can you?' she huffed. 'You've got to be disgusting.'

'What can I say? It's a talent.'

She huffed and tutted, but turned away. At least they weren't arguing. Something about the view made arguing impossible. Rolling meadows of impossibly-green grass over rumbling hills as far as the eye could see, stretching away to the glittering line of Long Lake in the distance, visible even from here. The waves of the green tide rose and fell, the blades caressed with a warm west wind into a hundred swirling shapes as they swayed and wove in the breeze. Scattered around were the black smudges of grazing cattle enjoying Enadir's gifts, while swifts swooped and glided over the land, their pointed wingtips a fraction of an inch from the ground, their graceful acrobatics admired by jealous grouse and partridges squawking and chirping to one another in the brush.

He closed his eyes. Peace.

Ma's bloated, tuberous face flashed in his head, her ravaged skin blistering and oozing black pus, her neck contorted and twisted at right angles, stretched out on Lusur's dissecting table, her abdominal cavity opened up and pillaged of its organs.

Stifling a yelp, he sat bolt upright.

'Alright?' Ffed frowned, cheese-laden cracker halfway to her mouth.

'Fine,' he lied, wiping the cold sweat from his brows. 'Just a thorn in my arm.'

'Well here comes the thorn in our side,' Dem grumbled, nodding to their left.

Turning, he clambered to his feet and beckoned Nari over with a shout. The rogue didn't smile. He'd been in a mood since yesterday, Enadir only knew why. Perhaps he and Dem had another private argument while he slept. It seemed the most plausible explanation. Patting the ground next to them, he offered the spoils of their shopping trip.

'We've got loads of cheeses,' he pointed them out. 'Good bread, Ffed's got some crackers there, this is a cured sausage from Holevale, you've got to try it,' he cut a chunk from the significantly-diminished sausage and handed it over. 'Ffed doesn't eat it so we have plenty left. She might not share the soft cheese though.'

'Good on crackers,' the goblin mumbled round her mouthful.

'I can't stay,' Nari announced, remaining on his feet.

They stopped what they were doing and looked at him. Dem's face brightened with an ill-concealed grin. Ffed's remained impassive. He felt his own fall. What was he talking about?

'You want us to get going now?' he suggested.

'No. You do what you want. I have things of my own that need sorting.'

'Fair enough,' Dem nodded. 'Bye.'

He glared at her. After everything they'd been through together? Well, he wouldn't be so ungrateful.

237

'What's happened?'

Nari sighed. 'No point hiding it. I've run out of time. I hoped we'd make it back but Pit's damned blockade of the Halfmount Hills made it impossible. Now time's up and I need to settle my debts.'

He shook his head. It didn't make sense. 'But you can't settle your debts. We haven't paid you yet. Here,' he fished in his pockets for the last remaining coins from Yewbar. A meagre sum, the rest wasted on their provisions. 'Damn. All I have left are a few coppers. How about you, Dem?'

'Same,' she stretched and yawned. 'Guess we won't be able to pay you if you're leaving now. Pity.'

Nari nodded, ignoring her smug comments. 'I wanted to say goodbye. I hope your mother recovers with that medicine. Just follow the treeline north to the–'

'Clearbed River, yes we know the way home,' Dem smiled emptily and waved him away. 'Alright, hopefully we won't see you again.'

Ash stared at her. Was this really how she wanted to mark their departure, with sarcasm and disdain? After everything Nari had done. Granted, their first encounter had a rocky start, but since then he'd proved himself trustworthy and honest.

'Where are you going?' he asked.

'I'll be heading over to Redgate Ruins to settle the score,' he smiled thinly.

'Why not just come with us, get your money, then head back there?' he asked. 'Surely a few more days won't make that much of a difference?'

Nari shook his head. 'I've got three days to get there. Can't be late for this, I'm afraid.'

'Nope, too long to go both ways,' Dem nodded enthusiastically. 'Best start making your way, really.'

Glancing at her from the corner of his eye, Nari chewed his cheek for a second, then flashed another thin smile. What a way to end things, as enemies until the very last word. Say one thing about Dem; she could hold a grudge.

'Well I'm glad you know the way back because I have a favour to ask in lieu of my payment,' Nari turned to Ffed. 'I wondered if you'd come with me? I could use your help.'

Ash raised his brows and looked between the goblin and the rogue. What was going on? He tried catching either of their eyes, but they kept their gazes on one another, some unspoken communication between the two. Dem did the same, her previous faux smile replaced with a grimace, as if she'd eaten the rotten grape of the bunch.

'Ffed stay,' she finally yipped. 'Protect children.'

Nari's shoulders slumped. 'I could really use your help.'

Ffed nodded sympathetically. 'Bad men.'

'That's right.'

She spread her hands. 'Bad men in forest. Children go home.'

He nodded again and forced a smile. 'I understand. Thank you for considering it, anyway.'

She nodded solemnly and took another cracker. Dem's smug grin returned and she took an arrogant swig of cordial. Something in her face turned his stomach. A good man asked for help and here she sat, relishing in his rejection? Bile burned his throat as he fought the urge to condemn her. She glanced at him, her smug grin fading to a scowl, her eyes widening under her glowering frown. She knew what was in his head before he did, cutting the idea apart before he could voice it and make it real. His throat settled, his clenched hands relaxed, and he sat back on his haunches in defeat.

'Well, if that's all, I think you should leave,' Dem took one of Ffed's crackers and spread it liberally with cheese.

'Seems so,' Nari wiped his hands on his front and turned to him, putting his hand on his shoulder. 'Alright Ash, it's been a pleasure getting to know you. Take care of each other and your mother. Oh, and before I forget' he stopped and grinned, 'stick to crafting. Being a woodsman isn't for everyone.'

Putting his hand over Nari's, he gave it a squeeze. 'Thanks for everything. Try visiting us sometime if you can?'

Nari smiled softly and gave his shoulder a final squeeze before pulling away. With one last nod to Ffed, he turned and trudged away.

'Winds! I thought he'd never leave. Like a bad smell,' Dem lay back and popped the cracker whole into her mouth, crunching away contentedly.

'Did you have to be like that?' he snapped.

Dem stopped chewing and looked at him, fury and contempt taking equal control of her features. 'Like what?'

'You know. He's been good to us.'

'Good to us?' she laughed falsely, nostrils flared and mouth curled in disgust. 'He robbed us blind and left us for dead. Never forget that. Scum of Enadir, that's all he is, how many times do we need to go have the same tired conversation?'

'He saved us over and over again,' he retorted, ignoring the warning in her tone. 'He's done more than enough to redeem himself.'

'If you actually think someone like him deserves redemption, then you're as pathetic as he is.'

'Whether or not he deserves it, his actions speak for themselves.'

'They do. Drugging and robbing two children and leaving them for dead in the forest. *That's* what he did. He's a robber and a rogue. Sure, he can speak with honeyed words behind his syrupy smile, but I know what he is. So would you if you opened your eyes and paid attention for once, instead of following him around and hanging on to his every word. All these weeks and I've bitten my tongue about it, but you've pushed me now, you've asked for it. It's been quite sad, Ashil, quite sad to watch you scamper after him. You think he doesn't know that? He's got you wrapped around his little finger. If only you could see yourself. And look what he's turning you into; someone who goes snooping around places he shouldn't and risking Ma's health for it. What were you trying to prove? That you could be just as brave as a cowardly thief? Honestly, it makes me sick. I know *exactly* what's going through your head right now, I know *exactly* how much you want to go after him and keep playing a big man, as if we all didn't see you near enough piss your pants when Pit had you.'

'He's just asking for help, like he's helped us,' he muttered.

'Open your eyes. He's using you, playing with your guilt, grooming you to follow in his footsteps. He doesn't care about you. You might think he does, I know you want him to, but he doesn't.'

He played with a daisy between his feet. 'I care.'

Wrong thing to say. He could practically feel the rage pulsing out of her in hot waves. Ffed yipped something at them to calm them down, but he didn't hear her. All he could hear was Dem's anger. All he could see was the hatred in her sneer.

'Well if you care that much, go after him. If you care *that much*, just go ahead and piss off. You've done literally nothing useful this whole journey. We're better off without you. Ma's better off without you. You clearly care more about some random bastard than your own family.'

She shook her head, disgust and contempt in the curl of her lip. He sat in silence. What could he say in response to such a tirade? What good would it do to respond? She'd worked herself up into a hysteria, anything he said to contradict her accusations would be ignored. Nevertheless, he had to try.

'He needs our help.'

Her face changed. The sneer disappeared and the frown slackened. Her eyes glazed over. She looked at him but stopped seeing him.

'Go then. But if you do, you're no longer my brother.'

She turned away. He stared at her back, waiting for her to turn around and say something else. She didn't move. Ffed was saying something but he couldn't distinguish the words from the whirring in his head. Her wiry hands clasped around his wrist, pulling him back down. When did he stand? Dem was still turned away.

'Most of the provisions for home are in my pack,' he heard himself mumble, voice muffled and heavy in his ears, echoing through a hundred layers of wool. 'I'll take yours.'

No response. Just the blank wall at the back of her head. He took her pack, lighter than his. She didn't move. Ffed said something else, but it was lost in white noise. He uncurled her gnarled fingers from his wrist and pushed past the goblin. His ears strained for the slightest stir from Dem's direction, anything to suggest she might have turned to look at him, risen to stop him, but no. She was a statue. Ffed pulled sharply on his arm, making him stumble. He pulled back, wrenching his arm free. At any other time, he might have been surprised at his own strength, but now was not the time to marvel at personal achievements.

Each step he took, guilt pulled him back with a grip stronger than Ffed's, but an equal guilt pushed him forward again. It should have left him motionless, but a creeping visceral fear added to the force spurring him on, and his feet moved accordingly.

He was at a crossroads. Ma was down one road, Nari the other. Family against a friend. Both in need. Dem accused him of caring more for Nari than Ma, but it wasn't true. Ma had help coming to her, she had the healers there already while Dem and Ffed were on the way with the medicine. Nari had no-one. Nari was leaving to settle his debts with the dangerous criminals and thugs patrolling the woods, and he went empty-handed. He went to certain death. In a way, Nari leaving them was probably his way of protecting them so they wouldn't be entangled in the same mess by association like back in Trottmire. He was doing what he could to save them, they should do what they could in return. With a shaking breath, he kept moving forward. He'd done everything he could to save Ma, there was nothing else for him to do. Nothing except be there for her. Kneel at her bedside, wipe the sweat from her brow and the vomit from her chin, hold her hand and brush her hair. He paused. It might be his last chance to see her. To see her bloated, twisted, bruised body, to see the tubercules ravage her skin and eyes, to mop up the blood from her mouth, to prise apart her spasmic fingers and hold them with the gentleness she held him as a child. His last chance to see what memories he had of her twisted into new ones of a corpse destined for the dissecting table.

He couldn't do it. Not today or tomorrow. Dem could curse him all she liked, but she hadn't seen what he'd seen. Besides, Nari needed their help, and at least he had a chance of being saved.

*

Dem kept her eyes on the plains. It really was beautiful. Flocks of swifts flitted in never-ending spirals and swoops, herding unseen clouds of insects between them and snapping them out the air, working together, consciously or not, to keep their bellies full.

Ffed slumped next to her in silence.

He was gone, then.

She didn't turn around. What was the point? She knew what was there. The distant figure of her brother scampering after a criminal, abandoning their family.

Blinking furiously to disperse the tears as they formed, she steeled herself and stood. Good riddance. People like him were poison, and poison needed eliminating. Let him die in a hole with the rest of them. Ma didn't need him. She didn't need him.

With a nod to Ffed, she picked up Ash's abandoned pack. Heavier than expected! Home's supplies weighed it down, from the wheels of cheese to the bottles of cordial. She shifted it to her shoulders, nearly overbalancing as she did so. Well, if Ash could do it, she certainly would as well.

'Come on, no point staying around here.'

She took a few hesitant steps, flailing her arms slightly with the slope. The weight suddenly left her shoulders as Ffed took the pack.

'I take.'

'I can do it,' she tried moving away but Ffed held firm.

'Yes. I still take.'

She relinquished and took Ffed's. It was much lighter, with barely anything at all within.

'Alright, thank you,' she paused. 'Did he say anything?'

Ffed shook her head sadly.

Sniffing, she smiled grimly. It was better this way. A clean cut with no more parting words. She'd played her part and that was it, everything that needed saying was said. His actions spoke louder than any response he could have come up with.

'Alright. Just you and me. Ready to go?'

Ffed nodded. 'I come.'

Chapter 15

Nari smiled reassuringly. He was a good lad, offering his help. Companionship like this was rare, to turn away from his own mother to help a friend... he shook his head. Touching. He hadn't realised how much of an impression he'd made on the boy. No doubt, his sister's reaction would have been worlds apart from his own, but that was neither here nor there. It was a beautiful gesture, exactly what he needed before setting out to Redgate.

It was also a tad inconvenient.

Now, instead of just looking out for himself, he had the boy to contend with. When he swallowed his pride and asked the goblin for help, it wasn't his intention to acquire a tag-along in the form of the boy. Had he wanted his help, he would've asked for it.

'It'll be dangerous,' he repeated for the fifth time.

'I know.'

'I can't promise you won't get hurt.'

'Hence the danger.'

'I mean it, Ash. These are bad men I'm going to. It'll end in violence.'

'Again, I know. It's why you can't go alone.'

'We both know how things went in the swamp. I won't be able to protect you like I did last time. I'll have my brother to watch as well.'

'I'm here to help,' Ash set his jaw resolutely. 'I'm not letting you go on your own. You obviously need help otherwise you wouldn't have asked. I'm here,' he laughed. 'You don't have to feel guilty about it, I promise.'

He grimaced, at least the boy thought his trepidation was born of guilt rather than regret. Perhaps he could play on his guilt as well?

'What about your mother?'

Ash shrugged and kicked a stick. 'Dem and Ffed will get the medicine to her, Semon and Joli are probably there already. What good would I be? I can't do anything to help.'

'You don't need to do anything, you can just be there for her.'

'I don't think Dem would want me there now,' he snorted.

'Doesn't matter,' he paused. 'This might be your last chance to see her, lad.'

Ash sighed and sniffed. Perhaps this was it! He placed a reassuring hand on the boy's shoulder and gave it a squeeze. If piling on the guilt about his dying mother wasn't enough, he was stuck with him. Praise the four winds for a mother's love!

'That's what I'm afraid of,' he mumbled.

He deflated. That was a bad sign. 'What do you mean? Don't you want to be there with her at the end? She'd want to see you one last time.'

'Except she wouldn't see me,' he shook his head. 'I saw a dissection of a patient with the tubercle sickness at the infirmary,' he shuddered. 'It was awful. His eyes were like a bunch of grapes. If Ma's like that... I don't want to see it. She wouldn't know I was there anyway. Apparently it gets into your brain as well, did you know that? Drives you mad.'

'It might not be like that,' he attempted another reassuring smile.

'But it might. It probably is. The medicine might not work, either, Lusur said so. I can't do it,' he sniffed and wiped his eyes, then smiled up at him. 'Besides, my friend needed my help. You saved our lives in the swamp, it's only right I try to repay the favour.'

He looked him up and down. Hopeless. He was sticking to him like a limpet, it seemed. Nothing to do but try to make the most of it.

'Alright, lad. Thank you.'

Ash beamed through red eyes. It meant something to him as well. Perhaps another pair of eyes and hands would help, after all.

'We have three days to get back to Redgate,' he nodded along the path back to Clovercream. 'Plenty of time. I suggest we get there a bit earlier to scout the place out and set up a few tricks and traps, if we can. We're bound to be at a numbers disadvantage so we may as well utilise the terrain to compensate.'

'What's the plan?' Ash asked in breathless excitement, his mood brightening suddenly. 'How many are there?'

'I don't know,' he admitted. 'It's difficult to make a plan without knowing exactly what we're up against. I imagine it'll be along the lines of a group of angry rogues, Kirkin among them, with my brother tied up and gagged.'

'So we're going to break him free,' Ash nodded with a grin.

'We'll try.'

'Death or freedom,' the boy shoved him playfully.

'If we're lucky.'

He glanced at his wrists. Death or freedom. Either would be a good outcome. Either would be better than having these wrists encased in Cadaran's irons.

*

Two days later, they watched the ruins from the cover of the trees, the low-hanging branch of an alder providing their shelter from unsavoury eyes.

Not that there were any. The crumbling walls and towers of old Redgate castle were as lifeless as they'd been since the Cataclysmic War. Centuries of pilfering and recycling of the stones left it a perilous site of half-collapsed towers and walls, overgrown with a myriad of mosses, shrubberies, and grasses. Although nobody had set up a permanent residence in the wind-swept stones since its long-dead giant masters fell, it provided a temporary shelter for countless thousands of travellers as they passed through over the centuries, utilising the sprawling network of cellars and dungeons to hide from the elements. While the surface structures were subject to the erosions of time, wind, and water, the foundations remained strong. It would take another hundred lifetimes for these stones to finally be destroyed. In the meantime, folk would come and go as needed, giving silent thanks to their long-dead rulers for the gifts they left behind.

It didn't seem like there were any here today, but one could never be sure. The deep alcoves and arrow loops held dark shadows within the pink sandstone structures, and who could tell how many evil eyes peered from the cellar windows?

Shifting his weight, he pulled the branch lower to expose the runway over the dried half-moat. A bare path led up to the ruined gatehouse that gave the old castle its name. Easy and open, which made it dangerous. Any half-decent archer would pick them off before they were halfway across. He released the pressure and turned back to the walls. Still no movement.

'Well?'

'Not yet,' he kept his eyes on the ruins.

'I've not seen anything apart from a few house martins,' Ash muttered. 'I feel like they'd kick up more of a fuss if someone was among them.'

'Maybe,' he nodded, 'but these birds are probably used to visitors. I wouldn't rely on them to reveal anyone.'

Ash grunted in response and went back to watching the walls. He soon grew bored, however, and started preening the untidy fletching on Jod's arrows. It took discipline and patience to sit and watch like this, qualities the boy lacked. Not him. How many weeks of his life had he spent watching a road or a house, waiting for the perfect mark, the perfect time to strike? More than he was proud of, but it all counted for something.

He waited for another hour. It was only once he'd seen one of the aforementioned martins pass within a few feet of every wall in sight that he relaxed. As used to visitors as they may be, they were still unlikely to fly within grabbing-distance of one. They could just be deeper within the structures themselves, of course, but his caution was satisfied for the time being.

'Alright, keep low. Keep an arrow in your bow-hand in case you need to draw it quickly.'

'I still need practice.'

He shook his head. 'Don't worry about shooting it, the threat of a drawn bow is usually enough to make someone pause,' he pointed to a cleft in the outer wall where flocks of martins perched on either side. 'We'll go in through that crack in the walls, alright? It'll get steep on either side of the moat so be careful not to lose your footing.'

'Alright. Keep low,' Ash repeated, nodding enthusiastically.

'Good lad. Come on.'

They scampered out the trees. He half expected the thud of an arrow in his gut with every step. Their boots pounded the ground, sending up small clouds of dust from the arid summer earth. He kept his eyes on the cleft. If an arrow came, let it strike him without him knowing. Some fools spoke about facing your death, meeting it head-on. Not him. Let it take him unexpectedly, if possible, let him die with hope in his breast.

It didn't come.

Rough sandstone scraped his palms as he vaulted over a fallen block of battlements and into the cool shadows. Pinkgate would be more appropriate. Perhaps once it was a richer crimson than this pale pastel, but no more. When the final stone fell, centuries from today, all colour will undoubtedly be drained from its desaturated pores. Well, by the end of tomorrow's meeting at least a few specks of crimson death might add a bit of life to the stones.

Ash clambered in after him, as clumsy and ungainly as the day they'd met. First his bow caught between the cleft walls and his legs, then one of his straps on a jagged spur, then the quiver upended against the wall. Clattering arrows echoed from the shadows, the cacophony received and multiplied by the startled flock of martins taking flight from the ruined roof above.

'Sorry,' Ash mumbled, stooping to collect his arrows and losing his pack over his head in the process.

'Just sit still and be quiet for a moment.'

If anyone were here, any hope of secrecy was gone with those birds. He stood still, listening for approaching footsteps between breaks in the winds howling and groaning amid the ruins. Nobody came. Damned lucky. He released his held breath and stooped to gather Ash's arrows, pointing the final one at him.

'Any slips like that around Kirkin's lot and they'll eat us alive, got it?'

'Sorry,' Ash repeated, taking the arrow timidly.

'I know you're here to help but please, *try* to be careful.'

'I know.'

'Alright,' he nodded and forced a smile. 'At least we know we're first here, eh?'

Ash nodded, a sheepish grin replacing his guilty sulk. 'So what now?'

He paused, taking stock of the empty room with its ruined walls and collapsed roof. Rescuing Nat would never be as simple as springing a surprise attack and sweeping him up from their clutches. Among other things, they'd need a defensible position to give Nat time to break free from his bonds prior to escape. This was far from ideal, nothing but an old storeroom within the castle walls, with far too many openings to make a worthwhile fall-back should things turn sour.

'We'll have a look around, get familiar with the ruins. Once we have a better idea we can set up a few surprises and plan an escape route.'

'Sounds good,' the boy paused and looked at him. 'You've done this before? Rescue missions and that?'

'Never. I'm normally the one breaking into somewhere or robbing someone,' he paused and shrugged. 'I guess it's not so different, though?'

Redgate ruins' walls were built for the moderate defence of a giant lord of similar importance. Only one of its four high walls retained its original imposing height, while the other three were reduced to variable states of collapse, the eastern wall being the worst at little more than three feet tall. Granted, what it lost in stone, the east wall had more than made up for in vegetation, with an impenetrable tangle of brambles forming a new, natural wall that was probably a more formidable barrier than the other three. All four walls were hollow, with narrow corridors between the internal and external faces ascending to pressing stairs leading up to the various arrow loops and battlemented parapets. At each corner were circular towers, all collapsed, two of them so full of rubble you could walk up the mountain of fallen rock and mortar straight up to the third floor, the stairwell to the fourth long-since collapsed, leaving the upper levels for the martins. The northeast tower was still fully intact apart from a section of wall on its second floor that left it open to the elements. Otherwise, you were free to climb the stairs from the turreted, bat-faeces riddled attic all the way down to the sprawling cellars. Its opposite southwest tower was similarly open, only its missing upper three floors provided a more modest view of the surrounding lands. The gatehouse and its associated southern wall were in a steady state of half-decay, the namesake doors long-rotted and abandoned, leaving only rusted and twisted hinges after some scavenger's unsuccessful attempts at removal. At the opposite side, abutting the intact northern wall was the keep. Once upon a time, it must have been a grand old building. No more. Large sections of stone were collapsed both inwards and outwards into the courtyard, exposing the internal designs of the old stronghold, from privy-rooms to bedchambers. There was even the remnants of a marble bathing-room on the lower floor, missing several of the heavy, polished slabs from its cold floor. Scattered among it all were the creeping vines, hedges, and mosses of Dailas Forest's attempts at claiming the castle for its own, including a carpet of delicate wildflowers taking root among the sandstone blocks and rubble of the open courtyard.

He wandered and circled them all four times over, embedding a mental map of the place into his brain. By the end, he knew where the stones were slick underfoot, where the footing was uneven, where the corridors twisted suddenly or dropped away. He knew where the ceiling dropped deceptively low and where the masonry holding the walls together was little more than dust between precarious granite blocks, balancing on millimetre-thick fragments. He knew how far along each wall were the gaping holes large enough to slip through, and what kind of landing to expect on the opposite side. Most importantly, he knew the best route out was the same way they'd come in, provided they could slip through the cleft without Ash blocking the way.

Regrouping, they sat and shared some of the boy's provisions.

'Happy?'

'As much as I can be,' he grunted.

'You have a plan for tomorrow, then?'

'Vaguely. As I said, it'll depend on what we face. Now, look here,' he sketched a rough map of the castle in the dirt. 'After food, we'll put tripwires here and here, and pile up some rocks around here. Not enough time for any pits and stakes and all that nonsense. After that, you and me are going to sit here and talk through the layout.'

'Talk it through?'

'That's right. Again and again until you can recite the layout like the names of your siblings. This storeroom is our number one exit.'

'Is there a number two?'

'Main gate. It's open as anything, but if we get cut off from here, at least the main entrance is easy to reach and run through. We just have to hope they don't have any decent archers.'

Ash nodded, lifting a trembling handful of cheese and sausage to his mouth.

'It's normal to be nervous. I'm scared shitless, to be frank.'

Ash grinned, face sickly pale. 'I'm more excited than nervous. I think.'

He clapped his shoulder. 'We won't stay up too late. We'll need to be on the lookout for when they arrive.'

*

Another bright morning greeted him, head throbbing from his paltry few hours of stolen sleep. Sunlight danced between the petals of the courtyard's wildflower garden, illuminating the haze of mist coiling around their stalks from the evaporating morning dew, forming and iridescent blanket of blue, pink, and purple over a shimmering golden cloud. Any other day, he might have marvelled at its beauty. Not today. He wished the sun never rose and yesterday lasted a lifetime. He breathed deeply, steadying his trembling hands and racing heart. Despite doing everything he could to avoid it, the day for confrontation with Kirkin was here.

Ash slept peacefully next to him. No point waking the boy yet, at least one of them should get a proper sleep.

He left their storeroom and wandered the now-familiar route to the northeast tower, ascending the twisting stairs to the attic. Ignoring the nattering and squealing cloud of bats above his head, he wandered from window to window, searching the woods for any sign of approach. He couldn't see much. Long ago, the land would have been carefully cultivated to maximise visibility from these towers, but no more. The wild Dailas Forest grew too close to the castle walls, its canopy too thick to see the forest floor expect for a few sparse clearings, and even then the low sun cast too deep a shadow to see anything properly. It didn't stop him from trying. Even if it gave him but half a second's warning, he'd rather know. Before long, the bats settled in their rafters, the sun crept higher, and dawn stretched to mid-

251

morning. The boy would be waking soon. With a final glance at the sea of foliage, a thousand shades of green and brown mixed into an ever-changing palate, he descended.

Their plan was for Ash to take a position in the keep with his bow while he waited in the courtyard and did the talking. There'd be very little negotiation, of course, the terms were already agreed on in the act of turning up. He just needed an opening, a half-chance to escape with Nat.

He reached the second floor and nearly stumbled. The crumbled wall provided a complete view of the courtyard and gatehouse. Between the twisted iron hinges stood a familiar, unwelcome face. Pit. By the grace of the four winds, he hadn't seen him, his eyes instead scanning the parapet walls as more rogues walked up behind him. Heart in mouth, he ducked low and descended all the way down to the cellar, where a short series of twists and turns took him back to the narrow passage within the west wall. Skipping over a tripwire, he jumped through the narrow opening into their storeroom.

Predictably, Ash was still asleep. He covered his mouth with his hand and woke him as gently as his shaking hands could. No time to think about what was happening, they'd done all their thinking last night. Now was the time to act. It didn't stop his body reacting, though. He could practically taste the adrenaline in his mouth, the sour stench of his own nervous sweat filling his nostrils.

Ash woke wide-eyed and confused, but settled within a few seconds.

'They're here, lad. Up and about.'

Ideally, they'd spend a bit more time watching them, identifying and getting to know their foes, but there was no time. If they didn't move quickly, they might not be able to choose the circumstances of their meeting. To his credit, he worked quickly, pulling on his boots and tying the quiver to his belt in seconds. Bow in hand, he followed like a faithful hound as he led him back to the cellars and up again to the keep.

'You know where you're going?' he asked.

'Second floor,' Ash nodded, breathlessly. 'Old bedroom, keep hidden until you give the signal.'

'Which is?'

'Open palm to your temple.'

He nodded and clapped him on the shoulder. It needed to be an obvious signal. Anything too subtle risked being missed, especially in someone as inexperienced as him. They parted ways, Ash scrambling upstairs while he left at ground level, picking his way through the dusty ground floor bathroom, his boots clacking and scraping against the fragmented marble, and out through the ruined wall into the courtyard.

They didn't see him at first. Four of them. Pit, Reger, a woman called Lia, and a big problem. Nembe, the grey dreyad. Kirkin must be particularly annoyed if he brought him. Like Damid, Nembe was once one of King Stolach's scouts, however where Damid retired after completing his years of service, Nembe was expelled from the grey dreyad company on account of his... misadventures. The fact he wasn't executed for his crimes was solely thanks to his race and the king's reluctance to garner any hostility from the other grey dreyads in his elite scouting company. Exactly what those crimes were was a source of infinite gossip and rumour within Kirkin's gangs, he'd heard accounts ranging from mass murder to extreme torture of civilians to arson. Whatever the initial crime was, he'd certainly committed each rumoured offence at least once under Kirkin's leadership as his cruellest enforcer. It was people like the dreyad who put the fear of Enadir's wrath into every rogue operating under Kirkin's name.

Well, he was here. No point running from it now.

'Looking for me?' he called out, leaning against a section of ruined wall.

Four pairs of eyes snapped to him, four glares and scowls. Eight hands twitched to their weapons.

'You turned up!' Pit grinned.

'I was sent a lovely invitation, couldn't possibly say no.'

Pit sneered. 'Who found you?'

'Damid.'

'Bah!' Reger wheezed and spat. 'Should've gutted you.'

'But then Kirkin would miss this reunion,' he shrugged with a nonchalance he wished he felt. 'Where is he, anyway? I wouldn't mind seeing my brother.'

'Let him know,' Pit grunted to the others. Reger scowled at him before turning and trudging back to the ruined gatehouse, wheezing faintly with each step.

Lia and Nembe took up positions on either side of Pit, sizing him up. He attempted a grin at Lia, she raised a disapproving eyebrow in response, resting her hands on the hilts of her twin smallswords. No love lost there, it seemed. Pit maintained his malicious smile, leaning on his mace. He avoided looking directly at Nembe, but could see him taking swipes at the abundant wildflower carpet with his falchion, clipping the heads off them with deft turns of the wrist, neatly chopping the decapitated heads in two before they hit the floor. A damned good swordsman. Far better than him. On the bright side, at least they didn't have any bows.

'What's wrong with him, anyway?' he nodded after Reger. 'Sounds like he's been puffing away at one too many pipes for the last thirty years.'

'Your goblin bitch did him pretty well,' Pit's smile faltered for a second. 'She here?'

Nari smiled, blowing away a fly hovering around the corner of his mouth. 'Might be.'

Pit scoffed and shook his head in disbelief, but the flick of his eyes to the surrounding ruins betrayed his nerves.

'I hope she is, Nari. Naz died that night, you know. Choked on his own blood as he slept. That's two of us she killed; Naz and Jod. Nembe wants to meet her.'

Winds! If only she really were here. Even Nembe would be less frightening with her at his side. But perhaps she'd already done enough. Reger's wheeze was still audible, even with him out of sight on the other side of the gates, and Pit's posture seemed odd, his right shoulder dipped, his mace held in his left hand not right. If his suspicions were true, Pit might well have lost function in his right arm.

'Nariton! I'm impressed!'

Kirkin's rough voice cracked like thunder, making them all turn to the gate. In he walked, arms spread as wide as his crooked grin, the gold crowns of his upper incisors gleaming in the sun. Reger puffed behind him with two others in tow. Kirkin's bodyguard; Ikit Jalbai the southlander, walking purposefully and resolutely in his brigandine, his poleaxe over his shoulder, and his brother. Nat. He looked awful. Eyes sunken and dark from a combination of sleep deprivation and bruising, his hair was matted with sweat, muck, and blood. His chin was covered in a sticky film of bloodstained saliva drooling from his gagged mouth, spilling around the filthy rag stuffed between his teeth. Three of his fingers were clearly broken, poking beyond the binds at his wrist. He limped barefoot, left knee buckling with every step. Damn. In this state, making a run for it was impossible, not unless he planned on carrying him the whole way. The fly returned, trying to land on his sweaty upper lip, but he blew it away again, licking his lips to dry them. Things weren't looking good.

'Bugger me, you look like shit,' Kirkin curled his lip. 'What happened to your face?'

He touched his cheek and ran his tongue over the empty sockets of his broken teeth. 'Pit gave me a tickle a few weeks ago, I'm sure you heard.'

'I did,' he winked. 'Just thought I should remind you.'

He snorted. What a bastard. 'Ain't too easy to forget.'

'True, true. Never mind your ruined smile, you won't be around for too much longer to worry about it,' he chuckled cheerfully. 'You had everyone convinced you'd abandon dear old Nat to Cadaran's pits,' Kirkin shook his head in disbelief. 'You never fail to surprise me, for good or bad. I guess there's a morsel of honour left in that black heart of yours after all.'

'Well, I'm here,' he shrugged, looking between them all. With Kirkin and Ikit, their odds of success were plummeting. An oversight on his part, to be honest. He should've anticipated the southlander coming, and completely forgot about Kirkin as a physical adversary in addition to being the puppeteer. His hopes of escaping with their lives trickled away and died.

'Honourable,' Kirkin nodded sympathetically. 'Well, no point beating about the bush with it. Kill this one and tie him up,' he pointed between him and his brother. 'I have other things to do.'

'Wait!' he raised his hands as Ikit shoved Nat to his knees, his brother's pitiful whimpers and protests muffled by his gag. 'Give me one more week, Kirkin, one more week. I'll get you all the money, I promise.'

'Nari, Nari, Nari. Who delivered the message? I made it clear to everyone that there was no room for negotiation,' he shook his head in disapproval.

'Damid, apparently,' grunted Pit.

'Of course it would be,' Kirkin rolled his eyes. 'Always tries to give them a bit of hope, the cruel bastard.'

'I know what the message was,' he interrupted. The fly buzzed again at his ear as another bead of sweat trickled from his scalp and down the back of his neck.

'Then you know this isn't a discussion. I already gave you an extension. I don't give out extensions often, do I? *You* failed, despite my generosity. That'll teach me for being nice.'

'Look, can I just... speak to my brother again?'

Kirkin laughed. 'I'm not a monster, Nari. Have your say.'

'I trust I can talk to him without fear of a club in the back of my head?' he nodded to Pit and Reger.

Kirkin tapped his fingers rhythmically against his round midriff. 'Can't make any promises, I'm afraid. They're upset with you after your friend killed two of their crew,' he pulled a face and looked him up and down. 'Is that what you've stooped to, Nari? Goblins? Even I have standards.'

'Can he come to me?' he asked. 'I just want a private few words between brothers. Please.'

Kirkin made a show of thinking it over, chewing his cheeks and tapping his stubbled chin dramatically. 'I suppose so, go and have a chat with your brother, Nat.'

Pit frowned and shook his head, turning to him. 'Sir, I don't think we should–'

'Nonsense!' Kirkin lifted Nat by his armpits and shoved him to Nari, sending him sprawling in the dirt. 'What's he going to do? He can't run, we made sure of that.'

His grin made his blood boil. He must've known he was planning something. No chance of anything good happening now, all he could do was hope for a chance to die here, today, instead of in the pits. If he could get close to Kirkin, he might be able to get at least one swing before Ikit pummelled him to the ground, hopefully for good.

Nat half stumbled and half crawled over to him. Reger followed a few paces behind, holding his cudgel with white-knuckled ferocity. His brother fell into his embrace, his bound hands placed awkwardly between them. Reaching up, he removed the gag.

'Good to see you,' he smiled, unexpected tears springing to his eyes.

'You should've run,' Nat coughed and spluttered. 'Winds! That thing tastes bad. I'm sure Pit was using it to mop the sweat from his arse the other day.'

'I thought about it,' he admitted. 'I dunno, I sort of thought we could worm our way out of it and make a run for it.'

'Out of this?' Nat scoffed. 'No chance. They cut off my toes, Nari. Last night. Gagged me so I wouldn't scream. Cut off my toes and knocked my knee in.'

He looked at his boots. What he presumed were mud-stains around the toes was dried blood seeping from within. He glared over his brother's shoulder at Kirkin, who grinned broadly and gave a sarcastic wave. For all his insults and feigned surprise, he expected him to return, after all, why else would he maim his brother so?

'Bastard,' he growled.

'He is. Winds! I would've run if I were you.'

'Couldn't let you rot in Cadaran, could I?'

Nat shook his head. 'So what? I get an easy death so you can suffer in my place? What a way to die.'

'If things go well, nobody goes to Cadaran,' he steeled himself, lowering his voice to a whisper. 'We'll walk back to Kirkin now, me supporting you. Once we get close, I'll drop you and have a go at him.'

'Ikit will get you,' Nat snorted.

'Hopefully. At least then we both go the same way.'

'What's to stop them from just chucking me into Cadaran instead of killing me?'

'They wouldn't take you now,' he pointed to his feet. 'You'd be a useless slave, can't even walk.'

'Ah, they'd find something for me.'

He shrugged. 'Then you'd better do something to justify them sticking you here and now.'

'Aye, guess so.'

He glanced back at Kirkin. 'Ready?'

'I suppose I am,' he paused. 'Nari? Thanks for coming back.'

'Of course.'

Wrapping his arm around him, he took the majority of his weight and started the slow walk back to Kirkin. Reger sneered at him as they passed, resting his hand on his shoulder. Perfect. Had anyone else done it, he might have worried, but Reger seemed less than half the rogue he was two weeks ago. If anything, he was protecting him from the more dangerous ones.

Nat breathed hard beside him, rivalling Reger's wheeze. He lifted him higher, doing everything he could to lessen the load on his mutilated feet. Kirkin grinned cruelly at their awkward hopscotch.

They passed Pit, Lia, and Nembe, each of them glaring daggers into his back. Hopefully they'd bury a few in there as well, for good measure.

Less than ten steps to Kirkin. His sword was at his side, pressed between him and his brother. Another few steps and he'd swing his brother around into Reger to tangle him up and free his hands to draw his blade and jump at Kirkin. He wasn't wearing any armour. His fat belly was like a bulging wine-skin, ripe and ready to be spilled.

Sweat trickled from his hairline and down his neck. The fly buzzed behind his ear, eager to have a taste. He swiped it away to stop its tickling.

A shrill shout came from behind, making them all pause. An arrow whistled through the air and struck a section of ruins, ricocheting into Ikit's brigandine and making him grunt.

Pandemonium erupted.

'Ambush!' Pit roared, diving for cover with the others. Kirkin disappeared behind the same ruins the arrow struck, joined soon after by Ikit, his armour sparing him from any harm.

Reger's hand dragged him back by the shoulder. He twisted, bringing Nat with him and pushing him into the rogue. Landing heavily on top of him, they drove the wind out of his remaining good lung, leaving the rogue red-faced and spluttering.

'Up top! The boy from the swamp!' Pit announced. 'Watch out for the goblin! I knew she'd be here!'

Another arrow clattered harmlessly off the ruins, making them duck.

He'd forgotten about Ash in his lofty position. The boy must've gotten nervous and loosed his arrow. Damn it all, now the opportunity to stick Kirkin in the gut was lost. But perhaps another opportunity arose.

'Come on!' hoisting Nat back to his feet, he gave Reger a final kick in the stomach for good measure and half-dragged half-carried his brother to the safety of the ruined keep.

'Winds! What's happening?' Nat gasped.

'We might get a chance after all,' he panted, hurrying past the crouched figures of Pit, Lia, and Nembe, their attention split between them, Ash, and the rest of the ruins for Ffed's fearsome phantom.

Another of Ash's wildly inaccurate arrows stuck into the ground just behind them. By the four winds, he'd feel safer once they were behind the boy's frantic arch of fire.

Back to the keep, to the cellar, to the tunnels and their traps, and they might just be able to find a place to hold up for a while. Thanks to the boy's mistake, it wasn't over.

*

Ffed sat bolt upright, making Dem jump. The navy night sky was dotted with flickering stars without a cloud in sight. A prevailing warmth from the day's heat kept the air pleasant enough to sleep without a blanket, still weeks away from autumn's chill. Yet she shivered.

'What is it? I've still got another hour on my watch,' Dem grumbled, watching her. 'You've got to stop doing this, I'm more than capable of staying up for a few hours and you need at least *some* sleep to–'

'Quiet!' she hissed her warning. Dem did as she was told, freezing in place like a rabbit in the hawk's shadow.

Her heart thundered, her hands shook, her broad ears quivered as they searched for a sound beneath the ambient noise of the forest. The wiry hair covering her body stood upright to attention, as if each individual strand were as eager as she was to catch a glimpse of the forest's shadows.

Invisible claws tugged at her breast, hunger panged in her stomach.

It was back.

'Get things,' she commanded. Dem sprang to action in nervous silence, clambering around their campsite to stuff their supplies back into their packs. She knew to trust her. The Clearbed gurgled away to their right, obscuring the finer sounds, but the forest was otherwise quiet. No rodents rustling in the undergrowth on their nocturnal foraging exploits, no hooting owls or churring nightjars, no buzzing flies or clicking crickets. Dailas held its breath. She drew her knife and held her hatchet close, trying to keep loose and avoid her muscles seizing and cramping, trying to keep escape a viable option.

Dem patted her shoulder to indicate their things were packed. With a single nod, she directed her to the riverbank, careful feet treading lightly as they backed away, her eyes and ears flitting from one shadow to the next.

Breaking from the trees, they made it to the riverbank, feet sinking into the soft ground. Her chest tightened. It was close. There was nothing obvious to say as much, but she sensed it nonetheless. She could see its malevolence in the gloomy darkness between the trunks, could feel its evil intent in the warm breeze, like the Great Hunter's charnel breath on her cheek.

They were so close! Only a few hours away from home, but they needed rest, walking on borrowed energy yesterday, limbs aching and feet blistering. They hadn't stopped anywhere since Clovercream, not even the little town of Squell on one of the Clearbed's tributaries. Straight and true as an arrow, they marched by the shortest possible route home. Even she found it taxing, worsened by the summer heat blazing down on their heads. Despite the clear skies, the cloud of Ash's departure hung over them. He didn't listen to her protests as he walked trance-like after Nari, his ears deaf to her protests, but what could she have done? More, probably. She could have pinned him down and beat sense into him. She could have bound his hands and legs and dragged him back by the scruff of his neck, but she didn't. He made his choice. Without her to protect him, the inevitable waited with open arms, and one of the Great Hunter's many jaws undoubtedly slavered in anticipation in his footsteps. Now all she could do was protect Dem, give her one day more to get back to her mother. It was all they needed. One day more.

'What is it?' Dem hissed, a trailing foot slipping into the river with a soft splash.

'Follower.'

Dem's sharp inhale confirmed her understanding.

Starforge was only a few hours away. She'd avoided the follower for entire nights around the infirmary. On familiar ground, they should be able to make it. But all those times she'd been alone, now there was a child to account for on top of her own life. Stomach twisted into a fist tighter than Dem's white-knuckled grip on her sleeve, she motioned the girl upriver. All they could do was try.

The going was slow. Dem took Ash's pack to give her more freedom should it come to a fight, but it made them slower, with the girl teetering with every other step, her exhausted limbs trembling like a foal. It couldn't be helped. Those fractions of a second she might lose in discarding the pack could mean the difference between life and death.

Metres turned into miles as they crawled along the riverbank. At times the tightness in her chest abated, other times it rose to the point where she could barely force her granite ribs to move. On either side, the foreboding trees towered above, every knot in the trunk or twist in the boughs taking a new life as the follower's hunched body, every pale leaf into its malign stare. Cold, sour sweat drenched her from neck to groin, but she couldn't risk stooping to wash it off. Its acrid stench stung her nostrils. The smell of her own terror. Dem was the same, her own horror a slightly different scent to her own, but no less repulsive. Every animal with half a nose would be able to track them. With every step, the follower surely relished in the intensity of their fear.

The forest slowly became increasingly familiar. They skirted around a basin in the riverbed that formed a natural pool where the village children bathed on warm days such as these. A shadow beside a rock made her pause and raise her axe, but it was only a forgotten blanket, damp with beads of dew clinging to its fibres.

'We're close,' Dem breathed, wide-eyed.

She ushered her on. No point lingering over a discarded cloth. Night pressed around them, the closeness of the heat and the dark suffocating. Even the sky, once navy and dotted with stars, seemed suddenly an impenetrable face of coal, choking them with its weight, blinding them with its clouds of dust. Everywhere she turned, she felt its eyes at her back, heard the scuttle of its stalking claws. Every moment this storm of terror blistered around her, thundering dread in her ears, flashing forked tongues of horror in the corners of her eyes.

A familiar broad meander approached, the far bank lost in the black belly of the night. It was where panners such as Lelan Nalbens knelt with stooped backs, filtering the water for any loose scraps of silver ore from the mines further upriver. Even Dem recognised it, whimpering with relief at the sight. Her whimper broke into a strangled cough as she stumbled back, lifting a quivering, wavering hand to the far bank.

'Ffed,' her cut-throat croak sent a chill to her soul.

She saw it then. The watcher, the follower, the dark ghoul of fear at their heels. A pale wight in the shadow of the forest, its sinister smile visible even when the rest of it remained concealed.

'Kolgatha.'

Chapter 16

He didn't know what he was doing.

Ash fumbled with another arrow, nocked it to the bowstring, drew it until the head touched the bow, and released. It clattered noisily against the stone blocks, ricocheting between them.

His clumsy hands grabbed another, missing the string on his first few attempts to nock it, then drawing too far and letting it fall to the floor. Shaking hands retrieved it automatically and repeated the movement, sending the missile zipping into the courtyard.

He only had five left, the other ten scattered randomly throughout the rocks and wildflowers below. He hadn't hit anyone since that first shot ricocheted harmlessly into the southlander's armour, all the others struck nothing but stone or petal, sometimes both. Nevertheless, the sheer randomness of his shooting kept the rogues pinned, for fear of catching a loose arrow by a stroke of absolute bad luck. It didn't matter, his haphazard shooting gave Nari the time to get his brother to the cover of the keep.

He'd seen the whole thing, and although he could only hear Kirkin's half of the conversation, it was enough to test the limits of his courage. He was safe as he was, unseen and unheard. He could just watch from a safe distance and steal away once they were gone, no harm done. But what sort of cowardly move was that? Nari set the example by coming here for his brother, putting his life on the line for companionship and brotherhood. He had to follow suit. Nari's actions were confusing, heading towards Kirkin instead of breaking away like he'd expected, but there was no mistaking the signal. He was supposed to just jump out and threaten them with the bow, but his sweaty hands slipped on the string, releasing it prematurely. He hoped Nari wouldn't be too angry, that his clumsy actions hadn't doomed them.

The woman and the dreyad glared hatefully up at him, grim determination in their stares. He swung his bow around at each of them, hoping to make them duck, if nothing else to break their stare. It worked on the woman, who dipped her head half-heartedly behind her rock, but not the dreyad. He remained as he was, falchion resting on the rock in front of him, challenging him with his unblinking stare.

Ash drew the string further, to the full length of the arrow. The dreyad stared back. A hatred suddenly sparked in his gut, born of fear and panic. With a growl, he released. It flew straight and true, cutting through the air with a whistle. It missed the dreyad by two metres, thudding lamely into the turf.

Gnarled face breaking into a grin, the dreyad strolled casually from behind his cover, pointing the tip of his sword up at him.

His bladder contracted suddenly, sending a gush of warmth down his leg. He hardly noticed. His whole world was in the tip of that blade and the victory in those eyes.

A sudden clatter behind him made him scream unashamedly. More of them! Snuck around the back while they were distracted. But no, it was just Nari.

'Come on, lad. With me.'

He stared dumbly for a second. Nari grunted and grabbed his arm, pulling him through to the passageway.

'Come on! Go! Go! Go! Into the tunnels. Nat's waiting.'

Stumbling on his weak legs, he allowed Nari to lead him through. A sudden crash rocked the crumbling walls, followed by a string of muffled curses from below. They kept going, coughing and spluttering through a corridor filled with plumes of dust.

'First tripwire triggered,' Nari grunted from behind. 'Rigged it to one of the collapsing walls. It'll slow them for a bit.'

They turned into the corridor between the north walls, passing an arrow loop on their way to descend the stairs. A waiting figure at the bottom made him pause and yelp, struggling to untangle his bow and quiver in the narrow space, but Nari caught his arm and pushed him forward.

'It's alright, just my brother. Don't stop.'

They reached the bottom. Nat leaned heavily against the wall, breathing hard as he waved his bound hands to disperse the dust.

'Right, back to the storeroom,' Nari looped his arm around his brother and nodded back to the narrow corridor. 'Remember the way?'

'I…' he paused. It was gone. There was nothing there, his head as empty as a beggar's tin.

'Not much to it, lad, just follow the corridor. Two tripwires on the way. Go. Go!'

He kicked him lightly on the back of his legs, spurring him like a rider whipped his horse. Suppressing sobs, he scurried along the corridor, the narrow walls pressing him on all sides, the darkness broken only by the glimmer at the opposite end. Tears streamed from his eyes, tears of fear, of panic, of confusion, of irritation from the lingering dust clouds. Nat's laboured breathing filled the tunnel, half-dragged by his brother along the way.

They reached another set of stairs, one going up and one going down. He paused, staring dumbly at the two.

'Down,' Nari grunted, shoving him in the right direction.

They descended. There were no handrails to steady him, nothing but the rough walls.

'Smells like piss,' Nat grunted between ragged gasps.

'Boy wet himself,' Nari grunted back.

'Ah.'

His ears burned in shame. It wasn't enough to be scared senseless, now everyone knew he was a spineless worm, unable to control even the most basic of bodily functions. But he couldn't deny the stench, or the uncomfortable cling of his trousers to his inner thighs.

On reaching the cellar, the stink of damp and mould added to the reek of his garments. They paused for a second at the bottom, taking stock of the high-ceilinged chambers.

'You good?' Nari asked.

'Fine,' he grunted, turning away to hide his face.

'Not you, lad.'

His cheeks burned hotter again. Of course he wasn't talking to him, not when he had a bound and beaten brother to care for.

'Not good, Nari,' Nat groaned. 'I don't have much left in me.'

'Not much further,' Nari drew his sword and cut his brother's binds. 'Alright? Let's go. I think I heard them coming. After you, Ash.'

It was all the motivation he needed. Pushing down his shame, he led them on to the western stairs, a vague memory finally pushing through the fog to light the way. Up two flights, turn back on themselves in the first floor to the southwest tower, down the stairs again and through the door to the storeroom. He scrambled up the stairs, using his spare hand to vault himself up. Nari and Nat panted behind. He didn't know what the plan involved once they reached the storeroom, Nat didn't seem in a fit state to run through the cleft and into the woods, but he trusted Nari had a plan.

On the second floor corridor, it was only Nari's sharp pull on the back of his shirt that kept him from triggering the tripwire. He stepped over it sheepishly, acutely aware of the rogue's judgmental frown on the back of his head. Winds curse him, he couldn't do anything right! Well, the next wire was on the stairway of the southwest tower, *that* at least he remembered.

Distant shouts of their pursuers echoed up from behind, bouncing and reverberating from the close walls, filling the tunnel with their hate. Mouth dry and heart skipping every other beat in its haste, he glanced over his shoulder at Nari.

'That's them. Don't stop!'

He scrambled on, the foul taste in his mouth impossible to swallow. One thing was for sure, he wouldn't die in this stone coffin of a tunnel. The tunnel opened up before them, daylight streaming in through the opening. After the suffocating, pressing darkness, its promise of open air was a blessing. He ran through, oblivious to Nari's warning.

Open and exposed to the weather, the floor of the southwest tower was slick with the passing seasons, the stone worn to a glass-like sheen by the passing of countless boots and entire seas of rain. A gruff shout came from the courtyard as soon as he shot out, enough to make him slip and fall heavily on his rear.

'Southwest tower!' Kirkin's voice boomed. 'Get the bastards!'

'Damn it, lad, there's no cover,' Nari growled, momentarily letting go of his brother to lift him back to his feet. 'Can't just go clattering through!'

'Sorry,' he wheezed.

'Don't be sorry, be ready! They'll be coming now.'

'Winds! Shoot the bastard,' Nat pointed at Kirkin, rushing between the ruins to their tower.

He nocked another arrow and sighted down the shaft, but he couldn't keep his arm still, it kept weaving and bobbing, his fingers threatening to slip from the bowstring at any point.

'I can't,' he whimpered, releasing the tension. 'I'll miss.'

'Damn it, Nari, where'd you get him? Give it here,' Nat snatched the bow and arrow from his hands, face red enough to burst.

'He's just a boy, Nat. He's trying to help,' Nari murmured, watching his brother sight down the shaft.

'Then he needs to do better...' he released the arrow with a soft breath. 'Damn it!' he broke into a series of ragged coughs as the arrow glanced harmlessly from the ruins a hands-breadth from Kirkin's face. A good shot, by any measure, but not good enough.

'It's alright, enough time for another,' Nari handed him another arrow, only two remaining in the quiver.

'Just a little... bah!'

At the exact moment he released the arrow, Kirkin stumbled, letting it pass harmlessly over his shoulder. At this point, the rogue ducked for good behind another pile of rubble, correctly identifying the skill of the new archer as far superior to the first.

Nari turned to him for another arrow, then gasped and pushed him aside. Ikit's poleaxe crashed into the ruined wall, showering him with sparks and stone splinters. He barely had time to roll away before Nari was up and swinging with his sword, his blade meeting the poleaxe's shaft in ugly clangs above his head. Struggling to his feet, Nat joined with a roar, swinging the bow like a cudgel, one hand on the ruins to steady himself. Ash covered his head and watched in terror as the three battled, Nari jabbing and cutting, Nat swinging, and Ikit knocking their blows aside with powerful sweeps of his axe.

Eager as the brothers may be, Ikit outmatched them in speed and strength, more often than not ignoring Nat's blows completely, absorbing the bow's strikes on his flanks and powerful shoulders, leaving him largely free to deal with Nari.

More cries and bellows sounded from the tunnel as their pursuers fell afoul of the other tripwire. Ash glanced at the opening, anticipating their imminent arrival to aid Ikit. The duellists circled like spitting cats, jabbing and hissing, each passing second bringing the rest of Kirkin's crew closer and closer.

The brothers fell into a rhythm, Nari's sharp grunts punctuated by Nat's rumbling gasps. Nat started using his bow more effectively, striking high at Ikit's exposed head where the bow would sting, while Nari's jabs and stabs kept the business end of the poleaxe occupied. They regained control, driving him around the exposed tower floor. Ash recoiled, driving him straight towards him! He scrambled on his rear, boots flailing as he tried to find purchase in the slick stone. He had no weapon. Nothing to defend himself with. He tried catching Nari's eye to warn him, but he was too focussed on the duel. They drove him within two metres of him, closer, the air humming above his head with the sweeps of the poleaxe.

The southlander's heavy boot stepped on his leg, making him howl and snatch it back. Suddenly overbalanced, Ikit gasped and flailed his arms. Nari pounced, lunging with his sword and striking the southlander hard in the gut. His sword clanged against the brigandine's iron plate, but the harm was done. Limbs flailing, Ikit's centre of balance took him over the edge and plummeting to the courtyard with a dull thump. Nat jammed the bow into one of the remaining stone blocks and threw his body against it, levering it over the edge to tumble after the southlander for good measure. The crack of broken stone echoed around the ruins, startling the house martins into flight.

'Not bad,' Nari nodded, panting.

'Didn't think we'd get him,' Nat gasped, leaning heavily against the crumbling wall. 'Need a minute.'

Rising voices from the tunnel made them turn.

'Nope. Come on!'

Once again, his arms wrapped around his brother, dragging him puffing and blowing to the stairwell. Ash struggled to his feet behind, legs limp and shaking. Another shout from the darkness of the tunnel and Pit burst out, mace at the ready, followed by the woman and dreyad. Lips curled in a fierce snarl, Pit made a beeline for him. Panic lent strength to his tired legs, spurring them to move. Scrambling on all fours, he ducked under Pit's grasping hands and scurried down the stairs, his pursuers hot on his heels, close enough to hear their breathless panting, to feel the thud of their boots on the stone steps. Nari struggled with Nat a few paces ahead, somehow already at the bottom of the stairs.

A hand closed around his arm followed by a triumphant bark of victory. Yelping and sobbing, he twisted free, limbs flailing like Ikit's only a moment before as he half-fell down the steps. He caught Nari's eye as he happened a glance over his shoulder, begging him to drop his brother and come to his aid, to spare him from the vengeful blades of his foe.

'Ash watch out!'

Too late. His foot caught the forgotten tripwire, pulling it free with a crack and sending him tumbling head over heels down the last few steps. Stars erupted before his eyes as his jaw cracked on the stone, and the whole world disintegrated into grey dust.

*

Coughing and spluttering, Nari dragged his brother to the storeroom, nothing but his memory to guide him through the blinding cloud. Depositing him against a wall, he went back through for the boy. He was here somewhere, beneath the rubble.

As the seconds passed, the drifting pinkish-grey flurries settled, leaving a faint lingering haze. Once the rumble of shaken foundations eased and the clatter of precariously-placed fragments died, groans and muffled curses took their place, and he was able to appreciate his handiwork.

The central column of the spiral staircase was destroyed, along with the stairs themselves and the central roof. Who'd have thought such simple measures as a tripwire around a weight-bearing fragment could cause such destruction?

His boots caught on something soft. Stooping, he cleared the rubble and pushed a couple of blocks away. Ash groaned beneath, a laceration in his chin and a set of newly-broken teeth to accompany it. Alive, at least. That was a start. He worked quickly to uncover the rest of him, acutely aware of the shifting stones and rubble-piles further ahead as the rogues recovered.

269

'Come on, wake up!'

'Nari,' Ash groaned, opening his eyes and staring up at him. 'I don't want to do any more.'

'That's fine, you've already done well getting us here. Come on, through to Nat.'

The boy gasped as the final block was pushed from his legs, revealing a nasty gash on his shins, gleaming bone exposed. Nothing seemed grossly displaced, but there was really no telling from such a cursory glance.

'Can't breathe,' Ash gasped, face strained with pain.

'Why, pain?'

Ash nodded, pointing feebly to his lateral chest wall. He placed a gentle hand on his flank, making the boy gasp again.

'Try again for me, just a shallow one. A bit deeper. Stop when it's painful. Just there?'

'Yes,' Ash wheezed, coughing feebly.

'You've probably broken a rib or two. Come on. Let me help you up.'

A wheeze like a stuck pig greeted his attempts to heave him to his feet, the boy a dead weight in his arms.

'You're gonna have to help me a bit,' he grunted, hands linked around his chest.

Ash wheezed again, raising a limp hand ahead. 'Watch out!'

Lia stumbled towards them, one hand held to her temple, the other grasping blindly ahead. He shuffled his hands to free his sword-arm, but too late, she was already on them... and beyond. She stumbled like a drunkard, ragged breath coming quickly. Ash's trailing legs caught her feet, sending her tumbling again with a pitiful cry. As she hit the floor, her face turned to them. Battered and bleeding, one eye was a scarlet gelatinous mass amid a sea of fractured bone, while the other sported a two-inch stone splinter through the globe itself. Her mouth dripped blood, her breath the tempo of poorly-controlled panic as she got to grips with her new, black world.

Dragging Ash the final few steps to the storeroom, he set him next to his brother, both wheezing and panting as much as the other. Sword ready, he returned to Lai. She hadn't moved, breathing as quickly and faintly as before, propped up on one elbow, the other hand still clutching her broken face.

'Pit?' she croaked, voice quavering and cracking. 'That you?'

He remained silent, his sword heavy in hand. He'd never killed in cold blood before, only ever out of necessity. But she was still an enemy, no matter how incapacitated. She had her own debts to Kirkin. Without eyes, what were her chances of repaying them? Wouldn't he just condemn her to a far worse fate?

He sighed softly. No choice in the matter. Lifting his sword with both hands, he struck hard and he struck clean. Lai dropped and lay still.

'Bastard!'

There was no mistaking Pit's growl. He dropped and twisted, anticipating the swing of his mace, but it didn't come. Pit crouched five paces away, red eyes glaring past his dirt-encrusted lids. No, not crouching, but still buried up to his mid-thigh in crumbled masonry, his left hand caught between two blocks, pinning him in place. Nari relaxed and approached cautiously, eyeing the mace in his right hand.

'You've always said as much,' he shrugged.

'Aye, and you've always been a bastard,' Pit spat. 'Lai never did you any harm.'

'But she was here to do it.'

'I should've killed you long ago.'

Nari stopped three paces away. 'Why don't you give it a try now?'

Pit sneered, his right hand closing around the shaft of his mace, but his arm remained still. Nari leaned closer.

'Go on. Give me a swing.'

'Bastard,' Pit hissed, spitting a pink gobbet into his face.

Lifting a finger, he flicked the sputum from his cheek and wiped it on the ground, lips pursed in disapproval. Pit scowled back at him, heaving his maimed shoulder uselessly. Nari straightened and circled the trapped rogue, twisting his neck to keep him in sight.

'Guess not,' he sighed. 'The goblin has a strong arm behind her axe, doesn't she? Not like you. I guess you should've seen it.'

'Get it over with.'

271

'Gladly.'

'I'll die knowing you and your son-of-a-whore brother–'

He didn't find out what the end of the sentence was. His sword knocked the rest of the sentence out of him in a guttural gasp as it plunged beneath his collarbone and deep into his thorax. Pit gurgled into silence, slumping haphazardly against the imprisoning stone blocks. A bad death for a worse man. He had no regrets.

Only Nembe left. Wiping his sword clean on Pit's carcass, he scrambled over the rubble, searching for the dryad. Now was the opportunity to deal with him, with his lungs filled with dust and his limbs trapped in rubble. But where was he? Scrambling over the haphazard mound of fallen stone and mortar, tossing aside handfuls of splinters and rolling aside blocks the size of his torso, he searched for a sign the dryad might be dealt with. Nothing. He stopped at the other side of the rubble-mound, his gaze wandering to the gaping hole in the roof. Surely not?

*

Snatching shallow breaths between stabs of pain, he listened to Nari and Pit's muffled voices, and winced at the latter's final choking splutters. A fitting demise. His only regret was not putting an end to him himself. That would have been the proper way to do it, poetic justice and all that.

But it wasn't to be.

He glanced at Nat, panting like a sick dog, his bow held loosely in limp fingers. He knelt across to take it from him, only for Nat to snatch it away.

'What you doing, lad?'

He tried grabbing the bow a second time, Nat snatched it away again. 'I need my bow.'

His voice was muffled, the floor of his mouth thick and swollen, limiting his tongue movements.

'No no, I'll be looking after this.'

'I need it.'

Nat barked a short laugh. 'How about leaving it with someone who can actually shoot?'

'It's mine,' his cheeks burned. He wasn't going to be caught empty-handed if Kirkin or the dryad came looking. He needed the bow's protection. Had he not pinned them in place in the courtyard with his archery? Had he not given Nat and Nari time to get to safety?

'How about this,' Nat wheezed. 'I'll take the arrows and the bow and I can protect you.'

'Just give it!' he lunged, missed, and sprawled on the floor, arcs of pain coursing from his chest, chin, and leg, worsened by the tangled mess of the quiver beneath him.

Nat's hands fell on him, grappling for the arrows. 'Give me the arrows, lad.'

'No!' he grunted, curling into a ball, ignoring the new urgency in Nat's voice.

'Now!'

The grappling hands grew rougher, pulling his arms aside, straining his aching ribcage. The pain only made him angrier, stronger. Gritting his teeth, he curled tighter, growling like a cornered dog.

A movement in the corner of his eye made him look up. From the cleft in the outside wall peered a familiar hateful gaze, eyeing them up with gleeful anticipation. Nat's hands withdrew abruptly, gripping the bow with two hands as the dreyad jumped in, falchion drawn. Whimpering, Ash dropped to the floor and covered his eyes.

He heard them clash, the thud of steel against wood. Nat cried out desperately for his brother. Whistling air cut by blade and bow, the scuff of feet, one pair nimble, the other clumsy and heavy. He felt the brush of displaced air as someone jumped over him, and the clash of metal as Nari joined the fray. Curling into a tighter ball, he screwed his eyes shut and clamped his hands over his ears, doing anything he could to mask the grunts, the curses, the arrogant scoffs of the dreyad and the grim curses of the brothers.

Is this what he left Dem and Ffed for? Is this all he was good for? Cowering like a baby as the men battled for their lives. He'd been useless this entire journey. Dem was right; he wouldn't have given the proper information to the healers, he wouldn't have known what the fungus looked like, he was a liability in the swamp, jeopardised Ma's medicine by wandering the infirmary's cellars, and now he'd doomed

273

them all by releasing his arrow and provoking Kirkin. At every moment, he needed someone to hold his hand and guide him through. If there was an opportunity to be useless, he was guaranteed to take it. If there was a chance of jeopardising their safety, he was guaranteed to put them at risk.

Gritting his teeth, he pushed himself to his hands and knees, untangling the quiver and its two remaining arrows from between his legs. This was his final opportunity to be more than just a child.

Staggering to a crouch, fighting the urge to vomit, he faced the fighters.

Nat was bent double, clutching his stomach, the bow in two halves on the ground in front of him and held together only by the bowstring. Nari bled from several wounds on his cheek, his arm, his left hand held awkwardly across his body, his left hip oozing a stream of blood. The dreyad moved gracefully around Nari's flailing blade, flicking it aside with casual twists of the wrist, countering with blinding ferocity that left Nari ever more bloodied. As he watched, Nat gathered a handful of rocks to give his brother respite, driving the dreyad back with bouncing thuds into his bark-like skin and clanging musically off his blade. It was enough for Nari to regroup with his brother, gulping mouthfuls of air. The dreyad sneered, batting away the last of Nat's projectiles. As soon as he stooped to gather more, he pounced again, pressing Nari hard, landing blow after blow. It was a different battle to the one with Ikit. A new level of desperation, the disparity in skill between the combatants stark. Nari's strikes grew clumsier, taking more and more time to recover after each blow, grunting and snorting foully, strings of bloodstained drool dangling from the corner of his mouth. Finally, he collapsed after a particularly clumsy swing, gasping as his knee struck awkwardly on the floor. The dreyad stood triumphantly over him as he crawled back to his brother, sword held casually between easy fingers.

'You got me, Nembe,' Nari chuckled falsely. 'Never had a chance in a swordfight, did I?'

'Insulted you ever thought you might,' Nembe growled, his voice like a hundred layers of crunching autumn leaves set alight by a rogue match.

'Do me a favour and make it quick?' Nari nodded back to the collapsed stairwell. 'I gave Pit and Lai the courtesy.'

'Quick?' Nembe frowned and shook his head. 'That sapling died when you tried it on. We expected as much.'

Nari's face paled and slackened. 'So what?' he whispered.

'Cadaran for you both.'

The brothers shared a glance, the stench of their dread oozing in pulsating waves from their pores. With a sharp cry, Nari made a lame attempt at rushing the dreyad, only to be thrust back with a sharp kick to the shoulder. Nat tried the same and was dismissed equally easily. Growling, they lunged again, Nari swinging his clumsy sword, Nat practically throwing himself in front of the dreyad's blade as it parried, both flicked away as easily as before to crumple in a tangle of bleeding limbs.

Nembe tutted. 'No easy way out, boys. No chance of skewering yourselves on this sticker,' he twirled the falchion around his wrist. 'I decide who lives and dies, not you. An idiot like Pit might have bashed your heads in, but do you think I'm so dim? You boys need to learn your lesson... slowly.' he leaned forward, grinning evilly. 'That being said, I'm in a mind for killing. I reckon I'll give the archer boy the lucky end you're hoping for.'

He turned to face Ash, but only made it halfway. Broken halves of the bow in each hand, Ash jumped up from his creeping approach to the dreyad, throwing his hands up in a circle, jagged ends of the broken bow at the ready. Nembe reacted quickly, pushing him forcefully in the stomach to make room for his falchion to swing. He didn't see the loop of bowstring attaching the two halves fall around his neck, not until the noose tightened like a cheese-wire. The sword dropped in surprise from his lazy grip. His hands darted to his throat, clawing at the skin to find purchase beneath the string. Ash pulled tighter, panicked tears blinding his eyes. The dreyad's hands left his neck and barrelled forward, headbutting him in his lacerated chin, sending spikes of pain coursing through his aching skull. His grip loosened on one of the bow-halves. Nembe's wood-vice hands closed around his wrist, squeezing the muscles and tendons, forcing his fingers open. He fell away, expecting the string to fall loose and

Nembe to run him through with his sword. Instead, his arm holding the other bow-half jerked with tension as he reached his knees. Nat gripped the other half, pulling with his whole body weight to keep the tension in the string. Beads of blood erupted from Nembe's rough skin, trickling from his throat in scarlet rivulets. His eyes bulged. His face purpled. Nari's sword cracked into his skull, opening an awful gash in the scalp, blood popping out in a grisly fountain. Terrible sounds erupted from Nembe's strangled gullet, an awful keening choke, high-pitched like a wailing kitten. Nari struck again, bone crunching beneath his blade, blood spurting again. Nembe dropped to his knees. He would have fallen were his neck not suspended in the noose between Ash and Nat, quivering tongue lolling from his open mouth. Nari struck a final time, his sword passing smoothly through the fragmented skull and into the gelatinous mass within, and Nembe's keening finally stopped.

Nari collapsed to his knees, panting hard. Nat did the same, releasing the tension from his half of the bowstring. Ash didn't. His muscles had seized, he kept pulling, fingers locked around the bow, muscles spasming into a permanent contraction. The dreyad's hateful, hideous carcass was pulled towards him. Sobbing, he tried pulling away, only managing to drag him even closer.

'Easy, lad, let it go,' Nari approached and set a comforting hand on his shoulder. 'Take it easy. Let it go.'

He shook his head. His fingers were stuck. He'd be tied to him forever, locked in a death grip of his own making.

Nari's hands closed around his own, their calloused roughness instilling life into his locked fingers. They gradually eased open, and the bow-half dropped to the floor with a clatter.

'Well done,' Nari nodded reassuringly. 'Damned good job, lad.'

'Aye, solid effort,' Nat breathed, shaking hands retrieving the falchion from the ground and giving it a few practice swings.

Ash nodded dumbly. His mind was blank. He couldn't take his eyes from Nembe. The red, bulging eyes, the blue lips, the swollen face slowly returning to normal as blood oozed from the ugly mess of his cranium. Because of him.

'Come on, Kirkin's still out there,' Nari grunted, turning him forcefully away from the carcass. 'We can rest after.'

Despite their own injuries, they each took an arm around their shoulders and walked him through the rubble back out to the courtyard. A sorrier trio of limping, battered fools had probably never walked the wildflower clusters of Redgate. He closed his eyes against the brightness, but that only gave his mind a blank canvass to conjure Nembe's face again. He forced them open, enduring the false tranquillity of the flowers with their humming insects and delicate petals swaying in the breeze.

'Kirkin!' Nari called, setting him down in the middle of the courtyard, his arrows scattered around the blocks like feathered flowers. 'How about we renegotiate?'

'Piss off!' Kirkin's voice boomed from nearby. 'You think you can intimidate me? Me?'

'The rest of your cronies are dead,' Nat jeered, his breath gradually returning. 'Think you can take three of us?'

'You've always been slimy sons of whores,' Kirkin appeared from the base of the southwest tower, Ikit's polearm held in both hands. 'Just because you wriggled away from my men with your tricks doesn't mean you'll get the better of me. Me!' he beat his chest, face as purple as Nembe's had been. 'I rule these woods! No two-faced slimy bastard gets away from me!'

'Come on, then,' Nari beckoned him on. 'Show us how the ruler of the woods intends to take us to Cadaran.'

'No, no, now *I* kill you,' Kirkin shouted, spittle flying from his twisted lips.

'Yeah? With all your men dead?'

Kirkin paused and sneered, pointing the head of the polearm at them. 'Not all.'

A burst of fire erupted in Ash's flank, punching him just below the ribcage, coursing up to his stomach. He couldn't breathe, could hardly think. Something withdrew with a dull slurp. Strength left his body in pulses. The pain from his leg and chin dwindled to nothing, this new pain overwhelming them all. He hardly felt himself hit the ground. Blurred feet shuffled in front of him, muffled cries reached his uncaring ears, then nothing.

*

Nari watched open-mouthed as Ash slid to the floor, Reger stooping triumphantly over him, knife dripping the boy's blood. He heard Kirkin's boots thumping the earth behind as he charged, but his eyes were for Reger. Frail and pathetic as he was after his tangle with Ffed, he'd forgotten about him completely, discarding the threat of his evil mind. Before he knew what he was doing, he was already charging him, the pain from his wounds forgotten, blind rage pumping natural anaesthetic to numb the bite of torn skin.

Reger's cudgel swung clumsily, knocked aside with a contemptuous sweep of his sword. He caught his other hand as it jerked up with the bloodied knife and twisted it sharply up and behind the rogue's back. Reger gasped and yelped, his hand opening instinctively to drop the blade. His breath came quickly, panting and gasping, lips moving in incomprehensible pleas for mercy. Winds damn the bastard! That he could even consider asking for mercy churned his blood, set his heart humming with frenzy. The cudgel-hand swung half-heartedly at him, his sword met it at the wrist, biting deep, coming to a stop against the bone. Reger squealed, his hot breath foul and stinking against Nari's cheek. No amount of suffering would be enough.

Nat's yelps brought him back to reality. He stole a glance over his shoulder. Kirkin swung the poleaxe gracelessly, a bruiser with a heavy bit of metal, using his considerable bulk to add overwhelming force behind each blow. Nat leaned against the ruins, doing his best to keep the stone blocks between him and his foe, turning away the poleaxe as best he could with Nembe's falchion. But he was tiring, his mutilated feet clumsy, threatening to trip him up with each stumble.

Turning on his heel, Reger held in front of him as a shield, he approached. Kirkin noticed and broadened his sweeps, practically swinging the poleaxe over his head in ever-widening circles, building speed and momentum as he went. Nat backed a step away, avoiding the head by a hand's breadth. Nari kept moving forward, frogmarching

278

Reger ahead, still pleading and spluttering with pain from his twisted arm, too weak to resist Nari's hateful grip.

He waited for the arc of the poleaxe to pass in front of him and rushed forward, crouched behind Reger's squirming body. Kirkin twisted to correct the direction of his swing, bringing the heavy weapon from overhead in a murderous blow, but they were already within the arc of the weapon. The shaft crashed into Reger's shoulder, his clavicle and scapula crunching audibly as they took the force of the blow. With a wheezing gasp, Reger clattered into Kirkin and fell into a heap at his feet. Nari followed up with his lunging sword, burying it up to the hilt in Kirkin's broad stomach.

His eyes bulged, inches from his face. Nari gave the sword a twist and a jerk, making him belch a mouthful of blood. They sank to their knees together, his hands already slick with foul blood.

Kirkin's mouth opened and closed, as if trying to say something. Nari sneered. 'Can't hear you.'

Kirkin's face turned purple with effort, straining in vain to take a breath. He watched his eyes grow unfocussed. The pumping blood from the wound slowed to a trickle. There were no final words.

It took a lot of effort to extract the blade from his stomach, especially with the handle so soaked with gore. Eventually it slid out with a scarlet spurt. The fat man had a lot of blood in his bloated body, most of it pooling around him in a grisly puddle. But it wasn't over, not yet. Reger continued to squirm on the ground, sobbing silently and pawing a limp hand against his shattered shoulder. Nari kicked him over to lie on his belly and set his foot on the back of his head, forcing his nose and mouth into Kirkin's exsanguinated pool. He kicked and writhed in protest, but Nari's foot stood firm. He didn't remove it until the jerking spasms stopped, and Reger's remaining lung filled with his master's blood.

He collapsed against the ruins, adrenaline finally wearing out, exhaustion and pain returning with a vengeance. Nat nodded slowly, staring at Kirkin and Reger's corpses.

'Good riddance,' he glanced up at him. 'We're free.'

He nodded silently. Somehow, it felt empty, too soon after all the killing to consider a future, too soon after resigning himself to death to consider a life beyond today. His eyes wandered back to the middle of the courtyard. Freedom, but at what cost?

Groaning, he shuffled over to Ash, bending over the boy's crumpled body. Nat limped over, shaking his head sadly.

'A shame, Nari. Mighty shame. I had my doubts at first, but you picked a good lad. Where did you say you found him?'

Ash's chest fluttered briefly. The faintest tap of a pulse at his neck. Relief flooded his chest.

'He's alive!' Nari breathed, looking up at his brother, expecting joy, but Nat shook his head sadly.

'Aye, for now. Poor lad. He's got a gut wound, mate, deep one by the looks of it. He's finished,' he turned away and pointed to the main gates. 'I reckon south is our best bet. Might be a load of trouble at the start now Kirkin's gone, but I bet Pahag'll send someone else up to take control before long. We can head out to the Jagged Isles from Morgenal, what do you reckon?'

'We need to get help.'

'Damn it, Nari!' he paused for breath, face shining with the effort. 'I get you feel guilty about it, but that's just how it is. If you hire a man for a job you have to expect casualties. We can't save him. Kirkin's cronies will still be out for us, the ones who aren't here, and everyone got the message he was meeting you here. I don't fancy hanging around for someone to come looking.'

'He wasn't hired. He's a child, Nat, a child I robbed. Him and his sister were out in the woods looking to find medicine for their sick mother. He asked to come along to help.'

Nat spread his arms, 'And I'm sure you warned him of the dangers. He knew and came anyway.'

Nari raised a warning finger. 'You're my brother Nat and I love you, but you're pushing it. We have to help him.'

Nat stared at him for a few seconds, gaze flicking intermittently to Ash, clinging to life. His features softened. 'Fine. What do we do?'

He looked at him, eyes fluttering fitfully behind their pale lids.

'I know a place.'

Chapter 17

'Behind me,' she murmured, extending her hand to push Dem to safety. She did as she was told, trembling under her touch, keeping her eyes on the far bank and the partially-concealed figure within.

Dark eyes glimmered in gleeful malevolence. Awful childish laughter filtered through the heavy summer night to chill her spine and set her heart fluttering. Dem's gasping attempts at restraining her sobs were a welcome distraction from the sibilant tones of their foe. An unholy melody of false innocence, veiling the darkness within.

'Know way back?'

'Yes.'

'Go. Leave pack. Make you slow.'

'What about you?'

A touching gesture to ask, but the girl didn't care. Even if she told her she stayed to sacrifice her life, Dem would give no protest. If she told her it may end in indescribable agony as the follower's jagged teeth and dirty claws raked a thousand stinging furrows into her skin, leaving her screaming for the Great Hunter's merciful jaws, the girl would still turn and run. Her terror was palpable. Evident in her pale cheeks and dilated pupils, in the flare of her nostrils and the stiffness in her limbs. It was taking all of her self-control not to bolt and abandon her this very second. A touching gesture, but a gesture nonetheless.

'I stay.'

Dem nodded slowly, slipping the pack from her shoulders. It hit the ground with a thump, an unnatural sound after the stillness of the forest, disturbing the follower's eerie giggles.

The leaves parted as it pushed forward, eyes and teeth shining like tapers in the dark. It was too much for Dem. Sobbing, she fled upriver, clogs of damp earth flying in her wake.

It didn't follow the girl. It had eyes only for her. She knew it would be like this, from their first meeting in the forest, she knew. Something connected them, some ancestral instinct in her blood called for it, for whatever made it. Its shadow lingered in the abandoned Whitewater place, saturated the forests around the Holevale infirmary, and grew overwhelmingly potent within its cellars. Now was the time to rid herself of its pull, to cut the cord attaching one to the other and set them adrift, to let it drown in the shadows of its own malice.

The leaves made no sound as they parted before it, even the trees too terrified to let their voices be heard. She felt the Great Hunter prowl behind her. Make yourself ready, my friend, there will be bones to lick clean by dawn.

Springing the branches back into place, it ducked suddenly back into the shadows, laughing as it disappeared. She crouched, axe and knife at the ready, steadying mind and body for its return.

What brought it here? Was it waiting for her? Planning and plotting with its dark master, setting a trap to ensnare her, to bind her one last time before the end. Is that why it waited until she was so close to home, to relish in shattered hopes? In a twisted way, it made sense. After all, she'd already fallen into the deadliest trap for any goblin by considering the future, by imagining tomorrow. She should have remembered that all Enadir was against her kind, and this kolgatha was but one of a thousand enemies. Enemies hoping to cut her down and desecrate her corpse. Time with the children had influenced her, all their dangerous planning for future events planting the seed of doom in her brain. It was allowed for them, of course, it was right for humans to consider days to come, but not her. For goblins, there was no tomorrow. All she could do was see what the next moment would bring and enjoy the breath while it lasted in her lungs. Yesterday could have been her last for any number of reasons. Despite the exhausting run and resurgence of the follower, today was still another day worth having.

A splash from downriver. She didn't turn. A trick, nothing more. A pebble thrown into the water to distract her, to test her vigilance. Giggles followed after a few seconds, echoing among the twisting boughs and into the night.

They'd done well to make it this far. So many foes lay in their wake. Empty buildings, skies full of lightning, robberies, swamps, rogues, sibling bickering. All overcome. She'd given the children so many days to keep breathing, to keep living. Every one of them worth it. Even the dark days like when Ash left after Nari, with one of the

Great Hunter's jaws looming over him with each step he took away from her protection. He might have avoided it by staying with her, but the Great Hunter was inevitable. One could only hide one's scent for so long. Hers was well and truly in its nostrils tonight. She had no fear of it, no regret. It was the way of the world, and her demise was long-overdue.

A twig snapped upriver, followed by a rustle of branches further ahead. She remained where she was. It wanted her to follow, to think it was pursuing Dem. Not so. The girl was a human, not a goblin, she was allowed a future. Her dreams of reaching home, medicine in pocket, were to be realised. Enadir welcomed such plans from the other races. For Ffed, on the other hand, her thoughts of reaching home and playing with Jal were doomed to fail for the simple fact she'd considered them. It was not her place to do so.

Another splash as a rock landed in the river a few feet in front of her. That was more like it. No more games. If it wanted her, it would have to come and get her.

Perhaps that's what it was; an agent of Enadir. Daemons, after all, were the souls of Enadir. If the kolgatha were indeed a servant of the Negotiators, would that not make it a servant of Enadir? Could it be her punishment for considering thoughts that were not permitted to one of her race? The sickly feeling in her stomach denied it. Rumours and stories were just that. Who was she to trust, a fat cheese-seller's outlandish claims or her own tried and tested instinct? The Negotiators were of nature, while this thing was a corruption of nature, not a servant of it. Enadir wasn't punishing her with it. Perhaps it was testing her by putting it in front of her to destroy. A chance for redemption for her transgressions of ambition.

The branches parted again. Tired of its one-sided game, the follower confronted its non-participating opponent.

A child. Not a child. A corruption.

Pale arms and thighs darkened to black forearms and legs. Half-rotten clothes clung limply to its decrepit and emaciated body, a head seemingly too large for its body suspended from a bobbing, scraggly neck. Red lips drew its unnaturally wide mouth into a slavering grin, black teeth shining as an obsidian wall in the moonlight. It giggled, body heaving and quivering, the sinister sound jumping unnaturally and grotesquely from its narrow chest, though its black eyes remained still and unmoving.

An abomination.

It waded into the water, its clawed feet cutting through the ripples as keenly as a blade, its giggle fading into a revolting clicking from the back of its twisted throat. Black eyes ensnared her with a noose of terror. Her hands were locked at her sides, her fingers losing their grip on axe and knife.

The water parted before it, each droplet running from its limbs as soon as they broke the surface, unwilling to be caught or absorbed by the otherworldly thing in its depths, leaving it as dry as the moment it entered.

Overwhelming silence smothered her, its oppressive folds muting everything beyond the ten-foot radius they occupied in the river. Invisible hooks tore at her chest, pulling her forward, dragging her unwilling body to this awful mimicry of a human child. Her body quivered in a whimper, but if a sound came with it she never heard it, her ears muffled and heavy as if she were under a hundred feet of water, the crushing pressure paralysing her eardrums.

Her reluctant legs mirrored each step it took, bringing its wide and monstrous mouth ever closer.

A twitch of her finger finally released the whittling-knife, which dropped silently into the Clearbed, the ripples of its fall lapping gently against her heavy calves. She was a marionette, dancing to the twisted tune of the hideous creature before her. At least her wide ears were free to flutter and twist, searching for a sound amid the stifling stillness of its spell. But no, nothing. An even greater chill ran down her spine at an awful realisation. For the first time in forever, even the Great Hunter's padding footsteps were gone, chased away by the ominous miasma exuded by the follower. Her ever-present companion, from as early as she could recall, sometimes close, sometimes far, but always with her. No more. What sort of abhorrent fiend had such an ability to chase away the keeper of her race?

Heart pounding, chest heaving, the kolgatha drew closer still. Her pulse thundered in her ears, the sound, terrible as it may be, somehow better than the dreadful silence it followed. It brought her back to reality, gave her something to concentrate on. With it came more senses. The shaft of her hatchet, smooth beneath her fingers apart from a rough bit of splintering at its very end. The warmth of the night on her cheeks. Even the smell of her own acrid sweat, trickling in steady streams down her flanks. A haze lifted from before her, the follower's black eyes and teeth apparently shrinking, allowing her to see beyond it, to remember where she was. It approached with ragged gasps of anticipation, a new stench like rotten carrion reaching her nostrils with each breath it took. Gleeful excitement glittered in its eyes as it flexed its black claws. A few more steps and they'd be touching hands. Her pulse was a hum in her ears, her chest fit to burst. The hatchet was heavy, her limbs feeble. She couldn't blink, eyes burning, its grotesque features growing closer, closer.

The swing of the axe caught the follower's hand, taking a twisted claw clean off.

Its banshee shriek tore through her ears, nearly making her collapse. Its opposite hand flew in a blur, catching her chin and sending her flying.

She splashed in the shallows, world upside down. There was no time to recover, barely time to breathe. It was on her again, teeth snapping, arms swinging, back legs kicking like a cat. She felt the claws dig into her flesh. She felt her skin rip as it tore through her, opening up gaping furrows in her body.

Ferocity like she'd never encountered. A caged, rabid animal unleashed on its master's foes. A hound sent to tear and ravage the fox to shreds.

She managed to hold up and arm to stave off an attack, pushing the shaft of her hatchet up against it. Obsidian teeth clamped around it, only narrowly missing her fingers, growling and slavering. The once-gleeful eyes were black pits of malice, deep as the abyss. Fury incarnate, its baleful face blazed inches from her own. Despite it all, Ffed smiled. Its spell was broken, the silence shattered by its screams and grunts. Somewhere behind, she heard the Great Hunter's footsteps return, prowling around, preparing its mighty jaws for the final strike.

285

Her arm grew weaker as blood flowed from her wounds, joining the Clearbed's flow as a black streak in the moonlight.

The Hunter's padded paws approached, its hot breath on her hair. Finally, her time was now.

The follower drew back suddenly, raising its arms and screaming in her face, charnel breath reeking of the grave, grey spittle flying from its inky teeth. If it was meant to terrify, it failed. She was beyond terror. Her keeper was here, its warm belly awaiting her body. Her hatchet was still in her hand, her failing strength somehow keeping it suspended between her and her foe. In a final act of defiance, she swung.

The kolgatha shrieked as its claws descended.

Her arm jarred, the handle slipping from her grip.

The Great Hunter's jaws snapped shut.

The abomination toppled into the river, her hatchet lodged squarely between its black eyes.

Silence at last.

She flinched. No, not silence. The Great Hunter padded slowly away into the forest, away but never out of earshot, its appetite satisfied for today.

More sounds joined its padding steps. Boots. Cries for help. Dem's cries. She tried mustering the energy to sit up. Impossible. She was too weak. Collapsing back into the river, she waited for them to arrive.

She didn't wait long. Dem knelt by her side, eyes wide, mouth open in shock. Ffed tried lifting a hand to comfort her, but no. Her body declined the motion.

Gruff shouts filled the air. Cries of horror, of outrage. She strained her ears to listen, exhaustion threatening to send her into unconsciousness at any moment.

'Winds! A child! Just a child!'

'Murdered him!'

'Goblin scum!'

Suddenly, rough hands brushed Dem aside, her cries falling on deaf ears. Gauntlets closed around her neck, squeezing ever tighter. Dem's frightened face appeared over the shoulder of the armoured, helmeted guard crouched in the shallows. Her blood thundered in her ears. Her pulse turned rhythmic, steady, like the pacing of prowling paws. She kept smiling, and slipped into darkness.

Chapter 18

'It'll be difficult,' Anten warned as his acolytes bustled about Ash's still form. 'I can't guarantee anything.'

'I know.'

'Even in Gerath's hands, the prognosis–'

'I know,' Nari cut across. 'You just have to try.'

Anten sighed. 'It'll be Gerath's choice to operate or not. He's already beyond my capabilities.'

'Will he do it?'

'I don't know. We'll see when he gets there.'

They watched the acolytes wheel him down the corridor, the boy's strained face so pale it was nearly lost in the white bedsheets. Holding his hands behind his head, he exhaled forcefully. North winds save him. Please.

Anten's hand touched his shoulder. 'Come. You and your brother need seeing to as well.'

He shook his head. 'We can't afford it.'

Anten shrugged. 'For your part with the children, we'll do it free of charge. Come. I can help.'

Ash's bed disappeared around a bend. With a heavy sigh, he nodded and followed the healer to the upper levels, Nat limping in tow.

*

Cold. Icy sweat covering his weak body, numbing his fingers and nose, making him shiver uncontrollably.

Hot. Burning streams of molten iron from his flank to his gut, biting and searing the skin, turning his inside into blistered sores.

He couldn't move his limbs. Manacles held them in place. He couldn't speak. His mouth was gagged, tongue pushed back into his throat. No, not gagged, a funnel attached to a tube, he could feel it rubbing against his gullet when he tried to swallow, sitting uncomfortably in his aching stomach. His eyes, at least, were open. Free to take in the horror of his surroundings. The dark cellar, walls dripping with moisture. His ears were clear, open to the moans of the other patients.

Another voice joined the choir of moans. Legible, for once, though only snatched phrases could be heard from this distance. A new chill spread over his body, raising his hairs into goosebumps.

'Successful surgery... surprising? I agree... technique... report on this could be... just a short study, give me a few months... late-stage failures...'

The speaker grew more agitated and he recognised the voice. Healer Gerath, arguing with someone, presumably over him.

'...of my intervention is why he's here... I can do with something like this! Please... be for nothing... too old for what you want... nearly a man, it's never been done with someone his age... said younger ones were more suitable for... going to die!'

Something struck his stomach. Not from without, but within. A punch of fear, a stab of dread coiling his wounded gut into a knot. Gerath's voice trailed away, the frustration dissipating into meek murmurs of placation.

Silence settled, the other patients falling still in an instant. The ward held its breath. He struggled against his bonds, but only managed a feeble wriggle of the torso. The sound of the rustling bedsheets seemed deafening in the silent room. Trapped.

He knew what was coming.

A shadow from the corner of his eye. His heart hammered in his chest, desperate to break free from his ribcage and flee before the darkness reached. His breath, difficult as it was with the feeding tube in place, turned impossible, seizing in his throat in a choking gurgle. His shoulders jerked helplessly in silent sobs. The vile stench of soiled bedclothes filled his nostrils as his body simultaneously lost control of bladder and bowel. He squirmed in vain. Nowhere to run. Nowhere to hide.

The shadow approached. A black silhouette against the grey walls. Nothing monstrous in its form, nothing strange in its movement, but that only made it more frightening. An unexplained hatred pulsed through his burning veins. He clenched his broken teeth around the metal tube. He couldn't even drown himself with a bitten tongue. No relief, no respite. The shadow approached. Unstoppable. Inevitable. A stench worse than the one from between his legs filled the air. Visceral and all-consuming, it worked its repulsive way from his nose into every inch of his body, quivering and convalescing as much as his bonds allowed. Regurgitated food bubbled up the feeding tube then fell back down to his stomach, followed by a foul belch, his stomach desperate to purge the pestilent stink from his body. His rolling eyes stung with tears. A smell of death and decay, it paralysed him with its oppressive weight. Charnel and rotten, the smell of evil deeds and black intent. A miasma of corruption, enfolding him in its evil haze.

Indigo eyes burned from the darkness, transfixing his feverish gaze in place. The familiar voice set his heart in a silent scream.

'Alive and returned to me. How tenacious.'

Chapter 19

'It's *my* treat!'

'Want it!'

'It's mine!'

'Want it!'

Tears erupted. Dem rolled her eyes. Inevitable. Elain plonked herself down on the grass, red-faced and howling as Hent hastily stuffed the last strawberry tart into his mouth, jam and crumbs sticking to the corners of his lips. Kneeling next to her little sister, she scooped her up in her arms.

'Now, now,' she soothed. 'Now, now. You both had the same amount. We have to learn to share fairly, don't we?'

'Wanted it!' Elain blubbered between her sobs, little face contorted into a disproportionately complex and intense range of emotions over such a small thing.

'I know, but you ate yours earlier, didn't you? H kept his for later, like we told you to.'

'Isn't fair!' she howled ever louder.

'I know it feels unfair,' she rocked her back and forth, stroking her hair. 'Things often feel that way.'

Elain pushed her away with her podgy little hands, weeping unconsolably. 'Want Ma!'

'I know,' she soothed.

'Want Ma!'

'She'll be back from work soon,' she reassured, wiping her beetroot cheeks with the hem of her sleeve. 'Then you can tell her how unfair and horrible I've been.'

Her sobs continued, loud and unashamedly, blubbering enough to silence the birds. Hent caught her eye and shrugged, looking guiltily down at his feet.

'Sorry, Dem,' he mumbled. 'I wanted my treat.'

'No need to apologise,' she smiled. 'It was yours to enjoy. I'm the one who's sorry you had to stuff it all in at once instead of enjoying it properly!'

291

He giggled and ran around them in circles, his antics enough to pause Elain's sobs, settling down into whimpering little hiccups. Hent flapped his arms and whistled as he ran, jumping over logs and swinging from low branches.

'I'm a buzzard! A lucky buzzard!'

He screeched and squawked, flapping ever harder. Elain giggled and wriggled out of Dem's grip to chase him, tears turned to laughter in the space of a few seconds.

She couldn't help but smile as she watched them.

Another morning spent looking after Elain. Heb was too busy to look after her between minding the house and taking her new place with the panners in the river. Ma could only work a few hours a day. She grimaced. Truth be told, she shouldn't even be doing that. She'd heard the whispers in the market and in the shops concerning Ma's inefficiency. It was always said under the breath, of course, and always dripping with sympathy, but how long would that last? Nobody bore her any ill will, not yet at least, they could all see the lasting effects of the illness and its medicine.

Three months since their return. Three months since scrambling red-faced and screaming like Elain into the hands of the Starforge guards on duty that night. Three months since bursting through home's front door with Healer Gerath's miracle cure in hand, and seeing just how far Ma's sickness had progressed.

Healer Semon and Joli did what they could. They'd excised several tubercles from her skin and kept her body functioning, but who knew what was going on inside? For a whole month, Dem pretended to know what she was doing with Gerath's medicine, administering it as per his instruction, fighting the urge to retch at the putrid stench of the bitter concoction. Healer Semon was initially dubious about it, but he couldn't argue with the results. What they couldn't decide on was which of the existing symptoms were a result of the medicine and which were the lasting effects of the illness. Her skin was yet to recover, hanging in yellow folds from her bones. There was a new squint in her left eye, practically losing sight in it completely, and her spine had a new scoliotic curvature that set her hips and shoulders at odd angles. They pretended not to notice when she woke up early to wash her bedsheets. They pretended not to notice how long it took for a cut to stop bleeding or a new bruise to disappear. They pretended not to notice how many teeth she had left, or how soft her meagre portions of food needed to be. She, in turn, pretended all was well and back to normal.

How could anything be normal again?

'Watch out or you'll hurt yourselves,' she warned to deaf ears, the children giggling and screaming with glee. No point. They were far too excited. Shaking her head, her eyes caught the threatening grey clouds gathering above the leafy canopy. 'Alright, time to go home now, Ma'll be waiting for us.'

They groaned in disappointment, little heads dropping and lower lips protruding in miserable defiance.

'Just a bit longer?' Hent whined, shuffling his feet.

'A *bit* longer?' she exclaimed, stooping down and wiggling her fingers. 'A *bit* longer? You can stay if you want, but the tickle monster will be here!'

Growling mockingly, she chased them for a few seconds, scooping them up squealing and kicking, tears of joy streaming down hot cheeks. She let them go, using the game to shepherd them back to the village. Every now and then she'd scoop them up again for more punishing tickles if they strayed too far, weaving through the trees on the familiar path to home.

'Can Ffed come out today?' Hent asked, pointing through a gap in the boughs to the ramshackle hut. Silly of her to take them this way, but a part of her wanted to see it as well, to punish herself.

She led him away, averting her eyes from the building. 'Not today.'

'Is she still sick?' he asked, looking over his shoulder at the empty hammock between the hornbeams.

'That's right,' she lied.

'I hope she gets better soon. I want to play with Jal. At least Mister Awne is looking after her,' he waved to the guard, whose spear dropped back at ease once they went by.

'That's exactly what he's doing,' she forced a smile, a lump forming in her throat. Three months since they'd beaten Ffed senseless and clapped her battered and bleeding body in irons, misunderstanding her babbling pleas for help that night. Her testimony did no good. All they saw was a goblin and a dead child. They couldn't differentiate which was the monster. Only when the body was inspected further by the captain of the guard did they pause to reconsider, but by then public opinion was inflamed by wild accusations and falsified accounts. Mysterious eye-witnesses were apparently interviewed, swearing blind they'd seen the goblin attack her and this unknown orphan child. Even the guards on duty that night swore blind she came running to them, tears of terror in her eyes and murmurs of bloody goblins trying to murder her. Nonsense, of course, but it didn't matter. Whispers turned to bellows of rage as the stupid and prejudiced joined hands to round up their followers, demanding Ffed's head on a stick, her heart in a jar, her hands on spikes. To her shame, she was too deeply occupied with Ma to offer much more than her initial testimony for Ffed's innocence, which was quickly brushed aside as dissent and rumours gathered momentum. If anything, it was a good thing Ffed was so badly wounded in her battle with the follower, spending the first two months under Oskra's daily attention as she was slowly nursed back to life. The villagers only tolerated it on the assurance her current state was too weak to fully appreciate and suffer the punishment for her perceived crimes. Now she remained confined to her hut, guards rotated every six hours, awaiting the time of her reckoning.

Of those who saw the body, not one said a word. The guards who'd recovered it were rotated to other villages, the elders who'd inspected it exchanged nervous looks but no more, even Oskra remained tight-lipped and jumpy whenever the subject was brought up.

Another trial was mentioned a few times now that Ffed was capable of relaying her own account of events, but for whatever reason, nobody seemed keen on the idea. Their minds were made, their judgements already passed. Now that Ma was slightly better, they might take into account her role in delivering the medicine to the village and look at her more kindly. Perhaps. Then again, she'd heard rumours that Ffed herself was responsible for the sickness, and the whole thing was a ruse to lure the children into the woods, after all, had Ash not mysteriously disappeared?

She shook herself. Best not to think about him. But the painful twist of the knife always returned when her feet inexorably brought her here.

Back to the Clearbed, the children splashed each other in the shallows, kicking up clogs of mud to splatter each other's clothes before she had a chance to stop them. She scolded them, but they ignored her, splashing around and soaking their boots. No matter. Their damp clothes in autumn's chill would be punishment enough. True to form, Elain's cheeks were soon puffy and red again as she prepared for another blubbering complaint, little shoulders shivering with cold. Not even the tickle monster could save this situation. To make matters worse, the grey clouds finally followed through on their threats and dumped countless gallons of rain on their heads, fat droplets splattering on leaf, bough, and sorry villager alike.

Soaking and brooding, they approached Starforge's gate. Guards leaned nonchalantly against the palisade, tucking their chins into their scarves to hide from the downpour. The rhythmic clack and clatter of a mule-drawn cart caught up with them, the approaching travellers no doubt making ready for the soldiers' inspection. She ushered the children to one side to make room for it to pass, stepping patiently into the grass on the side of the pebbled road.

The cart drew near, its driver hanging his head low, his nod of thanks barely perceptible. She smiled politely up at him in acknowledgment. The mule ignored them, struggling gamely on with its load.

'Dem?'

She jumped. She knew that voice. The driver pulled on the mule's reins, coming to a sudden stop in front of them. Two of them on the cart, one in the driver's seat, the other with its cargo. Her heart skipped. For a second, it was as paralysed as the rest of her body, then jumped back to action twice as quickly to compensate for the pause. The familiar, hated face stared at her beneath his dripping hood.

'Dem?'

295

She looked over his shoulder at the one cowering behind him, his features concealed by hood and scarf. Her hands shook, but not for the cold. Was it relief? Was it anger? Equal amounts of both, surging in retaliatory waves, battle lines of emotion clashing in her chest.

They stared down from their cart, she stared right back up at them. The silence grew. Hent tried chancing a glance around her legs, but she pushed him back. She wouldn't let another boy be corrupted by his honeyed words.

Hood low, the one in the back continued to avoid her eyes. Coward. She had a hundred things to say, lectures and beratements she'd practiced every night since his departure, hoping and dreaming for the moment she could finally say all the things she should have said before he left. A hundred cutting remarks followed by a hundred welcomes, a hundred reprimands and a hundred declarations of joy. It built up like water behind a crumbling dam, bubbling and frothing up from the pit of her stomach, rushing into her chest, expanding and swelling in preparation for the explosion to come. She opened her mouth to scream, but nothing came out but a whimper, barely heard over the rain. Her tongue was in knots, her brain a jumble of half-formed sentences practiced countless times but now the opportunity was here to voice them, suddenly silent and incomplete.

'I don't really know what to say,' Nari's twisted face trembled. Enadir damn him. His remorse was meaningless, even less welcome than his foul features. She ignored him, her eyes on the lanky one behind, waiting for his apology, wondering how she'd react when it came.

'Want to go home,' Elain tugged at her sleeve, hiding behind her legs as she stared up at the rogue.

She pushed her further behind her legs. He'd corrupted one sibling, winds be damned if she'd give him the opportunity to sink his foul claws into another.

'We're going, don't worry,' she managed to untangle her tongue, still staring over Nari's shoulder.

'I'm sorry. I wanted to find you to let you know, it's good you're here,' Nari mumbled, head hanging low, his companion still hiding behind him, unwilling to step forward. 'I… you needed to know.'

'That you're sorry?' she spat. Why wasn't he coming? It was one thing to be ashamed, but hiding behind Nari like Elain and Hent hid behind her wasn't helpful. 'Just send him over and piss off, I'm getting soaked.'

'Send him over?' Nari frowned.

'Don't forget to piss off before I call the soldiers,' she gestured over her shoulder to the village gate, where the guards were starting to take interest in the motionless cart blocking the road.

'But–'

She shut him up with a raised finger. 'Just. Go.'

She felt his eyes on her. Nobody moved. He was probably too embarrassed to come. He should be, for all the pain he'd caused them, but standing out in the rain wasn't making it any better.

Elain tugged at her sleeve again. 'Dem?' she mumbled, drawing out her name in a whine. Untangling her fingers from her sleeve, she gave her sister's hand a squeeze.

'Yes, we're going,' she looked over Nari's shoulder. 'Well?'

Nari sighed heavily and jumped from the driver's seat. She flinched. Damn it. Now he'd think he had something over her, some power. Why do it? To have one final eye-to-eye with her before relinquishing her brother? Pathetic rodent, squaring up to a girl.

She held her chin high, preparing for the confrontation, for this final battle of wills.

He walked right by her and around to the rear of the cart, head low, shoulders slumped. Unexpected. What was he doing? Helping Ash off the cart like a precious little flower? She shook her head and suppressed a derisive chuckle.

Nari flicked the latch to let the rear hatch drop and leaned against the cart, breathing heavily. She tapped her foot impatiently. They were really dragging this out. She snapped her fingers up at the cart and gestured to the village.

'Come on. Let's get inside.'

Nari looked up at her again, his frown deepening. 'Nat's staying with me, Dem. I'm trying to tell you about your brother.'

297

Nat?

She stared at the figure on the cart. Lanky, tall, ungainly. Sensing the need to clarify, he raised his hand and pushed the sodden scarf beneath his chin. Her heart fluttered again. Her cheeks flushed. Elain whimpered as she tightened her grip into a fist.

'Dem. Hurts,' she blubbered.

She hardly heard it, the surging wave of emotion building in her body suddenly dissipating into a void.

'Where is he?'

Nari's head dropped.

'Where?'

The brothers glanced at each other uneasily and into the back of the cart. Nari drew a long breath as if preparing an answer. She waited, hands trembling, Elain squirmed to break free. Hent whimpered, sensing things were amiss.

'Where?' she barked, but she already knew the answer. She'd known for three months.

'I'm sorry.'

Nari gestured with his chin into the cart. She took a shuddering breath and forced her heavy feet to move. Like moving blocks of lead through treacle, she fought the urge to give in, to stop, to turn away. She couldn't. This was happening. There was no running from the inevitable. Rounding the cart's rear wheel, she peered over the edge at its contents.

Black and terrible in its box-like simplicity. A coffin.

She would have sunk to her knees in the middle of the road, but her whole body was frozen. Only her hands moved, shaking like leaves in a storm.

'He got hurt saving Nat,' Nari mumbled, his words floating to her half-deaf ears. 'We took him back to the infirmary but… I'm sorry. Gerath did everything he could.'

Nothing. She had nothing to say, nothing more to feel. Her heart was lost in the abyss, the growing void in her chest consuming her mind, devouring her soul.

'Dem. Hurts,' Elain managed to wriggle free. Her hand fell helplessly by her side. Limp as a carcass. Ash's carcass.

298

'We did everything we could,' Nari continued, empty words trying in vain to fill the deepening darkness within her. 'He saved both our lives. We really tried to do the same. I promise we did everything we could. I'm sorry. Got him the best treatment. Even if you don't believe us, you trusted Gerath's abilities with your mother. We did everything we could.'

'Want to go *home*.'

'I'm sorry–'

'Dem–'

'We did everything we could–'

'Home–'

'Tried our best–'

'Getting wet–'

'Nothing we could have–'

She screamed. Nothing specific. There was nothing to be said. No way of putting it into words. The growing emptiness inside her demanded release. Bubbling and spitting like a pot of boiling milk, it surged from her throat in an indecipherable screech. Elain clapped her hands over her ears, Hent wailed in childish confusion. Nat vaulted from the cart, hand shooting to the folds of his cloak. Nari flinched and closed his eyes, but remained where he stood. She wanted to hit him, to scratch his eyes out and dig her thumbs into the bleeding sockets. She wanted to push his face into the puddles in the road, to place her heel on the back of his head and grind it into the mud. It was all his fault. All of it. But she couldn't move. If she moved she'd only fall.

The guards broke into a run, spears held ready, drawn to action by the sound of her distress.

'Dem,' Nari raised his hands, sorrow glazing his eyes and tugging the corners of his mouth into a grimace.

'Go away,' she whispered, ushering Elain and Hent back behind her.

'I wanted to tell you, to deliver him back to you.'

'Go away!' she screamed.

Boots pounded on the road, reverberating in the cart's ramshackle wheels. The mule whined at the excitement. Nat

299

whispered something to his brother and promptly disappeared into the woods. Nari remained as he was for a second, holding her gaze. He was trying to tell her something, trying to convey his regret, his sorrow, searching for a semblance of companionship in his grief, for forgiveness. He wouldn't find it. Not from her. Let him search until he croaked his final damned breath and faded into oblivion, but she had nothing more for him. He'd taken her brother.

His eyes flicked away to the approaching soldiers. A final glance at her, a final unanswered plea for absolution. He disappeared after his brother.

Soldiers surrounded her, some continuing after the two rogues, some remaining. Their questions bounced back and forth. She couldn't answer them, didn't even look at them. She placed her hands on the coffin, its splinters and uneven boards rough against her fingertips. Elain clung to her legs, sobbing again. Rain continued to fall, running down her cheeks after silent tears.

*

It was time.

Jal was restless, squawking and flapping her wings in frustration as she circled the hut. They'd get going soon. Ffed checked her belongings a final time. It was all there, everything she needed for the journey.

Where was she going? What would she do when she got there? Meaningless questions. It didn't matter. Making the journey is what mattered. Breaking out of this new prison is what mattered.

The guard leaned on his heavy spear, hauberk glistening in the rain. Another person might have been insulted by Starforge's betrayal, by the wild accusations and terrible stories they told about her. Another person might have sunk into a depression or worse, a rage, losing their minds to anger and dreams of retribution. Not her. Such an outcome was expected, inevitable. All goblins knew the whole world was their enemy. They'd tolerated her company for long enough, and now was the inevitable end. Forget the fact she'd saved one of their daughters from the follower, forget the fact she'd brought the medicine back for Lelan. One excuse was all they needed.

What she couldn't forgive was this attempt at imprisoning her, at clapping her back in irons, chaffing and grating the twisted scars on her wrists.

She reached into a pouch for a handful of peas. Jal quacked happily and waddled over, tail wagging like a dog as she devoured the food directly from her hand. Good duck. She might follow her into the woods, she might not. It was her choice. She'd tolerate no lead or collar to ensnare her, just as no manacle or cage would ever contain her again. The villagers might think they had her under arrest, but she was only biding her time, recovering after her ordeal. These naïve guards on their pointless rotation would be better served elsewhere, she'd had enough of Starforge and its villagers, she wouldn't have approached its walls even if they allowed it. Better to wander again, to live with the trees and the animals away from the civilisations of other races.

True, living near Starforge had its benefits. Oskra, for example. Her expertise and gentle hand nursed her back to health after the skirmish with the follower, closing the gaping wounds in her body, stuffing her entrails back into place and sewing up her flesh on top of it. The scars were still tight, rough lines of hypertrophic tissues marking where they'd leaked foul pus from infection borne on the follower's rancid claws, but her body fought through it all. For whatever reason, the Great Hunter had no appetite for her. Perhaps its consumption of the follower gave it a bad stomach. It was the only possible explanation for surviving such gruesome wounds. Nevertheless, it continued to prowl after her, panting and sniffing, awaiting its next opportunity.

The trapdoor in the corner opened to the narrow space beneath her stilted floor, barely two feet high. She dropped the bag through first. No hatchet, no knife. Prisoners weren't allowed such luxuries. At one point, she half-hoped Dem might visit with a secret parcel for her containing her old weapons, but no, the girl had better things to do than visit the likes of her. She didn't blame her, of course, she bore her no ill will. Such was simply the way of things.

Lowering herself into the space, she crawled over the hard-packed earth to the vent in the back. Concealed by the intervening hut, the guard wouldn't see her leave. They probably wouldn't even know she was gone. The floor turned muddier the closer she came to the vent as it absorbed the pooling rain outside. Kicking the loose sticks free, she watched the waves come down, saturating the earth and muting the colours of the forest into greys and browns. There was a rustle behind her, followed by the rhythmic slap of Jal's webbed feet on the floor. Her little head popped up by the crook of her arm, inspecting the pounding rain outside. She gave a series of soft quacks before waddling out, head and tail wriggling with a life of their own as they got used to the rain. With a sniff, she manoeuvred her body through the tight space, drawing in her belly and twisting her hips and shoulder to make it through.

There was peace in the rain. Tranquillity. No thunder and lightning, no howling winds or sweeping gales to set the tall trees into their violent swaying dance. Just a steady patter of raindrops on leaf and bough, rock and dirt, dancing from puddles and streams in its cool autumn shower. Almost through, she drew in her belly and wriggled forward. A rat scurried past, then a jackdaw landed on a branch. She paid them no heed, going about their daily business in the rain, scurrying and hopping back and forth to their hides and homes. Why would she ever want anything more than this? She needed no heading, no goal, no direction save for the one the forest dictated.

Just a final twist of the hips and she'd be free, free to wander and live as one with the forest, away from the complications and distractions of the villages. They would never see her again in Starforge, Muddylan, Clovercream, Yewbar, or any of the others. Hers would be a life of bark and dirt, leaf and loam. Her and Jal, and any other animal who decided to join her. If they headed due north, they'd get to the foothills of Iadden. The woods grew particularly deep around there, mossy barks growing so close together one could barely squeeze between them, where neighbouring trees curled around each other like embracing snakes. Apart from a few red dryads, she wouldn't have much company.

With a final scramble, she drew her legs through and stood. Free at last.

A familiar, unwelcome claw tugged her chest, and was gone.

302

She caught the wall of her hut to steady herself.

Impossible.

Her chest tightened. Her heart fluttered. Her gut knotted and squirmed beneath her scars. But there was no mistaking it. Even Jal felt it, scurrying back to cower between her legs.

It was dead. Oskra confirmed it on her visits, her hushed questions concerning the carcass floating through the blur of fevered recovery. It's why she was so vilified by the villagers, why she was here in the first place. Nothing could have survived the hatchet-blow between the eyes. She felt its skull crumble beneath the iron, the squelch of its brain macerated by her blow.

And yet... there was no mistaking the gnawing hunger in her belly.

She scanned the forest. Elm, oak, alder, chestnut, brooding shadows beneath their spreading boughs. Towering redwoods and black pines sheltered squat hazel and blackthorns between them, but nothing else.

Another tug and she fell to one knee, only her grip on the wall keeping her upright. Jal quivered beneath her.

Her mouth was dry, making swallowing impossible, impossible to dispel the lump in her bobbing throat. Her cheeks felt hot, hot enough to make her throw down her hood and cast her face to the skies, willing the falling rain to cool her burning face. Her hands trembled, no comforting hatchet of knife handle to steady them. Her neck prickled, malicious eyes causing her hairs to stand on end.

She turned slowly, peering into the ferns beneath a spreading fir. Black against the grey. Her ears fluttered. A laugh, deeper than before, but no less sinister. It crouched between the leaves, the rain pattering the leaves around it but somehow leaving the evil shadow untouched.

A whimper broke from her throat.

It rose. Taller than before. Tall as a man. Gangly limbs pushed the boughs aside, moving as fluidly as a cat. A shadowed face drew her gaze, familiar despite its repulsive corruption.

Laughter echoed, muffled by the cascading rain. Her heart raced, fluttered, and stopped for a second. She was on her knees,

303

gasping for breath, open mouth and impotent chest paralyzed in shock. She dropped, bent double, face-down in the mud. Agony pulsed in her breast, searing fire and boiling oil coursing through her body. It ripped up her gut and into her throat, stabbed between her eyes and into her brain, twisted her fingers and toes into unnatural contortions. An abyss of despair opened before her blind eyes, beckoning her on, to fall to its infinite depths. The cackle of unknown enemies echoed in memories she didn't possess, locking her thoughts behind black iron bars, her mind wrapped in suffocating chains.

*

Dem sat in the silent room. It was worse than the deafening sound of Ma and Heb's wails. Worse by far. It was lonely, empty, an uncomfortable reflection of how she felt inside, awfully familiar, exactly how it was after Da.

They were both in their rooms. Elain with Heb, Ma on her own. She should go to her, hold her, let her know it wasn't her fault, let her tell her it wasn't hers either. She needed to know. It was all Nari's fault. All of it. She knew it in her heart, but the splinter of doubt worked its way deeper each time she tried to rub it free. Was it because of her?

Her brain wasn't working properly. She tried recalling all their conversations on the journey, tried understanding what sentence or combination of words pushed him under Nari's poisonous spell, but she couldn't. She could hardly recall a single thing she said to him. She could hardly conjure his face.

A few brief wails echoed around the house, then were silent again. She stared at the kitchen floor, smashed dishes still strewn over the rug where they'd been pushed off the table. She'd better pick them up in case someone hurt themselves.

Gathering the pan and brush, she crawled around the table legs, sweeping up the glass and ceramic remnants of their dishes, careful not to cut herself, even more careful to ignore the coffin that pushed them all off to cause the mess. At least now Elain wouldn't need sutures if she tripped.

Enadir only knew what they'd do next. There'd be a service, of course, final farewells as they committed his body back to Enadir.

Then that would be the end of it. No more wondering, no more hoping. They'd be able to get on with their lives.

She caught her sob in her chest before it burst out.

Not today. She would be strong today. Resolute. He'd made his choices, this was the consequence. There'd be no more tears for a boy who abandoned his family, not from her.

Shards all cleared, she turned her attention to the boot-prints on the floor. The guards were gracious enough to escort them to their home and bring the cart's load into the kitchen. The cart and mule were then promptly confiscated as possessions of known criminals, and the dirty floor, smashed plates, and shattered family left alone. A good job well done, by their standards.

It took a while to clean it up, with two buckets of soapy water and more than a fair share of elbow-grease, but it was done. Resetting the chairs around the table, she inspected the room. As if nothing had ever happened. Except for the coffin. You couldn't miss that.

Another sob threatened. She forced it back down. Not today. Damn it all, not today. Not for him. Not after he'd abandoned them.

She tried remembering the look on his face when he left. Did he smile or frown? Did he clench his teeth and set his jaw like he usually did when following his stubborn ways, or was it a difficult decision for him? She couldn't remember. She couldn't picture it.

Strange. She'd spent her whole life with him, but now his face was nothing but a blur, a half-formed memory. It kept morphing into other faces whenever she tried bringing it up. Da's. Nari's. Hent's.

She glanced at the coffin.

It wouldn't do her any harm.

Running her hands down the lid, she searched for purchase. Rough, uneven boards. Made in bulk, no doubt, as part of an assembly line with another few bodies waiting a similar treatment. Basic and plain, built for function with no love or respect for the craft. He'd have hated it.

Curling her fingers, she lifted the lid a fraction. Perhaps she should wait for the others to come down, to face this thing together as the broken remnants of the family. No. This was between him and her. A private moment. She needed it, needed to see his face.

Nari mentioned he'd been hurt saving his brother. How badly? Ugly wounds? Severed limbs? Headless? She didn't know how she felt. No, that wasn't true. She just felt empty.

She threw the lid aside.

Empty. Empty as her heart, as her soul, nothing but clay shards and dust to fill its four wooden walls.

She lifted one of them from the depths of the coffin. Sharp edges, like the plates she'd cleaned up moments ago, only much thicker. She picked up another, and another, staring between them with tired, confused eyes. Smashed and broken pots, nothing more. Useless junk. She threw them back in. Where was he? Was this his and Nari's twisted idea of cutting ties with his family, by faking his own death with a debris-filled coffin and hoping nobody would check its contents? A final insult, that they weren't even good enough for the truth of his betrayal?

No. She shook her head, sitting in a chair. Nari was remorseful, no doubt about it. He thought her brother was dead. More than that, he *knew* it. He genuinely believed he was delivering the body to her. So what was this?

Standing again, she took out one of the shards. Straight edges. She rummaged around. A corner piece, no mistaking it. She took more out, trying them together like pieces of a puzzle.

Her heart skipped as two pieces slotted together almost perfectly. She was right. Shattered remnants of a box. She glanced at the mass in the coffin. If she had the time to put it all together, she already knew what it was. A clay box. Big enough to fit a person.

She sat back down on the chair. Why? Healer Gerath and his acolytes would have done it in their mortuary. Why send an empty coffin to her? A sign of some sort? A message?

A chill ran down her spine. Her eyes left the coffin and wandered to the dresser. On the top shelf, half-hidden where she'd left it following Hent's prompt rejection of the unwanted gift, Ash's faceless doll stared down at her, featureless and empty as her memories of her brother.

Snatches of conversation with the woman in Clovercream came back, replacing the void in her heart with pulsating dread.

Tucking her knees to her chin, she wrapped her arms around them and closed her eyes. It wasn't enough. Even through her lids, she saw the blind stick doll's mocking gaze flitting between her and Ash's empty coffin, its false innocence suddenly repulsive, its twisted limbs as hateful as the evil it beckoned.

Chapter 20

Something touched her cheek. Again. Heavy lids fluttered open. Jal's bill pecked her nose.

Ffed stirred and forced herself to her knees. Rain continued to fall. Her chest was light, free, released from the crush of the shadow's oppressive grip. She took long, steady breaths, relishing the free flow of air into her lungs. Another blessed breath.

The shadows and ferns beneath the fir were empty again, no more darkness within the greys and browns of the waterlogged forest. She shuddered with relief, one hand clutching her breast, the other stroking Jal's head.

She stood, hauling herself up with heavy limbs. Closing her eyes, she shuddered, but the sight was burned into her eyes like the after-glow from a searing flame. Black eyes deeper than oblivion, obsidian teeth flashed in a grotesque grin. The boy's corrupted face twisted into a hungry grimace to mock her memory. She thought it was the Great Hunter who would claim him when he left her protection. Not so. After everything she'd seen, everything she'd felt in those forests around the infirmary, she should have known better, should have seen what would happen. The appetite of the evil lurking in the shadows claimed all it desired, with no escape from the inevitable.

She turned back to Starforge. For a moment, she considered returning to warn them of the evil in the forest, of the corruption circling their little haven. She turned back. The wise goblin knew not to tempt the Great Hunter. What would be, would be, no point worrying about tomorrow. By the grace of his claws and fangs, she'd been given the gift of another day, another breath. She looked to the forest, tranquil and fresh in the pouring rain, its open leaves and busy undergrowth inviting her in. It was in there, sure enough, soft paws stalking, eyes watching for the right time, but not now. Now it was happy to wait, to lord over its subject, to give her another day of precious life in the darkness of the world.

As all goblins knew, another day was always worth having.

The End

308

Milton Keynes UK
Ingram Content Group UK Ltd.
UKHW010724180823
427095UK00004B/140